HONOURKEEPER

'Heave!' Morek bellowed above the thunder. The dwarf's voice resonated through the bronze mask of his helmet as he urged his warriors again.

'Heave with all your strength. Grungni is watching you!'

And all thirty of his hearth guard warriors did.

Beneath the gromril-plated roof of a battering ram, the armoured dwarfs pulled the ram back for another charge. Runes etched down its iron shaft blazed as the gromril ram-head, forged into the bearded visage of the ancestor god Grungni, smashed into the gate.

More Warhammer adventure from the Black Library

GRUDGE BEARER
by Gav Thorpe

OATHBREAKER
by Nick Kyme

GOTREK & FELIX: THE FIRST OMNIBUS
(Contains the first three Gotrek & Felix novels: *Trollslayer,
Skavenslayer* and *Daemonslayer*)
by William King

GOTREK & FELIX: THE SECOND OMNIBUS
(Contains books four to six in the series: *Dragonslayer,
Beastslayer* and *Vampireslayer*)
by William King

Book 7 – **GIANTSLAYER**
by William King

Book 8 – **ORCSLAYER**
by Nathan Long

Book 9 – **MANSLAYER**
by Nathan Long

Book 10 – **ELFSLAYER**
by Nathan Long

GUARDIANS OF THE FOREST
by Graham McNeill

DEFENDERS OF ULTHUAN
by Graham McNeill

MASTERS OF MAGIC
by Chris Wraight

EMPIRE IN CHAOS
by Anthony Reynolds

A WARHAMMER NOVEL

HONOURKEEPER

NICK KYME

For my clan; for Louise and Shakespeare.

A BLACK LIBRARY PUBLICATION

First published in Great Britain in 2009 by
BL Publishing,
Games Workshop Ltd.,
Willow Road, Nottingham,
NG7 2WS, UK

10 9 8 7 6 5 4 3 2 1

Cover illustration by Clint Langley
Map by Nuala Kinrade.

A CIP record for this book is available from the British Library.

ISBN 13: 978 1 84416 684 8
ISBN 10: 1 84416 684 8

Distributed in the US by Simon & Schuster
1230 Avenue of the Americas, New York, NY 10020.

See the Black Library on the Internet at
www.blacklibrary.com

Find out more about Games Workshop
and the world of Warhammer at
www.games-workshop.com

Printed and bound in the US.

CENTURIES BEFORE SIGMAR united the tribes of man and forged the Empire, dwarfs and elves held sway over the Old World.

BENEATH THE MOUNTAINS of this land lies the great realm of the dwarfs. A proud and venerable race, dwarfs have ruled over their subterranean holds for thousands of years. Their kingdom stretches the length and breadth of the Old World and the majesty of their artifice stands boldly for all to see, hewn into the very earth itself.

MINERS AND ENGINEERS beyond compare, dwarfs are expert craftsmen who share a great love of gold, but so do other creatures. Greenskins, ratmen and still deadlier beasts that dwell in the darkest depths of the world regard the riches of the dwarfs with envious eyes.

AT THE HEIGHT of their Golden Age the dwarfs enjoyed dominion over all that they surveyed, but bitter war against the elves and the ravages of earthquakes put paid to this halcyon era. Ruled over by the High King of Karaz-a-Karak, the greatest of their holds, the dwarfs now nurse the bitter memories of defeat, clinging desperately to the last vestiges of their once proud kingdom, striving to protect their rocky borders from enemies above and below the earth.

ACT ONE
Wrought in Iron

CHAPTER ONE
Beginnings and Endings

BEYOND ARCHER RANGE, King Bagrik surveyed the carnage of the battlefield from atop a ridge of stone. Across a muddy valley riddled with trenches, earthworks and abatis his army gave their blood, sweat and steel. Sat astride his ancestral war shield, carried by two of his stoutest hearth guard warriors, the king of Karak Ungor had an unparalleled view.

The silver moat the elves had fashioned shimmered like an iridescent ribbon, reflecting the flames of burning towers. Bagrik watched keenly as gromril-plated bridges were dropped over it, landing like felled trees for the siege towers and warriors with scaling ladders to cross. On the opposite side of the ridge where it fell away into a shallow ravine, Bagrik could hear the heartening din of smiths at their forge fires, toiling in the dwarf encampment making more bridges, bolts for the ballista, quarrels and pavises. The smell of soot and iron drifting on the breeze was like a taste of home.

Bagrik's expression hardened as a siege tower lurched and slipped on one of the bridges, falling into the molten moat and taking most of its crew with it. Others had better fortune, and battles erupted across the length of the elven wall with spear, hammer and axe.

He swelled with pride at the sight of it, all of his hearth brothers locked in furious battle with a powerful foe. Sorrow tempered that pride, and wrath crushed both emotions as Bagrik glowered at the city.

Tor Eorfith the elves called it. Eyrie Rock. It was well named, for the towers at the zenith of the city had soared far into the sky, piercing cloud and seemingly touching the stars. They were the dominion of mages, great observatories where the elven sorcerers could contemplate the constellations and allegedly portend future events.

Bagrik wagered they had not seen this coming.

He had no love for sky, cloud and stars; his domain was the earth and its solidity beneath and about him gave him comfort. The earth contained the essence of the ancestor gods, for it was to the heart of the world that they had returned once their task was done. They had taught the dwarfs how to work ore to forge structures, armour and weapons.

Grungni together with his sons, Smednir and Thungni had shown them the true nature of magic, how to capture it within the rune and etch it indelibly upon blades, talismans and armour in order to fashion artefacts of power. Bagrik had no love for the ephemeral sorcery of elves. Manipulating the true elements of the world in such a way was disharmonious. At best attempting to control them smacked of hubris, at worst it was disrespectful. No, Bagrik held no truck with such transient things. It angered him. The mage towers had been the first to go.

Crushed by hefty chunks of rock flung by dwarf stone throwers, the towers had exploded in a conflagration of myriad colours as they were destroyed, the arcane secrets and the alchemy of their denizens turned against them, and only serving to affirm Bagrik's vehement beliefs. They were just blackened spikes of stone now, broken fingers thrust into an uncaring sky, their communion with the stars at an end.

It was a fitting epitaph.

For the briefest of moments the air was on fire as elven sorcery met dwarf runecraft, forcing Bagrik back to the present. Further down the ridge, their litanies to the ancestors solemn and resonant, the runesmiths worked at their anvils. Not mere forgesmiths' anvils, no. These were runic artefacts – the Anvils of Doom. Agrin Oakenheart, venerable rune lord of Karak Ungor led his two apprentices, esteemed master runesmiths in their own right, in the rites of power as they dissipated hostile elven magicks and unleashed chained lightning upon the foe. With each arcing bolt, Bagrik felt his beard bristle as the charge ran through his ancestral armour.

Death wreathed the battlefield like a sombre shroud, but it was at the gatehouse where its greatest harvest would be reaped.

Break the gate, break the elves. Bagrik clenched his fist as his gaze fell upon the battle being fought there. He would settle for nothing less…

'HEAVE!' MOREK BELLOWED above the thunder. The dwarf's voice resonated through the bronze mask of his helmet as he urged his warriors again.

'Heave with all your strength. Grungni is watching you!'

And all thirty of his hearth guard warriors did.

Beneath the gromril-plated roof of a battering ram, the armoured dwarfs pulled the ram back for another charge. Runes etched down its iron shaft blazed as the gromril ram-head, forged into the bearded visage of the ancestor god Grungni, smashed into the gate. It was a barrier the likes of which Morek had never known, adorned with gemstones and carved from seemingly unbreakable wood. The eagle device upon the gate barely showed a scratch. The elves, despite his initial beliefs, knew their craft. Morek was determined that it would not avail them. Sweating beneath his armour, his orders were relentless.

'Again! There will be no rest until this gate is down!'

Shock waves ran down the iron with the impact as dwarf tenacity met elven resistance and found each other at an impasse.

Breathing hard as he wiped his beard with the back of his glove, Morek paused a moment and detected the groan of metal high above. It was the third day of the siege; he'd had plenty of time to survey the city's defences. The elves had cauldrons above the gatehouse.

'Shields!' he roared, long and loud.

The hearth guard reacted as one, creating a near-impenetrable shield wall to protect the vulnerable flanks of the battering ram.

Near-impenetrable but not invincible.

There was a whoosh of flame and an actinic stink permeated Morek's nose guard as the elves released their alchemical fire.

Screaming drowned out the roar of the conflagration as hearth guard warriors burned down like candles with shortened wicks. Reflected on the underside of his shield Morek saw a blurred shape fall from the narrow bridge where they made their assault and land in the moat beneath. A pillar of blue-white fire spiralled skyward as the burning dwarf struck the moat, so high it touched cloud. The elves, employing more of their thrice-cursed sorcery, had filled a deep trench around their city with molten silver and the alchemical fire's reaction with the shimmering liquid was spectacular yet terrifying.

A second deluge of the deadly liquid smashed against the battering ram, as the elves vented their stocks in desperation. Heat came through Morek's shield in a wave, pricking his skin despite his armour. He grit his teeth against the onslaught, watching iridescent sparks crackle and die upon the stone at his feet as the elven siege deterrent spilled away.

No screams this time. The attack abated. Two cauldrons had been expended. The elves had no more. It would take time for them to replenish the deadly liquid fire. In the brief respite, Morek took stock and smiled grimly. Only three hearth guard dead: his warriors had closed ranks quickly. But the elves had more. As the battering of the gate resumed, a flurry of white-fletched arrows whickered down at the dwarfs from above, thudding into shields and plate. Despite the armoured canopy of the ram, Morek took one in the pauldron. The dwarf at his flank, Hagri, was struck incredibly between gorget and face-guard, and died gurgling blood. Morek chewed his beard in anger. Hagri had fought at Morek's side for over seventy years. It was no way for such a noble warrior to die.

The arrow storm was relentless, the dwarfs effectively pinned as they raised shields again, unable to work the ram and protect themselves at the same time. Peering upwards through a crack between shield tip and the ram canopy, Morek saw white-robed elves – stern of face with silver swan helmets gleaming – loose steel-fanged death with ruthless purpose. Archers lined the battlements and as Morek scanned across he saw one of the elven mages incanting soundlessly as the battle din eclipsed his eldritch tongue. In a thunderclap of power, the mage was illuminated by a crackling cerulean aura. Forked lightning arced from his luminous form and the mage's silver hair stood on end as the energy was expulsed, straight towards Morek and his warriors. But before the bolts could strike they hit an invisible barrier and were deflected away. Blinking back the savage after flare, and muttering thanks to Agrin Oakenheart's rune-smiths, Morek tracked the bolt's erratic deviation.

One of the distant dwarf siege towers assaulting the eastern wall exploded as the lightning found a new target and vented its wrath. Dwarfs plunged earthward from the high parapet of the tower, mouthing silent screams. The assault ramp and the upper tower hoarding were utterly destroyed. Fire ravaged it within and without, and the siege tower came to a grinding halt. In its place though, three more towers moved into position, dragged and pushed by hordes of dwarf warriors, those at the front protected by large moveable pavises of iron and wood. As one, the heavy armoured ramps crashed down upon the elven parapets, crushing them before disgorging throngs of clansdwarfs.

All across the churned earth, as far as the deepening black of oncoming night in the distant east and west, the dwarfs marched in droves. Teams of sappers flung grapnels, heaving as they found purchase to tear down ruined sections of tower and wall. Quarrellers, crouching behind barricades or within shallow trench lines, kept up a steady barrage of bolts in an effort to stymie the heavy death toll being reaped by the elven archers and ballista. On the bloody ramps of the siege towers, and battling hard upon scaling ladders, dwarf warriors fought and died. But it was at the great gate, the principal entrance to the elven city, that the fighting was fiercest. Knowing this would be so, Morek had taken his finest hearth guard warriors and told his king he would break it. He had no intention of failing in that oath.

'We are like stuck grobi sat out here,' said Fundin Ironfinger, a hearth guard warrior crouched behind Morek, his shield locked with that of his thane.

Morek had to shout to be heard above the insistent thud of raining arrows.

'Bah, this is nothing, lad – a light shower, no more than that. They can't shoot at us forever, and once the elgi run out of arrows we'll have this gate down. Then they'll taste dawi steel–' Morek was forced to duck down as the storm intensified.

'Eh, lad?' he said during a short lull in the arrow fire, looking back at Fundin.

The hearth guard didn't answer. He was dead; shot through the eye.

Dutifully, another hearth guard moved up the line to take his place and Fundin's body was edged beyond the relative protection of the canopy to be punctured with further arrows.

No, Morek thought grimly, he had no intention of failing in his oath but if the arrow storm didn't end soon, he'd have no warriors left to break down the gate and fulfil it. Touching the runic amulet around his neck, he made a pledge to Grungni that this would not be so.

* * *

THE AIR WAS thick with arrows, bolts, fire, lightning and
stone. Bagrik watched as a battery of mangonels flung
massive chunks of rock that had been hewn from the
hillside and smashed them into Tor Eorfith, shattering
walls and pulverising flesh and bone. With grim satisfaction, he saw one missile strike the central arch of the
elven gatehouse where his hearth guard stood beleaguered beneath their battering ram.

Elven bodies fell like white rain.

CHEERS GREETED THE destruction of the gatehouse, the
arrow storm brought to an abrupt and bloody halt.
Debris fell along with the elven dead, fat pieces of rock
and limp bodies bouncing off the gromril roof of the
battering ram.

Morek urged the hearth guard on to even greater
efforts. They swung and pushed, swung and pushed with
the thunderous insistence of an angry giant. At last, the
runes upon the ram-head were doing their work, forcing
cracks into the sorcerous wards that galvanised the gate.
Magic permeated all that the elves did; it was even seeped
into the very rock and wood of their settlements. Tor Eorfith was no different. It had been enchantment that had
repulsed the dwarfs for this long. That protection had
ended with the life of the silver-haired mage, now nothing more than a shattered footnote in history, dead and
broken at the foot of the outer gatehouse wall.

Thickening cracks appeared in the eagle gate as it
finally yielded to the punishing efforts of the hearth
guard.

Morek could sense they were close.

'One last pull!'

With an almighty splintering of wood, the elven gate
was split in two. Through the rough-hewn gap, Morek

glimpsed azure robes and shining elven mail. A cohort of spearmen faced them; tips angled outward like a forest of razor spikes. Then as one the elves parted like a crystal sea to reveal a pair of bolt throwers of ivory-stained wood, and both fashioned into an effigy of a hawk.

The dwarfs raised shields as the javelin-like projectiles flew at them. Three more of the hearth guard were killed, impaled on the sharp missiles. Morek swung his axe once the barrage was over, working out the stiffness from his shoulder. The spearmen had closed ranks again, ready to skewer the foe. Morek raised his axe, runes upon the blade shimmering, and signalled the charge.

BAGRIK WATCHED THE gatehouse fall and the hearth guard rush forward to meet the elven spearmen within. The high ridge was an excellent vantage point to view the battle from and the king took in the full spectacle. Even as the elves fought, as they spat arrows from their tower walls, unleashed arcane fire and lightning and thrust with gleaming spears and swords, Bagrik could tell that this was the final push. The dwarf army was on the brink of breaking through.

Three long days, and the cusp of victory was within his grasp. It did nothing to satisfy him, it did not slake his thirst for vengeance, nor did it quieten his anger. No protracted siege this; no picket lines had been erected, no wells blocked or provisions destroyed or tainted. Full assault. That was all. Come his reckoning at Gazul's Gate, the final portal before admittance into the Halls of Ancestors and the dwarf afterlife, Bagrik would be held to account for the blood expended.

He cared not.

'My king,' the voice of Grikk Ironbeard, captain of the ironbreakers, interrupted Bagrik's thoughts. Grikk bowed low before his king as he announced himself. Not one inch of the ironbreaker's body could be seen beneath the all-encompassing suit of gromril. Even his face was concealed behind a stylised dwarf mask. Only Grikk's wiry black beard was visible. It was a necessary precaution. As an ironbreaker, Grikk was responsible for guarding the dwarf underway, a dangerous underground road between the holds that was fraught with many monsters. Today, Grikk had a different task. But it was one for which his ironbreaker armour and his skills as a tunnel fighter were ideally suited.

'Rugnir and the sappers are ready. The final assault can commence.'

Bagrik nodded, his gaze drifting over to the south wall of the city where Rugnir and the hold's engineers were tunnelling in preparation to undermine it. Bagrik had five throngs of clan warriors held in reserve, together with the hold's longbeards to exploit the breach when it came.

Bagrik's gaze remained fixed as he replied gruffly.

'Secure the tunnel, kill any opposition.'

'Yes, my king.'

Grikk departed swiftly, the sound of clanking armour left in his wake.

Bagrik watched a moment longer before he gave the order to advance. An entire phalanx stood upon the flat ridge, clan warriors and hearth guard all. Ten thousand more dwarfs. The hammer with which to crush the elves beneath the anvil of warriors already breaking through the elven defences below. War horns blared down the line one after the other, raising a thunderous clamour. The dwarfs' march towards the elven city was resolute and relentless. Bagrik went with them, brought to the forefront of the attack and into the cauldron of battle by his shield bearers.

Regarding the bloody fire-wreathed vista, the swathes of dead, the wanton destruction levelled at two great civilisations, Bagrik couldn't help wonder.

How did it all come to this?

CHAPTER TWO
Fateful Meetings

KARAK UNGOR WAS the northern-most fastness of all the mountain holds of the Karaz Ankor, the everlasting realm of the dwarfs. The rocky edifice of stone and bronze was a monument of dwarf tenacity and their expertise in the building of impregnable fortresses. For over two thousand years, Karak Ungor had stood stalwart against ice storms, cataclysm and the predations of greenskins. In the eyes of the dwarfs, this was but an eye blink in the grand chronology of history, for the mountain dwellers made things to last and endure the capricious ravages of time and conquest.

In the vastness of the hold's outer gateway hall, a small welcoming committee awaited their guests from across the Great Ocean. These dwarfs were little more than specks in a huge expanse of stone, standing before the immense gate that led out of the hold and into the northern Worlds Edge Mountains.

Gigantic figureheads of the ancestor gods that were carved into the rock of the mountain loomed over them. Grungni, Valaya and Grimnir, the greatest of all the ancient deities of the dwarfs, each dominated one of the three open walls of the chamber. Craggy-featured, the ancestors were stern and imposing as they regarded their descendants as if in silent appraisal. No dwarf would ever wish to be found wanting under their gaze.

The fourth wall was taken up almost entirely by the great gate. It was encompassed by a sweeping arch of bronze, and inlaid with runes of gold and myriad gem-stones dug from the mountain. The gate itself was a huge slab of smoothed stone with copper filigree describing an effigy of two dwarf kings upon their thrones. It was a magnificent sight and the main entrance into and out of the hold. Either side of it were a pair of statuesque hearth guard, their faces hardly vis-ible beneath their stout, half-face helmets and braided beards. Each carried a broad-bladed axe, resting against the pauldron of their ancient armour, their stillness belying their readiness. One bore a large bronze-rimmed warhorn at rest next to his chest. He was the gate warden and the hold's chief herald.

Above the quartet of warriors, patrolling a stone plat-form that rose over the great gate arch, were ten quarrellers with crossbows slung across their backs. These dwarfs were the interior gate guard, the first line of defence of the hold and from whom the call to arms would be raised should it come under attack.

Morek, at the edge of the welcoming party, fidgeted restlessly in his armour. He had wanted to double the troops on the gate and supplement it with a cohort of thirty more hearth guard by way of a show of strength and intent, but the queen would not have it – they were negotiating trade with the elves, not war.

Queen Brunvilda, wife of the great king Bagrik, was at Morek's right, occupying the centre of the delegation. She was royally attired with deep blue robes, fringed with gold and threaded with runes of copper and bronze. Upon her brow she wore a simple mitre with a single ruby in the middle. Her long hair was the colour of tanned leather, bound up in concentric knots and pinned in place invisibly. Around her waist was a bodice of leather that squeezed her matronly figure and accentuated her ample bosom. It was augmented by a gilded and bejewelled cincture. Her eyes were grey like slate but held warmth akin to the forge fires of the lower deeps. All told, Morek thought she was a remarkable woman.

The dwarf thane had his own claim to royalty, albeit a weak one. His clan was a distant cousin to that of High King Gotrek Starbreaker. There was noble blood in his veins, though he had never sought a regal claim, always content to serve the kings and queens of Ungor.

To the queen's right was Kandor Silverbeard, a merchant, diplomat and the royal treasurer. Kandor wore expensive garments of emerald and tan, a testament to the profit of his gold gathering and silver-laced tongue. He was festooned with gilded accoutrements, including a lacquered wood cane encrusted with gemstones. Though Morek had no clue why Kandor needed it; the merchant could walk perfectly well without a stick. Kandor's reddish beard was well groomed and immaculately braided, his hair combed and pristine. Despite himself, Morek brushed down his armour surreptitiously with a gloved hand in an effort to make its gleam more lustrous. He saw the merchant look askance at him, halting Morek's pre-emptive preening in its tracks. The captain of the hearth guard's response was gruff and inaudible.

The rest of the party was made up of ten more hearth guard, the only additional warriors the queen had conceded to, imposing in their ranks behind them. None of the dwarfs had spoken for some time since their arrival in the outer gateway hall, though a dulcet chorus of hammers striking anvils carried from the lower deeps on air heavy with the smell of soot and thick with forge-warmth.

Morek broke the silence.

'Your elgi guests are late.'

Kandor Silverbeard didn't look over as he answered.

'They will arrive soon enough, Morek. Don't you have any patience?'

'Aye, I've plenty. I could stand here until Grimnir returned from the Northern Wastes and still wait another fifty years if needs be,' barked Morek, feeling challenged as he levelled his steely gaze at the imperious merchant.

'They are guests of our hold, Thane Stonehammer, not merely that of Kandor Silverbeard's,' said Queen Brunvilda, her tone soft yet powerful.

'Of course, my queen.' Chastened, Morek averted his gaze from her, feeling a sudden burning at his cheeks, and was glad his armour largely hid his face. 'But we dwarfs have strict habits and routines. All I'm saying is lateness is no way to gain our favour.'

'Their ways are not our ways,' the queen counselled, though she didn't need to remind Morek of the fact. To his mind, elves were utterly unlike the dwarfs in both appearance and demeanour. These stargazing explorers were not content in their own lands it seemed, and deliberately sought out others to satisfy some innate wanderlust. Morek thought them effete and brittle; he fancied they would be ill-suited to life within the hold. He smirked beneath his faceplate at the thought of their discomfort and hoped they would soon leave as a result of it.

'It begs the question then, my lady, how we ever think an agreement can be reached between our peoples?' Morek returned, choosing his words carefully so as not to offend his queen.

Kandor answered for her.

'You are a warrior, Morek, so I shall leave the defence of the realm to you,' he said, turning to look at the captain of the hearth guard. 'But I am a merchant and ambassador, so I ask you leave matters of trade and diplomacy to me. This pact will succeed. What's more, it will strengthen our realm and ensure its continued prosperity.'

'You'd do well to remember that all dwarfs are charged with the protection of the hold,' Morek replied. 'And do not think me so foolish as to be unaware of your eye for profit in this.'

'As royal treasurer, it is for the wealth of the clans of Ungor that I—'

'Enough!' said Queen Brunvilda, halting Kandor's retort before it could continue, 'Our guests are here.'

Slowly, a portal within the great gate was opening. Much smaller than the gate itself, the portal was the true entryway into the hold. The grand doorway of Karak Ungor had not been opened in over two thousand years, not since it had first been founded and the entirety of the hold's armies had marched forth to join the forces of the then High King, the venerable Snorri Whitebeard. Dwarfs and elves had come together then, too, but despite the intractable nature of the dwarfs, things had changed during that time and alliances were now being forged anew.

A clarion call resonated throughout the large chamber as the gate warden blew hard on his warhorn, announcing the arrival of the elves. At his signal, his fellow warriors stood to attention, the stamp of their booted feet in perfect unison, and the quarrellers stopped patrolling as they observed an honourable stillness before their new allies from across the sea.

The elves were fey creatures, tall and proud, whose pale skin shimmered with an otherworldly lustre. They glided across the dwarf flagstones as light as air, their white and azure robes fluttering on some unseen breeze. There was a stark and wondrous beauty about them, powerful and frightening at the same time. Yet to Morek's eyes, they seemed delicate and thin. Despite their unearthly aura, what could these lofty creatures possess that the dwarfs had any need of?

The party of elves was led by what Morek assumed was an ambassador amongst their people. He was dressed in white robes. Golden vambraces, worn for decoration, gleamed beneath wide sleeves trimmed with tiny sapphires. The ambassador's hair was the colour of silver and rested upon either shoulder evenly, and though his smile was benign, sadness lingered behind his eyes that he could not hide.

A warrior wearing ceremonial half-armour of fluted plate and overlapping scale of glimmering silver followed closely behind. His eyes, almond-shaped like the rest of his kin, seemed perpetually narrowed, and a long angular nose spoke of royal bearing. A slender sword, its hilt encrusted with rubies, was scabbarded at a plaited belt at the elf's waist. Golden hair cascaded from his stern countenance, and a gilded crown set with gem-stones framed the elf's brow as he regarded the hall with haughty indifference. This then was their leader, Morek decided, the elf prince.

Two others came in the prince's wake, also nobles. One was a male with long, black hair, also enrobed, though his garb was ostensibly more opulent than that of the ambassador. This one had an ill-favoured look about him, and Morek saw the implied threat in the way the elf toyed idly with the hilt of the sword that he wore at his waist.

His companion was a female, similarly attired, though she wore a small circlet of silver around her head. The pair were muttering quietly, in such close consort that Morek found it uncomfortable to watch them. Certainly, the female possessed a… *presence* that the hearth guard was at once attracted to and repelled by. He had to fight to stop himself from lowering his gaze. The male alongside her, walking with a disdainful swagger, seemed to notice the dwarf's discomfort and whispered something into the female's ear to which she laughed quietly. Morek felt his cheeks redden and his annoyance grow.

One other elf stood out from the rest of the entourage that trailed in after the nobles in pairs, an entourage that consisted of musicians, gift bearers, pennant carriers, servants and some fifty elven spearmen. He was bigger than the rest, not just taller, but broader too, and seemed the most ill at ease with their newfound surroundings. His straw-coloured hair was wild and bound into a series of plaited tails. A thick pelt of white fur was draped over his muscled shoulders and he wore scale armour over which was a gilt breastplate. A long dagger was sheathed at his hip and a doubled-bladed axe slung across his back.

The bodyguard, Morek thought, noting the way that this elf surveyed the chamber, searching every darkened alcove for threats and enemies. Perhaps, Morek wondered, not all elves were so weak and fanciful. Was it possible he had misjudged them?

PRINCE ITHALRED WRINKLED his nose at the foul stench of the dwarfs' domain. A 'magnificent hold' he had been told. It looked like little more than a tomb buried into the earth, gladly forgotten but now exhumed for some unconscionable reason. This 'great gate' Malbeth had spoken of was little more than roughly hewn stone peppered with gemstones. It had none of the flowing lines, the smoothness and artful consideration of elvish architecture. Worse still, the air was stiflingly hot and thick with acrid fumes. Ithalred smelled oil, tasted soot in his mouth and at once longed for the high silver towers of his realm at Tor Eorfith.

What is this place you have brought us to, Malbeth? he thought, his eyes upon the ambassador's back as he led them to the awaiting dwarfs.

'They call this hole in the ground a *kingdom*?' Lethralmir whispered to Arthelas, echoing his prince's thoughts as he strode behind him. The seeress laughed quietly, her musical voice arousing more than just the simple pleasure of companionship in the blade-master.

'They build such grand chambers, though, Lethralmir,' she whispered back.

'Mighty indeed,' the elf replied sarcastically, casting his gaze about in the gloom. 'Yet *they* are so diminutive. Do you think, perhaps, that they are compensating for something?' he added, smirking.

Arthelas laughed out loud, unable to control herself. A scathing glance from Prince Ithalred silenced them both.

'Your brother is ever the serious diplomat, is he not, dear Arthelas?' scoffed Lethralmir in an undertone.

The seeress smiled demurely, and the elven blade-master felt his ardour deepen.

'WELCOME DEAR FRIENDS, to Karak Ungor,' said Kandor, bowing before the elf ambassador. The dwarf merchant's gaze extended the greeting to all, in particular the prince, who seemed unmoved by the gesture.

'*Tromm*, Kandor Silverbeard,' said the ambassador warmly, in rudimentary Khazalid, and clasped Kandor's hand firmly.

'Tromm, Malbeth. You honour us with these words,' Kandor returned, glowing outwardly at the elf's use of the dwarfs' native tongue – 'tromm' was used by way of greeting and a mark of respect amongst dwarfs at the length and quality of their beards. The incongruousness of an elf saying it was not lost on Morek, however.

Honour us? Kandor, you are a grobi-fondling wazzock, the elgi has no beard! If anything, he besmirches us with his hairless chin, thought Morek, gritting his teeth at the merchant's obsequiousness, and wondering if Kandor's ancestral line was tainted with elf blood.

This was not Malbeth's first visit to the hold. The elf was a ranger, as well as an ambassador, and had travelled from Yvresse on the east coast of Ulthuan, across the Great Ocean and to the Old World. There he had met Kandor Silverbeard, who was delivering shipments of ore southwards to the other holds of the Worlds Edge Mountains. The two had struck up a firm friendship, echoing that of the elf lord, Malekith, and the first High King of the dwarfs, Snorri Whitebeard. It was but an echo of that halcyon time. That former alliance was now cast in an inauspicious light, the traitorous son of

Aenarion the Defender having fled Ulthuan before the might of Caledor the First, and now seeking succour in the lands of Naggaroth.

Such things were not of consequence, however, and talk between dwarf and elf had soon turned to trade, and after accompanying Kandor as far south as Mount Gunbad, they had returned north to Karak Ungor. The elf's stay had been brief, and Morek had never met the ambassador during that time, though he looked as effeminate as he had imagined.

'We too are honoured, by your generous hospitality,' the elf, Malbeth, replied before turning to the dwarf queen.

'Noble Queen Brunvilda,' he said, bowing. 'It seems like only yesterday when I was last a guest in these halls.'

'Aye, Malbeth,' began the queen, 'It has only been twenty-three years, little more than a shift in the wind,' she said, smiling broadly.

Malbeth returned the gesture, before announcing the rest of his kin. 'May I present Arthelas, seeress of Tor Eorfith and the prince's sister.' The demure elf came forward and gave a shallow bow to the queen, before Malbeth continued, 'Lethralmir, of the prince's court.' The ambassador's gaze seemed to harden as it fell upon the lean-faced blade-master, who gave an overly extravagant bow towards their dwarf hosts. 'This is Korhvale of Chrace, the prince's champion,' Malbeth added. The muscular elf preferred to stand as he was, with his prince in eyeshot, and only nodded sternly.

'Finally,' said Malbeth, stepping back, 'Prince Ithalred of Tor Eorfith.'

The prince came forward of his own accord, eyeing each of the dwarfs in turn, his gaze lingering on the warriors especially.

'I do not see your king,' said Ithalred abruptly, dispensing with all bonhomie as if it were an enemy run through on his sword.

Morek bristled at the elf's impertinence, about to speak before a glance from Queen Brunvilda stopped him.

'I am Queen Brunvilda of Karak Ungor,' she said to the prince, stepping forward and inclining her head in greeting. 'The king will meet us in the Great Hall once you are settled. Alas, an old wound makes walking for my liege lord difficult and I was sent to greet you in his place.'

Prince Ithalred glanced around, not deigning to look the queen in the eye as he replied. 'I look forward to our first meeting,' he said, his own mastery of the dwarf language, unlike Malbeth's, was crude as if the words were uneasy on his tongue.

'He dishonours our queen!' Morek hissed to Kandor who had retreated to stand alongside the hearth guard captain.

'They do not know our customs, that is all,' Kandor snapped back in a harsh whisper, his withering gaze demanding silence.

Ithalred seemed not to hear and turned and spoke in elvish to his attendants. Upon his beckoning, the servants and gift bearers came forward.

'We bring riches from our island realm as a token of our friendship.' The prince's words were neither warm nor obviously sincere, though the array of gifts was fine indeed with belts of silks, beauteous elf potteries, opulent furs and spices.

'We are honoured by these tokens,' said the queen, still observing due deference to the prince.

'Yes,' Prince Ithalred answered, 'and yet I see your hospitality extends to meeting us with armed guards.'

A slight ripple of indignation crossed the queen's face but she did not act on it.

'They are the ceremonial honour guard of Karak Ungor,' she explained carefully, her tone calm but taut. 'In our traditions, these warriors greet kings and nobles of other holds. So it is the same with you, good prince.'

'Are we to be "guarded" then, whilst we visit this… *hold*?' the elf continued. 'Under house arrest until we are due to return? This does not smack of alliance, being met by warriors at your kingdom's gate like an enemy laying siege to its walls.'

'It is a great honour to be received by the royal hearth guard!' bellowed Morek suddenly, unable to keep his patience any longer.

'Captain Morek,' snapped Queen Brunvilda, before the elves could reply. 'Hold your tongue!'

Ithalred was fashioning a retort when Malbeth intervened. 'Please, there is no need. My prince is tired from our journey and acknowledges this gracious welcome,' he said with a glance at Ithalred, who, to the ambassador's apparent relief, seemed suddenly disinterested in the exchange. Though Malbeth also caught a look from the black-haired elf, the one called Lethralmir, who smiled mirthlessly at him. The ambassador averted his gaze, focussing his attention back to the dwarf queen.

'Perhaps we can be shown to our quarters?' Malbeth suggested. 'A rest will clear all our heads of fatigue.'

'Of course,' Queen Brunvilda said politely, turning to Kandor.

'We have prepared extensive chambers for you and your party,' the merchant said quickly, his relief at the crisis having been averted obvious on his face.

'They expect us to dwell in caves like them, no doubt,' hissed the black-haired elf.

Morek found his distaste towards Lethralmir deepening by the moment as he spoke to the eldritch female, Arthelas. She seemed to wane as the talk went on, her beauty slowly fracturing as if the travails of the elves' journey were taking a heavy toll.

Kandor seemed not to hear the black-haired elf's remark, or least he chose to ignore it, determined as he was to win over the delegation.

'If you would follow me,' he said courteously.

Cringing wattock, thought Morek then said, 'Wait,' and showed his palm. 'No weapons may be carried by an outsider beyond the outer gateway hall,' he told the elves, 'You must relinquish them here.'

At a signal from their captain, the hearth guard came forward to collect the elves' spears, bows and blades. At the same time, the one wearing the furs, Korhvale, stepped between his prince and the advancing dwarfs. Though he didn't speak, his intentions were clear. No elf would be handing over their arms.

The prince muttered something in elvish to the warrior who stepped back, though his eyes never left the hearth guard.

'Is this how you establish a bond of trust, by surrounding your allies with troops and then demanding they submit their weapons?' the prince asked with growing agitation.

'We request it only,' said Kandor, still trying to recover the situation. 'Your weapons would be stored in a private armoury.'

'Private?' queried the prince, waving away his ambassador's nascent protests, 'I see little privacy or consideration here, *dwarf*.'

'Even still,' Morek asserted, stepping forward in spite of the six elf spearmen that had come swiftly, almost unnoticeably, to their prince's side and were brandishing their arms with meaning. 'You *will* be disarmed before you enter the hold proper.'

Though Morek was over three feet shorter than the elves, he stood before them unshakeable like a mountain and would not be disobeyed.

The elven bodyguard, Korhvale, interceded again, knuckles clenched and aggression written across his face.

'Then you shall have to *take* them from us,' he muttered, his elven accent thick as he struggled to pronounce the words. This time Ithalred was content to let it play out, his face a mask of stone. Behind him, the black-haired elf watched with profound amusement, an ugly smile upon his lips, whilst the female seemed suddenly fearful and unsure of where the confrontation was heading.

Morek had no such concerns.

'By Grungni, I *will* do it,' he snarled belligerently, reaching for his axe. His hearth guard moved up behind him, enclosing the other dwarf nobles and preparing to brandish their own weapons.

'Thane Stonehammer!' bellowed Queen Brunvilda, who had kept her silence throughout the heated exchange until now. 'Do not dare draw your weapon in anger before me,' she ordered. 'Return your hearth guard to the west hall barracks at once.'

Morek turned and made a face behind his armoured mask, the substance of his mood obvious in his eyes.

'I would not leave you... *unattended* my queen,' he protested with a fierce glance at the glowering elves. 'No hearth guard in the history of the hold has ever–'

'I am well aware of our hold's history, my thane, and have lived many long years within its halls. What need have I of warriors at my side with you as my honour guard,' she added with a thin smile, by way of maintaining Morek's reputation and standing. 'Your concern is unnecessary. Now, please dismiss the hearth guard.'

Morek opened his mouth again, made clear by the movement of his beard, but clamped it shut when the queen's own expression made it apparent that she would brook no further argument.

The captain of the hearth guard's shoulders sagged slightly, though he took care to fire a warning glare at Korhvale before he retreated.

You were close to tasting my axe, it said. Morek meant every word.

Morek bowed once in front of the queen, who nodded in turn, before ordering his warriors from the outer gateway hall. Dutifully the dwarfs departed, the sound of clanking armour echoing in their wake, and Morek went to stand back alongside his queen having to content himself with glowering at the elves.

'Now, dear *friends*,' Queen Brunvilda began anew, 'as queen of Karak Ungor, I humbly ask you to leave your blades and bows here. No armed force has ever entered Karak Ungor, save those of us dawi. I will not break with that tradition now,' she said, her voice soft but commanding. 'I, nor any of my warriors, shall take them from you. Rather you will be *asked* to relinquish them. There is an antechamber to this very hall where you may take your weapons until you are ready to leave us. Noble Prince Ithalred,' she added, facing the prince, 'your fine sword is clearly an heirloom and we dwarfs know the value and importance of such bonds. I would not ask you to part with it and, as such, I give you my personal sanction to carry it in this hold. A dwarf's oath is his bond,' she said, 'and it is stronger than stone.'

The prince was about to respond when a meaningful glare from his ambassador, Malbeth, made him hesitate. Understanding passed between them and when Ithalred spoke again, his truculent demeanour had abated.

'That is acceptable,' he said, this time looking her in the eye.

'Very well then,' replied the queen. 'You are invited to the Great Hall once you are settled in your quarters. The hold of Karak Ungor has prepared a feast and entertainments in your honour.'

'You are most gracious, noble queen,' Malbeth interjected.

With that Queen Brunvilda bowed again as did the elves in turn, passing slowly from the outer gateway hall to stow their weapons in the antechamber. After that was done, closely watched by Morek, they were then led by Kandor to their quarters.

Once she was alone with the hearth guard captain, Queen Brunvilda sighed deeply. The elves had barely got through their doors and already hostility was rife.

'That could have been worse,' said Morek honestly, aware that his own enmity towards the elves had only fuelled the fires of discord.

The queen offered only stern-faced silence by way of response.

'The elgi are rude and without honour,' Morek said to fill the uncomfortable silence.

'Yet, we managed to match them,' Queen Brunvilda replied, her gaze upon the disappearing train of elves as they walked down the long corridor to their quarters.

'But, my queen, they disrespect us… and in our own domain!' Morek cried, and regretted raising his voice at once.

Queen Brunvilda's glare was now fixed upon him, and laden with steel.

'They disrespected *you*, my queen,' the captain of the hearth guard said, his voice tender as he looked into the matriarch's eyes.

For a moment, Queen Brunvilda's expression softened, then, as if catching herself, her stone-like disposition returned together with her anger at Morek.

'Let us hope that their mood improves,' she said quietly, and headed off to the Great Hall where her king was waiting for her.

'THIS DANK, THIS dark, I feel it seeping into my very marrow,' said Prince Ithalred, a scowl creasing his face as he watched the elven artisans erect his grand marquee.

Kandor, the dwarf merchant, had brought the elves to what he described as the 'Hall of Belgrad' in the eastern wing of the hold. These 'quarters' consisted of an expansive central chamber, where it was presumed the elf prince and his entourage would stay, flanked by two wide galleries where his warriors could be barracked, and four antechambers, two each feeding off the barrack rooms, for servants and storage.

Though long abandoned by the dwarfs when the seams of ore nearby were exhausted, the rooms were still magnificent and lavishly decorated. Flagstones of ochre and tan decked the floors and were polished to a lustrous sheen. Gilt archways, glittering with jewels, soared overhead into vaulted ceilings supported by thick, stone columns inlaid with silver and bronze. Flickering torches, ensconced along the walls, cast a warm glow that shimmered like burnished gold. This 'opulence' had failed to move or impress the elves, and once the dwarf had taken his leave, the prince was quick to set his servants to work.

According to Kandor, the Hall of Belgrad was formerly the dwelling of a long-dead dwarf noble. At least that was as much as Ithalred could discern with the few words of Khazalid he knew.

'It is every inch the crypt that the dwarf described,' he said, as the cohorts of servants laboured hard to fashion something more to his liking.

Belts of flowing white silk were unfurled across the flagstone floor then taken up and affixed to wooden stanchions to make large tents. Elven designs had been stitched into the luxurious cloth: runes of Lileath, Isha and Kurnous, preying hawks and soaring eagles, the rising phoenix and rampant dragon. They represented Ulthuan, their gods and the symbols of their power.

Once the tents were up they were filled with thick rugs and furs, hanging tapestries and carved wood furnishings such as beds, stools and chests decorated with elven imagery and fine jewels. Ithalred had brought several draught horses and elven carts with him from Eataine. This baggage train had entered the hold with the servants, and its horses were housed within the overground stables of the dwarfs – elvish steeds ill-suited to life under the earth.

Each of the marquees the elves had brought with them that were reserved for the nobles had several rooms. They were sumptuously decorated according to their specific tastes with pillows and pennants. Long velvet curtains contained the aroma from silver dishes of slowly burning spices intended to ward off the stench of soot and oil from the underground hold.

As ambassador to the prince, Malbeth, too, was afforded a separate abode. The remainder of the elven cohort had less grandiose accommodations, their tents smaller and bereft of the outrageous finery and luxury prevalent in the grand marquees, but not without comforts of their own.

'It is not what we're… *used to*, my prince but this hall obviously has some significance to the dwarfs. By granting us such accommodations they are bestowing great honour,' counselled Malbeth, the inauspicious start to their visit at the forefront of his mind.

'Malbeth, are you so beguiled by this soot-stained race that you cannot see the cave we are meant to dwell in, or has Loec tricked you with some glamour that hides the truth of the matter?' Lethralmir asked, arriving at the prince's side with Arthelas in tow.

The ambassador stiffened at the noble's presence but bit his tongue when he felt his heart quicken with anger. Lethralmir was Ithalred's closest companion, his best friend. They had shared swords on the field of battle many times over and a bond forged in blood was unwise to challenge. Malbeth would only lose Ithalred's favour if he spoke out against the blade-master, and he would need the prince on side if they were to come to any agreement with the dwarfs.

'An honour you say?' Lethralmir continued. 'I do not see it as such. These earth-dwellers may be content to roll around in muck, even consign their royal households to such ignominy, but the purebloods of Ulthuan will not bow down to such debased levels.'

Arthelas giggled quietly. Even Ithalred suppressed a smile at the blade-master's remark.

A servant approached before Lethralmir could speak further, though he did manage to flash a furtive grin at Arthelas. It was not so secretive that it escaped Ithalred's notice, however, or that of his towering bodyguard, Korhvale, who had appeared silently behind them.

'My lord,' said the servant, bowing as he addressed the prince, 'where should I put this?' The plain-robed elf carried a small chest of dwarf design, one that was obviously intended for the prince. From the clinking sound emanating within, it seemed that there were bottles of some description inside.

Ithalred stared at the item as if it were something unpleasant he had stepped in.

'Put it with the rest,' he said, and looked away. The servant took it as a gesture to leave.

Malbeth watched him take the dwarf chest into one of the antechambers where he saw the shadowy outline of other furnishings and victuals from their hosts. The dwarfs had laid on a small banquet of food and drink, together with stools and tables that their guests could use. The elves had swept it all away swiftly, stashing the items unceremoniously where they'd be out of the way and out of sight. It pained Malbeth to see it. He had hoped Ithalred would have tried to embrace the dwarfs' culture. It seemed, though, that he had no desire to.

Even the dwarf torches had been doused, the prince complaining of the smell and the smoke they exuded. In their place the servants had hung elven lanterns from gossamer-thin cords of silver. Immaculately carved wooden stanchions supported the loping lengths of silver that carried the lanterns and these in turn were decorated with some of the native flora of Ulthuan. The scent of the flowers did, in part, mask the heady stench of soot, oil and damp stone that permeated the air, and were supplemented by incense burners, great golden cauldrons set around the main hall, that cast an eldritch glow.

Once they were finished, it was as if the elves had created a small corner of Tor Eorfith within the subterranean halls of Karak Ungor.

'It will have to do,' said Prince Ithalred, striding towards his marquee. 'Lethralmir,' he added. The other noble stopped in his tracks as he sidled up to the prince's sister.

Korhvale's face darkened abruptly when the blade-master approached Arthelas.

'Yes, Ithalred?' said Lethralmir.

'Have my servants pour me a bath, and send a maiden to bathe me. I have need for this stink to be washed from my body.'

'Of course, my prince,' Lethralmir replied, masking his annoyance well as he stalked off to gather the servants.

'What of the trade pact, Ithalred?' Malbeth interjected, just as the prince was about to disappear through the door flap of his tent. 'We have much to discuss.'

'I will attend to it later... over wine,' he replied, and entered his dwelling without looking back.

Korhvale was quick to follow, though he stopped short of going inside, contenting himself to standing at the door. He was a White Lion, the traditional body-guard of the nobles of Ulthuan, and a native of the mountainous region of Chrace. Malbeth liked Korhvale. Though sullen and taciturn, he spoke plainly and hon-estly, and without the venom-tongued bile that Lethralmir favoured. The ambassador noticed the White Lion linger a little too long on Arthelas as she departed to her tent, averting his gaze when she made eye con-tact.

It seems you have many would-be suitors, thought Malbeth as he retired to his own dwelling, *a fact that will displease your brother, seeress.*

THE TENT FLAP closed behind him and Malbeth sighed deeply, before dismissing his servants so that he could be alone. He had worked hard to forge this meeting with the dwarfs, in spite of Ithalred's resistance. He knew it would not be easy, that his greatest obstacle would be the prince's attitude, his arrogance. As a child of Eataine, his blood carried within it the royalty of Ulthuan and Ithalred was as noble and proud as any of his forebears. His grandfather had even fought alongside Aenarion himself, aiding the greatest and arguably most tragic of all the elf heroes to cast the daemon hordes back into the abyss that had spawned them.

History was not the only thing working in Ithalred's favour. The estates of his father and uncle were extensive, his family amongst the most affluent of all the Inner Kingdoms. Ithalred, though, had no desire to cement his fortune in lands and title, he was an explorer, and in that he and Malbeth were kindred souls. Small wonder having seen the Glittering Tower – that glorious spike of purest silver, blazing like an eternal beacon before the Emerald Gate of Lothern – that Ithalred had turned to the life of the wayfarer and desired to set sail for lands across the Great Ocean. He could no more deny its call than a dwarf could suppress his urge to dig into the earth and explore the mountains. It was in his blood.

Malbeth knew it had been personally hard for the prince to come to the dwarfs, even under the mask of a trade agreement, but come he had and now they needed to make the best of things, to ingratiate their hosts if they could. Ithalred's narrow-mindedness, his imperious superiority was always going to make things difficult, but Malbeth had fostered hopes that the first meeting with the dwarfs would have gone better in spite of all that.

Their need was a dire one, if only the prince would acknowledge it. Establishing a trade pact with the dwarfs was a small but necessary thing; without it the elves would never get what they truly wanted from them.

CHAPTER THREE
Goblin Hunting

SIX DWARFS STALKED down a narrow, rocky gorge. Despite a distance of some several miles, the towering peaks of Karak Ungor still loomed in the background like rocky sentinels watching the party's progress. The dwarfs moved in single file, against the wind, their cloaks fluttering in a chill breeze. Wearing tunics over shirts of mail, each with a low slung crossbow over his back, the dwarfs were hunting, and their prey was not far.

'We are close, Prince Nagrim,' said Brondrik at the head of the group. He was crouched by a cluster of rocks jutting out on the snow-dappled trail. He eyed the edge of the gorge ahead, the scree path rising to a natural plateau.

Nagrim nodded at the old pathfinder, watching him sniff the cold mountain air, his nose wrinkling as he detected the scent of greenskins.

'Their foul stink is heaviest here,' added Brondrik, spitting onto the ground as if the stench had left a bitter taste in his mouth.

'How many?' asked Nagrim, peering through the fitful drifts of snow funnelled down the ravine by the wind.

'Nineteen, I think,' Brondrik replied, before moving on. 'Very near, now.'

Brondrik wore his ranger's garb, a green-grey tunic with a small cloak of *hruk* wool. The hruk were a hardy breed of mountain goat that the dwarfs reared on overground farms and mining settlements. The beasts produced hard-wearing wool, perfect for ranging over the crags of the mountains. Brondrik wore scars too, across his cheek and right ear. His beard was tan with flecks of grey, left to grow as it will. When the venerable pathfinder had smelled the goblin musk, he'd snarled, showing three missing teeth.

Nagrim grinned broadly as he thought of the quarry just ahead.

He would beat his father's tally this day.

The dwarf prince, in contrast to the pathfinder, was dressed in a deep blue tunic. Its hue indicated his heritage and the legacy he carried as a member of the royal household of Karak Ungor. Thick bronze vambraces were clapped around Nagrim's wrists, whilst copper torques banded his muscled arms, and gold ingot pins secured his plaited dark brown beard. Over his shoulders sat bronze pauldrons, the mantle of his ranger's cloak clasped to them. He was armed for the hunt, his crossbow slung over his broad back, and a hand axe cinctured at his waist by a strip of leather.

The hunting party reached the end of the rocky gorge, filing out onto a barren plateau of rock. Out of the narrow defile they could see the mountains again. There in the open, the wind whipping about them, it was as if the dwarfs stood at the zenith of the world.

'Magnificent...' breathed Brondrik, misting the air as a tear ran down his face.

The lofty crags of the Worlds Edge Mountains were wreathed in white, and encroached upon the horizon like broad, rocky fingers. Snow peeled off the distant peaks like a phantom veil, shawling the thick clusters of lowland pine below. Melt waters shimmered like frozen glass as they fed into valleys and basin lakes; thin trails of silver-grey veining the mountainside. Clouds gathered overhead in a steel sky pregnant with the threat of a heavy snowfall. The trail behind the dwarfs was dusted with the drifts, several booted footprints disappearing slowly as the errant snow filled them.

A slighter-built dwarf, armed only with a small hand axe and dressed in a silken coat and velveteen breeches, tramped after the prince.

Nagrim had approached the edge of the plateau, and gazed down the long, winding road that led into a forested valley scattered with rocks.

'Our quarry is close, eh, Tringrom?' said the prince as the smaller dwarf reached him. Wisps of snow caught on Nagrim's beard as he smiled warmly at his kinsdwarf.

'We'd best hope so, Prince Nagrim. We cannot be late for the feast. Your father would shear a foot from my beard if I allowed that,' Tringrom replied. The royal aide wore a permanent scowl, ill-suited to ranging outside the hold. He'd been ungainly as he'd trekked through the chasm, his once fine clothes ripped and scuffed by the rocks and brush. Even now, standing beside the prince, he worried at the gold trim of his coat that had snagged on a clawed branch, the stitching partly torn.

'Finding it hard going?' said Nagrim, watching the royal aide with amusement as he huffed and puffed at the ragged trim of his coat.

'How much longer are we staying out here?' he grumbled. 'King Bagrik expects us back before nightfall to meet the elves. It would not–'

'Aye, and we'll bring back a host of grobi trophies to impress the pointy ears, eh, ufdi?' bellowed a red-faced dwarf appearing beside Tringrom. From the slur in his voice he was obviously drunk and stomped about the trail with all the subtlety of an ogre. He was clad in worn clothes, and his fingers were covered in tarnished rings that might once have been beautiful. His tattered attire and drunken disposition conspired to give the dwarf a decidedly unkempt appearance.

'My *name* is Tringrom,' said the royal aide through gritted teeth, 'of the Copperback Clan, and my family have been attendants to the royal line of Ungor for over a thousand years, Rugnir *Goldfallow*.'

The red-faced dwarf, Rugnir, stiffened with anger at the insult, but the reaction was fleeting. His ire seemed to vanish with the breeze and he was quickly his bawdy self again.

'Calm down, lad,' said Rugnir. 'You'll always be an ufdi to me.' The dwarf gave a wide grin that showed off his teeth. 'Pretty as a winter's bloom with your pressed silks and perfumed beard, a preening red-feathered crag sparrow,' he said. 'If I didn't know better...' he added, closing one eye as he appraised the dwarf mockingly, '...I'd say you were a rinn!' Rugnir laughed uproariously, clapping Tringrom hard on the back. The royal aide was inspecting the damage done to his coat and ripped off the gold trim completely when his drunken kinsdwarf smacked him.

'Quiet down!' snarled Brondrik from part way down the valley path, whirling around to fix them both with a fierce stare. 'The wind is shifting, and our voices will soon carry into the lowlands,' he warned, adding, 'And the grobkul will last until we find the grobi and burn their nest.' The pathfinder patted a bulging leather satchel, slung over his shoulder, at this last remark, before moving on.

Tringrom's straw-coloured beard bristled as he flushed with embarrassment at Brondrik's admonishment. Rugnir on the other hand, his own beard rust-red like his drunk-blushed cheeks and ringed eyes, merely chuckled and held up a hand to show his compliance with the pathfinder's wishes. For his part, Nagrim grinned over at the ebullient Rugnir. The two were constant companions and drinking fellows.

There was none better than Rugnir during a feast or celebration. The prince liked his boisterous demeanour and easy company. It was welcome relief from the intensity of his father, the king, and the royal flunkies he insisted on having accompany Nagrim whenever he left the hold. It was only by the prince's request that Rugnir had joined the hunting party. Many in the hold who knew him did not like him, claiming he was destitute and a *wazlik*, an honourless dwarf that borrowed gold from another and did not pay it back.

Wealth, for a dwarf, was a measure of success and therefore prestige. With that came respect. Rugnir's clan, once Goldmaster, but now referred to in whispers as Gold*fallow*, were once vaunted members of the Miner's Guild and renowned as the greatest lore finders and tunnel-hewers in all of the northern holds. Their fame had even stretched as far as Karak Eight Peaks, the

Vala-Azrilungol, one of the southernmost kingdoms of the Worlds Edge Mountains. Fate, though, had been cruel to the Goldmaster clan, and the great fortune amassed by Kraggin and Buldrin Goldmaster, Rugnir's father and grandfather, was eroded over the years. Tunnel collapses, flooding and a series of bad investments had all but left them destitute, and their holdings worthless. Rugnir, the last of the Goldmasters of Karak Ungor, after his father was slain by trolls, had frittered what funds remained on beer and gambling. The Goldmaster coffers had dried up.

Now Rugnir satisfied himself with Nagrim's patronage, which paid for his debts and wagers and kept him fed, much to the distaste of the other dwarfs of the hold. The shadow of his ignominy was long indeed, and some feared it would touch the prince before long. Nagrim would not hear of it, however, and so Rugnir had accompanied the hunters into the mountains.

'Tringrom,' said Nagrim, venturing after Brondrik once he'd seen that the rest of their party, two of the pathfinder's rangers, Harig and Thom, had caught up. They followed in Rugnir's wake, taking great pains to cover the rowdy dwarf's tracks, lest they attract attention. There were deadlier things than goblins lurking in the mountains and it was wise to be cautious, or sooner or later the hunter would become the hunted. Though the dwarfs held sway beneath the earth, they did not have such dominance over the mountain crags that they could tread with impunity.

The royal aide had tucked the gold trim of his silken coat in his pocket and was somewhat disconsolate as he followed the prince.

'What is my father's tally?' Nagrim asked.

Tringrom took a heavy-looking, leather-bound book from a satchel slung over his shoulder. Using his body and cloak to shield it from the worst of the wind and snow, he started to leaf through its pages. Finding what he was looking for, he stopped and read aloud.

'Lo did Bagrik Boarbrow, of only seventy winters, reach a tally of five hundreds and three score plus one grobi.'

'And what is my tally?'

'Your tally, Prince Nagrim, is only five short of that,' said Tringrom.

'Six grobi,' Nagrim thought aloud, grinning broadly. 'Do you think I can beat my father's count, Brondrik? Is there enough quarry for that?' the prince called out to the pathfinder who was crouched by a fork in the valley road, inspecting tracks invisible to the others.

'Aye, my prince, they'll be enough grobi for that,' he answered gruffly, and stood up. 'This way,' he said. 'And no more talk. The grobi stink is very strong, my eyes water with it.'

'Are you sure your nose isn't too close to your arse, pathfinder?' Rugnir asked, and roared with laughter.

Brondrik turned on his heel and unslung his crossbow. His eyes were like granite, his mouth a thin, hard line of anger.

'Have your travelling companion be quiet or I will shoot him myself,' he said to Nagrim.

'Easy, Brondrik,' said the prince, showing his palms, a look over his shoulder at Rugnir warning the ex-miner to keep his mouth shut from here on in. The colour drained from the drunken dwarf's face when he saw the loaded crossbow pointed at him and the apoplexy on Brondrik's face.

'Can we move on?' asked Nagrim. 'There are grobi to kill and precious little light left to do it in.'

The low winter sun was setting behind him, filling the valley path with shadows. They had but an hour, maybe less.

Brondrik saw it, too, and nodded, stowing his crossbow and leading the dwarfs onward to their prey.

'Brondrik,' Nagrim whispered, settling down into a comfortable position amongst the rocks. His kinsdwarfs were close by, hidden well in the crags.

The fork at the long valley path had led them to a high, boulder-strewn ridge. Snow fell readily from the sky now and draped the craggy rise. The goblin camp was below them, down a shallow slope, at the base of a wide canyon. The vermin had made their nest in a small cave, their crude daubings marking it from the outside. There were no guards. Only dung and the gnawed bones of lesser creatures – rats, birds and elk calves – lay outside the greenskins' lair.

Closing one eye, Nagrim sighted down the shaft of his crossbow and took aim on the cave mouth. 'Hurl the *zharrum*, now,' he said.

The venerable pathfinder did as asked, reaching into the satchel he carried and taking out a small round keg with a length of fuse poking through the lid. Lighting the fuse quickly with flint and steel, Brondrik launched the fire bomb into the air. The lit fuse fizzled dangerously as the bomb's parabola took it just outside the cave, only for it to clank against the ground and then roll in.

Nagrim and his fellow hunters winced as the fire bomb exploded. Jagged silhouettes were revealed in the ephemeral blast of light that followed. A chorus of high-pitched screams came from inside the cave, together with a plume of issuing smoke. Moments later, the first goblin came scurrying out, patting his head frantically to try and put out the flames in his topknot.

Nagrim put the creature down with a bolt through its neck.

'Tally-marker,' he shouted to Tringrom, who cradled the leather-bound tome in his arm, a quill at the ready, 'scratch one up for Nagrim Boarbrowson!'

Three more goblins emerged from the cave with scorched faces, coughing up phlegm.

'He's mine!' roared Rugnir, nearly slipping over in his enthusiasm to peg a greenskin drooling black snot from its bulbous nose. The dwarf had been going for the head but his aim was off and he only succeeded in pitching the creature's furred helmet off. Confused, the goblin first patted its skull to find out why it felt suddenly cold then, realising he'd lost something, turned in a circle to try and find it.

Nagrim stood, eschewing the cover of the rocks for a better target, and put a bolt through the hapless creature's eye. The impact spun it around and it fell face-forward into the dirt.

'Ha!' he cheered loudly. 'Are we shooting grobi or just playing with them, Rugnir?'

The ex-miner muttered drunkenly beneath his breath.

As the flames within took hold in earnest, burning straw, leather and whatever else the greenskins kept in their foul abodes, a stream of goblins came staggering from the cave. Some, the paltry few with their wits about them, loosed arrows from crude short bows at the dwarfs, but most fell pitifully short of the target or broke against the rocks.

With the fleeing goblins in disarray, Nagrim and the rangers came out of their hiding places, loosing quarrels with deadly accuracy at the yelping greenskins. The dwarfs made their way steadily down the ridge, disturbed scree tumbling ahead of them as they closed on the nadir of the canyon, and the goblins' lair. Only Rugnir slipped, and tumbled headfirst down the slope. He laughed as he landed on his rump in front of the others. He quickly flung a throwing axe at a screeching goblin that had tried to skewer the dwarf on its spear. The greenskin took the axe blade in the face, blood spurting from the wound, and lay still.

'That one counts,' Rugnir hollered, as he struggled to his feet and set off after the other goblins.

After Rugnir's unceremonious arrival at the base of the canyon, Nagrim was next to level ground. Blinded by the flames, a burnt greenskin blundered past him, heedless of its surroundings. Nagrim unslung his axe and buried it in the creature's skull, tearing the weapon out with a wet crunch of bone. Another was running back into the cave, despite the raging conflagration within, and Nagrim changed weapons again, lifting his crossbow and puncturing the creature's back with his shot. It fell dead just before the cave mouth.

Breathing heavily, the prince was aware of the other rangers alongside him, making their kills and calling them out to their tally-marker, Tringrom. The ufdi's fine silken tunic and velvet breeches, already ruined from the trek through the gorge, were covered in dirt and grobi blood. A bulging knapsack at his waist held goblin ears, noses and teeth, and when the hunters threw their trophies to him he'd not been fast enough to stop the blood from marring his clothes.

'Maiming doesn't count,' shouted Nagrim, beheading one of Rugnir's 'kills' that still had some life in it.

The drunken dwarf muttered something in reply that was lost in the scream of another goblin cut down by his axe.

The slaughter lasted only minutes, just as well given the sun had all but faded in the sky. Goblin corpses lay everywhere, the dwarfs moving amongst them removing further trophies.

'Eighteen, all told,' announced Brondrik, sucking his teeth before he muttered, 'Could've sworn by Grimnir there were more…'

'How did we fare, Tringrom?' Nagrim asked, wiping the blade of his axe on one of the steaming greenskin corpses.

The royal aide paused in his shovelling of the trophies into his knapsack to refer to his leather tome.

'A score of six for you, Prince Nagrim,' he told him.

Nagrim glowed inwardly. He had beaten his father's tally.

'Four for Brondrik,' the royal aide continued, 'and three each for Harig and Thom.'

'And what of Rugnir,' said the drunken ex-miner, 'what of his tally, eh?' he asked eagerly.

'Two,' Tringrom replied, stony-faced.

'Eh? Two? Two? I slew more than that!' he raged, stomping towards Tringrom for a better look at his tally-marking.

'Two!' the royal aide confirmed, slamming the tome shut and locking the clasp.

Rugnir was incensed, balled fists on his hips as he glowered at Tringrom.

'There is falsehood here,' he growled, before turning away in disgust.

'What was it?' said Nagrim, 'Fifty pieces of copper that you'd outshoot me?'

Rugnir grumbled again, looking into the distance.

'Wait, I see one!' he declared suddenly, fumbling to get his crossbow to a shooting position. Brondrik had been right – there was a survivor. The last remaining goblin had somehow evaded the dwarfs and was scampering madly back up the valley road. When a furtive glance behind it revealed that the dwarfs had seen it, the goblin redoubled its efforts.

'Double or nothing that I can peg this grobi swine,' said Rugnir, boastfully.

'Be my guest,' Nagrim replied, gesturing for him to proceed.

'One hundred copper pieces you'll owe me, lad,' he grinned, sighting down the crossbow.

Rugnir missed by a yard.

'A good effort,' said Nagrim with false sincerity. He took up his own crossbow, the goblin a diminishing green smudge in his eye-line by now, and fired.

'Yes!' he cried, making a fist in triumph as the goblin was pitched off its feet by the shot and lay dead on the trail.

'Mark that as seven kills, tally-marker,' said Nagrim, before he turned to look at Rugnir.

'Impossible…' breathed the dwarf, the drunken ruddiness of his face paling suddenly.

'A hundred copper, then…' Nagrim goaded him.

'Er… perhaps you'll let me owe you it, prince?' Rugnir asked, hopefully.

Nagrim looked serious at first but then laughed out loud, slapping Rugnir hard on the back.

'Don't worry old friend, your copper is no good to me.'

'*What copper?*' Tringrom mumbled to himself, still scowling.

'Which, er… reminds me,' said the ex-miner, ignoring the remark. 'I have certain outstanding… financial obligations to Godri Stonefinger and Ungrin Ungrinson…'

'How much?' sighed the prince.

'Twenty silver pieces each,' Rugnir replied.

'Tringrom,' Nagrim said to the royal aide. 'Have the amount taken from my coffers and settle the debts upon our return.'

'Yes, Prince Nagrim,' said Tringrom, his eyes like daggers as they fell upon Rugnir, who was careful to avert his gaze.

'Lead us back to the hold, Brondrik,' said Nagrim. 'I must tell my father his grobi tally has been beaten! There is celebrating to be done, and I must drink quickly if I'm to catch my friend here,' he added, throwing his arm around Rugnir's back in comradely fashion and laughing loudly.

'Indeed you must, my prince,' muttered the pathfinder, who fired a withering glance at Rugnir before heading back up the trail. The ex-miner didn't notice and laughed along with Nagrim. His smile faded when he saw the disapproving glances of the other dwarfs.

CHAPTER FOUR
Pacts

KING BAGRIK SAT in his counting house, surrounded by the month's revenue from the clans of the hold. Smoke drifted from a pipe pinched between his teeth, filling the room with the heady scent of tobacco. The king was dressed in a simple brown tunic, his bald pate reflecting the glow from the ensconced torches set around the room. He pored over the stone tablets and curling parchments strewn across the table in front of him, sat bent-backed in a broad throne, which, like the table, was fashioned from lacquered wutroth, a rare and incredibly strong dwarf wood. The bare stone walls of the small austere chamber were carved with the klinkarhun, the numerical dwarf alphabet.

Pieces of gold, silver and copper – some made into coins stamped with the royal rune of Ungor, others nuggets of purest ore gathered in bags – were stacked around the king, their order fathomable to Bagrik alone. With careful deliberation, the king checked off the tributes and taxes of the clans, the leaseholds on mines and overground farms, statutory beard tax and ale tithes. As liege lord of the realm, a percentage of all the hold's remunerations went to the king and Bagrik was meticulous about its acquisition.

'How do we fare so far with the taxes, Kandor?' asked the king, his voice deep and gruff as he sifted through the requisitions.

'The Firehand and Flinteye clans still owe thirty pieces of gold each for anvils and picks,' the merchant replied, sat behind a smaller desk next to the king's, checking parchment and tablets of his own. As royal treasurer it was part of Kandor's duty that he attend the monthly gold gathering, to log in taxes and dispatch reckoners, the king's bailiffs, to reclaim late payments or act on the behalf of other clans who had cause for grudgement against their fellow dwarfs.

'Mark that!' bellowed the king. Bagrik's edict was followed by the measured scratching of a quill from one corner of the room where Grumkaz Grimbrow, his chief grudgemaster, was sitting shrouded in shadow. The longbeard recorded each and every late or missing payment in the form of grudges, writ in the king's blood and set down in the massive tome resting on a stone lectern next to the venerable dwarf.

'I have here a claim from the Ironfingers, who say they were sold knackered ore ponies by the Leatherbeards and lost a day's tunnelling on account,' said Kandor, leafing through the pile of papers.

'Denied!' said Bagrik. 'The Ironfingers should learn to better examine their stock before buying.'

'Another from Grubbi Threefinger, a reckoner, requests remuneration for worn boot leather in prosecution of the king's duties.'

'Granted–' the king began, but then turned swiftly to the shadowy form of Grumkaz, who was halfway through noting the king's order.

'How much in taxes has Grubbi recovered this past month?' he asked.

The grudgemaster leafed back through the hold's records.

'One hundred and fifty-three gold pieces, fifteen short of his required tally,' the grudgemaster announced.

'Denied!' the king bellowed again, and went back to the parchments on his desk as the sound of frantic scratching came from the grudgemaster as he made an abrupt adjustment.

'Tell me, Kandor,' Bagrik said after a moment, his head still in the parchments on his desk, 'what do you think of these elgi? Is there trade to be had between us?'

The merchant set down a stone tablet, surprised at the sudden question.

'They have travelled far, my king and the elgi, Malbeth, has much honour. I do not think they would have done so if they meant to waste our time,' he said.

'I care not for their ambassador,' the king responded curtly. 'What about their prince, this… Ithalred? It is he that holds power amongst the elgi. Morek tells me he is an arrogant bastard.'

'Morek knows nothing of diplomacy–' Kandor began, before the king interrupted.

'Neither do I, Thane Silverbeard. That's why I'm asking you.'

Kandor's reply was frank.

'The elves are utterly unlike us in every way, my liege, and… *difficulties* between our cultures are inevitable, but open trade between us could be very profitable for

Karak Ungor. We would be foolish not to at least listen to what they propose.'

'You do not think me a fool then, Kandor?' Bagrik asked, looking up from his tallying.

'Of course not, my liege,' Kandor blathered, face reddening with sudden concern.

'Then you'll know that I'm aware of the disrespect they've shown towards my queen, that they have turned the Hall of Belgrad into an elgi dwelling, yes?'

'My liege, I–'

Bagrik scowled, and waved his hand for silence.

'I trust your judgement, Kandor. Aye, I do, as sure as stone,' Bagrik told him. 'And a king's trust is no small thing. I know you won't have brought these elgi to my halls without good reason. And I know your talent for gold making. But know this, too,' he added with a steel-edged glare, 'If I receive word of our guests dishonouring my queen again, or besmirching her in any way, I will have them thrown out. And your beard will be shorn, Kandor of the Silverbeard clan, for bringing them to my gates in the first place!'

'Please accept my apologies, liege. I've spoken to Malbeth and made it clear to him that such behaviour will not be tolerated again,' said Kandor, trying to sooth the king's sudden ire.

'You are right. It will not,' Bagrik added simply, staring at Kandor a moment longer to make his point, before turning his attention back to the taxes piled on his desk.

'All seems in order here,' he said. 'Dispatch reckoners to the Firehands and Flinteyes to settle their accounts, and add on ten pieces of copper each for late payment.'

'At once, King Bagrik,' Kandor replied, quietly relieved that he'd escaped with only a mild tongue-lashing.

'Go then to you duties!' bawled the king. 'And make your oaths to Grungni that these elgi put me in a better mood.'

Kandor bowed and left the parchments where they were on the ground.

'It shall be done, my king,' he said, and as he was leaving met Queen Brunvilda with Tringrom in tow coming the other way. He bowed to them both before walking on and out of the counting house.

'My queen,' Bagrik said warmly to his wife as she approached. Brunvilda bowed once she'd reached her husband. The king then dismissed Grumkaz who shuffled quietly out of the room, his work done for now.

'And Tringrom,' added the king, 'you look like a wanaz.'

'My lord, Tringrom has been on a grobkul with your son,' said the queen before the royal aide could reply. 'Late, again,' she added, stern of face. 'He is being readied for the feast, as should you be.'

'Bah! I'll be ready soon enough,' Bagrik snapped, 'But tell me, Tringrom,' he added, conspiratorially, 'how did my son fare?'

'He has beaten your tally, my liege,' the royal aide replied.

'Ha!' cried the king, slapping his hands down upon the desk and sending parchments spilling onto the ground. 'Barely sixty-nine winters, and he beats his father's tally,' Bagrik said proudly. 'Go... mark it in the Book of Deeds, so all shall know of my son's achievement!'

'At once, my king,' Tringrom replied and left his king and queen alone, gazing longingly at one another.

'Our son, he will make a fine king,' said Bagrik, once the royal aide was gone.

'Indeed he will,' Brunvilda replied, resting a hand upon her husband's shoulder. 'But he is reckless, and I do not like his friendship with Rugnir, either. Brondrik has made a damning report to Morek that you should hear.'

'He is young,' counselled the king, 'it is to be expected. And as for Rugnir,' said the king, seizing his queen around the waist, who yelped mildly in surprise and delight, and pulling her close, 'let the captain of the hearth guard deal with it.'

'Bagrik Boarbrow, unhand me at once!' cried Brunvilda, though her demand was distinctly half-hearted as she looked lovingly into the eyes of her husband.

'Is that really what you want me to do, lass?' he asked.

'No…' she answered demurely, smoothing down his beard with the palms of her hands.

'You smell like hops and honey,' he said, breathing in her scent like it was nectar.

'And you reek of gold, my king…' she replied, smiling. 'Bagrik?' she asked after a moment.

'Yes, my queen,' he replied, voice husky with the ardour of their embrace.

'I would like to see our son.'

'You will see him,' Bagrik replied, nonplussed. 'He will be at the feast, Grungni willing he is ready in time.'

'No, not Nagrim…' Brunvilda said quietly, shaking her head.

Bagrik's face darkened as soon as he realised what she meant. Silently, he released his grip and gently let her go.

'That… *thing* is no son of mine,' he said, his voice now hard like stone.

'He *is* your son, whether you care to admit it or not,' insisted Brunvilda, stepping back into Bagrik's eye-line when the king averted his gaze to stare at parchments he had already read. 'I will not abandon him, even if you have disowned him,' she continued.

'Abandoned?' said the king, facing her again. 'Yes, he should have been abandoned. Cast out at birth and left in the mountains for wild beasts to devour!'

Brunvilda's faced was pinched with anger, and tears were welling in her eyes at the king's harsh words. Bagrik regretted them at once and tried in vain to make amends.

'I'm sorry, but the answer is no. I have agreed to stay my hand, and I've honoured that pact. But that is all I will do.'

'He is your son,' the queen repeated, imploringly.

Bagrik hobbled from his throne, wincing in pain at an old leg wound, and turned his back on her.

'I will speak on it no further,' he whispered.

Queen Brunvilda said nothing more. Bagrik heard her footsteps clacking on the stone, fading as she left, and felt his heart ache once she was gone.

CHAPTER FIVE
The Serpent Host

ULFJARL OF THE Skaeling tribe stood upon the skull-headed prow of his Wolfship and bellowed defiantly at the gods.

Crimson lightning answered, flashing across the storm-wracked horizon and turning the sky the colour of blood. Massive waves, churned up by the wind, rolled over the surface of the thrashing Sea of Claws and sent stinging spray into Ulfjarl's face and body. The Norscan warlord ignored it, exultant as the power of the terrible storm filled him.

Nothing would stop him reaching the mainland. There lay the Old World and the silver tower of the elves that haunted his dreams. Upon those white shores, Ulfjarl would find his destiny.

Bondsmen fought the rumble of thunder with their dour baritones, pulling at the oars with determined fury and bringing the Norscan warlord back from his reverie. Stoic, fur-clad huscarls sat beside them, clutching axes and spears, their round wooden shields strapped to their arms. Norsca, their frozen homeland, and the rest of the Skaeling tribe, was a distant memory now as they drove across the ocean with a ragged fleet of thirty other Wolfships. Their black sails, daubed with the symbol of a coiled crimson snake with three heads, bulged with the hellish gales, the mast pennants snapping like dragon tongues.

Ulfjarl had the same snake symbol seared into the skin of his bare and muscled chest. It was the icon of his army, the Serpent Host. He wore a mantle of furs thrown over his massive shoulders. Skins covered his wrists and ankles, leaving his legs and arms, fraught with battle scars, naked to the elements. Furred boots covered Ulfjarl's feet and were bound with chains. A war helm, festooned with spikes and wrought of dark metal, sat upon his head crested by two curling horns. Only the warlord's eyes were visible through a narrow cross-shaped slit, hard like rock beneath a jutting brow.

The beat of drums kept the oarsmen in time. It echoed the pounding of Ulfjarl's feral heart. Every pull brought them closer to the mainland, and through the boiling clouds he could just see it as a thickening black line, lit sporadically by the storm. Neither man nor elf nor daemon could keep him from it. The fire-blackened wrecks of the elven catamarans, left burning in their wake, were testament to that. Ulfjarl had lost no less than five ships to the immortals, who'd fought with skill and desperation. It was a small price. Ulfjarl had cut their warchief's head from his shoulders with his axe, shearing the elf's silver mail as if it were bare flesh.

Like his war helm, Ulfjarl's blade was forged from the ore of a black meteorite that had destroyed his village in fire and fury. Its coming was heralded in the stars, the impetus for his conquest, and he had gathered warriors at once. The Norscan had never seen the metal's like before, his crude mouth could not even form the words to describe it.

Obsid...

Ulfjarl cared not. It slew his enemies well. The elf had learned that lesson to his cost; his flayed skull was now tied to the Norscan's belt as a trophy. Destiny, Ulfjarl's glorious fate, lay at journey's end. Veorik had promised it, seen in a vision, and the shaman was never wrong.

Ulfjarl gazed up to the crow's nest. Eldritch green light crackled and spat like a miniature thunderhead as Veorik used his sorcery to guide them through the storm, just as he had through the ice flows, maelstroms and razor-sharp bergs of the Norscan coast.

Screams pierced the rising tumult of the storm as another ship was lost, swallowed whole beneath a mammoth wave. Ulfjarl watched the mast splinter and crack, watched the tearing sails and scattered rigging, as the vessel was pulled asunder with its crew. Some cast themselves into the sea, flailing as they struggled for life, but endless wet oblivion claimed them all.

Ulfjarl knew each and every one who drowned beneath the waves. He gave their names as sacrifices to Shornaal, one of the Dark Gods, that he would reach land unscathed. The muttered pledges had barely passed his lips when a huge curtain of water, crested by frothing surf, loomed up before the ship.

It seemed the gods had answered.

He saw faces in the watery blackness; a host of daemon visages with needle-pointed teeth and hollow eyes hungering for his soul and the souls of his men. Ulfjarl roared in defiance of it, as if it were an enemy that could be cowed by his fury. He heard the oarsmaster urge his charges to row harder, and they pulled with all their might. Some sang lamentations, others screamed in maddened terror as they faced their doom. Ulfjarl merely laughed, long and loud into the wind, his cry echoing across the sky where it could be heard by heathen gods. He felt the prow rising as the Wolfship surged up the monstrous wave and roared again at the stygian sea, bellowing his name.

Hard and fast they raced up the thrashing waters, nearly pitching prow over stern so severe was the angle of their approach. Ulfjarl ran forward to the very tip of the prow as they rode higher and higher. Misshapen hands with taloned nails seemed to reach out for him as the waters closed. Sibilant threats, half-heard in a tongue he did not understand, filled his ears. Ulfjarl ignored them, his cry of triumph eclipsing the daemon voices as they crested the apex of the wave before it broke.

Smashing down on the other side, foaming water engulfed the Wolfship and for a moment the vessel was swallowed beneath the sea before it emerged again like a cork in a barrel, water cascading from its sails and rigging.

Drenched from head to foot, Ulfjarl beat his chest with a mighty fist and bellowed at Tchar, god of storms and the bringer of change, daring his wrath. His warriors cheered with him, the relief at their survival violent and palpable. Raging winds ripped at the sails, driving them harder, and rain lashed down against the Norscans like knives of ice. Ulfjarl saw another Wolfship draw up alongside them. The warriors onboard yelled and cried in reckless victory. Expressions of triumph turned to horror as the wooden hull of their ship tore open and a huge, serpentine creature surged from the ocean through the debris.

The beast, its silver-blue scales shimmering as the water peeled away from it, towered above the Norscan ships, its broad snout flaring with rage and hunger. Flanged fins, edged in poisonous spikes and attached to a long saurian head, flared as the monstrous serpent regarded prey. The warriors of the stricken Wolfship mewled in abject terror, their pathetic vessel cleft in two, its jagged halves sinking into the murky waters. The beast roared. Its keening cry smothered the thunder and shook the very ocean, before it dove down onto the hapless Norscans and cast their broken bodies aside like tinder.

Ulfjarl saw a barbed tail disappear beneath the waves, before a curious silence reigned in the creature's wake. He knew this monster. He had heard tales of its terror. It was an ancient denizen of the deep – an ice drake. Stirred from a long slumber beneath the Sea of Claws, it was angry.

Clambering to the edge of the skull-headed prow Ulfjarl leaned over, searching the water for some sign of the creature; a plume of foam, a shadow, anything. But there was nothing. Nothing until the monster erupted from the thrashing sea near the prow on Ulfjarl's blind-side, its razor-snout shearing through the surface like a spear. The Norscan warlord staggered back, craning his neck to see the towering ice drake. Black eyes, like pools of endless hate, regarded him as he retreated slowly to get a more secure footing on the deck. It was an epic sight. Man facing monster as the maelstrom of the storm whirled around them.

Ulfjarl took a throwing axe from his belt, bracing his legs for balance as he tested the weapon's weight. Just as he was about to fling the blade, the ice drake dove into the depths again. Ulfjarl spun around, running further onto the deck and screaming for his warriors.

The beast emerged on the Wolfship's starboard side, bellowing its fury. Those bondsmen not unmanned by the terrible creature loosed arrows, and hurled spears and axes, only for the weapons to shatter and rebound from the monster's thick, armoured hide. Thordrak, a jarl chieftain, shouted orders above the tumult of the storm and a group of his bondsmen grabbed rope and barbed bone hooks. Roaring oaths to the gods, Jarl Thordrak and his bondsmen loosed their hooks, desperate to snag the monster's scales or bite into flesh that they might bring it down to the deck to let the huscarls do their grisly work.

A cheer went up as several of the barbed hooks took hold. Thordrak roared for his men to heave. The thick ropes attached to the weapons went taut as the warriors pulled, the ice drake screeching as it resisted them. For a moment the beast appeared cowed as its head dipped, but this false hope was fleeting as it surged upright again with a bellow of power. The ropes snapped, and warriors were yanked off their feet and cast overboard with the force of the monster's escape. Thordrak groaned in anguish as the drake twisted free of the biting snares. Like quicksilver, the beast's head flew deck-ward, smashing into the jarl and what remained of his warriors. He and a clutch of bondsmen were crushed in the ice drake's jaws as its neck snapped straight again. Throwing back its head, the hapless Norscans were tipped down into the beast's gullet and devoured whole. The rest were scattered across the deck, bloodied and with bones broken.

A band of huscarls hefting spears and bearded axes, charged at the creature, shouting war cries. The ice drake came level with the deck and roared back, exhaling a blast of deathly frost from its gaping maw. The huscarls were engulfed in a cloud of frost. As it dissipated the Norscan warriors were left frozen solid, belated screams forever etched on their faces. The deck became a sheet of ice in the wake of the attack, and bondsmen slipped and fell as they fled and fought.

Grabbing a baleen spear, and a length of rope that he slung over his shoulder, Ulfjarl fought his way through the carnage, beheading a screaming bondsman who had lost his mind to terror, and heaving him over the side of the ship. He smashed the corpse of a frozen huscarl to ice shards with his axe as he strove to reach the Wolfship's mast through the chaos. As he slid to the mast and launched himself at the rigging, Ulfjarl heard the oarsmaster extol his charges with threats and curses. Even if they slew the beast, the Sea of Claws might yet drag them all to its watery hells. Ulfjarl would yield to neither, and climbed the bone-hard rigging that was chilled with frost, hand over hand, muscles bunching with effort. Above, he saw the crackling magicks of Veorik in the crow's nest, the shaman lost in a magical trance as he guided the ship despite the deadly battle. A sideways glance revealed the creature was close. Its dank breath reeked of cold and dead blood as it exhaled over the deck, and tore bondsmen apart with its jaws.

Reaching the top of the sail, Ulfjarl heaved himself up and stood on the vertical spar of the mast, ramming the baleen spear into the wood and then lashing himself to it. The ice drake was ravaging the Wolfship, tearing chunks from the hull and butchering Ulfjarl's warriors. The deck was slick with ice and blood. Men slipped and were flung over the side into the raging waters as the Wolfship pitched and yawed.

Hefting a hurling axe, Ulfjarl waited until the ice drake turned its ugly head towards him then threw it with all his strength. The monster screeched in agony as the blade pierced one of its eyes, purple-black blood gushing from the wound. Overcoming its pain, the beast found its attacker and roared at Ulfjarl who was battered back by the fury of its cry. As the ice drake came at him, the Norscan tore the baleen spear free and lunged. The monster recoiled then came at Ulfjarl again, who fought hard to keep it at bay. A fierce jab opened up a gash in the creature's flanged fin and it twisted forward in pain. Seeing his chance, Ulfjarl rammed the spearhead through its other eye, burying the weapon halfway up the haft.

Blinded, the creature thrashed about in a rage, ripping apart the rigging and smashing the mast. Ulfjarl cut himself loose before the spar collapsed, snapped in two by the ice drake, and leapt onto the creature's back. Its long neck was thick like a tree trunk, but ridged and not so wide that Ulfjarl couldn't grasp it. He found purchase beneath its scales as the creature bucked and thrashed to try and shake him loose.

With his free hand Ulfjarl drew his axe and hacked into the beast's hide. Chunks of scale sheared away and soon he was cutting into meat. Below, the huscarls and bondsmen continued to throw spears and loose arrows. Some found chinks in the creature's armoured hide. Ulfjarl felt it weakening as he clove into it, and rode the beast as it sagged downward.

Crashing against the deck, Ulfjarl was thrown off the ice drake. Taking up a fallen spear as he got to his feet, left by a slain huscarl, Ulfjarl impaled the monster through the neck. He rammed another through its upper jaw, a third through its snout, pinning it to the deck. Swinging his axe in a wide arc, he brought it down against the ice drake's neck, again and again, until it was severed. Burying the axe into the deck, Ulfjarl gripped the ice drake's jaw and tore its head away from its neck, thick threads of skin, scale and flesh splitting with his grunting efforts. Raising the head aloft, he roared in triumph, the beast's shedding arteries bathing him in blood. The creature's decapitated body slid off the deck and was swallowed by the sea.

Through the clamour of warriors surrounding him, baying in adulation, Ulfjarl saw the twisted form of Veorik. The shaman hobbled over slowly, parting the throng with his mere presence, and stood before his king in supplication. He took a cup, made from a child's skull, from beneath the ragged skins of his robes. Plunging it into the pooling blood and gore beneath Ulfjarl, the shaman drank deep. Veorik's eyes flashed with power within the shadows of his hood, and he smiled.

Now the Serpent Host had dominion over the ice drakes of the deep...

CHAPTER SIX
An Uneasy Alliance

THE GREAT HALL of Karak Ungor thronged with dwarfs. Clans from throughout the hold had been summoned by their king for an audience with their eldritch guests from across the Great Ocean. Soot-faced miners of the Rockcutter, Stonehand and Goldgather clans sat alongside the blacksmiths of the Ironbrows, Anvilbacks and Copperfists. Fletchers, brewmasters, gold and silver smiths talked loud and readily with venerable runelords, engineer guildmasters, merchants and iron-breakers.

Truly the gathering of dwarfs that night was one of the largest ever in the long and prestigious history of Ungor.

The room was filled with many broad tables, low wooden benches set alongside them and occupied by the dwarfs. Brewmasters surveyed the Great Hall with beady eyes, watching their apprentices dispense immense barrels of ale. Never was a tankard to run dry, a stein to be empty. Flickering torches cast shadowy light onto a bawdy scene as dwarfs spoke and drank, wrestled and boasted. A thick syrup of smoke lay heavy just above the heads of the merry makers, a greyish fug exuding from numerous pipes that flared in the half-light.

In the middle of the vast and impressive chamber was a massive fire-pit, the coals within glowing warmly, filling the place with the heady aroma of rock and ash. Wrought from bronze and inlaid with strips of silver and copper, the ornate basin was sunk partly into the ground and set inside a ring of flat stones inscribed with runes of fire and burning.

The edge of the chamber had a series of stone ledges, fringed with shadow, where the musicians, victualers and other servants were sitting. The Great Hall had three doorways: two led to the east and west halls, the oaken portals banded with iron and protected by a pair of hearth guard each; the third entrance was the grand gate of the hall itself. This massive, wooden door was inlaid with gemstones, its magnificent, sweeping arch rendered in gold and chased with silver filigree. It, too, was stout and defensible, for the dwarfs were concerned with the practical as much as they were the grandiose. The splendour of that fine ingress into the king's vaulted chamber said much of dwarf ambition and pragmatism.

A stone platform, reachable only by a central stairway of red carpeted rock, rose at the back of the hall and it was here that the king and his charges were seated. The King's Table, as it was known, was broad and long. It stretched almost the length of the stone platform and was fashioned from dark wutroth with gilt tracery, its stout feet made into effigies of dragons, griffons and eagles. Banners and standards capped with ancestor badges hung behind it on bronze chains. Together they described a tapestry of battles, heroic deeds and the hold's founding, taken directly from the ancient chronicles of the dwarfs.

The great Bagrik was in attendance, surveying all that fell beneath his beetling brow. A tunic of red and gold swathed his kingly form, with a coat of shining silver mail beneath. Vambraces of polished bronze, inlaid with ruby studs, clasped his forearms. Rings with emeralds, malachite and agate festooned his broad fingers and a great talisman, wrought from gold with a single giant ruby at its heart, hung around his neck. Across his shoulders and head sat a dried boar pelt, of which Bagrik took his honorific, Boarbrow. Beneath the dead beast's skin, under the sweeping tusks capped with silver tips, was the crown of Ungor and symbol of Bagrik's lordship over his realm.

Beside him was his queen, bedecked in her own royal finery, the same attire she had worn to greet the elves at the outer gateway hall. Nagrim, his son, was also at Bagrik's table sitting to his father's right as was the custom for heirs apparent. Lamentably, Rugnir was with him, bawdier and more raucous than the entire host of dwarfs put together. Bagrik noted with distaste, as the penniless miner taunted Tringrom who stood biting his tongue in the background, that Rugnir had quaffed more ale than anyone else in the room. He suspected, with reluctant praise, that the wanaz could probably drink Heganbour, the king's chief brewmaster, under the table.

Next to the King's Table was the Seat of the Wise, as occupied by the venerable longbeards of the hold, and then came the lords and thanes, then the priests of the

Ancestors, Grungni, Valaya and Grimnir. The last table upon the stone platform was that of the Masters, the vaunted leaders of the dwarf craftguilds. Here sat the runelords, the engineer guildmasters, chief lodewardens and the captains of the hold's warrior brotherhoods, the hearth guard and the ironbreakers. In the Great Hall proximity to the king was an indication of wealth, prestige and respect. The closer a dwarf was to the table of his liege, the more power he possessed. These then were the greatest of the dwarfs. It was no small matter that Bagrik had allowed the elves to sit at his table. It was the greatest gesture of honour he could afford them. He hoped, sourly, that they would live up to it.

The sounding of horns reverberated around the chamber, announcing the arrival of the elves. Under Bagrik's withering appraisal, the assembled clans ceased their merrymaking at once, observing dutiful silence as all eyes turned to the gate of the Great Hall.

With the scrape of stone and the groaning of ancient wood, the doors eased open and the elven delegation from Tor Eorfith came through. A small cohort of dwarfs led them in with Kandor striding at their head, followed closely by Morek and the king's banner bearer, Haggar Anvilfist. The dwarfs were dressed in shining gromril mail with open-faced helms and glimmering beard locks. Crimson cloaks, trimmed with silver, sat upon their shoulders. Haggar bore the king's banner, held in both hands, one flesh and blood, the other forged from bronze and bearing runes of power.

The great standard of Karak Ungor was fashioned into an effigy of Grungni, the ancestor god depicted in his form as the miner, wielding hammer and chisel. Below this gilded icon was the stylised image of a red dragon, coiled in on itself and stitched into the cloth banner. It was surrounded by a knotted band of gold, with the royal runes of Bagrik's household woven into it. The banner was a relic, as ancient as any in the king's possession, and it was a great honour to bear it.

Their booted feet clanked loudly against the stone, as the dwarfs tramped into the chamber. The elves were close behind them, dressed in white robes with silver adornments. Though he had not met them face-to-face, Bagrik had listened intently to his queen's descriptions of them, her mood still icy following their argument in the counting house. Bagrik resolved to try and make it up to her later. For now, he was intent on his guests.

Prince Ithalred strode imperiously into the chamber, as was the wont of the elves. He carried a sword at his hip and wore a crown upon his forehead. An azure cloak that seemed to shimmer with an enchanted lustre was draped over his shoulders. He kept his gaze ahead, his cold face unreadable. His sister, the one Brunvilda had said was called Arthelas, and the raven-haired Lethralmir stood either side, seemingly serene. Malbeth the ambassador, who was just behind the dwarfs, smiled warmly at his hosts, exchanging the occasional nod with clansmen who seemed to remember him from his previous visit to the hold. The muscular brute, bulky for an elf and who eyed the room with suspicion, was obviously Korhvale. He seemed ill at ease to Bagrik and kept his fists clenched, regarding the dwarfs like a threat.

The elves seemed to move slowly and regally, yet crossed the vast carpeted aisle that led to the King's Table with the utmost swiftness. They were strange creatures, like drifting white veils or half-glimpsed shadows. It was like they were made of air and light, their voices musical and yet ancient all at once. Bagrik had only had a few dealings with elves, but each was chiselled onto his mind, a memory carved in stone.

Together with the royal household of Tor Eorfith, were a host of servants, gift bearers and the prince's warriors. As Ithalred gained the steps to the stone platform, the servants stopped, arranging themselves upon the carpeted concourse in two lines. The warriors peeled away from the royal entourage, too, taking up their positions next to tables below. It had been the suggestion of Kandor and Malbeth to split the elves thusly, to allow the warriors of the two races to mix with one another and feel able to speak freely outside of the presence of their liege lords.

Kandor, Morek and Haggar halted before their king, and bowed deeply. Bagrik nodded back, grumbling for them to take up their positions. The dwarfs obeyed dutifully, Kandor and Morek assuming their places at the King's Table, while Haggar stood behind the throne with Tringrom and Bagrik's hearth guard shieldbearers.

'Noble King Bagrik,' said Kandor, who had remained standing. 'May I present Prince Ithalred of Tor Eorfith.'

'You may,' Bagrik said impatiently, 'now be seated. I am sure the prince and his charges did not come to my hold to stand on ceremony before a foreign lord, am I right, Prince Ithalred?'

The corner of Ithalred's mouth twitched in what could have been a smile, before the elf nodded slightly and took his place at the King's Table. The rest of the royal household followed, though they were careful not to sit before their prince had taken his own seat.

'I am King Bagrik Boarbrow,' Bagrik declared proudly, 'and you and your kin are welcome here, elgi.' He noticed Ithalred's lip curl in distaste as he regarded him, but he chose to ignore it for now.

Following the king's declaration, Kandor and Malbeth made the rest of the introductions respectively. With these formal observances out of the way, the rest of the elves, the warriors in the lower section of the Great Hall, were seated. An awkward silence descended, the total opposite of the bawdy bonhomie that had been prevalent before the elves' arrival, and Bagrik clapped his hands loudly to break it.

'Behold, Prince Ithalred,' he said, gesturing a servant carrying an ornate iron chest over to him, 'a token of our forthcoming alliance.' Bagrik took the chest, dismissing the servant with a scowl, and opened it to reveal a gold drinking horn. The wondrous artefact was festooned with gemstones and fashioned into the likeness of a rampant dragon with emeralds for eyes.

'May you drink to many victories from it,' added Bagrik as Ithalred received it. The elf clearly found the item unwieldy, and was quick to pass it to Malbeth for safekeeping.

'The chest comes with it,' explained the king, somewhat curiously.

Ithalred nodded, as if he had known this all along, and took the chest, passing that to Malbeth also.

'And here,' the king continued, as another dwarf servant came forward, 'is a mantle of finest gromril scale.' Bagrik held the garment before him, which shimmered goldenly in the torchlight. A looping chain of silver was held in place against the cloak with burnished bronze clasps wrought into the faces of dwarf ancestors.

This, too, the prince took gingerly as if uncertain what he was supposed to do with it and promptly dumped the cloak on Malbeth, who had since got the attention of two elven servants to take the gifts and look after them until his prince was ready to inspect them further.

'You honour me, King Bagrik,' said Ithalred by way of reply, his sincerity unconvincing. 'With these fine... offerings,' he struggled, 'Allow me to return the favour.' He turned and gestured to the gaggle of gift-bearing servants below him.

'This bow,' the elven prince began as the gift bearers hurried up the steps to his side, 'was carved with wood taken from the forests of Eataine, its string woven from the hair of elven maidens.'

Bagrik took the weapon as it was proffered. It was smaller than a conventional elven longbow and obviously finely wrought, but Bagrik held it like it was a fragile thing in his thick fingers, his expression wary as if he expected it to break at any second. After a moment he twanged the string, much to Ithalred's horror, and smiled.

'It makes a curious sound this instrument,' Bagrik told him. 'A weapon, you say?' he asked.

'One of the finest ever crafted in all of the Outer Kingdoms of Ulthuan,' the prince replied, paling with disbelief.

Bagrik shrugged, passing the gift to one of his servants.

'Spices,' said the prince hurriedly, indicating a trio of large, silver urns brought forth by more servants, 'from beyond these shores.'

Bagrik eyed the urns suspiciously in turn, before licking his finger and plunging it inside one.

Ithalred went from pale white to incensed crimson as he watched Bagrik root around the spice urn with his saliva-coated finger.

Malbeth, noticing his prince's building apoplexy, interceded quickly on Ithalred's behalf.

'The spices, noble king,' he began, 'are particularly aromatic. Perhaps,' he ventured, 'you might like to sample their scents first?'

Bagrik looked up at the ambassador, and gave an almost inaudible grunt as he pulled his fist from the urn he'd chosen, fragments of spice clinging to his skin, and sniffed deeply. Bagrik's expression went from disinterest to distaste in a moment, his nose and brow wrinkling with the heady scents of the spices.

'Pungent,' he remarked with a scowl. 'Intended for cooking, yes,' he added, plunging the spice-laden finger into his mouth and sucking off the contents. Bagrik smacked his lips and flicked his tongue, a scowl upon his face as he experienced the taste. Then his face reddened and a sudden hacking cough wracked his body. Bagrik slammed his fist onto the table, upending tankards and goblets, as he tried to master his coughing fit.

'The king is poisoned!' cried Morek, leaping from his seat with his axe drawn. The hearth guard throne bearers were beside him in an instant, Haggar too. A commotion erupted from the Great Hall below at the hearth guard captain's pronouncement. Angry voices were taken up as elf and dwarf shouted at each other in their native tongues.

Prince Ithalred was stunned into enraged silence, while Malbeth and Kandor tried desperately to calm the situation, though their assurances only seemed to enflame the opposite race. Korhvale was on his feet immediately, stepping between his prince and the axe-wielding Morek. Lethralmir and Arthelas merely laughed at the absurdity of it all, the elves and dwarfs in the grand chamber at sudden unexpected loggerheads.

'Morek!' a stern voice rose above the clamour, 'put your weapon away and get back to your post beside your king.' Brunvilda was up, and glowered at the captain of the hearth guard, stopped in his tracks by the queen's anger. 'Do it at once!' she ordered.

Morek obeyed, stowing his axe, and retreating to the throne. The others dwarfs went with him, red-faced before the fury of their queen. The impassioned bickering stopped, and all eyes were on the dwarf king as he slowly recovered from his coughing fit.

Queen Brunvilda was quickly at her husband's side.

'I'm fine, my queen,' he said as she rubbed his back.

She was concerned, but still carried the ire of their earlier words spoken before the feast.

Bagrik averted his gaze as she went back to her place. Looking at Ithalred, the king smiled. 'Your spices have a mighty kick, elgi…'

A moment of charged silence descended, before the king's smile broadened and he roared with laughter. At first, the elves seemed shocked by his reaction but as the other dwarfs joined in the icy mood thawed and all could relax again. Malbeth laughed heartily, encouraging his kin to do the same, though it was mirth tinged with relief that another potential disaster had been averted. Only Ithalred was not amused, though his agitation seemed to have drained away for the time being.

'Perhaps, it would be wise,' the king announced to all, 'if we were to leave gift giving until later. For I suspect the hall is hungry,' he added, struggling to his feet, 'Am I right?'

A cheer erupted from the dwarf throng, much to the elves' alarm. Korhvale, having previously retaken his seat was almost on his feet again as if he feared another attack. Malbeth had a swift but harsh word in his ear before the White Lion relaxed, but even then he was still wary.

'Then bring the feast!' the king bellowed in response to the roar of his kin.

The two side portals to the hold were thrown open and dwarf victualers filed in bearing metal platters of rare beef on the bone, hunks of seared goat flesh, shanks of lamb and thick ham hocks dripping with juice. Heat shimmered off the succulent meats as they were paraded around the chamber, the victualers converging first on the King's Table, followed by those nearest to it, until they came to the tables in the lower part of the Great Hall. A pair of dwarfs followed the initial entourage of chefs, a spitted boar carried between them over their shoulders. It was a massive beast, though paled in comparison to the skin hung about Bagrik's shoulders, and was brought to the central fire-pit where it would cook slowly as it was flensed by the victualers. Dwarfs carrying baskets of earth and stone-bread followed the boar carriers, together with another four servants who laboured with a stout iron cauldron, a meaty mould broth slopping within. This, too, was placed over the fire-pit on a metal frame, the vast basin more than capable of accommodating both dishes.

Apprentice brewmasters worked alongside the victualers, refilling tankards and flagons, and bringing out fresh casks from the hold's ale stores. Though the elves had brought wine from the vineyards of Ellyrion, Eataine and Yvresse, they were encouraged to try some of the milder brews offered by the dwarfs.

'Here...' said the king, taking a keg from one of the passing brewmasters and filling a goblet for Ithalred, 'Gilded Tongue. It is light and flavoured with honey, delicate enough for even your fair palate I'd warrant, dear prince.'

Ithalred set down a goblet of wine, already poured by one of his servants, reluctantly and took the vessel offered by Bagrik.

'Malbeth,' he said curtly, passing the goblet to his ambassador and ignoring the affronted expression wrinkling the dwarf king's face as he did it.

Malbeth bowed to his host and then to the prince before sipping.

'Bah! That is no way to quaff ale,' a voice slurred from the far end of the table. It was Rugnir, the dwarf's cheeks already ruddy with the consumption of alcohol. 'Tip it down, lad!' he bellowed.

Bagrik was inclined to agree and only watched.

The elf nodded, smiling nervously as he drank. Swilling the ale down, Malbeth's eyes widened before watering profusely.

'Potent...' he rasped.

'That's it, elgi,' said the king, a fierce look out of the corner of his eye reserved for Ithalred. 'That is how we dwarfs drink our ale.'

The elf prince seemed unmoved and nonchalant as he sipped at his wine.

This will be a long evening, thought Bagrik ruefully.

WITH THE INTRODUCTION of the meat, a heady flavoursome aroma had soon filled the Great Hall. Though the elves found the notion of eating with their hands distasteful, whilst the dwarfs gleefully licked grease off their fingers and supped spilled broth from their beards, the food itself was well received. Copious amounts of ale and wine warmed the stilted atmosphere and it was not long before all were talking readily, both races curious as to the habits and mores of the other.

Discrete pockets of conversation sprang up throughout the Great Hall, as the elves and dwarfs began to debate in small groups. The King's Table was no exception.

'Yes, we are troubled by the greenskin around these parts. There is no hold of the Karaz Ankor that is not,' explained Bagrik, his mood dark. 'They are vermin and grow in number each year–'

'More for us to hunt, eh, father?' Nagrim chipped in.

As they ate and drank, Bagrik had begun to talk at length to Ithalred about the history of the hold and the long, proud legacy of Ungor. For his part, the elf prince had said little, though listened intently, only mentioning once the greenskins that a party of his warriors had slaughtered in the mountains during their journey to the hold. Bagrik had greeted this news warmly, but then his demeanour had turned bitter as he recalled the encroachments of orcs and goblins upon the dwarf realm.

'That's right, lad,' said Bagrik, his mood lightening at once, throwing his arm around his son's shoulder and seizing him in a fierce grip.

Ithalred looked nonplussed, as if he didn't understand the tactile gesture.

'You kill the beasts for sport, then?' the elf prince ventured.

'Aye, he does,' Bagrik said for his son. 'In fact, earlier this evening, the lad beat his father's tally and before his seventieth winter! A fine deed, eh?' the king exclaimed, turning about to regard those dwarfs in earshot.

Queen Brunvilda nodded politely, a beaming smile reserved for her son, though her eyes carried a small measure of sadness. She had been attending to her husband's words dutifully, but had seldom spoken. Her mind was on other things. She loved Nagrim, and he was worthy of their praise, but whenever Bagrik extolled the virtues of his son, she could not help but think of the other, the one bereft of his father's love and devotion.

Dissatisfied with his queen's muted response, Bagrik looked to his hearth guard captain, whose stern gaze was fixed upon the ebullient Rugnir, further down the King's Table, the ex-miner showing the elves how easy it was to quaff two tankards at once without spilling a drop. To his credit, the wanaz achieved the feat with aplomb.

'Eh, Morek?' the king prompted.

'Yes, my king. None in the history of Karak Ungor have killed so many. I doubt it will ever be bested, though I'd be happier if we had another one hundred score to that amount. The greenskin overrun the mountains like ants,' he said.

'Indeed,' Bagrik agreed, a little crestfallen as he released Nagrim from his grasp. Morek's dour response wasn't exactly the affirmation he had been looking for.

'And I plan to add to that tally,' Nagrim told the prince, puffing his chest proudly beneath the red and gold tunic that echoed that worn by his father. 'Good Brondrik, the hold's finest and most venerable ranger has offered to take another party into the mountains after the winter. The mines north of the hold are ever plagued. I'll mount a fair few more grobi heads upon my mantle that day, I promise you,' said the dwarf prince, his eyes alight with the prospect of further glory.

'You take trophies off the creatures?' asked Ithalred with slight distaste.

'Teeth, noses, ears,' replied Nagrim. 'Heads, too, if you can carry them all,' he added with relish.

'If the greenskin are so numerous, do you not worry that they will overwhelm you?'

'Bah,' interjected Bagrik, 'They are base and dimwitted beasts. What has the heir of Ungor to fear from them?' he said, clapping Nagrim on the back and smiling broadly.

'And what of you, Prince Ithalred,' said Bagrik, 'do you hunt in your native lands?'

'Yes,' the elf muttered darkly, 'I hunt. Though of late, the quarry has not been to my taste.' Ithalred stared into space, lost in some dark memory.

'You speak of the troubles in your land, the kinslaying?' asked Bagrik, his tone low.

Word had reached the dwarfs, some months prior to the elves' landfall, and the colonisation of Tor Eorfith, of the civil war in Ulthuan and the treachery of the one they knew as Malekith. It was he that had first brokered peace between elves and dwarfs. It was Malekith that had befriended Snorri Whitebeard, the first of the High Kings of Karaz-a-Karak, capital of the Karaz Ankor. Yes, the dwarfs knew of Malekith. The elves had a different name for him now.

'In my youth, I hunted stag, deer and even pheasant in the forests of Eataine,' Ithalred explained in a rare moment of candour. 'Those days are done.'

An ugly silence came over them, as if a small storm cloud shrouded that part of the King's Table, the rest of the elves and dwarfs seated there conversing easily.

'You are among allies here, Prince Ithalred,' Bagrik told him, saddened by the elf's melancholy but also glad at the bitterness they both understood and shared, albeit for different foes.

'Of course,' replied the prince, his taciturn mask slipping back onto his face again.

The sudden awkwardness was broken by the king's chief victualer and food taster, Magrinson, approaching the table. He had two apprentices in tow carrying the head of the giant boar between them on a silver platter, swimming in dark blood and fatty juices.

'My lord,' Magrinson began, his voice dry and gruff like grit, 'the boar's head.'

The chief victualer ushered his apprentices forward, who then placed the platter before their king. It was the custom of Karak Ungor for the hold's liege lord to eat the flesh of the great boar's head, the meat having cooked in its own juices until it was at its most succulent and flavoursome.

'A fine beast,' said Bagrik, nodding his thanks to Magrinson who bowed curtly and left the King's Table with his apprentices. 'What do you say, Prince Ithalred, are there creatures as fine as this in your forests?'

The elf looked aghast at the steaming boar head, the brute's beady eyes staring at him expectantly. He looked away but found only the skins that Bagrik wore over his shoulders.

'Yes, I ate this one too,' the dwarf king told him, noticing that Ithalred regarded the dried boar carcass that he wore. 'I was not much beyond a beardling when I encountered the beast in the lowland caves to the east of Black Water,' Bagrik explained. 'It was winter then, too, and the snow was foul that year. I was trapped, unable to find my way back to the hold in the growing drifts. So I sought refuge in a cave. Only it was already occupied. It was *his*, you see.' Bagrik tapped the head of the boar skin with something approaching reverence. 'He was a fierce beast, and did not take kindly to me trespassing in his lair. We fought, and he gored me with his tusks. But I slew him. The meat of his body sustained me and his skin warmed me, until I could be found by my father's rangers. Though I did not emerge from the battle unscathed. The wound it dealt me I still carry and I have not walked without pain since that day because of it.'

'Yes,' said Ithalred, seemingly unmoved by the story, 'your queen explained it was the reason for your absence at our arrival.' There was a barb in the elf's words, and Bagrik felt it keenly.

'Perhaps,' ventured the king, 'you would be more understanding if you, too, bore such an injury, elf.'

'I'm not sure I follow your meaning, dwarf,' Ithalred countered.

Kandor, who had paused in his own conversations to hear of what his king and the elf prince were talking about, chipped in quickly to dispel the sudden belligerent mood.

'You admire the line of kings?' he asked a little too loudly.

Malbeth, who had been doing no such thing, but caught onto his fellow diplomat's ploy immediately, looked around the room with feigned interest.

Arrayed around the Great Hall, cast in stark relief with the jagged fingers of firelight from the wall sconces, were statues of the royal clans of Karak Ungor.

'Yes, they are wondrous,' the elf replied with genuine humility, when he actually regarded the statues. 'Are they carved into the rock of the mountain?'

'That they are,' said the king. 'There for eternity, so that all would know of our proud lineage.'

Glad to have averted yet another disaster, Kandor pointed to one statue sat in a large dusty alcove. 'That is King Norkragg Fireheart,' he said, with a quick glance at his king to ensure that he was happy for him to go on. 'Norkragg was a king of the elder age, one of the first of Ungor,' he continued. 'So the Book of Remembering held, Norkragg was a miner at heart, even eschewing his royal duties to pursue his passion, a fact that left him without queen and heir. In his tenure, Norkragg hauled more coal from the rock face and to the under-forge than any since.'

'A great and noble lord was Norkragg. He had much respect for the traditions of us dawi,' added Bagrik, a meaningful glance at Ithalred to ram his point home.

'And this one,' said Malbeth quickly before the elf prince could reply, gesturing to the next statue in line. 'What is his tale?'

'Ah,' said Kandor, as he regarded the stooped shoulders, were it possible for a statue to stoop, of the liege lord alongside Norkragg. 'King Ranulf Shallowbrow. And to his right, Queen Helgi.'

Malbeth beheld a large and fearsome dwarf woman when he looked upon the effigy of Ranulf's queen.

'She is… *formidable*,' he said, choosing his words carefully.

Kandor went on.

'It was rumoured at the girthing ceremony that Ranulf had to wait another fifty years after his initial proposal of marriage before they could be wed. You see, according to dwarf law a suitor is required to wrap his beard around a rinn's waist twice over before the marriage can be made legal, and Helgi was a mighty woman.'

'It was also said,' Rugnir chipped in, 'that she was of such fine stock that she neared bankrupted poor old Ranulf when she sat upon the nuptial scales!'

The ex-miner laughed raucously, Nagrim alongside joining him.

Even King Bagrik raised a smile.

'Aye, Rugnir,' said the stern voice of Morek, who had been listening in to all the conversations around the King's Table, 'that it did, but what a queen Ranulf had. Any wife that you might make for yourself would be as waif thin as these elgi, such is your squandered fortune,' he added caustically.

Kandor balked at the hearth guard captain's remark, hoping that the elves did not take any offence. If they had, they didn't get the chance to voice it as Morek went on unabated.

'Kraggin will be wandering in limbo before Gazul's Gate because of your profligacy. It is no fate for one such as he; no fate at all.'

The entire table fell abruptly quiet at Morek's outburst. Even Rugnir's drunken humour seemed beaten out of him at the mention of his father's name.

'How is this so?' said Lethralmir, who had been apathetically swilling his wine around in his goblet before noticing the apparent discord and seizing upon an opportunity to exploit it. 'Surely, this fine… *individual* cannot be held responsible for the fate of his father. Did he not make his own destiny?'

Morek's face flushed and he clenched his teeth.

Malbeth interceded quickly when he realised what the raven-haired elf was trying to do.

'I think what my kinsmen means,' began the ambassador, 'is we are unfamiliar with dwarf belief. For instance, what is this gate you speak of? It is not a literal gate, like the entrance to this grand chamber, I assume?'

'No,' said Morek, looking daggers at Lethralmir, before switching his attention to Malbeth. 'Gazul's Gate bars the way to the dwarf afterlife and the Halls of the Ancestors,' he explained. 'Every dwarf must face those gates and balance his deeds before Gazul himself. Even if they are found worthy, and pass into the Halls, there is no guarantee they will remain so. The deeds of descendents can throw their place at the table of Grungni into jeopardy. So it is with some,' Morek said, looking askance and angry at Rugnir, 'where their ancestors will wander lost until amends have been made for dishonourable behaviour.'

'Surely, though, this dwarf, if he is indeed enduring purgatory, must have brought it upon himself?' Lethralmir pressed with a sly wink at Arthelas, who was enjoying the show sat alongside him.

'Kraggin was honourable and good,' Morek asserted passionately, 'How dare you besmirch his name!'

'Please, please,' said Malbeth, 'Lethralmir meant no offence, I'm sure. Did you?' he added, looking meaningfully at the dark-haired elf who returned his stern gaze with a look of indifference.

'No, of course not. I would never *besmirch* a dwarf,' he replied at length.

Morek's face darkened and he stood and turned to Bagrik, who was similarly unimpressed.

'My lord, I regret I must leave the King's Table to attend to my many duties,' said the hearth guard captain.

Bagrik was grave as he regarded the elves. It seemed the hope that his guests would live up to the honour of being at his table had been dashed. He sighed deeply, mastering his annoyance. Bagrik knew his hearth guard captain's views – they were not so dissimilar to his own – but he also had no desire to fuel the fire of Morek's anti-elf sentiment. He had promised Brunvilda he would try, and made a similar pledge to Kandor. As king of the hold, he would keep to his word. Yet with Morek in such a foul mood, he had little recourse but to give him leave.

'Granted,' Bagrik said at last.

Morek bowed swiftly, firing a dark glare in Lethralmir's direction before he left the Great Hall.

* * *

KORHVALE HAD NOT spoken a word since the elves had entered the Great Hall. He had watched all within the chamber diligently, though, his gaze lingering on Arthelas more than most. Only when she had noticed him looking did he turn away, abashed. He took greater care when watching her after that. It only served to exacerbate the discomfort he already felt. The White Lion did not like the dank halls of earth, the sense of the mountain on top of him. It felt like a threat waiting to make good on itself. Instead, he longed for the wide open spaces of Chrace, his homeland: to feel the breeze upon his face, the warmth of the sun against his skin, and to drink in the scents of the wild.

Korhvale, at his heart, was the beast he wore as a pelt across his shoulders. Wild and untamed, he desired to roam the forests and mountains of Ulthuan. This which he now endured, fettered within a cage of stone, was anathema to him.

'He was always highly strung, that one,' remarked a dwarf sitting alongside him. Korhvale saw he had a thick black beard and dark circles ringed his eyes. He had rough-looking hands, scarred and calloused. Clearly, he was a warrior. He wore a dark grey tunic and pinched a pipe between his lips as he offered a hand to the White Lion.

'Grikk Ironspike, Captain of the King's Ironbreakers.'

Korhvale shook hands with the dwarf, though the tactile gesture felt strange to him.

'Korhvale,' he muttered, uncertain in his use of Khazalid to say much more.

'I get the feeling that grand feasts are not for you, elgi,' said Grikk, struggling for conversation himself.

'No,' Korhvale replied.

'Me neither,' Grikk agreed. 'I would rather be alone in the Ungrin Ankor, the tunnels beneath the hold,' he explained. 'There are many beasts that inhabit them – that is true – but I know what is to be done about beasts,' he added with a glint in his eye.

Korhvale shrugged, unsure how to respond.

'It is at grand gatherings that I am at a loss,' the dwarf said.

'Yes,' the elf replied.

'Seems you and me both,' the ironbreaker muttered, after an uneasy silence, and folded his arms as he supped on his pipe.

A GREAT GONG echoed metallically throughout the Great Hall, struck by Haggar. It heralded the end of the feast and the onset on the entertainments provided by the dwarfs. The reverberant sound came as a welcome relief to both races – certainly Bagrik was glad of it. This Ithalred had proven himself every inch the arrogant warrior-prince that Bagrik supposed he would be. He wondered, as a veritable throng of servants issued into the grand chamber to clear plates and platters, whether or not it had been a wise move to listen to Kandor's counsel regarding the elves. The merchant guildmaster had insisted that a trade alliance between their peoples would bring about much prosperity, that the elves would be all too willing dwarffriends in light of the troubles that beset their own shores. So far, though, Bagrik had seen little to encourage him and would only bite his tongue so long.

The dwarf servants worked quickly, taking the remnants of the feast back to the hold's kitchens and lesser clan halls. As he watched them troop out with the giant broth cauldron and the fire-pit, Bagrik felt himself being raised aloft on his throne by his hearth guard.

The King's Table was moved from his path by a group of clansdwarfs, and he, together with Brunvilda and Nagrim, was carried to the edge of the stone platform overlooking the sunken floor of the vast hall. The other tables, the Seat of the Wise and that of the Masters and other dwarf nobility, had already been taken away to be stored. Below, a similar arrangement was taking place as a large open plaza started to appear where before there had been many tables.

The ledges that delineated the room were soon occupied, more dwarf servants providing plump velvet cushions with wooden backboards for the venerable or important. In short order, the Great Hall took on the aspect of a roofed amphitheatre, the stone plaza a natural focal point for the attention of the surrounding elves and dwarfs.

Once the transformation was complete, Bagrik turned again to Haggar who stood at the ready by the great gong in one corner of the hall. At the king's command, Haggar sounded the gong again and the hall, which up until then had been filled with a hubbub of low voices, fell silent. Bagrik then signalled to his banner bearer to begin the entertainments.

'Grikk Ironspike, Captain of the King's Ironbreakers!' Haggar declared, his voice resonating around the room like a clarion call.

The black-bearded dwarf came forward from the shadows at the edge of the Great Hall, approached his king and bowed on one knee, his clenched fists at either side of his body and touching the floor in the regal fashion of the dwarfs. He was no longer wearing his dark grey tunic, instead stripped to the waist and wearing leather breeches with a skirt of mail, bronze vambraces clapped around his wrists.

'Tromm, Grikk of the Ironspike clan,' said Bagrik to
his captain. 'What feats have you for us?'

'AXE HURLING, MY liege,' Malbeth heard the ironbreaker
reply, 'and anvil lifting.'

Sat next to Kandor, the elf ambassador watched as
clansdwarfs marched onto the plaza of stone in the
middle of the Great Hall carrying, first, a weapons rack
of dwarf hand axes and then a series of wooden stakes
on top of which had been rammed the heads of greenskins. Malbeth swallowed back his disgust at the grisly
targets, with their lolling tongues and glassy-eyed stares.
Ragged skin hung from their necks, together with strips
of desiccated flesh caked with dried blood.

They were repellent things, the elf decided, worrying
what Ithalred was thinking, who wore a perpetual grimace as he regarded the decapitated heads. As he fretted
over his prince, Malbeth also caught the venomous gaze
of Lethralmir, who was clearly enjoying the spectacle for
all the wrong reasons. Holding the elf ambassador's
gaze, the raven-haired blade-master whispered something into Arthelas's ear, who laughed quietly. Malbeth
noticed Korhvale, too, his attention rapt, but not on
Grikk who was approaching the weapon's rack for his
first axe, but rather on Arthelas.

That will not end well, Malbeth thought, and resolved
to speak with the White Lion later.

Fraught with concern and misgivings, he gave a false
smile to Kandor who gestured for him to watch, as the
display was about to begin in earnest.

GRIKK WAS LATHERED in sweat, a line of split greenskin
skulls and upturned anvils testament to his endeavours.
The dwarfs had cheered as one with each lifted weight,

with every orc or goblin head struck and maimed. Grikk never missed, not once, and no anvil, however large, could defeat him. Conversely, the elves seemed not to know what to do and were largely silent throughout, only clapping politely at the end as the ironbreaker captain bowed before his king and then his audience.

Haggar found the elgi to be strange creatures, who lacked the ready camaraderie of his kin. How could they fail to appreciate the skills of the ironbreaker captain? Grikk was one of the finest warriors in the hold, next only to Morek. Would that he, Haggar, be so great... For a moment, the dwarf's mind drifted to a time before, to a shame he must atone for. He eyed the banner of Ungor, resting in its place behind the throne of King Bagrik and felt the dishonour of that day anew.

Thagri, he said to himself, will your dishonour ever linger over me?

So deep was Haggar's remembrance that he very nearly missed the order of his king to announce the next entertainment.

Hurriedly, Haggar thrashed the gong and cried, 'The Miners' Guild Choir, led by Jodri Broadbellow!'

MALBETH WATCHED AS in filed the dwarf choristers, decked in their finest attire, the bronze buttons on their brown tunics gleaming, black metal mining caps polished to a dull lustre. Some wore tiny bells around their fingers, or had cloth tassels bound to their ankles and wrists. There were musicians, too, carrying instruments: large, brass horns curved to resemble coiling serpentine monsters; fat animal bladders, fitted with an array of copper pipes that sprang out at awkward-looking angles; orc-skin drums, rolled out onto the stone plaza; and a strange-looking barrel organ with yellowed-bone keys at one end and a metal turning crank at the other.

It was as bizarre an assemblage as Malbeth had ever seen, and he had been to the dwarf kingdoms before. However odd this array of dwarfs, though, the sight could not have prepared him for what happened next. A dour bass note began the proceedings, the head chorister singing *a cappella* at first, before his fellows joined him in complimentary baritone and tenor. As they sang, some ditty about firkins and a goblin's rump, as far as Malbeth could discern, the musicians struck up their instruments.

A horrific din assailed his senses, and the elf ambassador shut his eyes at first in the hope that the dwarfs had merely mistuned. After a few more seconds of the auditory torture, it became clear that they had not and, grimacing, Malbeth opened his eyes. Puffing cheeks red with effort, the dwarfs pumped out a sound akin to a throttled horse or bone scraped down metal. The elf ambassador noticed King Bagrik seemed to be enjoying himself, as did the rest of the dwarfs watching, slapping his thigh as the miners danced with strange, squatting motions, bells and tassels shaking with every syncopated movement.

Malbeth gritted his teeth, trying desperately at the same time to smile, and prayed to Isha, the elven god of mercy, that it would be over soon.

BAGRIK STOPPED DRUMMING the beat of the choristers' drums when he saw the expression on Ithalred's face. The elf prince looked as if he was in profound agony, his features screwed up so tight they might never revert back to their usual state of indifference.

Hurriedly, the dwarf king got the attention of his banner bearer and urged him vigorously to strike the gong.

After a moment's indecision, Haggar did as he was bidden, the reverberating sound of the gong cutting the performance of the Miners' Guild Choir abruptly short.

'Enough!' Bagrik snarled.

Confused, the miners stopped part way through the first verse of their ditty with a belated toot and crump of a pipe and accordion. Bagrik waved away the looks of the nonplussed miners agitatedly, and they tramped off in disconsolate fashion with a discordant clamour of instruments and much grumbling.

The king then turned swiftly to Haggar, his gaze questioning as to what was next. The dwarf merely shrugged, looking slightly panicked at the sudden interruption in the schedule.

Malbeth came to his rescue.

'PERHAPS, YOU WOULD allow us to grace you with a taste of our native culture,' said the elf ambassador, to Haggar's profound relief.

Bagrik muttered something in response, but then Kandor nodded, similarly relieved.

'Arthelas,' said the elf, turning to the pale maiden at Prince Ithalred's side, 'would you grace our generous hosts with a song of Eataine?'

Haggar saw the elf maiden nod demurely as she rose from her seat, and felt his face flush at her elegance and ethereal beauty. Never had he seen such a creature in all his days. So thin, so brittle, she was like the wind, the reflected light of sun against water, the glitter of gold. She glided down to the plaza, two elf harpists drifting silently to her side as she took her position in the middle of the plaza. The magnificence of the Great Hall seemed dulled in her radiant presence and all within fell silent as she began.

A lilting melody filled the air as Arthelas sang, a haunting, ephemeral sound that seemed to drift in and out of being, as the harpists plucked their instruments in accompaniment. Though he did not understand the words, Haggar felt warmth and a curious sense of lightness spread over his body as he heard them. The effect was bewitching. Time slowed and ceased to have meaning. It was like there was only her in the grand chamber, alone and singing just for Haggar. Her gaze connected with the dwarf's and the burden of his past faded away. Not even a lingering memory remained, there was only Arthelas.

When the song ended and she bowed her head in supplication before the crowd, stunned silence reigned. Haggar wiped tears from his eyes and breathed again. When he saw Arthelas collapse, his heart nearly stopped in his armoured chest.

KORHVALE WAS THE first to come to Arthelas's aid, vaulting down from his perch on the stone ledge, landing deftly, and at her side in a moment. Ithalred was close behind the White Lion, waving the harpists and other elves aside as he took her from his bodyguard and cradled her in his arms, before whispering softly in his sister's ear. She roused, opening her eyes slowly.

'What is wrong with her?' asked Malbeth, the elf ambassador having followed after his prince. A small cluster of other concerned onlookers had gathered, elves and dwarfs both.

'Is everything well, shall I summon the priests of Valaya?' asked Kandor, a little breathless.

'What goes on down there?' called Bagrik from his seat, the dwarf king unwilling to hobble down to see for himself.

'*We have no need of your priests!*' snapped Ithalred beneath his breath, as he flashed a scowl at the dwarf merchant.

'All is well, my friend,' said Malbeth, stepping between the prince and Kandor, and placing his hand on the dwarf's shoulder. 'Arthelas is merely tired from our journey. She feels it more than the rest of us,' he explained.

Kandor nodded slowly, catching a glimpse of Ithalred past Malbeth as he angrily summoned his servants, but did not appear reassured.

'All is well,' Malbeth said again much louder for the benefit of the entire assembly. 'The Lady Arthelas is only tired.'

'We are all tired,' came the voice of Lethralmir, his tone dark, as he emerged through the crowd like a viper. 'These… *games*,' he added, 'have gone on long enough.'

Malbeth was about to say something when Ithalred got up, carrying Arthelas in his arms.

'Lethralmir is right,' said the prince in elvish. 'This ridiculous display is over. I have endured enough of it.'

'But my lord, I'm sure if Arthelas returns to her–' Malbeth began.

'It is over, Malbeth,' Ithalred snapped, his tone brooking no argument.

The elf ambassador, halted in mid-flow, closed his mouth and nodded his assent. Out of the corner of his eye, he noticed Lethralmir quietly smirking to himself.

'Malbeth,' Ithalred said curtly, 'tell our hosts we are retiring for the evening.' At that he stalked out of the Great Hall, Korhvale, his face awash with concern, with him. A clutch of servants came after them, the muttered grumblings of the dwarfs left in their wake.

Lethralmir gave a series of sharp commands in elvish at which the warriors got to their feet and followed the prince with the rest of the servants. The raven-haired blade-master was about to move into step behind them when Malbeth grasped his arm.

'What do you think you're doing?' he hissed, angrily.

The raven-haired elf smiled darkly, 'Keeping my dignity and the dignity of our race,' he said.

'Khaine damn you, Lethralmir.'

The elf sniffed, as if he found Malbeth's remark amusing. 'You first,' he countered, looking down meaningfully at his arm where the ambassador still gripped it.

'Do you really want to make a scene before our generous hosts?' Lethralmir goaded him after a few seconds, and looked back down at his arm again. 'Remember that temper of yours…'

Malbeth let him go.

'What is going on?' asked Kandor, as the elves were trooping out of the Great Hall.

Malbeth turned, having recovered his composure.

'Tiredness has got the better of us all, it seems,' he replied weakly, then raised his voice to address the king.

'Regrettably, your majesty, we must retire for the evening. Prince Ithalred is exhausted, and must rest from his journey. He asked me to convey his appreciation at the fine feast and entertainments you so graciously provided, however.'

King Bagrik said something beneath his breath, clearly unconvinced, and Malbeth took that as his cue to leave.

BAGRIK SURVEYED THE pandemonium of his Great Hall left in the elves' wake: the dwarfs milling around the stone plaza scratching their heads and muttering amongst one another; the disgusted tones of the glowering longbeards, their pipes smoking furiously; the dark glances passing between the guildmasters, and the other clan lords and thanes, that he, Bagrik, had given sanction for this debacle.

He felt the presence of Brunvilda nearby, about to reassure him, and clenched his fists.

'Say nothing!' he snarled between his teeth, turning his furious gaze onto Kandor, who seemed somehow lost standing below him.

Rugnir's voice broke the tomb-like atmosphere.

'Who died?' he asked, jovially. 'Let the elgi get their beauty sleep, there is still more drinking to be done.'

A few of the younger clansdwarfs seemed to warm to the idea at once, Nagrim included.

Bagrik shattered the levity in an instant.

'No!' he raged, struggling to his feet and casting his steely gaze about the room. He had bent over backwards for these elves, allowed them into his home, turned a blind eye to their affronts, their arrogance and rudeness. They had thrown his hospitality in his face like grobi dung. Bagrik was incensed, and in no mood to make merry. 'Back to your clan halls, all of you, the party is over!'

CHAPTER SEVEN
Dark Secrets

IT WAS SEVERAL hours before Malbeth returned to the Hall of Belgrad, now turned into an elven enclave. After leaving the Great Hall, he had waited for Kandor. The dwarf merchant had emerged soon enough, having exchanged curt words with his king, or rather had words foisted upon him, which he had attended to in silence. Ashen-faced from his berating, the merchant had then taken the elf to his private halls and the two had discussed the evening at length, Kandor expressing the king's concerns over the elves' behaviour and Malbeth giving the dwarf his assurances that they were merely teething troubles and an accord could be reached over the trade agreement. The long debate had left the elf weary, but he had managed to convince Kandor that there was still an alliance to be salvaged from the carnage of the feast.

Even so, it was with some trepidation that Malbeth approached the tent of the prince. Korhvale was outside, the White Lion and a handful of other guards and servants the only ones yet to retire to their makeshift abodes. Malbeth knew Korhvale would stay at his post all night, eschewing sleep or even meditation, to watch over his master.

Arms folded like bands of iron, the muscular bodyguard grunted as Malbeth came near, stepping aside so that he could enter.

Low lamps burned within the tent, creating a warm, cloying atmosphere in the opulent surroundings. Ithalred was laid out on a pile of plump cushions and divested of his princely robes, bare-chested and wearing loose-fitting cotton breeches. A soft melody pervaded the room, the two harpists from earlier playing quietly nearby. Two further maidens, wearing precious little, but enough to preserve their dignity, were decanting wine into the prince's goblet and massaging his neck and shoulders. At Malbeth's appearance in the room they looked up and smiled lasciviously before continuing with their duties.

A blue-green smoke drenched the atmosphere, lingering about Malbeth's feet like autumnal glade mist. The elf ambassador saw Lethralmir sitting cross-legged as he supped from a long-handled marble pipe, a fifth maiden combing his long black hair.

The two nobles had been laughing as Malbeth had entered, enjoying the tail end of some jest he was not privy to. Still smiling, Lethralmir blew a large ring of smoke into the air. It held its form for a short while before it dispersed into lingering aroma.

'Prince Ithalred,' said Malbeth, his tone serious, 'we must talk about what happened at the feast. The dwarfs are unhappy.'

Ithalred closed his eyes and leaned further back, wallowing in the decadence of his private pavilion. He beckoned with his ringed fingers and one of the scant-ily-clad maidens came over with a platter of fruit, which the prince accepted with hedonistic torpor.

'The dwarfs are unhappy, *I* am unhappy,' he replied, nonchalant. 'Let us just be done with these trade talks so that we can return to Tor Eorfith and some sem-blance of civilisation. I swear by Asuryan, if I spend much longer in the burrows of these hirsute dwarfs, I shall be sprouting hair from my own chin.'

Lethralmir smirked.

Ithalred wasn't jesting.

'With respect,' said Malbeth, ignoring the blade-master, 'amends must be made if the trade talks are to go ahead.'

Ithalred sighed in agitation, waving away the servant girls as he levered himself up onto his elbows.

'What would you have me do, Malbeth? Our cultures are utterly opposite to one another. A clash was inevitable.'

'It is more than a clash,' said Malbeth with growing exasperation. 'We have offended our hosts in their very home! I, too, long for the lofty towers of Eorfith, for the sky and the wind and all that I hold dear about Ulthuan and Eataine, but there is too much at stake here to jeopardise in the name of selfish desire and petulance.'

He'd gone too far. The sneering smile spreading across Lethralmir's face, just visible in the corner of his eye, told Malbeth as much.

'You forget yourself, ambassador,' snapped Ithalred, sitting up and nearly tipping over his wine.

'I apologise, my prince,' Malbeth replied humbly, 'but the fact remains that Tor Eorfith will not survive with-out the dwarfs' aid.'

'We do not know that for certain,' said Lethralmir, even now stirring the pot.

Malbeth whirled around to face him, though he kept his anger at bay. But only just.

'We know it all too well, Lethralmir,' he said fiercely. 'Do not allow your arrogance to obscure your already clouded mind.

'Prince Ithalred,' Malbeth continued, turning back to his lord without waiting for a response from Lethralmir. 'I am *urging* you – apologise to the dwarfs, make amends for all that has transpired. You know as well as I what this trade pact truly represents, what we hope to gain from it. Please… *please*, do not lose sight of that.'

Ithalred's expression promised another angry retort, but he stopped short as if realising the truth in Malbeth's words and at last capitulated.

'Very well. I'll do as you ask, Malbeth. I will regain the respect of the dwarfs. It is my duty to safeguard the future of Tor Eorfith, so there is little else I can do, is there,' he added, clearly unhappy with the position he was in, with the position that they were all in. 'Now, go…' he said after a moment, his face suddenly darkening. 'It is late, and I tire of politics.'

One of the maidens, seeing her lord's distemper, slid over to resume massaging his neck.

'Leave it!' he snarled, and she shrank back as if scalded by his words. 'All of you,' he added, glaring around the room, 'get out!'

Hurriedly gathering their things, and some of their clothes, the quintet of maidens made a hasty exit, eyes down as they left the prince's private abode for fear of further reproach.

Lethralmir seemed bemused at Ithalred's reaction, particularly his dismissal of the wenches, whose company he had been enjoying profusely.

'Was that strictly necessary, Ithalred?' he asked, taking a long draw on his pipe and reaching for his wine.

'You too, Lethralmir,' the prince said quietly.

The raven-haired elf opened his mouth to protest but thought better of it.

'As you wish, my lord,' he said with forced deference, clearly incensed at being expelled from his prince's presence like a common slave.

Malbeth watched the entire display and felt no satisfaction. He saw only Ithalred at last coming to terms with the gravity of their situation and the stark reality that theirs was a precarious position indeed.

Bowing slightly, he departed immediately after Lethralmir had stormed out, his mood no better than when he had first entered the pavilion.

'WAIT...' CALLED MALBETH, once they were a few feet from the prince's tent and the imposing figure of Korhvale, '...I would speak with you, Lethralmir.'

The raven-haired elf turned. He was on the way to his own tent, determined to summon a pair of the wenches that Ithalred had just dismissed. He let Malbeth come to him before he gave his reply.

'I have nothing to say,' he told the ambassador, still smarting over the prince's rebuttal.

'Then merely listen,' Malbeth countered, guiding the blade-master by the shoulder around the side of one of the tents. Once out of Korhvale's eye-line, he seized Lethralmir by the arm and drew him close.

'Do not think your blatant attempts at sabotage have gone unnoticed,' said Malbeth, his eyes hard. 'I don't know what your reasons are, but it will stop... now. And you would do well to stay away from Arthelas,' he warned.

Lethralmir went rigid at her name. His cerulean eyes were like diamonds as they regarded the ambassador, his dark smile etched as if in ice.

'Your behaviour towards her is unseemly,' Malbeth continued. 'I have turned a blind eye to it for long enough. Do not think that Ithalred will continue to do so, either. The prince has no desire to see his sister sullied by one such as you. Her gifts, her sight – they are precious... I am telling you, Lethralmir–'

'No,' the raven-haired elf hissed, grabbing Malbeth's robes, all trace of his sarcastic vainglory evaporated, and in its place... malicious, undiluted bile. '*I* am the only one doing the *telling* here. Or do you want me to reveal your true nature to the prince, to your precious bearded swine?' He sneered hatefully, though his expression betrayed his fear.

Malbeth's loosened his grip, the sudden creeping dread of discovery shaking his resolve.

It was no idle threat. Lethralmir meant every word. There was anger in his eyes now, the same impotent fury that there had been all those years ago...

Malbeth still held him in his grasp, remembering the day they had first crossed swords, in the sheltered arboretum of his uncle's villa in Eataine, the pale sandstone walls flecked with darkness, Elethya dying in his arms. Her hot blood was a baptism for the rage and anguish that would manifest in Malbeth. And just like that, the feelings that he had fought so hard to repress, the fury that lay in his cursed soul, came boiling to the surface in a tempest.

Lethralmir saw it in the ambassador's eyes, saw him glance to the jewelled dagger the blade-master wore at his belt.

'Go on...' said the raven-haired elf, his lip curling in a sneer '...Do it.' Lethralmir released Malbeth's robe, let his arm drop in submission. 'Give in.'

It would be easy…

Elethya… dying in his arms…

Malbeth let him go, then turned away, heading towards his tent without saying another word.

LETHRALMIR SMOOTHED DOWN his robes, releasing a long breath as he tried to stop shaking. He told himself it was anger, but in truth he was afraid; afraid of what Malbeth might have done if pushed.

That could be useful, he thought, if properly channelled.

Recovering his composure, he managed to swagger off, imperiously staring down any servants that had seen or overheard his altercation with the ambassador and dared to meet his gaze. He was intent on finding the masseurs – their *attentions* would be a welcome distraction right now – when he changed his mind. He bypassed his own tent, and went straight for Arthelas's instead.

Bastard, Malbeth, threaten me will you?

Lethralmir's route took him back towards Ithalred's domicile and the stern-faced Korhvale, who glared at the raven-haired elf as he approached.

'The prince asked me to see how his sister was feeling,' he lied, flashing a broad smile in Korhvale's direction. The White Lion stiffened in response, his leather gauntlets cracking as he made fists.

Lethralmir gave him no further thought, passing by and continuing on to where Arthelas was waiting.

'I AM BORED,' Lethralmir declared, as he entered the tent, 'and I have charged you with entertaining me,' he added, sweeping into the room and down to Arthelas's side, where she reclined on a chaise-long of white wood, upholstered with sumptuous red velvet and fashioned into the image of a swan in repose. Lethralmir noticed several servants hovering at the periphery, their faces veiled by the thin cotton shrouds that hung throughout the room, and carrying silver carafes and broad, paper fans. There was no food in sight – the seeress seldom ate. Lethralmir dismissed the servants with a few curt commands.

'Finally alone…' he purred, once they were gone, letting the insinuation linger. He drew close to her, the scent of her in his nostrils more potent than any perfume as it enflamed his ardour.

Arthelas pushed him away, but her protest lacked conviction.

'My brother would have you killed if he knew what you were intending,' she said, sighing as she rested the back of her hand across her forehead in an overtly dramatic gesture. 'I am tired Lethralmir, and in no mood for your advances tonight.'

Lethralmir sniffed contemptuously, and recoiled.

'You are in a fouler mood than your brother, the prince,' he replied.

'He is a fool,' said Arthelas, looking at Lethralmir for the first time. There was darkness in her eyes, bitterness in her voice. 'I am a seeress first and a sister second to him. Ithalred's mood is foul because he does not like it when he doesn't get his way. He is annoyed because he must listen to Malbeth's counsel, because he must make parlay with these dwarfs.'

She almost spat the words through clenched teeth as the demure and elegant façade slipped completely.

Lethralmir gazed back at Arthelas, her words meaningless as he drank deep of her azure eyes, and became lost in their fathomless beauty. Determined to lighten the mood, he moved over to the tent flap by which he had entered.

'I have something that will cheer you,' he said, smiling conspiratorially and beckoning her over.

Arthelas exhaled loudly, sitting up, ostensibly annoyed as she padded over.

Lethralmir ignored the histrionics, opened the tent flap and gestured outside.

'Look…'

Arthelas sighed again, signalling her impatience, but did as she was asked. Peering through the flap, she saw Korhvale, brooding outside her brother's tent.

'No more than a crack,' Lethralmir warned, as the White Lion stared in her direction but then swiftly averted his gaze as if suddenly ashamed.

'Look how forlorn he is,' the raven-haired elf said sarcastically.

'I don't like the way he watches me.'

'The dumb and dutiful lion,' Lethralmir sneered, revealing his true feelings. 'His mawkish attempts to gain your favour are only marginally less laughable than the antics of the earth-dwellers,' he added, growing more serious. 'What need do the asur have for these diminutive swine? If Ithalred possessed any backbone at all he would raise the army at Tor Eorfith and turn back the northern hordes closing on our borders. Yet instead, at Malbeth's insistence,' he spat, 'he seeks to yoke the strength of these rough creatures and their crude ways. What will they do, bite the ankles of the northern savages? No,' he scoffed, 'there is nothing to fear from *men*.'

'I am not so certain…' said Arthelas, finding no more amusement in watching Korhvale, and closed the tent flap.

'Why?' Lethralmir asked. His eyes narrowed as he regarded her, suddenly understanding. 'What have you *seen?*'

In that moment, all expression seemed to vanish from Arthelas's face and her eyes glazed over like pale moons. The heady scent of her perfumed boudoir was gone, the smell of the sea, of cold, glacial air, and the tang of salt came in its place.

'Our ships,' said Arthelas, her voice far away, 'ablaze on the ocean…'

'Hasseled's Hawkships,' Lethralmir whispered, realising at once what she meant. Just before they had set off for the dwarf hold, Ithalred had ordered a defensive blockade to be erected far out at sea against northmen vessels the elves had seen from their watchtowers, sailing the Sea of Claws. Commander Hasseled was to lead them, assess the enemy's strength and destroy them if he could. It seemed the good commander had failed.

'Their crude vessels riding through a storm…' Arthelas continued. 'They make landfall… the sentinels are just the beginning…'

'The watchtowers are lost?' hissed Lethralmir.

Arthelas turned to him, vehement, fear in her eyes – the sense of it exaggerated by her dream-trance.

'They already burn… All are dead, all of them.'

She wept, the tears rushing down her face in a flood, and Lethralmir held her.

'Let it go,' he said softly, stroking her hair, 'Let it all go.'

Arthelas looked into his eyes, coming out of it at last.

'All dead…' she whimpered, softly.

Lethralmir took her chin gently, tilting Arthelas's head so she had to look into his eyes. He caressed her neck and drew in close.

'What are you doing?' she hissed, fear and excitement warring in her voice.

'Your brother has no need of a seer, anymore.'

'I can't,' she said in a cracked whisper.

'You must…' Lethralmir replied huskily, parting his lips and pressing them to hers…

Blood. Endless blood. The battlefield was soaked in it, a crimson-tinged isle of pounded dirt. Ragged banners fluttered on a fitful breeze that reeked of copper, and smoke from burning cities rendered into ruined shells by the carnage. Hollow, pleading cries and the clash-scrape of metal filled the rancid air, borne upon a hot wind that swirled about in tired eddies and whispered… death…

Malbeth awoke, lathered in sweat. He sat up sharply as if the pallet where he lay were a bed of spikes, and he'd just felt the first prick. His head was swimming, visions slipping in and out of focus – a war against creatures not of this world, screaming terror and a bloody-handed god exulting in the slaughter. A sense memory spoke of metal and fire, the stench of smoke lingering impossibly in Malbeth's nostrils.

The coldness of the dwarf stone, penetrating even the cushioned floor of his tent, brought him around. Sodden sheets clung to his body, and Malbeth cast them off like they were shackles that incarcerated him in the dream. Dull and resonant hammering, the ever-present din of the dwarf forges working day and night, reminded him again of the battlefield as Malbeth lost himself once more to memories that weren't his to recall.

A smoking sword of ruin thrust in a black anvil.

Daemons, their maws hungering, crouched before a dreaded altar.

The world ended in bloodshed and darkness.

Malbeth shook his head to banish the fever-dream images, snapping at the edge of his sight like lashing vipers. It was not his memory. It was the Blighted Isle and the final resting place of the Sword of Khaine, that most cursed of all artefacts, driven into the black anvil by Aenarion the Defender, the first Phoenix King, and arguably the greatest and most tragic of them all. By first drawing the sword, he had embraced Khaine utterly. In becoming a near god, he had saved the high elf race, and yet, at the same time, his actions had doomed them.

Malbeth got to his feet, revelling in the coolness of his naked form as his evaporating sweat chilled him, and padded over to a shrine devoted to the goddess Lileath. It was a simple thing, a statue upon a raised dais, set aside innocuously in one of the tent's antechambers. His heart was thudding loudly as he regarded her silver effigy, arms wide with her palms upward in acceptance. Malbeth lifted Lileath carefully from her silver, gem-stoned dais and placed her reverently by its side. With two hands, he then lifted off the disc of the dais itself, revealing a small compartment within that housed a wooden chest. Taking out the chest, he set it down on the ground and then sat crossed-legged with it in front of him. It was locked, but Malbeth had the key around his neck – a small golden rune, *elthrai*, attached to a gilt chain. It meant 'hope', but like much of elven symbolism it had a counter meaning, one that could also be interpreted as 'doom'.

Unlocking and opening the chest, Malbeth still felt the pull of anger, the arousal of killing, albeit experienced cathartically, from his dream. The verisimilitude of the battlefield was still strong. There were sixteen vials within, no larger than a finger joint, each containing a pale green milky liquid. With a trembling hand, Malbeth took one of them, ripping off the cork stopper and drinking it swiftly. Rivulets of the thick fluid ran down the curves in his mouth, and Malbeth wiped them away with the back of his hand. Slowing his breath, the thrashing in his heart, the violent desire, subsided and Malbeth began to feel better.

Something had broken in him the day that Elethya died. He'd found solace in rage and death, embracing the will of Khaine. All of the asur held the capacity for those traits embodied by the Bloody Handed God. Murder, hatred, war and destruction: they were part of the elven psyche, as insoluble as stubbornness and gold-hunger was to dwarfs. But it was tempered by peace and love and order – the elven philosophy that one element cannot exist without its counterpart. Malbeth did not possess the same balance that most other elves of Ulthuan did. To his mind, he was cursed, the bloodletting and reaving of his youth, barely justifiable, and an eternal stain upon his soul.

Malbeth returned the chest to its hiding place and remade the shrine. Sinking to his knees, he prayed fervently to Lileath for forgiveness. There were tears in his eyes when he'd finished. He stood wearily, reaching for a robe and soft boots, before drifting out of his tent without a sound.

Outside, Korhvale was the only one left awake. He was scribing something furtively by the dimmed glow of the eldritch lanterns and didn't notice Malbeth as he slipped by him silently.

I'll find no further sleep this night, thought Malbeth, heading out of the Hall of Belgrad and into the hold.

* * *

THE SWEEPS AND twists of the elven script were applied with the utmost care and attention. Korhvale took great pains to be exacting and neat in every detail. The wet ink glistened in the low lamp light, the pigments reacting with the oily luminescence that filled the former Hall of Belgrad. The shining runes reminded him of the light in her eyes and that then led to a remembrance of the shape of her lips, the glittering cascade of her golden hair.

He had loved Arthelas for as long as he had known her. A chance encounter with the Prince Ithalred, whilst he was out hunting sparhawks in the Annuli Mountains of northern Chrace, had led Korhvale to his service as a guide and, eventually, bodyguard. It was then that he had met Arthelas, and then that his heart had been lost.

Korhvale did not have the ready wit or charm of Lethralmir, nor the erudite intelligence of Malbeth; he was an intense and brooding soul, but beneath all that there was an artist that desired to be set free. As he sat upon a short, white, wooden stool, he scratched with a sparhawk quill upon a leaf of parchment, just one of many he had already filled as his ode to Arthelas grew. It was a work in progress, having undergone many revisions. He dared not speak his feelings out loud; to do so would reveal the inadequacy of his tongue, the shortfall in his eloquence and charm. Only in these words did Korhvale feel that the depth of his emotion could be expressed. Once finished, he then only needed the courage to show them to her…

The faintest scrape of leather against stone commanded the White Lion's attention and he stopped writing at once, immediately thrusting the leaves of parchment into a nearby knapsack. He stood, surveying the dark for any presence.

A dwarf, their captain of the hearth guard if Korhvale's memory served, appeared in the Hall of Belgrad, holding a lantern.

'Keeping the late watch, eh?' said Morek, moving into the light.

Korhvale noticed the axe, cinctured at his hip, immediately.

'I don't sleep,' he responded in Khazalid, forming the words crudely.

'Must be tiring,' Morek replied, idly casting his gaze about the chamber. The dwarf's expression hardened as his took in all the tents, the elven furnishing and subsequent obliteration of anything resembling dwarf culture.

'I need only to meditate,' said Korhvale.

Morek grumbled beneath his breath, before saying, 'All is well then.'

'All is well.'

'All is well,' the dwarf repeated, but it was as if he'd said the words to himself and with an air of speculation.

Silence fell, elf and dwarf staring at each other uncomfortably.

After a moment, Morek about-faced and tromped from the hall, lantern swinging lightly as he went.

AFTER WALKING THROUGH tunnels, passing galleries, kitchens and stores, Malbeth's wanderings had brought him to a massive, vaulted chamber. The room glowed with starlight, reflected from the upper world. The disparate shafts were diverted through a series of mirrored chambers and funnels until they converged on this place, bathing it in silver. The effect was wondrous, diamonds set around the room's six walls glittering like the celestial bodies whose light they refracted; lines of beaten gold shimmered like liquid and runes carved into the walls glowed with power.

Most impressive of all, though, was the monolithic statue that dominated the centre of the hexagonal chamber. It was a female dwarf, rendered in stone. She was dressed in simple robes; her hands rested across her body serenely, her countenance benevolent and wise, yet also possessing a sense of ageless fortitude.

From his studies, Malbeth knew this to be Valaya, one of the dwarf ancestor gods, in her aspect as teacher and mother. The gravitas invested in this temple, in the statue itself was humbling. There was peace here, Malbeth felt it at once, and whispered a blessing to the effigy of his benefactor.

'You elgi are light sleepers,' complained a voice from behind him, arresting his thoughts.

Malbeth turned to see Morek, one of King Bagrik's captains, regarding him sternly.

'Or do you merely 'meditate', as well?' said the dwarf, approaching the statue himself.

Malbeth looked nonplussed, and decided to ignore the remark. 'Elgi,' he said instead, 'I've heard that word several times. What does it mean?' he asked in good Khazalid.

If Morek appreciated the gesture he did not show it.

'It has two meanings; "elf" is one of them,' he replied.

Malbeth followed the dwarf's gaze to the statue.

'Valaya,' he said, changing the subject but confirming Malbeth's initial belief. 'She is the wife of Grungni, goddess of Hearth and Hold, one of our greatest ancestors.' The mood softened a little, as if the power of the goddess was affecting the pugnacious dwarf even through his mere presence in her temple.

'Grungni taught the dawi how to fashion metal into weapons, how to fight when the lands were shrouded in darkness, before the coming of *elves*.' Morek almost spat the last word, Valaya's influence upon him clearly fleeting. 'It is a sacred place,' he added, the implication in his words strong so as to leave no doubt at Malbeth's trespass.

'I meant no offence,' offered Malbeth.

Morek grumbled again, and turned away.

'Elgi; you said it had two meanings,' said the ambassador, 'elf and what else?'

Morek looked back briefly, a scowl on his face.

'Weak.'

The dwarf walked off, expecting Malbeth to follow.

THE ELF WAS not the only one abroad in secret that night, others more familiar with the myriad passageways and ancient, dust-drenched halls of Karak Ungor were also moving clandestinely amongst the shadows.

'I beg you, Queen Brunvilda, reconsider,' Grikk pleaded, a fettered lantern held in front of him in one hand, his ironbreaker's axe in the other.

'If the king finds out about this, I shall tell him I made my own way here,' replied Brunvilda, her gaze upon the armoured dwarf's back as he led them through the catacombs of the hold.

'Aye, my queen, and he'll then shear my beard for letting you walk the Grey Road alone.'

There was no pleasing some dwarfs, thought Brunvilda, and carried on her way.

These vaults, as they were known, were seldom trodden paths. It was as if eons of dust collected on every surface in an all-pervading patina, hence the name given to it by the ironbreakers, 'The Grey Road'. Every alcove, every statue fallen into ruin, every shattered tomb and reliquary was overlaid by a shroud of grey.

Known also as Delving Hold, Karak Ungor was the deepest of all the realms of the Karaz Ankor. Here, in the lowest habitable level it was as if time itself was held fast, like a body in tar. This far down, only ghosts and their whispers frequented the lonely corridors.

Though they were far below the clan halls and the royal quarters of the king, Brunvilda winced with every other thudding report of Grikk's armoured boots. The sound echoed rudely, as if the silence took umbrage at the disturbance. The darkness, too, seemed to shrink reluctantly from the lantern light, as if affronted by its presence. There was sentience in these walls. Dwarfs had lived here once, thousands of years ago. They had mined the rock, and built their lofty chambers until the ore had run dry, and they'd moved on. Only memory lingered. It was an ill-feeling; Bagrik knew it too. It was part of the reason the king had imprisoned *him* here, but it was also something that Brunvilda was prepared to endure.

A sudden draft wafted down the long, pitch-black tunnel. It smelled musty and bitter, the stench of it prickling Brunvilda's nose.

'Stay close to me, my queen,' said Grikk, his voice low as he turned his head slowly, surveying the route ahead. 'One of the fallen gates into the ungdrin ankor is nearby,' he told her in a whisper.

The underway, the subterranean road that linked all of the dwarf holds of the Worlds Edge Mountains, was divided by a series of gates, portals that were guarded and patrolled by the ironbreakers. Though generally considered safe, some of the gates had fallen, the dark creatures that lived beneath the mountain and who vied with the dwarfs for dominance of the underearth having destroyed them. Such gates were sometimes left alone, rather than retaken, clan miners despatched to close them off with controlled cave-ins. Not all of the gates stayed closed, and Grikk was ever mindful of the ones that weren't.

Brunvilda quickened her pace, looking left and right as dilapidated columns were revealed by the wan lantern light, along with the skeletal remains of disused torch sconces. She was so close to Grikk, and so preoccupied with her surroundings that when the ironbreaker finally stopped she barrelled right into him.

Grikk apologised profusely, his eyes wide with shame and embarrassment behind the full face plate of his gromril armour. Brunvilda waved it away with good humour, confessing it was her fault, brushing down her robes and doing her best to placate the mortified dwarf captain.

'We are here, my queen,' Grikk said at last, once he'd finished saying he was sorry.

Brunvilda looked past him to a short length of corridor, at the end of which was the faintest glow of another lantern.

'Thank you, Grikk. I can go the rest of the way by myself,' she said.

'But my queen–' he started to protest.

'Captain – that was not a request. I'll be just fine on my own from here. You need to get back to your duties. If the king finds you absent, he'll know that something is wrong. I have risked his anger once today, already; I will not do so a second time.' Brunvilda placed her hand against his pauldron. 'Your concern is touching – really,' she told him, genuinely, 'but leave me now, Grikk.'

The captain of the ironbreakers obeyed reluctantly, turning back the way they'd come. Brunvilda watched him all the way, until he'd disappeared around a corner. Satisfied he'd done as asked, she checked the satchel she had slung over her shoulder then took a deep breath and headed in a hurry towards the distant lantern and her destination.

Another ironbreaker greeted Brunvilda as she reached the lambent glow cast by his lantern. He was stood stock still in front of an oaken, ironbound door, the hinges embossed with the snarling visage of Grimnir. The dwarf looked shocked when he saw the queen approach from the gloom.

'Queen Brunvilda!' he said quickly, almost dropping the lantern. 'You're not supposed to be here.'

'I know that, ironbreaker,' she answered. 'Now let me pass.'

'I… can't, my queen. The king has forbidden it,' the dwarf answered, clearly flustered.

'Bagrik is not here, but I am, and as your queen I demand that you let me pass,' she pressed. Eyeing him sternly, she detected a chink in his resolve and took a step towards him.

'I cannot, milady. My duty is to guard the gate. None may enter without the king's sanction, I have sworn it.' Despite his protests, the ironbreaker took a half step back as Brunvilda advanced.

'Even still, let me through,' Brunvilda reasserted calmly. 'I have food here going to waste.'

The ironbreaker paused, the dilemma he faced rendering him momentarily mute.

'Let me through, and the king will not hear of it. You have my word,' she said, taking another step forward. 'I am queen of Karak Ungor,' she told him when the ironbreaker maintained his silence, 'and I will not be denied in my own hold.'

The ironbreaker faltered as he fought between the orders of his king and the wishes of his queen.

'It has already been fed,' he said in the end.

It was a poor choice of words that the ironbreaker regretted instantly.

'That is my son you speak of,' Brunvilda snapped.

'Of course, my queen, I didn't mean… it's just. I cannot let you pass,' he urged, his tone pleading. Yet still he did not yield.

'Do you think me weak, ironbreaker?' Brunvilda said after a moment.

'My queen, I only–'

'I ask again,' she said, cutting him off, 'Do you think me a weak queen?'

'No,' the ironbreaker said humbly, 'of course not.'

'Then you'll know I will not leave here until I've seen my son.'

Queen Brunvilda came right up to the armoured warrior, her chin almost touching his breastplate. Though he stood a good half-foot taller and was bristling with weapons, the ironbreaker seemed instantly diminished by her formidable presence.

'Let me pass. Now,' she said firmly.

The ironbreaker could only hold her gaze for a moment, then he nodded swiftly and turned towards the portal behind him. With a stout bronze key, held around his neck on a thick chain, he unlocked the door with a loud, metallic clunk and opened it.

At once, the reek of sweat and old meat assailed Brunvilda. It warred with the stagnant aroma of standing water and badly brewed ale. With a last scathing glance at the ironbreaker, she went inside, the door closing firmly behind her.

A small, roughly-hewn chamber lay beyond, guttering torches set at intervals upon the walls offering little light to alleviate the gloom. No statues here, no remnants of former days or remembrances of heroes. It was dank and barren. A hole in the middle of the room, like a crude well, was the only feature. Its purpose was obvious, despite what Bagrik and his ironbreakers might have said – it was a gaol.

Brunvilda steadied herself, trying to master her emotions and the stench wafting from the hole, as she stepped towards it. She got down to her knees in order to peer into the deeper gloom of the well. A faint shaft of light, issuing from some point high above, and reflected into the hole, illuminated a cell. A darkened figure, wearing scuffed dwarf boots and clad in ragged clothes shuffled out of the patch of light and lingered at the shadow's edge.

'Lothvar,' Brunvilda coaxed gently. 'Lothvar, I've brought you food.'

The shadow moved slightly, as if it recognised her voice and after a moment, came forward. It was a dwarf, or at least, some twisted parody of one. Patches of beard clung to his face in sporadic clumps and his eyes were albino pink. A deformed mouth made a jagged line across his features. A flattened nose, one of the nostrils wide and grotesque, sniffed at the air then detected the food in the satchel. As Lothvar shuffled towards the light, enticed by the aroma, Brunvilda saw the withered and twisted hand he held close to his body. His skin was pale, like alabaster, and though the light was weak, it clearly caused him discomfort to endure it.

'Mother…'

The sound of Lothvar's voice nearly broke her heart, and Brunvilda had to turn away.

The queen found her resolve quickly, crushing the sudden rush of guilt she felt at Lothvar's mistreatment, even his existence. She longed to free him of this place, but she had sworn to her king that she would not, and that word was a bond forged in iron.

There was a basket sitting next to the cell entrance. Brunvilda took it and attached it to a pulley system suspended above the well, putting the satchel in the basket before she lowered it. There were leftovers from the feast inside, just scraps, but Lothvar devoured them hungrily, and Brunvilda felt a fresh pang of anguish as she watched him.

'My father, is he with you?' asked Lothvar, his voice hopeful. The creature's intonation, for no other appellation was more suitable for it, was crude and ponderous. He formed his words slowly, as if struggling to grasp them, the droning quality hinting strongly at the malady that debilitated his mind as well as his body.

Lothvar was Brunvilda's first son and his arrival as Bagrik's heir and the future king of Karak Ungor was meant to be a joyous occasion. But Lothvar had developed poorly, his disfigurements obvious at birth and only worsening as he grew older. In spite of it, though, Brunvilda loved him and had pleaded with Bagrik not to cast him out, not to condemn him to death left alone in the mountains. Only a handful of dwarfs knew of Lothvar's existence – the king's captains, Morek and Grikk, and a select group of ironbreakers who would guard Lothvar's cell from interference. The rest of the hold, those that remembered, thought Lothvar dead, lost in childbirth. Great shame would be heaped upon Bagrik should the truth of his first son's survival be discovered. Mercy had stayed the king's hand that day, but the resentment of that decision festered still.

'No, my son, your father meets with the elgi. But he told me to say he loves you,' Brunvilda lied.

'The elgi are here?' Lothvar asked, working his mouth but making no sound as he fought to understand. 'I shall fight them alongside my father,' he said eventually, standing and thumping his chest.

Brunvilda smiled through her tears, glad of the darkness around her.

'No, Lothvar,' she said, 'the elgi are our friends. We will learn much from each other.'

Lothvar gazed up at her blankly.

'I will make him proud,' he said.

'Yes,' Brunvilda whispered, her voice cracking, 'he would be *so* proud.' Her face fell and for a moment she couldn't look at him for fear that her resolve would fail her completely.

'Mother?' Lothvar asked. 'Mother, are you crying?'

'No, Lothvar,' she managed after a long pause. 'I'm fine.' She turned and looked over her shoulder, calling out, 'Ironbreaker.'

'Ironbreaker!' she repeated more urgently, when a response wasn't forthcoming.

There was the clunk of the lock being set loose and then the door opened on creaking hinges to reveal the guard.

'Is everything all right, my queen?' he asked, brandishing his axe and surging into the room as if he expected Brunvilda to be in mortal danger.

'Put that weapon away!' she snarled.

The ironbreaker cinctured the axe quickly as if stung.

'I wish to go down and see my son,' she told him.

The ironbreaker's posture changed, becoming straight and intractable but it was the voice of another that spoke from beyond the doorway.

'I can't allow that.'

'I am your queen!' she insisted, tears in her eyes. 'Who is that? I demand to know who dares disobey me!'

'I think I had best get you back to your quarters, milady.' Morek stepped into the torch light. 'Wait for us outside,' the hearth guard captain said in an undertone to the ironbreaker.

Once they were alone, Morek walked to Brunvilda, risking a furtive glance into the gaol pit before quickly averting his gaze.

'Is he so repellent, Morek?' she said quietly, so that Lothvar could not hear her.

'He is your son, that is all,' the hearth guard captain replied plainly.

'I thought diplomacy was Kandor's arena,' Brunvilda said with a sad smile.

Morek crouched down on one knee and offered her his hand. 'Come now, my queen,' he said softly, 'you have lingered here long enough.'

Brunvilda's defiance evaporated. Taking Morek's hand gratefully, the hearth guard captain helped her to her feet.

'Are you leaving, mother?' asked Lothvar, disappointment in his voice, the sense of abandonment evident in his wretched and pitiable expression.

'I'll return soon, my love,' Brunvilda replied, 'I won't stay away so long, next time,' she said, forcing herself to turn away. Morek ushered her gently out of the room, the ironbreaker who awaited them outside closing the door and locking it behind them.

Brunvilda held her head high as she entered the darkness of the corridor again, the steel in her remade as she strode off towards the royal quarters, Morek in tow. Only when the captain had gone, when she was alone and divested of her royal trappings, when she became just a mother and a wife, and not a queen, only in the dark would she weep. For the dark hid many secrets.

CHAPTER EIGHT
Inexorable Destiny

A JAGGED SPUR of rock crumbled and fell away under Ulfjarl's grasp, and the Norscan was left hanging, one-handed, from the cliff face.

Below, a white-shrouded doom beckoned, the many hundreds of feet engulfed by the mist that had wreathed his ascent, swirling like marsh phantoms in an icy fog. More than once during his climb, Ulfjarl had seen faces in that mist; snarling, monstrous visages that bayed for his blood, and craved the heat of his soul-fire. The Norscan warlord had laughed out loud at every one and drove on through swathes of sleet, icy rain and buffeting winds that howled at his impudence.

With a bellow that matched the thunder ripping through the heavens, Ulfjarl swung his massive frame across the face of the storm-wracked bluffs and found another hand hold. From there he drove on, fork lightning filling every crevice, every cleft and gorge, with shadow as it set the sky alight. Ulfjarl was inured to the elements; they were merely obstacles to his inexorable destiny.

Finally, after three hours of climbing the savage face of the mountain, he reached over and found a stony plateau. Ulfjarl heaved his hulking body over the lip and drew himself to his full height. Veorik was waiting for him several feet from the edge. The mysterious shaman was sitting cross-legged, the cowl of his ragged flesh cloak pulled over his head. Thin slivers of jade, the faint glow of his eyes, were barely visible from beneath his hood. The Norscan couldn't fathom how Veorik had reached the summit – the shaman certainly hadn't climbed as he had, nor could he. The shaman's body was thin and wasted compared to the gargantuan Ulfjarl. Yet it possessed a wiry sort of brawn with coarse and scaly skin. His veins stood out like cords of rope, the sinews taut and unyielding.

Veorik had appeared mysteriously in Ulfjarl's village the day that fire had rained from the sky. Returning from a raid against the Bjornlings, the Norscan warlord had witnessed the arcing trail of flame cutting across the darkening sky like a portent. He'd killed the three others in the hunting party, a primal instinct driving his hand, and arrived at his village alone. Devastation greeted him. Ulfjarl's village was no more. Crude wooden huts burned like lonely signal fires, the stink of charred flesh redolent on the oily smoke. Blackened bodies lay twisted and broken in a morass of carnage; leather, metal and hair fused to skin. Ulfjarl stepped impassively across the scorched earth, incapable of remorse as he sought to comprehend what could have wrought such utter destruction. His furred boots disturbed wisps of smoke as they scraped at the dust and ash. The Norscan had soon found a long furrow that he followed to an immense smoking crater, a large meteorite burning within its blistered confines. This was the harbinger that had doomed his village. The heat of it had seared him, but he was drawn to the meteorite, to the night-black ore that shimmered like oily veins in the rock. It was then, his skin reddening, and lathered with sweat, that Ulfjarl had seen Veorik.

The shaman was like an ice wraith, detaching himself from the shadows surrounding the otherworldly meteorite as if he had once been a part of it. At first Ulfjarl had thought him a foe, gripping his stone axe and readying to kill the wizened spectre before he entranced him. But then Veorik had spoken. Though he did not know the shaman's tongue, the language sibilant and snake-like, a malicious susurration of old, dead sounds, Ulfjarl had understood its meaning and knew it was his destiny to follow this stranger. Ulfjarl had looked deep into his emerald eyes and felt impelled to thrust his palm against the rock. Pain, agony that tore into every fibre, coursed through the Norscan but when he finally withdrew his hand, a mark had been seared into his flesh. It was the symbol of his destiny – a three-headed serpent.

As the memories faded, Veorik beckoned Ulfjarl with a crooked talon. The Norscan warlord stepped purposely across the stone plateau until he reached the shaman and crouched down by his side. Veorik clutched three vipers that hissed and snapped in his skeletal fist. The shaman ignored their protests, intent on his ritual. Taking a curved dagger from within the folds of his robes, he sliced off the vipers' heads with a single, savage cut, spilling their blood onto the frost-bitten ground. Crimson smoke issued from the vital fluids and, casting the decapitated bodies aside, Veorik thrust his face over the visceral fumes and inhaled deeply. He then scraped his talon through the congealing blood, stone screeching under his scratched attentions, his finger moving as if of its own volition. When he was finished, Veorik looked up and exhaled, a jagged smile splitting his serpentine mouth. Ulfjarl was sure he'd seen a forked tongue, too, slipping out from between the shaman's thin lips and lathing the air. Whatever Ulfjarl had seen, it was clear from the shaman's expression that the auguries were good.

Veorik beckoned again, and this time Ulfjarl helped the shaman to his feet. His grip was as strong as stone, the wretch's apparent frailty belying his true strength. Veorik extended a bone-thin arm to the distant horizon. Ulfjarl followed his gaze and saw a glittering silver spire, fashioned like the watchtowers of the immortals that he had sacked when they'd made landfall, only this was larger, more grandiose. There was power in the bastion of the fey creatures, Ulfjarl could taste it, and the Norscan warlord meant to make it his own.

Impassive, Ulfjarl turned away and walked back to the edge of the plateau. Miraculously, though the Norscan warlord had not even heard him move, Veorik was already at Ulfjarl's side as he peered into the void, the mists receding as if on command. There below, he saw his army.

The Serpent Host had swelled since they'd reached the shore. Lines of warriors bearing the three-headed snake motif still tramped through the passes of the snow-kissed mountains, joining the hordes already taking up assembly at the foot of the cliff. Ragged fires burned like red wounds in the snow-shrouded plain directly below where the army gathered. Great beasts, their shaggy hides matted with frost, bayed and trumpeted as cruel wardens goaded them; whelp masters wrestled with savage hounds that frothed and strained at the leash. Brutish huscarls, bondsmen and the subjugated barbarian tribes held their banners aloft, and brandished spears and axes in honour of their lord.

It was a host of thousands, of hundreds of thousands. The watchtowers upon the shore, where they'd ran their ships aground with wild abandon as a bloodletting frenzy took them, were swept away like chaff. Ulfjarl had beheaded every enemy, had ordered every structure burned as a warning. Fear would range ahead of his host, weakening, sapping, draining. The barbarian tribes of this land had been quick to recognise his strength, quick to appreciate that fear. Every village passed had swelled the ravening horde further. The time for army building was at an end.

Ulfjarl raised his arms aloft and bellowed his name. A guttural chorus, thousands strong, answered, reverberating through the mountain. It was so terrible that the wind cowered, and the lightning fled, and the thunder balked.

War had come and it would engulf the elves completely.

THE ELGI ARE tenacious, I'll give them that, thought Morek, begrudgingly.

It was the fifth day of the trade talks, and the fifth day that the hearth guard captain had waited silently outside the huge gilded doors to the Elders Chamber as Bagrik made his deliberations with the elves. The Elders Chamber was where all the kings of Karak Ungor, Bagrik included, held council. It was a place of deliberation and of majesty, the atmosphere within heavy with the weight of history and the expectation of legacy.

Compared to many of the other halls and rooms of the holds, it was stark with simple square columns, rune-etched without gold or silver or gemstones. Austerity reminded all those within of their duty, and the severity which the dwarfs attributed to the weighty decisions of the king and his council. Morek had seen it many times, but only when considering matters of war or defence. There was an esteemed assembly of dwarfs in attendance today. Morek had watched them pile into the room one after the other, their demeanours a mix of gruff indifference and flint-eyed suspicion.

This was as fine and noble a group that had ever been gathered, with vaunted guildmasters like Chief Brew-master Heganbour, his many belts and plaited locks festooned with firkins, steins and tankards; Agrin Oak-enheart, runelord of Karak Ungor, his bare arms like tanned leather, tattooed with bands of runescript and sigils of power; and Kozdokk, lodemaster and head of the Miners' Guild, ever-present soot-rings beneath his eyes, an array of candles and lanterns affixed to his black pot helmet. In addition to the masters were the venerable longbeards of Bagrik's Council of Elders, whose wisdom was more valuable than gold.

The king had also included his son, Nagrim, in the proceedings. Morek thought this a prudent gesture, for it would be Nagrim that would govern the hold when his father had passed into the Halls of the Ancestors. Rugnir, the hearth guard captain noted, had not been invited, which was just as well. Like Bagrik, he too frowned upon the young prince's association with that wanaz. Kandor, of course, was the first to the table after his king, dressed in his finest tunic, beard preened like the prancing ufdi he was. Alongside him was his mentor, Thegg the Miser, who was as shrewd and cantankerous as any dwarf.

The elves came last of all, late as ever. Morek had scowled behind his beard as the elven prince had stalked into the Elders Chamber, ignorant of the import of that great room and all that had transpired there. The elf's ambassador and the other, raven-haired, lackey were in tow. They were followed by a gaggle of enrobed flunkies – treasurers, smiths and merchants by the look of them.

Servant hosts, dismissed before the council held session, brought silks and spices, silver metals forged into arrowheads and blunted blades, fettered falcons and hawks, and even songbirds – just some of the enticements through which the elves hoped to beguile and impress. What dwarfs needed with such items, Morek was at a loss to explain. Perhaps there were a more sizeable proportion of ufdis in Karak Ungor than he had first suspected. Such things, however, were not the captain's concern. Morek merely performed his duty as the king expected of him. Once the great and the good had been convened, the hearth guard captain sealed the golden doors, and was to allow none to enter until a bargain had been struck.

It rankled that he had been demoted to gate guardian and that Kandor, the feathered peahen, was admitted to the talks. Though begrudgingly, Morek did concede that the merchant thane knew his way around business negotiations. For all of his camaraderie and good nature with the elves, Kandor had deliberately drawn the trade talks out. It was a well-used dwarf tactic, designed to wear down the opposite party in order to get the best deal for the king and his hold. The elves, to their credit, had showed some resilience and had yet to capitulate – if the fact that talks were still ongoing was any barometer.

It was then, as Morek was yet again debating the merits of a union with the elves, albeit only for trade, that Haggar appeared at the end of the wide corridor that led to the Elders Chamber. The young thane was full of purpose as he marched towards the hearth guard captain, his helmet clasped under his arm, the runic hand gifted to him by Agrin Oakenheart gripping the pommel of his belt-slung hammer.

'Gnollengrom, Thane Stonehammer,' Haggar intoned, bowing as low as he could before he would lose his balance and fall.

Morek noticed he used the formal greeting, usually expressed only for elders.

'I am not so old that "tromm", will not suffice,' growled the hearth guard captain.

Morek's gaze lingered for a moment on the runic hand, a simulacrum of one of flesh and blood that had been forged for the young thane by old Agrin himself. Haggar came from the long and noble line of clan Skengdrang, his current appellation referring to the artefact he wore in place of a hand. It was due to his vaunted standing that Haggar had been gifted with it. Though, lamentably, there was a stain upon that once proud lineage. Morek saw it occasionally when the young dwarf thought he was not looking, a fleeting shadow behind his eyes, a severe cast to his face. It saddened the hearth guard captain to see it, and he hoped that one day Haggar would atone for the dishonour of his forebear.

'And call me "Morek", young Haggar,' he said, wrenching himself from remembrance. 'It is my name, after all, and it will do just fine.'

The other thane reddened against the older dwarf's mild admonishment and an embarrassed silence followed.

'I thought you were a statue, at first,' offered Haggar, by way of conversation. 'Three days I have passed the end of this corridor, and for three days I saw you move not an inch,' he added, clearly in awe of the captain.

'It was five days,' Morek corrected him, 'five days and counting,' he said.

Morek sniffed his nonchalance then cleared his throat, as he warmed to a theme.

'And a dwarf must know when to be still, lad,' he told him. 'Once, when I was hunting in the southern forests, three leagues north of Black Water, back when Brondrik was a beardling, I stumbled across a herd of wild hruk. The beasts were in season, rampant and amorous as only hruk can be.' Morek's eyes grew wide. 'They had my scent, and I knew I was in great peril. I could not slay the beasts; the goatherders would have sent the reckoners for me had I done that. Nor could I escape them. So, for seven days and seven nights, I stood stock still in that field, until the hruk moved on and I could return to the hold. I learnt the value of stillness that day,' Morek concluded.

Haggar nodded his appreciation at the imparted wisdom.

'Now, you tell me something,' Morek said.

'Anything, Thane Stonehammer,' said Haggar, his face screwed up in concentration as he devoted all of his attention to the hearth guard captain's query.

Morek sighed before asking, 'What are you doing here?'

'Ah, that is easy,' he said, his face brightening as soon as he realised he knew the answer. 'King Bagrik summoned me to wait for him here before the trade talks had ended. I am to accompany Kandor to the elgi settlement, take possession of any promised goods and return them to the hold.'

Morek couldn't hide the fact that this perturbed him. Why had the king entrusted such a deed to Haggar, and not him? Was he not chief of the king's warriors, aside perhaps from Grikk with whom he had equal standing – but his domain was the ungrin ankor. What if Bagrik had somehow gotten wind of his meeting with Brunvilda in the catacombs? The king would be greatly displeased that Morek had kept it from him. Still, Bagrik was not one to let his annoyances go unspoken...

'It's a pity you left the grand feast so early,' Haggar said, arresting Morek from his thoughts as he noticed the dwarf captain's furrowed brow and attempted to change the subject. 'You missed some fine entertainments. Grikk put on a great display and the elgi maiden, she was...' Haggar was lost for a moment in wistful remembrance.

'Grikk was there, eh?' Morek asked with mild interest, ignoring the elf comment.

'His axe hurling was worthy of the sagas of old,' Haggar adulated.

'I see,' Morek mumbled under his breath, adding, 'well he'll never beat my hammer throw, no dwarf will...'

Before Haggar could ask him to repeat himself, the dwarfs were interrupted by a clamour of armour emanating from the end of the corridor.

Six fully-armoured hearth guard emerged into the dwarfs' eye line; trooping towards them. A seventh figure, an elf, and not one of Ithalred's party, walked amongst them.

'Hearth guard, explain yourself!' bawled Morek to the first of the warriors that approached him, a veteran of the gate guard.

'Captain,' said the lead dwarf, thumping his chest in salute, 'this one claims he must speak to the elgi prince at once. I thought it best to bring him from the outer gateway hall directly.' At the hearth guard's remark, the elf, who wore silver mail and a cloak of fern and olive, came forward. Throwing back his hood, the elf's eyes sparkled with vehemence.

'My name is Ethandril, I am a ranger of Tor Eorfith and I must see Prince Ithalred on a matter of dire importance.'

Morek raised an eyebrow, noting that the elf was still armed. He cast a reproachful glance at the veteran hearth guard, who showed his palms in a gesture of contrition.

'There was no time to summon you,' pleaded the veteran.

Morek ignored him – he'd deal with him later – and focused his attention instead on the elf.

'Relinquish your arms, first – then you may see the prince,' he told him.

The elf seemed reluctant but he was obviously exhausted and in no mood to haggle, so handed over his bow, a quiver only half full of arrows and a long curved dagger.

'Please,' he implored, once it was done. 'Let me see the prince.'

Morek made a show of inspecting the elf for weapons one last time, a side glance at the lax veteran, who avoided his captain's gaze, before Morek muttered under his breath and turned to face the golden doors.

Haggar stood to one side. This was the hearth guard captain's 'honour' alone.

'He's not going to like this,' Morek muttered, before taking a deep breath and pushing against the doors.

The gilded doors to the Elders Chamber clanged and boomed as Morek heaved them open. All eyes turned to the hearth guard captain who beheld the king's chisellers going to work on a granite plaque. This, he knew, was the deed of agreement. An accord must have been reached with the elves and now those terms were being ratified and sealed in stone.

Kandor and Thegg the Miser were stooped over the chiseller's work, inspecting every blow, every cut, intent on the deed. The masters were in various states of attentiveness. Kozdokk held up a cage, a song bird twittering within. Whatever he had just said to the elf avian keeper had set an ashen cast to his already pale face. The venerable miner eyed the bird with interest, as he held it up to the light. Morek would learn later that the head of the Miners' Guild had proposed to use the birds to warn lodefinders of gaseous effusions in the mines. Given the mortality rate of this occupation, Kozdokk had suggested to King Bagrik that several hundred birds be traded. Evidently, this had offended the more artful and less pragmatic sentiments of the elf.

Several of the longbeards, slumped in plush chairs, had fallen asleep. One of the venerable elders appeared almost comatose and for the briefest moment, Morek feared he was dead. A nervous eyebrow twitch gave him away, though. Agrin Oakenheart was amongst the somnambulant dwarfs, snoring loudly in one corner. The pipe cinched in the runelord's mouth blew perfect smoke rings as he exhaled. Nagrim seemed interminably bored, chewing his beard, and picking at his teeth with a chisel. The elves looked worn from the deliberations, adding further credence to Kandor's strategy of negotiation by attrition. Malbeth, the elf ambassador, had his sleeves rolled up and a ragged look about him.

All were crowded around a large, slab-like table, its stone surface inscribed with effigies of Grungni and Valaya extolling the virtues of wisdom and temperance. Upon the table sat a huge pair of bronze scales, their use and meaning esoteric to the elves. This archaic device had existed since the early days of Karak Ungor. It was fashioned into the squatting figure of a dwarf goldmaster, his palms open and flat, his arms outstretched. Only the accepted members of the elder council were privy to its significance.

All of this Morek took in after he opened the gilded doors and surveyed the scene. His gaze, unsurprisingly, settled upon Bagrik last of all.

'What is the meaning of this?' bellowed the king from atop his throne on a stone plinth overlooking the Elders Chamber. He leaned forward as he barked at Morek, spittle flying from his lips. It was not wise to interrupt the king during his deliberations but the hearth guard captain had a sneaking suspicion that the elf ranger of Tor Eorfith brought bad news, and that meant the elves' departure from Karak Ungor. For Morek that couldn't happen soon enough. In his opinion, it was worth risking Bagrik's ire.

'Forgive the intrusion, my king,' Morek declared, bowing curtly with all due deference. 'It could not wait.'

Bagrik's stern expression suggested he doubted it.

'An elf, travelled from Tor Eorfith, seeks audience with Prince Ithalred.' Morek couldn't keep the scowl from his face when he mentioned the elf noble by name. He stepped aside, allowing the ranger to enter. The elf bowed stiffly.

'Bring ale,' Bagrik ordered. 'Our visitor has had an arduous journey by the look of him, and is in need of fortification.' One of the hearth guard, who was hovering outside the chamber next to Haggar, hurried off to find a servant.

'You are welcome here, elgi,' Bagrik told the ranger.

Morek chafed at his king's magnanimity, but his mood soured further at what the king said next.

'You, Morek, are not. Grumkaz, mark the hearth guard captain's name and enter a grudge in the kron.'

The king's grudgemaster, his ever present shadow, stirred from the corner of the chamber, so still and grey it was as if he were part of the rock, made animate by Bagrik's bidding. The scratching of his quill against the parchment ran down Morek's spine, making him wince.

'Ethandril.' It was Lethralmir who spoke next. The raven-haired elf came forward, heedless of any royal etiquette he might be besmirching, and beckoned the ranger to approach.

Ethandril did so, swiftly, speaking in hushed tones in their native language.

Morek's face reddened at what was deliberate subterfuge in his eyes, desperate to speak out against it and demand that the elves be open in the presence of the king. But he had affronted Bagrik once already, and even though the king's expression told him he was not impressed, Morek held his tongue.

Lethralmir then went to Prince Ithalred, relating the news in a similar manner to before. All the while, the dwarfs watched in stony silence, Agrin's snoring the only contribution to the susurrus of conversation between the elves.

Ithalred's face had darkened by the time Lethralmir had finished. He turned abruptly to the king, and said, 'With regret, your majesty, we must leave. At once.'

Bagrik's brow wrinkled.

'All is well, I hope?' he asked, his tone probing.

'Yes,' Ithalred replied. 'An urgent matter has arisen at Tor Eorfith that requires my personal attention. I'm sure you understand.'

'Of course,' said the king, though the look in his eyes said anything but. He glanced over at Kandor who was observing the chiseller, as he finished up.

'The deed is set. All is in order,' the merchant thane told Bagrik, as he looked up.

The king nodded, satisfied with the business done, despite the unconventional close to the deal and the subsequent upheaval.

'I give you leave to go back to your settlement, Prince Ithalred,' said Bagrik, once his attention was back on the elf, though Ithalred gave the impression he neither needed nor appreciated the dwarf king's sanction. 'As per our agreement,' Bagrik continued, 'Kandor Silverbeard and Haggar Anvilfist will accompany you as my representatives.' Haggar had entered the room by this time, and bowed at the mention of his name. 'They will bring the promised goods from my vaults and take charge of those offered by you upon your return.'

'As agreed,' snapped Ithalred, obviously distracted as he turned on his heel and stalked out of the Elders Chamber. Lethralmir followed him, deep in clandestine conversation with Ethandril.

Morek watched them go. He could not understand their words, but he was wily enough to discern the note of tension in them. The expression of the ranger, when he had been brought before the hearth guard captain, spoke volumes too. The elves were hiding something. Morek just didn't know what it was.

As they left, a panting dwarf servant rushed into the chamber, a foaming flagon balanced on a wooden dish.

'Ale, my lords,' he said humbly, casting his gaze about frantically for those in need.

'Give it here, lad,' said Bagrik, who quaffed the beer prodigiously, his steely glare fixed on the departing elves as he wiped his mouth with disdain.

'Haggar,' the king snarled, though his wrath was reserved for his former guests. The banner bearer thumped the cuirass of his armour in salute. 'Have a cohort of hearth guard make ready, you are leaving with the elves. You, too, Kandor, and be quick about it!'

The merchant nodded, gathering his things before muttering his respects to the masters and hurrying out of the chamber after the elves. Haggar turned and was about to troop off with him when Morek caught his arm.

'Eyes open, lad,' he said with a wink. 'Eyes open.'

Haggar nodded solemnly, catching on immediately. Whatever was bothering the elves, much like Morek, he had seen it too.

BAGRIK WATCHED FROM the craggy slit of the Dragon's Tooth, the highest watchtower of Karak Ungor, the rocky spire by which all of the ancient skybridges were connected. His expression was stern as he regarded the trail of dwarf carts and mules, diminishing into the mountain passes. He saw the long lines of the elf expedition that had come to his hold, too, and the cohort of twenty hearth guard warriors led by Haggar and accompanied by Kandor. The dwarfs led the group as they made their wending way northward to Tor Eorfith, their knowledge of the secret routes across the Worlds Edge making for a safer and more expedient journey.

A sharp wind was blowing from the north, unsettling the snow-shawled peaks and sending thick drifts across the trees and lowland roads. It blustered through the viewing port of the watchtower, insinuating its way through Bagrik's furs and tunic, chilling him. He suppressed a shiver and his gaze hardened. There was the scent of metal and smoke on the breeze. It did not bode well.

'There is no better vantage point over the northern reaches of the Worlds Edge than the Tooth, my liege.'

Bagrik did not turn to face the speaker. He merely sighed, his earlier anger long since fled to be replaced by concern and doubt.

'Aye, Morek, and it is also a place where a king might find some solitude.' Bagrik had long since dismissed the quarrellers patrolling the Dragon's Tooth and his personal hearth guard who had carried him up the many steps to the lofty watchtower.

'Forgive me, my king, but Queen Brunvilda was looking for you,' said Morek, moving to stand alongside Bagrik, he too now staring at the view beyond the hold.

'All the more reason for me to be up here,' Bagrik muttered, a note of tension creeping into his voice.

'The wind coming from the north is a harsh one,' the king said after a moment of silence, filled only with the howl of the breeze. 'I feel the coming of winter, Morek,' he confessed, no longer talking about the weather. 'I cannot even reach my towers without aid, and all my great deeds are eclipsed in memory, smothered by the dust of ages, soon to be forgotten.'

Morek maintained his silence for a spell, allowing the maudlin atmosphere to thin a little before he spoke.

'You have left a proud legacy, my king. All of us, our time is finite. Grungni calls us to his table in the Hall of Ancestors. Your place is waiting,' he said.

'Is it, Morek?' Bagrik asked, turning to the hearth guard captain for the first time.

Both dwarfs knew of what Bagrik spoke.

'Nagrim's time is dawning,' Morek replied, returning his king's gaze. '*He* is your legacy, my liege. In him the future of Karak Ungor is set in stone.'

Bagrik smiled, though his eyes were still sad. He felt somehow older in that moment.

'Yes, you are right,' he said, turning back to the view port. 'Nagrim is the future.'

'One thing I am less certain about,' Morek grumbled, as he too returned to looking out of the watchtower, the mule train finally disappearing from view, 'is these elgi. For a race that is longer lived than us dwarfs, they have little concept of patience.'

'Indeed,' Bagrik replied, his eyes narrowing. The old leg wound from the great boar gave a twinge. It was a sure sign of troubling times to come. 'They do not,' he concluded.

ACT TWO
Blood in the North

CHAPTER NINE
Legacy

THE IRON DEEP was akin to an armoury in that within its heavily-guarded confines there resided all the many martial heirlooms and artefacts of Bagrik's royal lineage. Each of the noble clans of Karak Ungor had such a rune vault, but none were as vast and grandiose as that of the Boarbrow's and the line of kings. The mighty room was staggering in its size and ambition. Cavernous in stature, five thousand dwarfs could have marched in and still had room enough to become lost in its numerous galleries and antechambers.

Stone columns, hewn into the image of kings and chased in bronze, shouldered an arched ceiling studded with diamonds. Mosaics were rendered into the walls, depicting ancient heroes and older deeds. The vault had several levels, and an expansive rectangular chasm fell away in the middle of each one, barring the deepest. These upper floors were spanned by bridges carved from the granite of the mountain. Dominating the

lowest level of the Iron Deep was the Zharrazak, the
Enduring Flame. Reputedly, or at least as far back as
records went, it had burned since Karak Ungor was
founded and had not once gone out. It was widely
postulated that should the Zharrazak ever fail it would
be a grave omen, foretelling the doom of the hold. It
was set in a simple copper basin and was so large that,
despite its depth, the fierce flame cast long, flickering
shadows around the entire vault's many nooks and
crannies.

Few had seen the Iron Deep, save for the kings of
Ungor and their runelords. Agrin Oakenheart was the
current custodian, and in addition to all the clan treasures, he kept three of the Anvils of Doom safe within
the vault. These artefacts had been forged five hundred
years earlier by the master runesmith, Kurgaz, at the
heart of Karag Dron. Only the volcanic fire of a mountain could have tempered such potent magical foci. The
runes inscribed upon the metal surface of the anvils had
only to be struck by a hammer, and for the runesmith
to intone the correct forging rite, for their power to be
unleashed. Such devices were venerated, and had to be
kept under runic seal, so it was with Agrin's Anvils of
Doom.

Save for the runelord himself, only King Bagrik had
the authority to order the Iron Deep unsealed. With
Nagrim in tow, he had done so with a specific purpose
in mind. For over an hour father and son had toured the
mighty vault, its many floors plunging down into the
mountain's core, the effect upon entering through the
iron-banded, ward-inscribed, gromril gate not unlike a
roofed amphitheatre. Gemstones punctuated the foot
and apex of each level in long lines and through them,
via some cunning device of the Engineers' Guild, natural

light was reflected and refracted creating an aura of myriad hues. Runes of power were described by the cornucopia of light emitted from the stones, wards of spell-baffling and sorcerous annulment that prevented harmful or insidious magic making a mockery of the otherwise stout safeguards.

As they walked, Bagrik showed Nagrim some of the treasures of the hold's long history, the gilded weapon racks, cradles for armour, iron-banded chests and bejewelled plinths stretching far in the glittering gloom.

'It is past time that we walked the Iron Deep together,' said Bagrik as he and Nagrim traversed a concourse of flagstones. Like much of the ancient chamber, it was rendered into a concentric knot pattern, the uniformity occasionally giving way to the artistic flourish of the original masons.

The king wore a simple blue tunic with silver trim and a short woollen cloak. It had been almost two months since Haggar and Kandor had set off with the elves. Winter still clung on tenaciously, reluctant to release its icy grip. Though the first thaws of the nascent spring were now emerging, evident in the subterranean reservoirs filling from the slowly melting mountain peaks, Bagrik still felt the cold and clasped his cloak tightly.

'See here,' said the king, ignoring the ache in his bones as he pointed out a weapons rack, 'the ancient spear wielded by Drekk that slew Kharanak, the great dragon ogre.'

'That must have been some throw to kill such a beast, and with a weapon such as this,' Nagrim remarked, taking in the sight of the simple flint-pointed wooden spear.

'Aye, lad,' Bagrik agreed. 'They did things differently in the elder days when the Karaz Ankor was newly forged, and dwarfs took their first faltering steps into the world.'

'Tromm,' Nagrim intoned respectfully, much to his father's pleasure. 'This Drekk must have been a great hunter. I would have liked to meet him at the grobkul.'

'Ha!' said Bagrik, slapping his son on the back, 'Ever eager to kill the grobi, eh my son?'

'I vow to rid the mountains of the green vermin, father,' Nagrim replied in all seriousness and stopped walking. 'And speaking of it, Brondrik is readying for another hunt. I wish to go with him. Rugnir, too.'

'Is it not enough that you've beaten me, must you crush your father's tally, also?' Bagrik joked, but then regarded his son with thoughtful eyes. He clapped his hands upon Nagrim's shoulders and, with a broad smile, the king nodded at some private affirmation.

'You will make me proud, Nagrim,' he said. 'You will make all of Karak Ungor proud, and your rule shall be the envy of the Karaz Ankor,' Bagrik declared boldly.

'You honour me, father–' Nagrim began.

'But…' said the king, 'I cannot condone of your friendship with Rugnir.'

Nagrim's expression soured and he stepped back from his father's embrace.

'He is a wazlik, son, and his presence by your side is a stain against the good name of this clan, even this hold,' Bagrik told him, wounded at Nagrim's rebuff.

'Have I not always been the son you wanted me to be, father,' said the prince. 'At sixty-nine winters, am I not the finest warrior and hunter this hold has ever known? Matters of clan and council, I will leave to others – Kandor is a more than capable mentor. You have said yourself that I possess the strength and wisdom to rule Karak Ungor, so trust my wisdom in this. Rugnir is my friend, his loyalty is beyond question. I will not forsake him because it raises the eyebrows of the masters and the longbeards.'

Bagrik was about to chastise Nagrim for his wilfulness and lack of proper veneration towards the clan elders, but stopped himself.

'I did not bring you here for us to fight, son,' he told him. 'Please,' he added, 'indulge me. Let us forget about Rugnir for now and walk on.'

Nagrim agreed and together they went further into the Iron Deep, where Bagrik regaled his son with further marvels like Garekk Dragonbane's shield – that which had repelled the flame of the wyrm, Skorbadd – resting on a golden plinth, its edges still scorched black; and the fabled Hammer of Logran, known also as Daemon-killer, glowing with a dull red light, the power of its runes still potent, if diminished. As great and fabulous as these heirlooms were, to Bagrik they paled in significance when compared to the artefact he had brought Nagrim to the Iron Deep to see.

'Your legacy lies ahead,' Bagrik said when they had reached the lowest level of the vault, so close to the Zharrazak they could feel the intensity of its flame, prickling their faces. The king stopped and pointed to another short pathway that led to a shadowed alcove.

Nagrim looked to his father with an expression of uncertainty, as if awaiting his permission.

'Take the road, Nagrim. Your destiny waits at the end of it.'

The dwarf prince obeyed and walked towards the alcove slowly, Bagrik following a few steps behind.

As Nagrim got close, a spit of flame surged from the Zharrazak, its flare so bright that it briefly lit the lower level with a fiery luminance. The light flooded the alcove, just as Nagrim reached it, peeling back the shadows like strips of black parchment. A wave of heat came with it that warmed the skin and set nerve endings tingling with vigour. Revealed in the glow was a suit of armour.

Gilded gromril plate, polished to a fine sheen, caught the light; the reflected flames of the Zharrazak making the surface seem as if it were ablaze. Even when the surge of fire died, the captured lustre in the armour did not. The golden pauldrons, vambraces and cuirass were burning brilliantly. In the glow of its self-made aura details of the armour's exquisite artifice were revealed.

Overlapping gromril plates were secured by ancestor studs, the visages of Grimnir and Grungni promising both strength and fortitude to the wearer. A crimson cloak of velvet hooked onto the breastplate and trailed down the back of the suit, trimmed in silver with runic talismans stitched into the lining. Plates covered the abdomen, and a skirt of gromril hung down like an impenetrable veil to sit just above the wearer's boots.

The ancestral armour was finished off by a full-face helmet, rendered into the stern countenance of a dwarf king of old and fastened to the cuirass by a ruby-studded gorget. Splayed eagle wings, hardened by wax before being gilded, spread from either temple of the war helm, the effect both regal and terrifying.

'This armour was meant for you,' Bagrik said softly, now standing alongside his humbled son. 'It is magnificent, isn't it?'

'I have never witnessed beauty such as this…' Nagrim had tears in his eyes. He reached a trembling hand towards the suit, hardly daring to touch it should he be found unworthy and coruscated in a sudden conflagration.

'It is yours, Nagrim,' Bagrik told him, 'Yours upon the advent of your seventieth winter, but a few short weeks from this day. It's the right of every heir apparent of Karak Ungor to wear it.'

Nagrim turned to his father, his outstretched hand still wavering. The prince's eyes held a question.

'Yes, my son. I wore it too, as did my father, and my father's father and so on to the very beginning of our line. Now it passes to you,' he added simply, gesturing towards the armour.

Nagrim looked back and this time he touched it with the strength of conviction that could only be born of a belief in legacy and destiny. The prince seemed at once uplifted, even empowered, as the physical connection to his ancestors coursed through his body.

'I have been no prouder of you than I am in this moment, Nagrim,' Bagrik told his son when he had turned back from the armour. Its lustre seemed to dim, the gleam only short lived, as if it 'knew' somehow that this was not its time, not yet.

'Thank you, my lord,' rasped Nagrim and went down on one knee to salute his father and his king.

'Rise,' said Bagrik, 'and help your old man back to the gate,' he added with a wry grin. 'We have lingered here long enough, I think. It is time to return to the upper deeps.'

Nagrim smiled, and together father and son made their way back up to the entrance of the Iron Deep, the solid gate slamming shut with thunderous resonance after they left, the dour and silent hearth guard retaining their eternal vigil over it.

Once they were out, Nagrim took his leave, eager to meet with Brondrik and the rangers at the outer gateway hall for the grobkul. Bagrik had his own duties to attend to. He was due in council to meet with the elders over the monthly matters of the hold. Even so, he tarried deliberately in the galleries above the Iron Deep, slowly hobbling the stairways and corridors, regarding the statues of his forebears. Soon his effigy would join them.

'I thought I might find you here,' said a soft voice from the shadows.

Bagrik turned to see his queen stepping into the brazier light.

'Trawling the corridors of the past?' asked the queen, as she approached her king.

'Aye, something like that,' Bagrik replied, stopping before the statue of his father, Thargrik. 'I am old, Brunvilda. I feel the bite of winter, the growing chill in my veins as if for the first time,' he said. 'Vigour abandons me. Age and atrophy creep into my bones and muscles like unseen assassins, making them feel like stone.' Bagrik clenched his fist, watching his fingers wrap themselves slowly together. 'Soon *I* will become stone,' he added, looking back at the granite statue of his father. 'A remembrance only, my body withering and decaying into dust in my tomb.'

Brunvilda laid her hand upon his hand, and the warmth of her touch spread like a rejuvenating salve.

'You are a great king,' she told him, 'who has done great deeds. I do not think your reign is over yet.'

Bagrik looked up at her. There were tears in Brunvilda's eyes.

'Your legacy is strong,' she said. '*That* is how you will be remembered.'

Bagrik smiled back at her.

'He is a worthy heir, is he not?'

'Yes, my king. Nagrim's deeds will also be great.'

For a short time, king and queen enjoyed the moment, allowing a comfortable silence to descend. Both knew it was not to last.

'It feels like you have been avoiding me,' said Brunvilda, her tone soft but candid.

'I have had much on my mind,' Bagrik replied, slipping from her grasp and turning to regard the statue of Thargrik again.

'You only ever seem happy when you are in the company of Nagrim,' she said, stepping forward but just falling short of touching her husband on the shoulder.

Bagrik maintained his silence. He knew what was coming.

'You lavish such love and attention on him, your favoured son,' she pressed.

Bagrik whirled around to challenge her.

'*Favoured* son?' he said, angrily. '*Only* son, you mean.'

Brunvilda's expression hardened. 'I have been to see Lothvar, as you should have done,' she told him. 'He dwells in a prison, surrounded by squalor. It is no way to treat a prince.'

'He is no prince!' Bagrik countered, becoming even more animated. 'He is a *nubunki*, and I should have had him exiled at birth, not compromised my rule with lies and dishonour.'

'He is your son,' Brunvilda maintained, determined to stand her ground in the face of Bagrik's growing fury. 'And the only reason you bestow such affection on Nagrim is your guilt over the treatment of Lothvar.' Brunvilda's mood softened then, as her defiance waned. 'All I ask is that you see him.'

'Never!' snarled Bagrik. 'That thing is no son of mine. He is barely a dawi at all.' The king hissed the words through clenched teeth, suddenly aware that others may be listening or might overhear their argument. Breathing heavily, he drew in close to Brunvilda, his face red with rage.

'Do not mention him in my presence ever again. Lothvar died when he was born, that is all.' Bagrik stared at her for a moment, making sure his words had sunk in. Then he turned and hobbled away, bellowing for his throne bearers.

'INCURSIONS BY THE grobi into the mines and overground farms have increased this last month,' Morek declared before the council of elders, speaking in his capacity as the king's general. 'The changing season has roused them from slumber, it would seem.'

The assembled longbeards of the council nodded sagely. They were arrayed around the stone table of the Elders Chamber, together with Heganbour and Kozdokk, the two guildmasters summoned to the monthly council meeting to discuss a land leasing dispute between the brewers and the miners. Tringrom, Bagrik's royal aide, was also present. Standing beside the glowering form of his king, who crouched upon his throne like a belligerent gargoyle, Tringrom had already announced the agenda. Beard taxes, ale tithes and the reckoners' ledger were all common fare at such gatherings. But it was the growing numbers of greenskins that demanded the council's attention now, an ever-present thorn in the collective side of all the holds of the Karaz Ankor.

Bagrik muttered beneath his breath at Morek's remarks, his mood more irascible than usual.

'What of the underway?' he growled. 'Do we need to purge the tunnels again?'

'The ungrin ankor is not so overrun with vermin, my king,' Grikk replied. It was a rarity for the captain of the ironbreakers to sit in on the council, but the orc and goblin infestation concerned him most of all. Should the greenskins attack the hold, it was through the underway that they would make their assault. 'All of the gates are holding and the ironbreakers report no incursions through the fallen portals,' added Grikk.

'And the *Grey Road*, is that also clear of intrusion?' asked Bagrik, his lip upcurled. The true meaning of his question was thinly veiled.

Grikk swallowed loudly, before answering.

'Quiet, my liege. Very quiet.'

Bagrik turned to Morek, who shifted uncomfortably beneath his king's gaze.

'We must trust in Brondrik and his rangers to thin the horde,' the king told him. 'Nagrim, my son, and soon to be heir of Ungor, hunts with him even now. He has vowed to rid the mountains of the greenskin, and I have no reason to doubt it.'

'Perhaps we need to take even more punitive measures in the extermination of the grobi,' suggested Morek. 'I could marshal the clan warriors and the rest of the rangers, have them scour the crags. One hunting party, however well led, cannot be expected to cleanse the mountainside single-handed.'

'And I suppose the king's treasury will pay for this campaign, will it, Morek?' growled Bagrik. 'You think my son will fail in his oath to me, is that it?'

'Nagrim is no umbaraki, my liege,' the hearth guard captain, said quickly. 'I only meant that–'

Morek's words would remain unspoken as a thunderous din coming from the golden doors of the Elders Chamber swallowed them.

'Are my private meetings to be constantly interrupted?' barked the king, glaring at the entrance to the room. 'Is this what the rule of Karak Ungor has come to?'

'Enter then,' he snarled after a moment of silence.

With a sound like churning iron, the great doors opened but a crack and the same hearth guard veteran that Morek had remonstrated during the trade talks with the elves stepped into the Elders Chamber, bowing profusely.

'Lords…' he said, catching his breath, having obviously run all the way from the outer gateway hall, 'forgive my trespass, but the elves and our kinsdwarfs… they have returned.'

BAGRIK AGREED TO meet with Prince Ithalred and his charges in his throne room. There, sat upon his throne, longbeards either side of him, he brooded silently. Surrounded by tapestries and mosaics of the grand deeds of Karak Ungor, Bagrik wondered what ill-news would undoubtedly follow the elves' sudden and unannounced arrival.

The Ithalred that marched into his kingly chamber had lost none of the imperious posturing that had so irked Bagrik in their initial meeting, but the haughty, arrogant noble in him had diminished. The elf prince and several of his kin had been brought directly from the outer gateway hall with all haste, so much so that they still had their weapons. Haggar and Kandor, together with the hearth guard, accompanied them by way of security. They had not – it had come to the king's attention – returned with either the promised goods of the elves or those originally sent by the dwarfs.

'Where is the promised trade, as given in the deed of agreement?' Bagrik's voice boomed like thunder in the vast throne room, the fire in the brazier fans flickering redly in concert with the king's wrath. 'You will answer!'

Kandor stepped forward. His face was ashen, eyes hooded with fatigue. The merchant's usually fastidious appearance was a shambles. Facing the accusatory glances of the longbeards, as well as the stern countenance of Morek, arms folded in disapproval, Kandor had to dig deep to find his voice and his courage.

'We did not bring them, sire,' he confessed.

'I can see that!' bawled the king, 'The empty carts clutter my outer gateway hall, even now. I am asking why that is, Thane Silverbeard.'

Haggar stepped forward before Kandor could answer. In the brazier light, Bagrik saw his banner bearer's armour was dented, some of the mail split. Dried blood spattered his face and tunic, creating a grisly visceral patchwork. There was weariness in his posture that came only from hard battle.

'We arrived at the elgi settlement to find it under attack,' said Haggar, his tone sombre, his face darkening with remembrance. 'A vast horde of heathen men, sailed from across the Sea of Claws, had gathered northwards of the city. By the time we knew what was going on, the elgi had already arrayed for battle. I led the hearth guard to join them, to see what manner of beasts these northmen were.'

'And you met them on the field of war, Haggar?' asked Morek. As general of the king's armies, the hearth guard were his responsibility.

'I did, my captain,' Haggar confessed, looking down at his boots.

'Do not lower your eyes from the king!' snapped Morek. 'Face the shame of your deeds with honour.'

Haggar looked up at once.

Morek scowled back at him.

'Tell me,' said King Bagrik, satisfied until now to let his hearth guard captain take the lead, 'what do the elgi have to say?'

Ithalred, silent until that point, came forth. The elf's eyes were haunted by death. Deep shadows pooled in the sockets and he too was battered and bloodied.

'My army was defeated,' he said simply. 'And it is only a matter of time before the northmen drive on further into the mainland and sack Tor Eorfith, too. I have risked much even coming back here, leaving the city in the hands of my captain, Valorian.'

'Risked?' Bagrik enquired. 'What is it that you think you have come here for, elgi?'

Ithalred unsheathed his sword. There was a clamour of weapons from the hearth guard, and Morek stepped in front of his king, axe at the ready. But the elf prince merely placed the ancient weapon on the ground, and knelt down with it in front of him. The mood relaxed. The hearth guard sheathed their weapons. Morek returned to his position beside the throne.

'King Bagrik Boarbrow, I, Ithalred of Tor Eorfith, Prince of Eataine, humbly beseech your aid,' said the elf. 'I lay down my arms in a gesture of supplication. I cannot defeat the northmen on my own. Join me with your armies so that together we might rid this blight from our lands.'

The room fell into abject silence.

Bagrik smiled cruelly. Leaning forward on his throne, he said, 'That could not have been easy.'

The hard line of Ithalred's mouth, the nerve twitching in his cheek, gave the dwarf king the answer he sought.

'And without the honeyed words of your ambassador or the thinly-veiled slights of the black-haired noble to hide behind,' Bagrik added, a dark glance at Malbeth, who waited in the shadows behind the prince. Lethralmir was not present. It seemed he had not accompanied his lord.

A wise move, thought the king.

'Yes, I believe that was very hard for you to do.' Bagrik stared at Ithalred who, to the elf's credit, returned his gaze without faltering. 'No sovereign would wish to beg at the feet of another.' Ithalred grit his teeth at the remark. 'For make no mistake, that is where you find yourself.'

Bagrik stood up, shooing Morek and his throne bearers away as he hobbled down the three broad steps that led to the throne room's flagstoned aisle, until he was face-to-face with the elf.

'You came into my hold, my kingdom, and offered only scorn and derision. You mocked our customs and besmirched our culture. For these deeds alone you are already entered into the book of grudges, and this dear elgi is severe indeed.' The dwarf king paused, allowing the import of his words to sink in, before he went on.

'Now, you are before me pleading for aid, to fight a foe that harries not my borders, but yours. And in so doing I have learned of a further misdeed. That your trade alliance was nothing but pretence for what you truly wanted, but did not care to admit even to yourself…' Bagrik let the words hang for a moment, the calmness in his voice more unsettling than any rage he could have mustered; '…the might of Karak Ungor.'

Ithalred's expression turned to defiance, and anger. The elf had his answer. The dwarf king was merely making a point.

'Through deception you have tried to garner my favour,' Bagrik continued. 'These northmen will not bother us. We dawi are shielded in our bastions of stone. Let them come – the mountain is our protector. They will shatter against it like twigs against the bulwark of a cliff. No, Prince Ithalred,' Bagrik said at length, turning and hobbling back up to his throne, 'I will not wage war for you,' the dwarf king added once he was seated again. 'We will honour the trade pact, should you survive this trial. Return to me with talk of that, not of war.'

Bagrik sighed deeply, the king grown suddenly weary of talk.

'Now, go,' he said. 'Back to your city, if it still stands.'

Ithalred rose to his feet, still elegant and defiant in spite of it all, picking up his sword and sheathing it. Though his face was contorted with suppressed fury, he managed to bow to the dwarf king before he turned and took his leave. The rest of the elves followed in his wake, escorted by the hearth guard.

'Not you, Haggar,' intoned the king, as the elves departed.

The banner bearer remained where he was, Kandor too.

Only once the elves were gone did Bagrik speak again.

'You saw the forces of this enemy, these *north-men*?' asked the king.

Haggar nodded sternly.

'Tell us of them, now. Spare no detail. I would know what manner of foe we face should their reaving bring them to our walls. And Morek,' added the king, turning to his hearth guard captain. 'Send out rangers to find my son. I will not have him caught up in this war by mistake.'

CHAPTER TEN
Casualties of War

FAR FROM THE throne room of Karak Ungor, high in the fastness of the northern Worlds Edge Mountains, Nagrim hunted greenskins. He was not aware that the dwarfs had returned to the hold and he did not know about the pleas of the elf prince. Nagrim was oblivious to the politics of Karak Ungor. It did not interest him. Let Kandor and Tringrom deal with such matters. Thinking of them now, he was glad that the royal aide had been unable to accompany them. The ufdi only slowed them down. The loremaster would have to record his tally in the book of deeds upon their return. Though, if the current count was any measure, he would have precious little to attribute to any of the hunters on the grobkul.

'Slim pickings,' grumbled Brondrik, cutting the nose off the solitary grobi he'd caught defecating in some brush. The steam of the greenskins' dung was still rising from where it'd squatted before being stuck by the pathfinder's crossbow bolt.

'Aye,' agreed Rugnir, his own axe as of yet unbloodied. 'You've killed too many grobi, Nagrim. Perhaps we should have brought that ufdi with us, his perfumed beard locks seemed to enflame their ardour and brought them running.' The dwarf's roaring laughter echoed across the peaks, carried on the warming winter breeze.

Nagrim didn't join in the banter. He had journeyed from his hold to slay goblins, not trek through the mountain passes.

'We head north-east,' he said without humour. 'There are caves there that may yet harbour greenskin.'

The prince noticed the other rangers in their hunting party, Thom and Harig, exchange wary glances. Even, Brondrik raised an eyebrow. Rugnir said aloud what they were all thinking.

'North-east, eh lad? That is far from the hold. Are you trying to narrow my girth, Nagrim? The rinns like a dwarf with a bit of meat on him, if you get my meaning,' he laughed thunderously.

Nagrim cut the merriment short, the half-hearted chuckles dying in Rugnir's throat.

'North-east,' he said, ignoring Rugnir's disappointment as the words of his father came back to him. He had been in a strange mood ever since he'd left the Iron Deep and set out into the mountains. When he had touched the ancestral armour of his forebears, the weight of legacy had fallen upon his shoulders like an anvil. His father's time was ending. Soon he would be king of Karak Ungor. The thought, he confessed to himself, filled Nagrim with dread.

'Brondrik, mark our trail,' ordered the prince, checking the load in his crossbow, before slinging the weapon back over his shoulder.

The venerable pathfinder nodded, before something on the ground caught his attention.

'There are other tracks besides grobi here,' he told Nagrim, who came over and crouched beside him. 'See…' said Brondrik, using a gnarled finger, the nail chipped and encrusted with dirt, to describe the irregular pattern in the earth and snow, '…booted feet and larger than grobi.'

'Urk?' the prince suggested, thinking of the goblins' larger and more brutish cousins.

'No,' Brondrik replied, shaking his head. 'No, I don't think it's urk.'

'Which way were they headed?' Nagrim asked. 'They may have driven the grobi in the same direction.'

The pathfinder sighed before he looked up at the prince again. His eyes held a warning that would not be heeded.

'North-east.'

THE DWARFS TRAVELLED for an hour before they caught sight of any greenskins again. Further northward than they had ever ventured, even the wildlife in the barren crags that surrounded them seemed sparse. There were no rivers, the melt waters of the mountain having bled south; just dry, dusty basins. Any trees were reduced to isolated copses of brittle pine with dead brown leaves.

'This is a hollow place, my lord,' said Brondrik from the front of the group, his crossbow low slung and at the ready, 'We should turn back.' The pathfinder seemed wary of his own shadow, his instincts and confidence deserting him. The mood spread to the other rangers, too. Even Rugnir was not his usual ebullient self, and had fallen into a drunken melancholy.

'Come on, Nagrim,' he said, mustering some joviality. 'Let's return to the hold, I'll buy you a drink,' he added with a weak smile.

The prince exhaled his disappointment, and was about to admit defeat when he saw the grobi, scampering through the rocks, some rangy animal carcass gripped fast in its overbite.

'There!' he cried, barrelling off down the trail after the greenskin. 'With me!'

The other dwarfs gave chase reluctantly, especially Rugnir who muttered beneath his breath, something concerning hruk fondling.

For such a gangling wretch the goblin was nimble, picking its way through the crags with apparent ease. Nagrim was hard pressed to keep sight of it, let alone get close enough to catch the creature.

He plunged after it, down a steep-sided valley and into a deep gorge. Nagrim was so intent on slaying the goblin that he slipped, and nearly fell. When he got his footing again, there was no sign of his quarry. He slowed, looking left and right in the wide, flat basin of the gorge. It was scattered with displaced rocks and fallen rubble from the steep sides.

Brondrik was the first to catch up to him, a few moments later.

'I've lost it,' Nagrim hissed to the pathfinder, training his crossbow over the craggy rocks where the shadows were thickest.

'The wretched beast could have slipped out of the gorge unnoticed,' Brondrik suggested, surveying the uppermost ridges of the chasm as an ill-feeling spread over the entire party. 'Do you hear that?' he added.

'I hear nothing,' whispered Nagrim.

Eerie silence persisted in the nadir of the gorge. There were no bird cries; even the wind had died abruptly.

'Exactly,' Brondrik replied.

Rugnir swallowed. The loud noise made the hunters start suddenly. Four stern-faced dwarfs regarded him as one.

Rugnir smiled apologetically, before one of the rangers pointed towards a cluster of rocks at the foot of one of the steep sides of the ravine.

They had found their goblin. He was slumped against one of the rocks, a thick dark arrow with bloodied feathers protruding from his chest.

Out of the corner of his eye, Nagrim noticed Brondrik look up, smelling something on the breeze as the wind changed suddenly. He followed his gaze...

Shadows gathered at the ridge of the gorge on either side, too large to be goblins.

'Defend yourselves, we are under–' the warning died on Brondrik's lips, the arrow in his neck severing his vocal cords and killing the old dwarf a few blood-gurgling seconds later.

'Take cover in the rocks,' cried Nagrim as an arrow thunked in his chest and spun him off his feet.

'Nagrim!' shouted Rugnir, as the other rangers sighted down their crossbows to retaliate. Thom was struck through the eye, then in the arm and neck as he loosed harmlessly into the side of the gorge. Harig made it to the rocks before three arrows thudded into his back, and he slumped forward.

Nagrim was on his feet again. He tasted blood in his mouth, and was finding it hard to breathe. The barbed arrow head had nicked his lung. He fired his crossbow at one of the ambushers and a cry echoed in the mountains as he found a killing shot. Rugnir, having lost his

crossbow in the confusion, flung a hand axe, slaying a
second. It was never going to be enough. Three arrows
put him down: two in the body, one in the leg. Another
struck Nagrim in the arm, and he dropped his weapon.

Unable to shoot back and down to one, the dwarf was
easy prey. The ambushers knew this and were emboldened, emerging from their hiding places in the crags at
the top of the gorge. Moving down the steep slope,
spilling scree and with arrows knocked, Nagrim saw the
ambushers clearly for the first and last time. The dwarf's
vision was fading. His tunic and chainmail was slick
with his own blood.

'Grungni…' he breathed, eyes widening.

The creak of bow strings split the air and then the
arrow storm began.

CHAPTER ELEVEN
The Death of Legacy

By the time Morek and the Clan Cragfoot rangers had arrived at the gorge, the ambushers were gone. Blood was splattered everywhere in the dry canyon, thick and black. Arrow shafts stuck out of the ground where they had missed their targets, like feathered grave markers. Dwarf weapons lay strewn about, dropped or abandoned in the chaos.

'This was a massacre,' Morek muttered under his breath as he crouched by the body of a dead ranger. He didn't know the dwarf, but closed his eyes for him as they stared glassily at the clouds scudding across the sky above.

Back at the hold, as he gathered the rangers, the hearth guard captain had been approached by Queen Brunvilda. She had asked him to lead the search party for her son, knowing this is what the king would want. Secretly she feared for Nagrim, but Bagrik would never allow his pride to admit that. Morek had gladly obeyed, amassing the dwarfs with haste and leaving Karak Ungor as soon as they were ready.

Though not as accomplished as Brondrik, the hearth guard captain had spent many summers with the clan rangers and was an excellent tracker. He had found the hunting party's trail quickly. Though, it seemed, it had not been nearly quick enough.

'Another dead, here,' one of the Cragfoots, a dwarf by the name of Lodri, called out. He was standing by the twisted body of a ranger with an arrow embedded through his eye. 'Grungni's oath…' he breathed, when he saw the barbed tip sticking out of the back of the dead dwarf's helmet.

'A grobi, too,' said another, having found a goblin slumped against a rock.

Morek's face only darkened further. He got to his feet and tried to survey the scene. His gaze rose to the ridge line, where another group of rangers patrolled.

'They were lured here, their murderers lying in wait at the ridgeline. They had high ground, surprise and likely outnumbered them,' the captain said, more to himself than any of the other dwarfs present. 'Nagrim,' he hissed, 'how could you have let yourself be goaded?'

Morek had been one of Nagrim's mentors, teaching him the ways of axe-craft and battle tactics when he was but a beardling. The prince was a gifted student, and had excelled in his studies. To see him outwitted and drawn into a death trap like the gorge was galling in the extreme.

'I can find no sign of the prince,' said Lodri as he approached the hearth guard captain. 'He could still be alive.'

Morek surveyed the grim vista again, took in the spilt blood and the disturbed rock and brush as the beleaguered dwarfs had fought desperately but to no avail.

'No,' he uttered sadly. It was one of the hardest things he'd ever had to admit to himself. 'See, there are no tracks leading from the battle, just some rough furrows. Likely the ambushers fled when they were finished, filthy *thagi*, covering up their tracks as they went. This trail here,' he said, indicating the furrows, 'looks like drag marks, possibly from some wild beast...' He stopped, seeing the logical conclusion to his words realised in the ranger's eyes, and decided not to articulate it. Morek did not wish to imagine the prince of Karak Ungor being gnawed upon by some cave-dwelling creature of the mountain. He made an oath to Grungni that none were alive if that was their fate.

'Could he have been captured, then?' Lodri offered. 'For ransom, perhaps?'

'Hmm, it's possible,' Morek's tone gave away that he thought this was a slim hope at best. 'I have heard that northmen covet gold and relish plunder, but taking hostages seems out of character for these beasts.'

As they continued to survey the scene and rationalise the possibility of Nagrim's survival, however remote, another ranger cried out.

Morek's heart caught in his mouth.

It was another body.

The hearth guard captain hurried over, though his haste was utterly unnecessary – all the dwarfs in the gorge were beyond help now. Not even Valaya could save them. The third corpse was face down, and peppered with arrows. Judging by the trail he had left and the position of the body so far from the main battlesite, the dead dwarf had obviously crawled along the ground in spite of heinous injuries. Morek noted with a deepening sense of sadness and outrage that the dwarf's hand, his fingers outstretched and reaching, was just inches from his bloodied crossbow. The hearth guard captain nodded to two rangers standing by the body to turn it over. Morek's heart sank and he felt something die within him in that moment. Perhaps it was hope. The dead dwarf was Nagrim.

Despite what he'd said to Lodri, Morek had still held on to the slight chance that the prince was still alive, that he'd fallen down a chasm and broken his leg, or become lost on an unfamiliar trail – anything but this. Now the irrefutable evidence of Nagrim's demise was before him, it struck like a hammer blow.

'Get them up,' he breathed, finding his voice choked with emotion. Lodri reached out and Morek grasped his arm just before he was about to touch the prince. 'Like the most venerated and fragile heirloom of your clan,' he said, 'Carry him like that.'

Nagrim was raised aloft on the shoulders of four rangers, another four, together with Morek, providing an honour guard as they carried him back up the trail and out of the defile to where a mule-drawn cart was waiting.

Reaching the ridgeline, the path widened out and there was the cart with a cohort of dauntless hearth guard stood at the ready to receive him. Morek had taken no chances with the search party, especially given the possibility of foreign invaders in the mountains, and had brought over thirty dwarfs with him.

As Nagrim was lowered gently onto the cart, the two other slain rangers set down after him, Morek wiped a tangle of dark brown hair that was matted with blood from the prince's face.

'I'm sorry, lad,' he whispered. 'Rest now, soon be home.'

'Dreng tromm, this is a dark day,' said Lodri, as they were leading off the mule.

'Yes,' answered Morek. 'I must find a way to tell the king that his son is dead.'

A SOLEMN PROCESSION of hearth guard carried Nagrim up the central aisle of the throne room upon a bier of shields. They bore him at shoulder height, the prince's hands clasped across his chest as he lay in quiet repose. The ashen complexion, his bloodied face, gave away the illusion that he was merely sleeping. Arrows were embedded in his body, the fatal one piercing his heart through his battered armour.

There were no sounds as Nagrim made his last journey, only the harsh *clack* of metal on stone from the hearth guards' boots. Even the forge hammers had stopped, the ever-present clang of the anvils held fast in respectful remembrance. Morek led the warriors down the central concourse of gilded flagstones, along the heavy path that would bring Nagrim to his disconsolate father.

Word had reached King Bagrik not long after Morek had entered the outer gateway hall, though none had yet related the precise details of what had happened or said explicitly that Nagrim was dead. It was unnecessary, the very manner of the prince's return made that fact abundantly clear.

When Morek finally reached the king, at the end of the long, wide aisle, his face was grave. The hearth guard captain was the only one not wearing his full-face helmet. He did so out of respect for Nagrim and to his king on account of the news he was about to give.

'We found him in a gorge, far to the north-east, beyond the grobi hunting trails,' said Morek in a subdued tone.

Bagrik stared down at the body of his son with ice-cold eyes, his expression neutral and unreadable. He reached out and was about to touch Nagrim's face, when he stopped and snatched his hand away as if scalded. To feel that gelid flesh, the chill of death beneath the skin… He would not be able to deny the truth before him. Bagrik felt a sudden tightness in his throat and rubbed it absent-mindedly.

Queen Brunvilda, alongside him, lightly squeezed her husband's hand. Bagrik reciprocated the gesture and held on as if for dear life, imagining all the strength dripping out of his fingers as mortality came to claim him, just as it had claimed his legacy. Kandor was the only other dwarf present. He was standing below the dais where Bagrik clung to his throne with claw-like fingers, knuckles white from the constant effort of gripping. The merchant thane had his head bowed, unable to bring himself to look upon the slain prince.

'Who was responsible for this?' the king demanded, his voice steady but carrying an undercurrent of threat. 'Who killed my son!' he cried out in anguish, coming down from his throne and slipping from Brunvilda's reassuring grasp to cradle Nagrim's head. 'My boy…' Gently, so gently, he stroked back Nagrim's hair, the tips of his fingers scarcely brushing the prince's cold skin. When Bagrik looked up at his hearth guard captain, there were tears in his eyes.

'It was not grobi,' Morek told him, taken aback at first by the reaction of his king. His expression darkened when he added, 'The arrows are that of the northmen, the ones plaguing the lands of the elgi.'

Bagrik's jaw line hardened as if carved of granite. A mask of calm fury came across his face, smothering his grief like a hand upon a candle flame. There was the briefest glimmer of rogue emotion in his eyes as he regarded Morek. Regret.

'Retribution,' rasped the king, 'I will have vengeance for this,' he promised, getting louder. 'Send word to the elgi. We'll fight their war for them and crush these heathen bastards, who think they can attack the royal clan of Ungor without fear of retaliation.

'Muster the armies. Every axe, every hammer…' Bagrik said, 'We are now at war.'

An aura of serenity existed in the Temple of Valaya. In the starlit gloom, a figure hunched over a stone slab below the mighty statue of the beneficent goddess. He was wrapped in a fur cloak, and his shoulders were slumped as if in defeat. Bagrik had ordered that his son be taken immediately from the throne room to the ancestor temple to await internment.

Following his declaration of war, the king had resumed his throne and gave curt orders for his bearers to take him to the temple after his son. To Morek he left the marshalling of the armies. Though grief and hurt unimaginable made him want to strike out, to bring swift retribution to Nagrim's slayers, he knew the mustering would take time. Armouries would have to be stocked, warriors summoned, war machines made ready.

Word had spread throughout the hold with all the force and purpose of an earthquake, the ripples of the king's anguish felt by all. From the hollow tunnels of the vaults to the busy workshops, guild chambers and clan halls, beards were tugged in despair and axes sharpened as all of Karak Ungor mourned and the thoughts of dwarfs turned to revenge.

Nick Kyme

Anger, hate – that would come. For now, Bagrik dwelt in a well of his own grief. Nagrim was laid before him, pale in death. The blood had been cleaned from his face by the priestesses, his hair was combed, his beard re-braided. The arrows that defiled the prince's body had been removed, the wounds sewn shut, and he wore a robe of deepest purple in place of his battered plate and mail. Alongside him, upon a stone plinth, was the ancestral armour from the Iron Deep. Bagrik hardly dared to look upon it such was the pain of loss he felt. It seemed like so long ago now that he had shown it to Nagrim. All that it once stood for, hope, pride and legacy, was gone like ash before the wind.

Bagrik bent forward, stooping to kiss his son tenderly on the forehead.

'Nagrim…' he whispered, voice choking, and wept. It was a horrible sound, empty and raw, as Bagrik vented his emotions, hollowing himself out until all that was left was granite.

When the king had finally stopped sobbing he looked up, realising that he was not alone.

'I have never seen you cry before,' said the voice of Brunvilda.

Bagrik turned to his queen. Morek had escorted her and was waiting patiently at the threshold of the temple. Brunvilda's eyes were full of pity and sorrow. All Bagrik could return was cold, hard stone.

'It will be the first and last time,' he replied sternly and started to walk past her, out of the temple.

'Your legacy need not end with Nagrim,' Brunvilda said. Her eyes conveyed her meaning.

Emotion returned like black clouds over a bright day, dark and full of promised thunder.

'I have no son,' snarled Bagrik, stopped next to Brunvilda, only a few inches from her face. He fashioned his vitriol into a bladed retort, 'My only son is dead.'

Bagrik stalked away, bellowing to Morek for his armour once he had left the sanctity of the temple.

Brunvilda shared a worried glance with the hearth guard captain, who knew his duty and followed the king.

CHAPTER TWELVE
Those Left Behind...

RUGNIR WAS ALIVE. Though when he awoke and opened his eyes he wished he wasn't. Pain seized his body before his blurring vision succumbed to clouds of black fog. It was like an anvil was resting on his chest, and he had to fight to breathe. Rugnir's skull pounded like iron worked beneath a hammer, an almighty hangover vying with his physical wounds for the prize of causing the dwarf the most hurt.

'Nagrim...' Rugnir's first intelligible words since his revival were rasped. He tried to get up but lances of agony brought him down again like a felled oak.

'Be still,' a voice told him, old, like grit worked over sandpaper. It had a cantankerous, chiding edge to it. Rugnir realised it was another dwarf.

His chest hard, like it was filled with too much bone, made his lungs tight, and his leg was stiff like petrified wood. Out of instinct, Rugnir reached down to the source of his pain. He got as far as the rough scrape of bandages before his wrist was seized by a hand that felt like gnarled wood and coarse leather.

'Be still, I said,' the gruff voice repeated.

Rugnir tried to see his saviour, but all he got for his efforts was spikes of hot pain and a vague silhouette. Abandoning that course of action, he closed his eyes and dimly recalled being struck by arrows, though the details were indistinct. He'd hit the ground hard, the stink of blood and metal filling his nose and mouth. That's when the darkness claimed him. Rugnir had expected to awake before Gazul's Gate, and for the ancestor of the dwarf afterlife to bar his passage into the Halls, and consign him to limbo for his contemptible deeds. This was not the Gate, nor was the hazy figure sat beside him Gazul, the son of Grungni and Valaya. This tenebrous chamber smelled of earth and stone and damp.

Howling wind told him he was still in the mountains, the noise oddly hollow and far away. Rugnir suspected his injuries, self-inflicted and otherwise, were to blame for that. Dripping water echoed dully, like he was lying at the bottom of a deep well or inside a cave, but boomed with a thunderous clamour. Rugnir grimaced at every drop, and that too caused him pain. Slowly, as his senses returned through the screaming wall of hurt, he realised he was not wearing his tunic and the softness beneath his recumbent body was from furs and skins.

A sudden panic gripped him as he remembered the gorge. The faces of the ambushers glared at him like ghosts. Rugnir tried to speak but found he lacked strength. Desperately, he fought to get up again but couldn't move.

'You're still weak,' the voice told him. The distinctive aroma of pipe smoke filled the air. 'Rest.'

Rugnir shaped a reply with his mouth, opening his eyes. Darkness swept over him, clawing its way into his vision and stilling his lips as he blacked out…

WHEN HE AWOKE again, Rugnir had no idea how much time had passed. It could not have been long; the other dwarf was still sitting beside him and smoking his pipe.

'I warned you,' he growled, getting to his feet and stomping over to what Rugnir's gradually returning eyesight discerned was a stove. The old dwarf picked up a steaming cup that had been resting on it and brought it over.

'Up,' he barked, crouching down and lifting Rugnir's head towards the proffered cup, so he could tip the contents into his mouth. 'Drink,' said the old dwarf.

It was some kind of broth, though the likes of which Rugnir had never tasted. Sweet, but with little flavour, it warmed his body and left an acrid aftertaste. Coughing and spluttering, Rugnir shied away from the cup but the old dwarf was insistent.

'All of it,' he growled, and held Rugnir's head fast. It would not have been difficult; he was so weak even the smallest beardling could have forced him. Only when he finished did the old dwarf let Rugnir go.

'What… what was that stuff?' he asked of the old dwarf, able to croak the words.

'Herbs, bark, hruk urine, all the good things a growing dwarf needs,' he replied. 'What does it matter what's in it? You'll drink it, that's all you need know.'

Rugnir's initial, half-comatose impression was right – he was an old, cantankerous bastard.

'You saved my life,' Rugnir continued, and with the affirmation came an overwhelming sense of grief. There was no one else in the cave with them. The others must have perished.

The old dwarf regarded him for a moment. His grey, unkempt, beard ruffled as he chewed on a piece of leather. He wore a dark green tunic with a cloak of furs, and a mail skirt hung down to his iron-shod boots. A mountaineer's cap perched on his head, stuck with sparhawk feathers, and a worn hand axe hung from a thick, brown belt around his waist.

'Keeps my pegs strong,' he said, grinding the leather and showing a perfect set of square teeth, albeit tarnished with age. 'Craggen,' the old dwarf added, tapping his chest with his pipe, before pointing the supping end at Rugnir.

'Rugnir,' the dwarf replied.

Craggen gave a shrug of his mouth, as if the name meant little, then clamped the pipe between his lips and said, 'I live alone in these mountains, hunting grobi, keeping out of the way. What's your excuse for being out here?'

Rugnir told him about the grobkul, about Nagrim and the other rangers. Then he described the ambush, though he left out the attackers. That was only for him to know.

'I must get back,' he said, struggling to rise before the old hermit pushed him down again.

'And waste all the time I've spent bringing you back from Gazul's door? Are you a wattock? You were half-dead when I found you beside the river. You'll last the time it takes for a grobi to stab you in your sleep!'

'River?' asked Rugnir, bleary-eyed. 'What river?'

'The river where I found you, that's what,' Craggen growled. 'Alone, I'm sorry to say,' he said sombrely, blowing out a thick plume of smoke as he considered the stricken dwarf. 'You can barely stand, let alone walk or trek the mountains. No, you'll remain here. The draught will heal you quickly. A few weeks and you'll be back on your feet; a few more and you'll be ready to leave.'

'A few weeks!' cried Rugnir, 'I must return to the karak, immediately,' he said, trying to get up again. His vision swam suddenly and Rugnir slumped back. The effort of even trying to get his shoulders off the ground was exhausting.

'I must get back...' he said, words slurring, his fading strength all but spent. Blackness enveloped Rugnir once more and he slipped into a fitful dream of blood and arrows and death.

BAGRIK'S ARMY MUSTERED at dawn. For the first time in over two thousand years, the great gates to Karak Ungor yawned open and lines of dwarfs emerged like armoured ants.

Word had already gone ahead to the elves, brought by the king's fastest runners, and was returned swiftly by carrier-hawk. One of the hold's mountain rangers had taken the message to the king. They would meet at Broken Anvil Hill, fifty miles south of Tor Eorfith.

With standards aloft, the gold, copper and bronze catching on the rising sun, the dwarfs trooped out with regimented discipline. Six columns deep, they marched in perfect time with pipe, drum and horn. No rousing chorus of voices, no stirring refrain accompanied the instruments – the choristers, heralds and minstrels kept a sombre silence out of respect for the dead. Rangers were dispatched ahead of the main force, swathed in their cloaks and armed with crossbows and throwing axes. They would pave the way for the army, rooting out any threats and securing the path ahead.

It was the hearth guard, though, that led the line, the stern countenances of their bronze masks gleaming dully. Morek marched in the middle of their ranks, first out of the great gate, the horns on his helmet marking him out as captain. Haggar was directly to his right, holding the grand banner of Karak Ungor high, the red dragon snapping in the breeze.

Next came the longbeards, clad in their ancestral armour, which, even though it bore the scars of a hundred or more battles, still shone with polished brilliance. Bagrik travelled with them, carried upon his war shield by the royal hearth guard bearers. The king's face was more severe than that of his bronze-masked bodyguards, as he rocked gently back and forth with the movement of the armoured warriors.

The longbeards were followed by the many clans, led in turn by their thanes and clan leaders. Warriors all, the hues and runes of the clans' fluttering banners described their heritage and craft – rockcutters, lantern-makers, metalsmiths all come together in a mutual cause. Amongst their number were the hold's quarrellers, crossbows shouldered as they marched beside their kin.

Between the massive phalanxes of warriors and longbeards was Hegbrak Thunderhand, master runesmith and former apprentice of Agrin Oakenheart. Though he was not part of the war host, the venerable runelord Agrin and his fellow runesmiths had toiled night and day in the build up to the mustering, fashioning rune weapons upon their anvils of power in the fuliginous depths of sweltering forges.

Hegbrak rode atop one of the anvils as it was heaved along by the Anvil Guard. Clad in rune-encrusted gromril, helmets wrought in the shape of their honorific, the

Anvil Guard were warrior elites, devoted solely to the Runesmiths' Guild, who wielded their great hammers with deadly efficiency. A youth compared to the venerable Agrin Oakenheart, Hegbrak was still a mighty runemaster, his rich tan hair fluttering in the breeze as he eyed the horizon.

Mule-trains brought up the rear of the vast column, hauling small carts heavy with baskets of crossbow bolts, axes, hammers and shields. There was ale, too, sloshing in broad casks, and chests of stonebread, oatmeal and other provisions.

War engines drawn by stout lode-ponies followed in the train – wooden stone throwers chased in bronze and brass, and hefty ballista with iron-headed bolts. They were accompanied by engineers, journeymen and warriors. Assorted victualers and brewers walked alongside the baggage train. Priestesses of Valaya, known as the Valakryn, were brought along too as battlefield surgeons. These ladies of the temple were warriors as well as healers, and carried axes and wore mail beneath their purple robes.

Last of all were the slayers, half-naked warrior fanatics that had sworn a death oath to seek their doom against the mightiest foe they could find or by performing the most insane feats of battle. The tattooed berserkers had attached themselves to the war host a few miles after it had left the hold, and acted as its unofficial rearguard.

The slayers were the only dwarfs to break the silence, bellowing oaths and war cries as they trooped along with their brothers. Some wore the skins of beasts like trophies: the shaggy furs of beastmen, hardened troll flesh, even dragon hide. Others painted their bodies to resemble bones and skulls. All wore their hair shaven into a blood-red crest, hardened with lime and grease, and gripped deathly sharp axes. Within their ranks moved the warrior-priests of Grimnir, the robed acolytes of the dwarfs' fiercest ancestor god, ready to swear in others to the cult during the heat of battle.

When the hundred thousand-strong army left Karak Ungor, the great gate had thundered shut in its wake. At the king's order Brunvilda had stayed behind, the queen watching from the Dragon's Tooth as her husband and his throng departed for war. Grikk remained too, together with his ironbreakers, there to protect the hold in the absence of most of its warriors.

Unsurprisingly, the dwarfs had met no resistance on the road and arrived at Broken Anvil Hill in less than three days.

THE MUSTER POINT of the two armies was well named. A huge, rectangular plain scattered with crags and grassy hollows stretched for over a mile. A rocky promontory jutted out at opposite ends, forming thirty foot bluffs that fell away into lowland valleys scattered with trees. It was these vantage points that gave the hill its shape and its name, together with a ten foot deep cleft that ranged partway down the middle.

Ithalred was waiting on one side of the cleft with his glittering host when the dwarfs had arrived, an army of silver knights on horse, light cavalry, chariots and vast ranks of spears and archers. His captains were alongside him, the raven-haired Lethralmir now wearing full armour forged from the elven star metal, ithilmar, a long bejewelled sword sheathed on his back; Korhvale, the White Lion, dressed in his hunter's garb and familiar scale with its golden cuirass. Malbeth, too, was with them, amongst a few other hitherto un-introduced elf warriors, the ambassador unarmed and wearing only robes.

At seeing this meeting of the two races across the cleft in Broken Anvil Hill, the casual onlooker might have supposed it to be a parlay before the onset of hostilities, rather than a greeting between allies. The mood had been tense, the diplomats of both races failing to thaw the ice. Bagrik and Ithalred had exchanged brief pleasantries of sorts, before retiring to their respective sides of the great hill and setting up separate camps.

It was nearing nightfall on the fourth day since the dwarfs had left Karak Ungor by the time the encampment was finished. The elves held the north side of the hill, their white silken pavilions and grand marquees in sharp contrast to the squat, angular dwellings of the dwarfs on the southern side of the cleft. Trails of smoke issued from the dwarf tents through carefully engineered vents in the roofs. They were made from coarse weave and dried animal hide, and lit by the glow of flaming coals heaped in iron braziers and cauldrons. The elves used their arcane lanterns to light the area around their own domiciles, strung between their campaign tents on silver thread.

Such was the lingering enmity between the two races that they seldom mixed. A few of the more curious occasionally ventured to the other side of the cleft but, when met with hard stares or muttered derision, were quick to return. Dwarfs kept to dwarfs and elves to elves, talking in huddled groups around fires, sharpening blades, stringing bows or simply lost in deep thought. Some, the balladeers, sang solemn tunes or dour lamentations; others prayed at small shrines. The lucky few, the oldest and wisest, slept. Tomorrow would be a hard day – there would be little, if any, time for rest once metal resounded against metal and the blood began to flow.

'Barely more than beasts,' growled Morek, the voice of the hearth guard captain coming from behind Haggar.

The banner bearer was sitting on a stool in front of a wooden bench, a series of tools unravelled from a leather belt on top of it. He had been alone prior to Morek's arrival, isolated upon the rocky promontory of Broken Anvil Hill that faced east.

'You mean the northmen,' Haggar replied, as he gripped his rune hand and twisted. Creaking metal split the air with his efforts, making him wince, before he had managed to unscrew the gromril hand and laid it next to the tool belt.

'Aye, lad,' breathed Morek, the scent of pipe smoke in the air as he spoke. 'You fought these dogs with the elgi, what were they like?' he asked.

Haggar's gaze shifted from his works, sweeping across the sloping plain, through swaying grasses and clusters of tightly bunched rock, until after a mile or so it settled upon the distant horizon and the waiting Norscans.

'Like you said, captain, they are beasts. They throw themselves into battle for the sake of bloodletting... 'tis a sobering sight.'

Something had changed in Haggar the day that he'd returned from Tor Eorfith. He'd only spoken once of the Norscan hordes he fought there alongside the elves, and only when the king had asked him expressly. After that, he'd kept his own counsel. This taciturn dwarf, so troubled and moribund, was as different again to the hopeful youth that had spoken to Morek outside the Elders Chamber several months ago.

Slipping into remembrance, Haggar watched the violet campfires of the Norscans burning into azure as they billowed high into the night, issuing spark-filled smoke. Shadows, mere silhouettes of imagined monsters and evil men who made their pacts with heathen gods, cavorted in the flickering light. Emerald lightning crackled sporadically as the sound of depraved pleasures and infernal tortures drifted on the breeze, redolent with the stench of cooking flesh.

'Even the wind is against us,' Morek grumbled, wrinkling his nose against the wretched smell as he came to stand alongside Haggar.

'It will be a hard fight tomorrow,' said the banner bearer, oiling the metal fingers of his rune hand fastidiously. 'I wish Nagrim were with us.'

'Aye, it will,' Morek offered with casual pragmatism. 'And so do I, lad,' he added wistfully. A moment of mournful silence persisted before Morek spoke again to dispel it. 'I'd sooner have the walls of the hold at my back than fight in that cauldron,' he said, indicating the open battlefield, fringed by the mountains on either side.

The Norscans had already set about clearing it, hewing trees in order to erect crude gibbets for their blood sacrifices. Bodies – goblins, beasts and other barbarian men – were splayed in cruciform, and could just be made out hanging limply from the grim scaffolds.

'They defile the very earth,' said Haggar, watching them darkly. 'What manner of beast are we facing, Morek?' he asked, though he already knew the answer.

'A hellish one it would seem, make no mistake of that,' replied the hearth guard captain.

'To bear the banner of Ungor is a great honour, Morek, but to me it feels like a tremendous burden,' Haggar confessed. 'What if I am found lacking?'

'Our great and noble banner is a symbol, Haggar. It is a symbol of our honour, of our resolve and our brotherhood. A symbol is a powerful thing. It can turn the tide when the odds seem impossible, turn defeat into victory…' Morek told him, pausing to put his hand on the banner bearer's shoulder. 'Don't fear failure, Haggar,' he said. 'I know your thoughts are of Thagri. Your destiny is not his; *you* are not him. You'll reclaim your honour come the morrow, lad. Grungni wills it.' Morek gripped the banner bearer's shoulder hard and then let him go.

Haggar turned, about to respond, but the hearth guard captain was already walking away to the camp and his tent. Instead Haggar returned to his labours, gratefully lost in the ritual taught to him by Agrin when he had first gifted him the hand. So consumed was he by his work, the meticulous cleaning and polishing, that Haggar failed to hear another figure approach until it was almost upon him. At first he thought it was Morek, come back because he'd forgotten something, but when he turned around Haggar saw that it was the elf seeress, Arthelas. He fumbled with his tools in sudden shock and made to stand before she raised her hand, stopping him.

'Please,' she said musically, sending the dwarf's heart thumping in his chest. Haggar was about to grip his chest, for fear that Arthelas would hear, when he stopped himself.

'Don't let me interrupt…' she said, pausing to regard the disembodied rune hand and the scattered tools, '…whatever it is you are doing.'

'It's nothing,' Haggar replied with gruff embarrassment, covering up the rune hand with the leather belt and shoving the stump of his wrist in his tunic.

'You've no need to hide,' Arthelas told him gently, seeming to glide alongside him. 'Let me see it.'

Haggar felt his face redden; he hadn't been this hot since he'd worked in Agrin's forge by way of gratitude for the runelord making his hand. Abashedly, he pulled his arm out from his tunic and showed Arthelas the wrist stump where a metal cap had been fused, a threaded hole bored into it in the centre.

The seeress took it gently in her hands – her lightest touch sent tiny tremors running through Haggar's body. Her face saddened as she looked back at the dwarf, eyes sparkling like captured stars.

'I…' Haggar began, feeling a strange compulsion to tell Arthelas its tale, but at a sudden loss for words. 'It was lost long ago,' he managed after gathering himself together, 'fighting grobi in the tunnels beneath my hold. King Bagrik appointed me his banner bearer that day when venerable Skardrin fell, and had Agrin, our venerable runelord, forge a new hand for me.'

'It is a grievous wound,' she said, letting Haggar go. 'And old…' Her eyes narrowed, as if she was seeing into his very soul, '…like another scar you bear, but one that runs much deeper and is still very raw.'

Haggar had kept the shame of his past to himself for nigh on a hundred years. But he could not resist. He was enraptured by this fey creature, and spoke in spite of his shame.

'My four-times grandsire, Thagri Skengdrang, once served Norkragg, one of the first kings of Karak Ungor. He was Norkragg's banner bearer, an esteemed and privileged position. When Karak Ungor went to war, Thagri went too, his task to protect the banner and keep it aloft.' Haggar's face darkened and he looked at his feet. 'Thagri failed in his oath,' he said. When he managed to raise his head again, his gaze was far away, lost to memory. 'During a battle against the greenskin tribes of the east, he allowed the grand banner to slip from his grasp and be sullied on the field. Desperate, he tried to retrieve it, but the enemy, foul urk swine,' he said, scowling, 'swarmed over it. With the banner lost, panic shuddered down the dawi ranks and many were slain. An entire chapter is devoted to them in the dammaz kron, our book of grudges. Thagri was amongst them, beheaded by an urk cleaver as he stooped for the banner. The day was won in the end. King Norkragg rallied the throng, whipping them up into a hateful fervour, but the stain of Thagri's shameful death could not be so easily undone,' said Haggar, blinking as he returned to the present. 'He wanders even now, headless, an unquiet spirit cursed to dwell forever in limbo. This shame has followed the Skengdrangs for over a thousand years. When Thagri failed in his oath, the honour of banner bearer passed to another clan. I am the first of my clan in four generations to reclaim it, and it falls to me to atone for Thagri's mistake by never allowing the banner to fall while I still live.'

Silence fell between them when Haggar had finished.

Arthelas, her expression shadowed with sadness, smiled, and the warmth of her countenance spread to the dwarf, nurturing the coldness within him back to life.

'I cannot pretend to understand your ways and customs, but I sense bravery in you, dwarf. I do not think you will fail in your promise,' Arthelas told him, then bent down and kissed the banner bearer on the cheek.

Haggar was emboldened at once, and seemed to stand straighter.

'There is a word, in my language...' he said, 'dawongi. It means 'dwarf-friend.''

Haggar went down on one knee. 'Tromm, dawongi,' he breathed, nodding slowly with the deepest of respect.

Arthelas smiled.

'Thank you,' she replied, returning the gesture as she took her leave.

Haggar watched her go, determined more than ever not to be found wanting, especially beneath her gaze. Come the morning, the banner of Karak Ungor would soar aloft and never fall until the battle was won or the blood in Haggar's veins had run cold.

ARTHELAS WAS TIRED as she walked back to her pavilion. She moved swiftly through the camp, passing the tents of warriors and knights engrossed in their pre-battle rituals. Those that did see her lowered their eyes respectfully and bowed until she had passed. Approaching her pavilion, Arthelas met the gaze of Korhvale, who was lingering nearby.

All too eager to follow my brother's every whim, she thought spitefully, but smiling benignly at the White Lion.

Korhvale frowned at Arthelas's appearance, her drawn features and weary posture suggesting fatigue. She didn't give him a chance to voice his concern, assuming he would have the confidence to speak it, moving on quickly and reaching her tent.

Upon entering through the narrow flap, Arthelas dismissed her servants and slumped down onto her bed. Stretching over to a small wooden chest, she took out a glass bottle filled with a silvery potion and drank the contents. It was a revitalising tonic, designed to take the edge off her recent exertions.

'You should have let me tour the encampment with you,' said a silky voice from the shadows. 'It isn't safe with all these... *lesser creatures* about.'

'I wanted to be alone,' Arthelas responded curtly.

'Yes, with the bearded swine. I saw that.'

'Are you following me?' The seeress's tone was accusing.

'Yes,' Lethralmir replied brazenly, a look of amusement on his face as he emerged into the lantern light.

Arthelas's annoyance was only feigned and she returned Lethralmir's smile with one of her own.

'You look powerful in your armour,' she said as he approached. When he was standing in front of her, she traced her fingers delicately over his breastplate and arm greaves.

'I am more powerful without it,' Lethralmir breathed lasciviously, leaning in to the seeress.

Arthelas pushed him back and stood up, the effects of the potion invigorating her. 'I cannot believe you were jealous of the dwarf,' she laughed.

Lethralmir sniffed his indifference and went to pour himself a goblet of wine from a silver carafe at Arthelas's bedside.

'I do believe that stunted brute has taken a shine to you,' he said, filling the goblet to the rim.

'He is repellent,' she declared, a wicked smile spreading across her lips. 'Perhaps, a change of *attire* would make us better suited though…'

A sudden flash of light filled the pavilion, not bright enough to attract attention but enough to make Lethralmir avert his gaze. When the raven-haired blademaster looked back Arthelas was gone, an actinic stench drenching the air. Before him stood a comely female dwarf, long plaited hair trailing over her ample bosom.

'Your brother would not approve of you using your magic so flippantly,' said Lethralmir, setting himself down on a plush velvet couch opposite the bed.

'Ithalred has no concept of my true power,' the dwarf replied, caustically. The tone was at odds with the appearance, though the timbre and language were authentic. Its body shimmered with an inner glow that exuded through the flesh, growing steadily brighter with each passing moment until it was utterly consumed by light. When the sorcerous aura died, Arthelas had returned to her true form.

'Let these hairy backed creatures rut with their own kind,' she said, eschewing the bed to recline on a chaise-long next to the velvet couch. 'I can scarcely imagine how such a race would procreate,' she added, taking Lethralmir's wine and drinking it as if to wash the foul taste from her mouth.

'You have beguiled him, though,' said Lethralmir, getting up and pouring himself another drink. 'And he is not the only one.'

'Korhvale,' said Arthelas with a sneer. 'He watches me like a hawk. I think my brother suspects something.'

That piqued Lethralmir's interest. 'Really?'

'Don't come here, for a while,' she told him.

Lethralmir drew close to her, his voice husky. 'But you have beguiled me, as well...'

'I know,' Arthelas replied teasingly, 'But now is not the time,' she hissed, pushing him hard back onto the couch.

Lethralmir frowned, wounded by the abrupt rejection.

'You are about to be summoned,' she said, by way of explanation.

He didn't catch on immediately and stared nonplussed.

'Get out,' Arthelas snapped, her ire lending Lethralmir purpose.

The blade-master got to his feet, swilling down the last of his wine and left with a lustful smile. Lethralmir was met outside by one of Ithalred's aides. The council of war with the dwarfs was in session and his presence was required.

Arthelas smiled to herself when they were gone.

'No,' she hissed, 'now is not the time.'

BAGRIK'S WAR TENT was the largest of all the dwarfs'. It had several chambers, in which the king could sleep, count his gold or eat. The greatest was given over to the war council, a sizeable wooden table dominating the centre and strewn with ragged parchment maps scribed by Bagrik's cartographers.

Flickering firelight from standing iron braziers revealed a crowded scene; dwarfs surrounded the war table, poring over the details of the coming battle, elves stooped next to them, bent-backed with the low ceiling. The aroma of roast pig filled the air, which was thick with pipe smoke, emanating from a spit in the corner of the room set over hot coals. Dripping fat hissed as it caught in the flame.

Bagrik crouched over the table, sat upon his throne in robes and furs. The boar pelt was slung over the back of it, dead eyes scrutinizing all. Morek, Haggar and a few other dwarf captains were standing nearby, smoking, chewing their beards or staring, furrow-browed and with fists on hips, at the maps. Of the elves, Ithalred and Lethralmir had a place beside the table. The other captains stood behind the dwarfs, peering easily over their shoulders.

'The northmen are here, to the east of our camp,' Morek addressed the allied captains, pointing to a place on the map that showed widely spread contours and downward sloping, flat plains almost bereft of any geographical features. The tacticians of the elves, given their recent sorties, had postulated that the Norscan's main camp was to the east, between Karak Ungor and Tor Eorfith. The movements of the Norscan army, and its appearance to the east of Broken Anvil Hill seemed to bear this out.

'Our rangers report a horde of some two-hundred thousand men, together with beasts and… other *creatures*.' Morek didn't elaborate. It wasn't needed. All gathered in Bagrik's tent knew what he meant. There were *daemons*, fell beings summoned from the Realm of Chaos, in the Norscan ranks.

'I suggest a strategy based on us holding this high ground,' Morek continued, setting a small gold marker stamped with a dwarf face on a raised slope indicated by the map. He added several more gold and bronze markers, shaped like coins, to the one he'd just positioned, that represented the other units in the dwarf army. 'We lure the Norscans with ranged attacks and wait for them to come to us. As they draw close, we pound them with our artillery,' he added, pushing forward a line of gold markers. 'When… If,' he corrected, 'they come through the barrage they'll hit a shield wall of hearth guard and elgi spear,' he said, placing a silver coin with an eagle wing on it in the line. 'The hammer and the anvil,' he announced proudly, leaning back and taking a long pull on his pipe, eminently satisfied. 'We won't even need our reserves.'

'Our force is mainly cavalry, what do you propose we do with them?' asked Lethralmir.

'They won't be needed,' Morek replied boldly, and folded his arms as if that was an end to it.

'You would have us linger by the sidelines as whatever ranged weapons the northmen can bring to bear kill us in our saddles? We are asur, dwarf,' he snarled, 'we too have our honour! And what about our spears, you are committing them to a battle of attrition. That way may suit dwarf ways of war, but it does not suit ours.'

'It's true,' countered Morek, rising to Lethralmir's bait, 'that you elgi are not so hardy. Would you like to hide behind our shields, instead?'

Lethralmir smiled mirthlessly, as he fashioned a rejoinder.

'I doubt they would provide much protection. What's to stop the northmen merely jumping over your heads? That's assuming they even see you.'

'Kruti-eating ufdi...' snarled Morek, shoving his way past the other dwarfs to reach Lethralmir, who merely recoiled with distaste.

'Morek,' snapped the king. It was the first time he had spoken during the council, but it was enough to send the hearth guard captain back to his place still fuming from the elf's insult.

Bagrik turned on his throne to address Ithalred. 'Perhaps there is a way to yoke the strength of both our armies,' he said. 'Are you familiar, prince, with the oblique line?'

Ithalred nodded. 'I am, yes.'

'Morek,' added the king, glaring at the dwarf, 'set the markers.'

The hearth guard captain obeyed, setting out a formation of gold and bronze markers upon the raised slope, several ranks deep. To them he added smaller cohorts of silver. Then he spread a long line of silver coins, bunched on one flank and hinged at the middle of the battle-line. When he was done, he stepped away from the table.

'Our south flank,' Bagrik said, 'will consist of our forces, artillery, infantry and quarrellers. Added to it are your archers and spears. On the north, your cavalry.' All eyes were upon the map and the tactical formation arranged by Morek as the king spoke. 'The plan is a simple one,' Bagrik continued. 'The south moves slowly, whilst its bows and machineries hold fast to maintain a barrage. The north will charge at full pace, and engage the enemy first. The attack will split their forces. One flank crushed by the cavalry, their opposite flank will move in support, but it will already have been decimated by our holding troops. Caught in a killing ground, they will falter. Attack the cavalry or march on the distant slope? Either choice is a fatal one, for by that time our slow moving flank will have reached them and they will be destroyed utterly,' Bagrik concluded. There was no relish in his tone, not even the satisfaction in the knowledge of a battle about to be won. There was only stone. 'We dawi call it the bear trap, and employed properly it is deadly.'

Lethralmir sniffed derisively and turned to his prince. 'This assumes, of course, that the northmen will simply attack as a horde. It seems to me our cavalry is greatly exposed by this plan.'

'No plan is without risk!' retorted Morek.

Ithalred ignored the bickering and held the gaze of the dwarf king.

'Very well,' he said. 'We will meet you on the field tomorrow at dawn.' With that he turned and walked out of the tent, his captains following suit.

* * *

LETHRALMIR STARED DARKLY at Morek as he left the king's war tent.

The dwarf's face was so red, his teeth gritted, that the elf thought he might immolate himself in a conflagration of his own anger. Lethralmir decided, once he was back out in the open, that he would have liked to have seen that.

'Lethralmir,' the tone in Ithalred's voice punctured the blade-master's good humour.

'Yes, Ithalred,' he replied with a disarming smile.

The prince was on the elven side of the cleft, and clearly did not share Lethralmir's mood as he beckoned the blade-master over.

'Is something wrong?' he asked, feigning concern.

'You were seen,' the prince told him, 'coming out of my sister's tent.'

Ithalred's aide. Lethralmir resolved to discover his name and punish him accordingly.

'Yes… I was merely–'

The elf prince didn't let him finish.

'Stay away from her,' he said meaningfully. 'She is a seer and must remain pure or she'll lose her gift,' he added, telling Lethralmir things that he already knew. 'Now, more than ever, I need her foresight.'

'You cannot shackle her forever, Ithalred,' Lethralmir replied.

The prince came forward, his face a mask of anger. 'Don't challenge me, or your *use* to this court will be at an end,' he promised, eyes wide.

Lethralmir backed off a little, false offence etched on his features.

'I thought we were friends, Ithalred. I would never do anything–'

'We are,' the prince replied, 'but that friendship does not extend to Arthelas. Are we clear about that?'

Lethralmir's expression was contrite, as if the notion of disobeying his prince was utterly beyond comprehension.

'Of course.'

In truth, the blade-master masked his furious chagrin, even keeping it from his eyes.

Ithalred was about to speak again, when he noticed a dwarf, one of the captains from the war council, watching them.

HAGGAR DIDN'T SPEAK the elf tongue, so he couldn't understand what the two nobles were saying. He had heard the name 'Arthelas' though, and it was apparent from their body language and tone that the elves were arguing. Upon seeing him they quickly became silent and went their separate ways. Haggar watched them go. Something wasn't right, and dissension on the eve of battle was a bad omen.

CHAPTER THIRTEEN
A Field of Blood

THE DWARF HORNS pierced the air in a dour baritone. The pounding of drums joined them, signalling the call to arms. Elven horns resounded, too. Combined with those of the dwarfs, it was a discordant cacophony.

Upon the southern edge of an immense sloping plain, vast regiments of dwarfs assembled. Their iron-shod boots churned the earth, and their armour clanked loudly as they tramped into position. A battery of stone throwers and ballista were hauled onto the shallow ridge by mules, the beasts of burden quickly led away once the machineries were in place. From their vantage point, engineers and their journeymen assessed distance and trajectory, making calculations on stone tablets with nubs of chalk.

Hegbrak was set upon an isolated hillock nearby, the stout wheels of his Anvil of Doom sinking a few inches into the soft earth, the Anvil Guard stood silently in front of him. The master runesmith swung his hammer to work the kinks from his shoulder, before tracing his fingers across the runes on the anvil to sense its power.

Just below the lip of the shallow ridge were a throng of quarrellers, smoking pipes and loading their crossbows. Some looked askance at the elf archers waiting nearby, standing in immaculately straight lines, every warrior a mirror image of the elf next to him, their longbows resting against their shoulders with an easy grace.

A sea of armour spread out in front of the bows, an impenetrable shield wall of hearth guard and dwarf clan warriors with standards held high. Rising above them all was the grand banner of Karak Ungor, and Haggar gripped it tightly as he muttered oaths to Grungni and Valaya.

Morek, fifty or more warriors down from the banner bearer, made his pledges too, for a good battle and a solid victory. His mind was conflicted though as he regarded the elf spears amongst their ranks. Led by the hunter, Korhvale, he hoped they would be able to hold the line.

A greater worry was the cavalry, far off to the northern flank, obscured by the glamour of the rising sun reflecting off their armour. Morek couldn't see their commander, the raven-haired Lethralmir, but knew he was there and felt his wrath deepen. He would use it, the dwarf decided, use it against the enemy. The hearth guard captain hefted his axe and awaited the call to advance.

BAGRIK SAT UPON his throne, several hundred feet from the battle-line on the highest point of the slope. Together with Ithalred, he watched the mustering with cold eyes. Dwarf king and elf prince were joined by their aides, diplomats and other observers, and shared an uneasy silence alongside one another. Each was protected by his own bodyguards and wearing their full panoply of war. Bagrik had a small cohort of hearth guard; Ithalred, despite being mounted, was surrounded by an array of heavily-armoured spearmen. Neither of them was to be involved in the battle. It was deemed too dangerous to risk them in an initial sortie when the enemy's strength was not yet gauged.

Ravens gathered in the sky over the battlefield.

Prince Ithalred scowled at them, muttering in elvish as he limned a ward in the air with his lithe fingers.

Bagrik sniffed at the ritual, dour-faced as the allied army moved into position, just as he had described in the war tent. If only all battles played out like those on the strategy table.

A GREAT CLAMOUR arose from the east as a vast and terrible horde came into view, observed at distance through Morek's telescope. Warriors decorated in blood, and clad in only furs and skins, hollered and raved. Men armed with blades fused into their bones, their faces bound in leather masks, and their skin studded with spikes, cavorted ahead of the main force. In their frenzy, the berserkers tugged at the chains that held them back, blood-flecked foam dripping off their chins from behind the masks they wore.

Snarling packs of feral dogs, their muscular flanks drenched in feverish sweat, strained at the leashes of their whelp masters on either side of the berserkers. One of the frenzied warriors strayed too close and was dragged down by a pack of hounds. His perverted screams were short-lived as the dogs rent him limb from limb in a grisly dark spray.

Hammered shields thrashed out a belligerent chorus as bondsmen and armoured huscarls tramped into view, laughing and roaring like madmen. The fierce din was eclipsed though by thunder as beasts swathed in thick, woollen fur and goaded by Norscans wielding long, barbed spears lumbered into view.

Morek had heard of the war mammoths of the icy north, but had never seen one, let alone fought it. He heard the slayers, given free rein to roam, roar with excitement at the sight of them. A death at the tusks or hooves of one of those beasts would be a worthy doom.

They are certainly ugly, Morek thought to himself as he regarded the mammoths taking up position opposite his flank through the dwarf's far-reaching lens, with their broad shaggy ears, long trailing snouts and beady eyes.

As he watched, Morek's attention was averted to the middle of the ragged Norscan battle-line, where a massive warlord astride another monster pushed his way forwards. He was a huge brute of a man, all brawn with sinew like rope. A black helmet almost encased his head, festooned with spikes, two curling horns surging from its temples. The beast he rode was a sabre-tusk, a muscular predator of the mountains. Morek had seen such a beast before. Feline, their bodies were an undulating mass of hard, slab-like muscles and their short coarse hair was grey-white to better blend in with the snowy peaks where they made their hunting ground.

Never had the dwarf seen somebody ride one.

Unlike the ravenous dogs, the sabre-tusk only eyed the nearby warriors that stood aside eagerly to let it pass. More remarkable still was its master had no lash around the creature's neck, no goad to cow it; the iron of his will alone ensured his dominance. Reaching the front of the horde he raised a mighty double-bladed axe, the haft of the weapon seemingly melded to his flesh, and roared a challenge. His army and the trumpeting of the mammoths echoed his cry. With the terrible sound reverberating around the mountains and across the plain the northmen came, and in their droves.

Horns blared down the dwarf and elf line as Bagrik, from his lofty vantage point, gave the order to advance.

The drums of the hearth guard beat loud and steady in response, a slow rhythm to guide the pace of the refused flank. The sound echoed inside Morek's helmet as the dwarfs began to move.

'Stay together, forward in good order,' Morek bellowed down the line, and heard the other captains echo him. 'We'll drive these dogs back to sea,' he promised, to a resounding cheer, his gaze on the closing Norscan hordes. Baying and howling, these depraved men were indeed the hellish beasts he had supposed them to be, and for a moment Morek's bravado held in his throat.

'Cold beer and soft rinns to any dwarf that stands with me,' he cried, finding his voice at last. More cheers erupted from the ranks. Only the longbeards grumbled, bemoaning falling standards and the bullishness of youth.

Still wet from the last vestiges of thawing winter, the wide plain shimmered in the morning sunlight as the elven cavalry began to canter, their shrilling war horns signalling the attack.

As the hearth guard and clan warrior cohorts made their slow trudge across the battlefield, Morek made out the dispersed groups of lightly-armoured horsemen ranging ahead of the deep wedges of elven knights and chariot squadrons. He was told that these were the horsemasters of Ellyrion, and there were no finer warriors in the saddle in the entire known world. To Morek, horses were for eating, or to draw heavy loads, not for riding. These elven ways of war were foreign to him. But he could not deny their efficacy as the Ellyrians loosed swathes of deadly arrows and launched darting feint attacks across the entire left flank of the Norscan horde, slowly drawing them out to break up their formation.

The heathens responded in kind, frustrated at their impotency to pin the skirmishers at close quarters, with slingers and javelin hurlers, but only a few of the elves were unhorsed. Behind them, Lethralmir and his knights were closing, with the chariots in support.

'Too fast, too fast,' Morek muttered beneath his breath as he recognised the eagerness of the elven knights to whet their blades with blood. The northmen still retained their coherency and the ranged barrage had yet to begin in earnest.

At that thought the skies suddenly darkened and the air was filled with the shriek of thousands of arrows and quarrels soaring overhead. The heavy *twang* and *thunk* of the dwarf war machines added a deeper, more resonant, chorus to the cacophony of death and for a few moments the sun was eclipsed by a storm of wood, iron and stone.

'Ha!' Morek punched the air in triumph as the deadly rain withered the distant Norscan ranks. Tightly packed groups of bondsmen were skewered where they stood, feathered shafts protruding from their bodies like spines. Armoured huscarls writhed in agony as they were pinioned in twos and threes by the immense iron-tipped bolts of ballista, or screamed in despair as the rocks of the stone throwers crushed them. The carnage was relentless, but in truth it was barely a scratch. The

Norscans continued to advance, in spite of the certain death that faced them, closing ranks and stepping over the dead and dying as their mighty warlord bellowed his rage.

Morek heard the familiar clarion of elven horns and his gaze moved northward again, to the elven knights riding up the flank.

The Ellyrian horse had withdrawn to allow the elven lancehead to attack. Dragon armour blazed red and hot as the knights charged, war horns screaming, and smashed into a thick square of bondsmen with all the force of a thunderclap. Northmen were crushed beneath flailing hooves, spitted on lances or cut down by swords as the elven mounted elite pressed their irresistible assault. None could get close, the elves' sheer speed and their shining ithilmar plate making them all but invincible.

Desperate to stem the slaughter, the cowardly already fleeing in their droves from the elves' fury, the Norscans unleashed their chained berserkers. Heedless of danger, seemingly impervious to pain, the masked warriors barrelled into the knights, blades hewing. Many were trampled, others cleaved amidst fountaining arcs of blood, but the sheer abandon with which the berserkers threw themselves upon their foes gouged a gory cleft of dead and wounded in the elven ranks, as knights were dragged off their horses, or had their steeds cut from under them by Norscan blades.

Morek observed the deadly skirmish with a small measure of grim satisfaction now that the elves weren't getting it all their own way.

Serves 'em right for going off half-cocked, he thought but was then forced to marvel as the knights marshalled their forces, one wedge breaking off from another to form a second wave with the newly arrived chariots. Together, they smashed into the rampant berserkers who were mown down by the chariots or scythed in two by their bladed wheels. Morek nodded his grudging respect at their prowess as the elves slaughtered the Norscans and reformed their lancehead to converge upon the remnants of the bondsmen.

With the dragon knights' small victory, Morek felt impatient for battle, swinging his axe as the Norscans closed.

'Come on,' he roared, the dwarf warriors echoing his belligerence.

All the way up the line the dwarfs marched, their elf allies small islands of silver in a sea of unyielding bronze and iron, whilst overhead the sky darkened again...

FROM ATOP THE slope, Bagrik watched the second ranged volley fill the air like a massive swarm of hard-nosed insects as it bore down on the advancing Norscan flank. Mere feet from reaping another deadly toll of skewered men, the missile storm struck an immense wave of green iridescent fire that surged violently from the very earth. Arrows burned to cinders and quarrels melted and died in the intense conflagration. Stones flung from the mangonels soared like scorched green meteorites through the wall of flame, cracking and shattering to dust as they hit raised Norscan shields.

'Sorcery,' spat Bagrik, as if the word left a bitter taste in his mouth.

The dwarf king saw Hegbrak come forward off the hillock, the runesmith's power grinding the wheels around and taking him down the slope. He heard the uttered rune rites captured upon Hegbrak's tongue as the runesmith's body was enveloped with the magic bound to the anvil. His hair and beard stood on end, as trickles of lightning coursed through it. A nimbus of raw energy, burning with azure brilliance, built around Hegbrak's sturdy frame. The runesmith, chanting all the while, focussed the power, channelling it into his hammer and holding it there for a moment before he cried out and struck the anvil.

Hegbrak's voice boomed like thunder, echoing across the battlefield as an arcing bolt of lightning was unleashed. It surged from the Anvil of Doom, crackling ferociously before it smashed into the oncoming horde that had been spared the arrow storm. Norscan bodies were flung into the air by the sheer destructive force of the blast, and a great smear of scorched earth and broken men was left in the wake of the terrible lightning.

Blinking back the afterflare, Bagrik searched the rampaging throng of warriors for the Norscan shaman. But before he could find him, a bestial cry rang out from the northern flank where the elven knights were fighting.

The bondsmen had crumbled against their attack, and fled all too easily before the rampant elves. The scattering Norscans revealed a bulky mass shawled with a crude tarp of stitched leather that had been previously obscured by the now fleeing warriors. Ropes tethering the mass were released and a gargantuan war mammoth reared up in front of the elves, trumpeting its fury.

Locked onto their inexorable course, the elven knights had no room to turn. Some tried to arrest their charge but were pushed forward by the warriors behind them or unhorsed in the carnage and trampled. Others rode harder with fatalistic abandon, their lances goring the flanks and chest of the mammoth. Colliding with its unyielding forelegs was like hitting rock, and the elves unable to twist aside crumpled against it, their dragon armour useless against such an immoveable force.

The mammoth howled in pain, swinging its tusks in a rage, stomping madly with its hooves. Further screams rent the air as chariots smashed like kindling against the beast or were upturned by its flailing tusks and snout. Knights, unhorsed in the suicidal charge, were crushed to paste, the gore of their bodies dripping from the mammoth's bloodied feet as they rose and fell.

Belatedly, a horn bearer tried to restore some order but the beast was running amok, the stabbing knights failing to even slow it, the denseness of the mammoth's furry hide repelling all but the most ardent of blows.

As they swarmed like confused insects around the creature, smashing into one another or being carried off by their terrified steeds, the bondsmen returned. The Norscans had regrouped and thundered into those knights and chariots that still retained some sense of coherency in the gruesome melee.

'GRUNGNI'S OATH...' MOREK breathed as he watched the slaughter from afar with detached horror. The anguished cries of the elves further down the line arrested his attention, tormented by the sight of their kinsmen being slain. Morek was more concerned with the fact that their northern flank was collapsing. Only the Ellyrian horsemen were kept in reserve, and their feeble efforts would not break the deadly grind in which the knights were mired. Even as they rallied to loose another flight of arrows, the Norscans unleashed more berserkers, who chased the Ellyrians down even as they were pummelled by slings and javelins.

Morek felt a tremor jolt him as it rippled down the line.

The elves were moving. Fast.

'Hold!' cried the hearth guard captain, 'Hold!' he implored them, but the dwarf's voice was lost in the madness.

Black, like sackcloth, volley after volley from the archers, quarrellers and machineries blanketed the sky. The Norscans were almost upon them now. Soon they would be too close to the allied battle-lines to risk a further barrage. Green fire flared intermittently, as the unseen shaman wrought his magicks, searing arrows to dust and fracturing stone. Hegbrak advanced in the face of it, keeping pace with Morek's slowly marching hearth guard. Lightning arcs crackled from the anvil with every strike of the runemaster's hammer. His face was set in a grimace of concentration, sweat lathering his beard as he shouted the rune rites with fury.

Still the elves moved forward, faster and faster, the spearmen eager to close on the foe so they could vanquish it and go to the aid of the beleaguered knights. Still Morek held the line, bellowing at his charges to keep pace and stay together. Haggar's voice added to that of the hearth guard captain, and the other dwarf leaders followed their example.

'Keep formation,' Morek cried, again and again, watching the approaching Norscan hordes, knowing that the time was nearing when they'd clash. He ducked, as the stone throwers flung a low barrage. Their deadly shadow had made them seem closer than they actually were and he reddened at his foolishness. Arrows and bolts followed swiftly and the eldritch flames of the Norscan shaman rose again to immolate them. Only this time a tapering smoke exuded in their wake, growing and coiling into a thick roiling mist. Clinging to the ground, the mist surged across the plain at a frightening pace, easily faster than the Norscans, and engulfed the foremost elves.

Strange shapes coalesced in that mist as it billowed into a rising fog. Morek's dwarf eyes discerned the lithe bodies of elf females, writhing within the bilious soup. The elf spearmen, ensnared by the tendrils of smoke, were seemingly beguiled. They cried out names in elvish – Morek could only assume they wailed for their loved ones – and more came forward, all of them dropping their weapons to the ground.

As the mist slowly dispersed, the dwarf saw the spearmen held in the embrace of the ethereal maidens of the mist, their expressions soporific as they became utterly enamoured.

'Valaya preserve us,' he gasped in awe and terror.

THE LINE WAS breaking. Bagrik could see it as plain as the bulbous nose on his face. Impassioned by the plight of their kin, the elf spear regiments in the refused flank had increased their pace; some were even running in order to close with the foe more quickly. Elven captains, the hunter in particular, shouted orders of restraint – Bagrik saw his dwarfs do the same – but it was as if a sudden urge had possessed the elves and forced them into desperate action.

'Is this discipline?' the king barked to Ithalred, who stood stony silent, a nerve tremor in his jaw suggesting his anger.

Slowly, but inevitably like a fraying rope whose threads could no longer bear a weight, the formation fragmented. Closely banded regiments drifted apart almost unconsciously, like floating islands in the grip of a turbulent sea. Where before there was harmony and cohesion, now there was disparateness and disorder working its way insidiously into the refused flank. A staggered formation of elven spear regiments jutted from the wavering line of iron and bronze like silvered teeth slowly being extracted from a giant maw. As they were drawn into the sorcerous mist, the elves became further stretched until even the individual units devolved into a ragged and incoherent mass.

The dwarf line tried to hold, but that only exacerbated the problem, as the elves pulled away and holes started appearing in the allies' wall of armour.

'Follow them, Morek,' Bagrik urged beneath his breath, seeing the danger for what it was. 'Damn the elgi!' snarled the king, heedless of Ithalred's presence and thumping his fist on the side of the throne. 'Damn them!' he cried.

MOREK GRIMACED AS he felt the taint of dark magic gnawing at his resolve. One of the hearth guard alongside him drifted forward out of his rank as the dwarfs' slow march brought them closer to the fading mist and the elven sirens dwelling within. Morek cuffed the warrior across the side of the helmet to bring the hearth guard to his senses.

'Back in line,' snarled the captain. Then Morek held his eyes shut for a moment as he tried to banish whatever sorcery was trying to affect him. When he opened them again, the glamour had lifted and he saw the maidens for what they truly were – foul daemons; female, but with their bodies perverted.

Wrists ended in claws. Pallid, scaled flesh, supple, but gelid and moist, shimmered with aberrant lustre. Their heads had crests or long tendril-like hair that thrashed

and coiled in a serpentine fashion. Bent-backed legs
ended in talons and the daemonettes' mouths were
black like tar pits, filled with tiny spine-like teeth.

The acquiescent elves saw them too, but their horrified realisation was much too late as the daemons tore
them apart with tooth and claw, gorging on their necks
or eviscerating their bodies with perverted glee. Those
elves following in the wake of their slain kinsmen at
first recoiled, but at Korhvale's urging found their
courage and fell in to the attack.

Morek could hold his forces no longer. The Norscans
were almost upon them and the daemonettes were
slashing the elves to ribbons. A second wall of spears
charged in, the hunter at their head. Through the spray-
ing blood and the frantic flash of blades and battered
shields, Morek could just make out Korhvale as he
strode into the daemon ranks, his double-bladed axe
swinging like a pendulum.

The hearth guard captain growled in anger. Their carefully laid plans were tearing apart like parchment in the
wind. But just as he was about to give the order to
attack, the reverberating hoot of warhorns erupted to
the south coming from the direction of the extreme
flank of the army.

From amongst a clutter of scattered rocks, those eroded
by time and weather from the mountain, there came a
ragged band of Norscan horsemen. Draped in furs, their
sloped brows and muscled bodies daubed in tattoos and
festooned with bronze rings and spikes, the warriors
hollered and cried out as they rode their brutish, snort-
ing steeds bareback. Wielding hooked chains,
long-handled bronze axes and flint-tipped spears, the
Norscan cavalry were heading straight for the raised
slope and the allied missile battery with deadly intent.

Morek was caught in no-man's land – halfway between reaching the elves and halfway from the beleaguered missile troops on the top of the slope. Even as he watched the elf archers, those troops at the outermost edge, trying to reform and face their attackers, he knew with stomach-churning certainty that they would not be able to redress their ranks in time. Without the bulwark of the refused flank to protect them, the archers were easy meat. A lightly armoured formation like that, caught to its flank and unable to bring its bows to bear would crumple against a determined cavalry charge, even one as ragged and undisciplined as the Norscans.

Morek had thought the mountains impenetrable. Yet somehow the northmen had found a passage through it and used that knowledge to outflank them. It was galling to think that these debased heathens had outmanoeuvred them. The allies would pay for their hubris with blood.

Yelling their feral war cries, the Norscans crashed into the unprepared elven archers. A paltry few were struck from their beasts by a futile scattering of arrows before the slaughter began. Irresistible, the Norscans ground through the elves like a plough through wheat, cutting off heads and flinging spears and axes with abandon. Bloodthirsty hounds, running with the Norscan horses and snapping at their hooves, fell upon the wounded eagerly, their wild eyes flashing as their maws became stained with gore.

Unable to weather the terrible attack, their ranks in disarray, the elves fled for their lives and the slow erosion of the missile battery began.

In that fleeting moment that heralded the arrival of the Norscan cavalry and the subsequent butchery of the elf archers, Morek imagined the entire back line crumbling like paper before a flame: quarrellers slain, war machines destroyed, the rear echelons of the entire allied army suddenly imperilled. The dwarf looked to Haggar but even in the brief lull of raging battle, he was too far away to be called. Morek turned to his sergeant.

'Narvag, take half the hearth guard and march them back to our lines,' he growled, even as the dwarfs were starting their advance towards the stricken elves battling the daemon horde.

'Captain?' Sergeant Narvag asked in obvious bemusement.

'Look to the rear!' Morek snapped, turning Narvag's head forcefully so he could see the Norscan horse and their continuing rampage, the dwarf quarrellers now bearing the brunt of their murderous attention.

'At once, my lord,' he responded quickly, ordering the horn blower to indicate the break in formation whilst shouting further instruction to the regiments now suddenly under his command.

Two cohorts, fifty strong each, separated from the dwarf throng and started their resolute march back to their lines and the now bloodied rise.

Morek's unyielding line of bronze and iron was weakened but there was nothing he could do. Drums pounding, horns blaring battle orders, the dwarf formation thinned to fill the gaps left by their departed brethren and Morek, with fire in his heart, pressed onward.

So close to the foe now, the black, soulless eyes of the daemonettes glistening wetly, the lesser northmen bearing down in their wake like wild dogs, there was but one thing for the hearth guard captain left to do.

'Khazuk!' Morek bellowed, ordering his warriors to charge.

The dwarfs tromped rather than ran, their heavy suits of iron and gromril armour clanking noisily. With the gathered momentum of the rear ranks, Morek's hearth guard fell upon the daemonettes with all the fury of Grimnir, even as the other dwarfs arrived in line alongside them, preparing to meet the onrushing Norscans.

Grunting, Morek took a blow on his shield, the claw of the daemonette nearly slicing right through it.

Valaya, they are fast… he thought as he was battered back. But the dwarf was not to be denied and clove the daemon in two, the runes on his axe flaring bright as they tasted its unnatural flesh. Black ichor drizzled from the wound like rotting syrup before the creature sloughed away and dissipated into the ether. A second daemon came at the hearth guard captain and he was nearly undone but for an armoured dwarf getting in its way. The daemonette eluded the warrior's clumsy strikes, its body undulating like a snake, before beheading the dwarf with a savage snip of its claws.

The dwarf's sacrifice was all that Morek needed. Still revelling in the kill, licking the blood lasciviously from its claws, Morek cut the creature in two, its waist spilling away from its lower body as it collapsed into a pool of ichorous sludge. With each daemonette slain, a puff of soporific musk exploded into the air, dulling the senses and slowing the body. The dwarfs held their breath against it and pressed on. The elves, too, had now reformed their ranks and were thrusting with their spears to deadly effect, impaling the screeching daemonettes before cutting off their heads.

The elves were swift and skilled, though the daemonettes matched them for pace and dexterity.

Where the dwarfs relied on their resilience to bring them through the battle, the spearmen attacked in a silver blur, darting left and right, parrying thrusting, fighting together as one perfect engine of war. The daemons, though deadly, were few in number. Together the elves and dwarfs slew every wretched one of them in a few frantic minutes, but the cost was high. Dwarf and elf dead littered the ground. Sweating, some warriors still shaken from their efforts, the allies closed ranks. They barely had enough time to catch a breath before the Norscans charged them, axes flailing.

'Lock shields!' Morek cried, above the rumble of the battle.

A thousand dwarfs ramming their shields together rose in a metallic clatter. A similar cry echoed from the elven quarter, and they lowered their spears, forming a deadly forest of sharpened silver death.

Like a foul wave of sweat, brawn and brute savagery, the northmen smashed against the dwarf shield wall or rushed the elven spears. At first it was a massacre as the northmen broke against a well-drilled line of bronze and iron or became impaled on silver spear tips, but their sheer masses quickly told as the front ranks of the allies were torn into, screaming elves and dwarfs brought down by crude axes or dragged out of their protective formations and butchered.

A burst of arterial spray resonated in Morek's ears as it struck his helmet, painting the faceplate red. He finished the bearded Norscan with a blow to the chest, ripping out his axe afterwards in a shower of bloody flesh chunks. A second came at him; a powerful hammer blow to the dwarf's pauldron sending spikes of hot pain all the way up his arm. Morek grit his teeth and smothered it, punching the northman in the mouth with an armoured gauntlet, shattering his jaw. Jabbing his axe blade in the warrior's stomach Morek despatched him, before cutting the arm off a third and burying his weapon in the fallen Norscan's head. The agonised scream was loud but brief. The battle whirled around him, a blur of red-ruin and metal-edged death. A dwarf to Morek's left fell, a spear lodged through the eyehole of his helmet. Another hearth guard from the rank behind filled in the gap. Another dwarf nearby was slain, his fate unknown to Morek. The rear rankers came forward again. And slowly, so slowly, the line narrowed.

'Uzkul a umgal!' cried Morek, rending and slaying as his muscles burned with effort.

Death to men! The words echoed in his mind. Another foe looking jealously upon the riches of the Karaz Ankor, another enemy to wear away at his race, another that possessed all the savage barbarity of the greenskins, but who seemed united in their purpose of calculated destruction.

The stink of blood was filling Morek's nostrils. Hot fluid sloshed in his heavy boots. The dwarf was not certain if it were his or that of the foe. The clamour of battle had become an ever-present din, gnawing at his resolve all the while it persisted. Warriors fell. Swords and axes flashed. Carnage churned the once fertile fields of the plains, weighing down the flowing grasses and staining them crimson.

For all the careful planning, for the subtle tactics argued and refined, it had become little more than a melee. Survival was all that drove Morek now, that and the desire to reap as many dead as his axe could take. Ahead, in the growing darkness of a building storm, he thought he saw the flash of lightning from Hegbrak's anvil. It was followed by the roar of some beast that haunted the suddenly benighted field – the sabre-tusk baying in fury at the will of its terrible master.

In the madness as he carved and cut and hewed, Morek thought he discerned the aged standard of the longbeards thrust alongside the banners of the rune-smith, together the venerable dwarfs having forged their bloody way through the Norscan ranks in order to bring the chieftain and his elite warriors into battle.

The runesmith's silhouette appeared in the flare of light, tearing back the layers of darkness that now suf-focated the field only briefly. Another figure was outlined in the azure flash, one far larger than Hegbrak and astride a beast that seemed dredged from the depths of the world. Two great warriors, dwarf rune-smith and Norscan warlord clashed and the ground shook with the fury of their thunder. As soon as it had come, the lightning flare died away and Morek could no longer see the epic confrontation.

Closer at hand was the fluttering standard of Karak Ungor, the dragon rampant still upraised proudly and defiantly by Haggar as he fought with fury alongside his warriors further down the steadily thinning line.

Keep it aloft, lad, thought Morek during a brief lull in the fighting. Keep it where we can see it.

As the relentless minutes ground on, even the stoic endurance of the dwarfs was being sorely tested.

Bagrik watched impotently from the ridge as his war-riors, both kith and kin, were slain. As he surveyed the faltering battle-line and the swirling melee into which the fight had devolved, his gaze went immediately to the raised slope and the plight of the war machines and quarrellers deployed there. But a few hundred feet away from his position, there was a deadly struggle being fought to reclaim it from the Norscan riders butchering there at will. The toll exacted in blood on that small hill had been heavy indeed.

By the time the cohorts of hearth guard had arrived, most of the elf archers were dead or had fled the field. Even now, they were being marshalled back by reserve forces and rallied for a second push. Ithalred's face had been grave as he'd seen them run. Of the two hundred elves, shimmering brilliant in silver and white at the outset of battle, a mere handful of bloodied souls, with robes dirt-encrusted and armour tarnished, remained.

Several of the war engines were damaged, though mercifully the Norscans lacked the skill or ingenuity to destroy them. But many crews were slain, journeymen and engineers that could not be easily replaced. A regiment of clan quarrellers lay cold on the field, having fought to the last, their defiance a bitter prelude to their inevitable demise.

With a roar of anger, Bagrik had ordered his body-guard to enter the fray with the diverted hearth guard. Thus combined, the dwarfs had now almost cleared the ridge, saving what quarrellers and machinery crews still lived. Those few Norscan horsemen not dead or having fled into the rocks, were slowly being corralled and put to the axe.

Bagrik maintained his angry demeanour.

It was but a pyrrhic victory on what was fast becoming a field of withering defeat.

In the centre of the plains, now blotted from view by the blood and bodies, the boiling mass of the battle was reaching its height. Lines of bronze and iron were dwindling as the ranks thinned rapidly. Dwarfs and elves lay head to foot in thickening pools of their own blood, face down in dirt: dead, dying and dismembered in the swelling quagmire of viscera.

For a fleeting moment, Bagrik felt his heart emboldened to see such defiance in the face of an implacable foe. Even the elves, he conceded, were unflinching in the face of death.

Even the bastard Lethralmir had distinguished himself, slaying the mammoth with his arcane elven blade and sending the ragged beast thundering to the ground. Its death throes had shaken the horde, but such numbers could not be denied and even now they pressed the elven knights hard, trying to surround them as they fell back. The chariots were utterly destroyed, now so much broken white timber, shattered wheels and twisted elven bodies. Norscan hounds, let slip by their whelpmasters, gorged themselves on the flesh of their slain and stricken steeds greedily.

Though their torn and bloodied banner was still aloft, the pride of Ulthuan was slowly dying in the desperate and protracted battle.

'We cannot win this fight,' said Ithalred through clenched teeth, as if the admission pained him greatly. 'There is no honour to be gained on these killing fields.'

Another agonising minute was allowed to lapse before Bagrik spoke again. His eyes were hard and cold as he observed the battle. For a fleeting second he thought of Nagrim and his stone heart softened.

'I know...' he whispered.

With clenched fists, the dwarf king turned to one of his military aides alongside him. Even as he had the other dwarf under his inscrutable gaze, he still hesitated.

'Sound the retreat,' he snarled at last. 'Withdraw all troops!'

CHAPTER FOURTEEN
Bloodied and Bowed

RUGNIR STIRRED OUT of unconsciousness. The pounding in his head had lessened to a dull throb and the hurt in his chest was easing. As he woke, reality washed over him like ice water. He tried to rise but found he was still too weak. After several painful efforts, Rugnir relented and stayed down. He was still in the cave. It was dark inside, perhaps it was night. The smell of Craggen's broth was heavy on the dank breeze. The old dwarf hermit was nowhere to be seen, though. Rugnir assumed he must be hunting. Rumbling stomach complaining loudly, he hoped that Craggen would bring back something tasty to fill it.

Grungni, I need a drink, Rugnir thought at the aching in his back, the dwarf taking little comfort from the worn furs beneath him. Drifting back into a fitful sleep, he was haunted by the dead faces of old friends.

* * *

'MAY VALAYA GUIDE you to the Gate,' Morek uttered softly. Closing the dying hearth guard's eyes, he snapped the dwarf's neck.

Mercy was all he could offer the warrior. His wounds were mortal. Though hardy enough to recover from most injuries, there were some that even dwarfs could not live through.

The withdrawal from the field had been a bitter blow. The armoured line had retreated by degrees, those warriors in more advanced positions helping isolated units like the elven knights break free of the enemy. It had been ordered but messy. At first the Norscans had pressed the advantage but with the upper slope cleared of the foe and the quarrellers and war machines rescued, the deadly missile volleys began again in earnest. Withering fire dampened much of the northmen's bloodthirsty ambition. Bands of slayers, still eager to find an honourable doom amidst the carnage, swept forward in a red-orange wave, axes flashing. Two more mammoths fell to their sharpened blades, now gore-slicked and notched.

In the end, the Norscans too had been dealt a blow of sorts, their dead and dying numbering in the thousands. Though Morek had not seen the warlord again, he'd heard the roar of his commands then echoed by crude Norscan warhorns. Both armies, bloodied and bowed, had quit the field leaving it to the carrion, the mewling wounded and the ghosts of the slain.

The decisive blow that had meant to crush the spine of the northmen and avenge the slaying of Nagrim had finished a bitter and blood-soaked draw. In truth, it was no better than a defeat.

Morek tried not to dwell on it and give in to his anger. He wasn't wearing his helmet, and he wiped a lather of sweat off his brow with the back of his hand. Thunder rumbled overhead in the aftermath of the battle, but it was a dry storm that heated the air and made it thick and stifling. Certainly it did nothing to assist him in the grave task ahead.

Across the bloodied field of churned earth and broken blades Morek and a small group of rangers, together with the Valakryn, moved swiftly and quietly in the doom-drenched night. Dispersed widely, but always in eyeshot of each other, they silenced the enemy wounded or dispensed mercy to those dwarfs and elves that would not recover from their injuries. The few that might survive were taken away by stretcher bearers to the gore-splattered and bone-weary chirurgeons that awaited them in the makeshift infirmary tents.

Besides the throaty thunder, the night was quiet but punctuated horribly by the screams of the injured and the fatalistic moans of the dying. Trekking through the mud and destruction, Morek saw the hafts of weapons jutting from the ground like broken teeth. He heard the guttural curse of a stricken northman silenced by the wet thud of an axe. Morek turned to regard the severe countenance of one of the Valakryn. The robes of the warrior priestess were flecked with blood as she went about her business stoically. Elsewhere, crews of stretcher bearers were ferrying the wounded away. They trailed solemnly from the field, the devotees of Valaya holding onto the grasping hands of the injured reassuringly or whispering benedictions in the name of the goddess.

Mercifully, the northmen had not returned. Though the rangers ensured that if any did they would be heralded and then dealt with swiftly. The barbarian hordes had no time or compassion for the dying. To Morek it

seemed a brutal culture. The dwarfs dragged the
Norscan corpses together, piling them up so that they
could be burned and some of their taint scoured from
the earth. In part it was to ward off disease, but it was
also because they'd retake the plains come the morrow
and no one amongst the allies desired to march across
the foetid carcasses of the slain.

As his gaze lingered briefly on one of the smoulder-
ing pyres, it struck the hearth guard captain that this
army was a mere taste of their numbers. The dwarf
shuddered to imagine the actual scale of the foe that
they were facing.

The 'mercy parties' were well advanced into the battlefield now, the fires of the Norscan encampment not
so distant or abstract anymore.

Tromping through the carnage, Morek saw a ranger
approach him swiftly with his crossbow low-slung and
ready.

'Ragenfel,' said Morek as the ranger reached him.

'Captain,' the ranger's face was ashen, his reply
breathless, 'we've found him.'

Morek shared a glance with one of the nearby
Valakryn, Hetga their matriarch. Her face was as grave as
he imagined his own to be.

'Take me there, lad,' he rasped, gripping the haft of his
rune axe for support.

Hegbrak lay across his Anvil of Doom, his back
clearly broken. Shards of gromril plates lay scattered
around him, stained dark with the runesmith's blood.
His once proud beard was matted with gore and a deep
and bloody gouge ran all the way up his open chest and
scarred his noble face. Hegbrak's eyes were wide, his
expression frozen in a rictus of agonised defiance. The
bodies of his Anvil Guard and several of the longbeards

lay strewn around him in various states of dismemberment.

'*Dreng tromm…*' the Valakryn whispered, and went immediately to her knees and wept for Hegbrak's passing, and the senseless deaths surrounding him.

Morek could see the horror in the ranger's eyes too. His wide-eyed expression suggested disbelief and the ending of something deep in his heart.

To many in the hold, much like Agrin his former master, Hegbrak had seemed immortal. Not so anymore.

'Ragenfel,' said Morek softly.

The ranger just kept staring.

'Ragenfel,' Morek repeated more forcefully, and the dwarf snapped out of it and turned to face his captain. 'Get the stretcher bearers, lad,' he added quietly. Ragenfel nodded curtly and went off to do as bidden.

When Morek turned back to the runesmith, lying broken at his feet, a tear ran down his dirty face. He wiped it away with his gauntlet. Already tired from the battle, the hearth guard captain felt his weariness deepen. Though this was not bodily, no; this was a weakening of the soul.

The Anvil of Doom was still hot. Morek could feel it as he extended a hand in the runic artefact's direction. The heat did not sear Hegbrak. It had actually kept the other Norscans at bay who might have attempted to mutilate him further. A veritable pyre of the heathens lay stacked around the runesmith and his slain guardians. It gave Morek scant comfort to learn that they had gone down fighting and exacted a heavy toll upon the enemy. The warlord, though, was not amongst them. Morek imagined the brute crowing at his victory, and felt a sudden rush for vengeance seize him. He and Hegbrak had grown up together as beardlings. Together with Kraggin Goldmaster, the three dwarfs had been firm friends since they'd each first held an axe. Now all of that was gone, condemned to bitter remembrance.

The arrival of the stretcher bearers interrupted Morek's reverie.

'Be careful, the anvil is still hot,' Morek warned the trio of Valakryn that came forward to lift Hegbrak onto the stretcher and carry him from the field.

'It burns with the anger of its master's passing,' said one of the priestesses as she stooped down, together with her sisters, to raise Hegbrak up. They bore him reverently. With a pang of painful remembrance, Morek suddenly thought of Nagrim and the slain heir of Ungor's arrival in the hall of his father.

So many dead… all in the name of retribution.

Morek pledged a thousand more until the debt of blood was fulfilled and the grudge against the northmen satisfied. He knew it would never be so, and that fact gave the dwarf captain grim comfort.

'Ragenfel,' Morek intoned. The ranger had returned with the Valakryn stretcher bearers. 'Round up six stout mules and bind the anvil with rope. I want it recovered from the field,' Morek ordered, waiting for the ranger to nod before following the departing Valakryn, Hegbrak carried between them.

MOREK BARGED INTO the command tent unannounced, stalking past the line of captains awaiting an audience with the king and then standing before Bagrik, his face set like stone.

'Hegbrak Thunderhand is dead,' he said, 'slain by the Norscan chief. His Anvil Guard, too.'

Bagrik paused in the scratching of his quill, the assembled thanes and clan leaders naming the dead so that their fates could be recorded in the book of grudges, and one day avenged. The list before Bagrik went to several pages, each name almost carved into the parchment with the vehemence of a vengeful king writing in his own blood.

Stern of face, the iron he placed there masking his deep lament, Bagrik added Hegbrak's name to the hundreds of others. A great many of the dead could not be accounted for. The slayers, cut down to a dwarf, were left unnamed. None in the war party knew them. Like so many of their ill-fated kind, the slayers were loners and had simply arrived unbidden as if Grimnir himself had growled in their ear that war was afoot. Their demise mattered not, it was a form of victory to the dwarfs' minds and in any case there were already more joining the cult, those who had fled the field to return in ignominy or had failed in their battle oaths. Beyond the king's tent, small groups of dwarfs were shaving their heads and dying their beards red. Stripping out of their armour and daubing their bodies with tattoos, they took up axes and swore their death oaths before the surviving priests of Grimnir.

Others, those besides the dead and the dying, licked their wounds and took stock of their losses. By all accounts it was a large tally, and a fell mood had descended upon Broken Anvil Hill as a result.

The elves, too, had lost a great many warriors. An entire cohort of chariots was no more. Morek had later learned that they had hailed from a realm known as Tiranoc, one of those that had suffered grievously during the elven war of strife. The land had been lost, engulfed by a great sundering. It struck the dwarf that these ill-fated chariot riders had been put asunder in much the same way. It was a harsh echo of a painful reality.

Lethralmir, much to Morek's bitter chagrin, had survived. Precious few of his silver knights and dragon armoured nobles joined him though, along with countless archers and spearmen. The elves had their own warriors prowling the battlefield, searching for the wounded, too. Their faces were cold and haunted, their dark hair fluttering in the languid breeze as they'd moved soundless and deadly amongst the fallen. The lines of their stretcher bearers had been just as long as those of the dwarfs, maybe even longer.

'Let it be known,' thundered King Bagrik once he'd finished scribing Hegbrak's name, 'that on this day was Hegbrak Thunderhand, Runemaster of Karak Ungor, slain by north-men. Ten thousand of their dead and the head of their chieftain shall atone for his passing,' he said, scowling, adding solemnly, 'Hegbrak will be remembered.'

The dwarf captains repeated their king's words with heads bowed, Morek amongst them. Every slain dwarf, regardless of his station was afforded the same reverence. All were to be honoured by their kin.

It would be a long night. Long and dark.

THERE WAS A palpable air of tension and barely suppressed anger about Bagrik's command tent early the next morning.

The king had wasted no time, once the Giving of Names was done and all the dead had been accounted for, in gathering together his finest captains and also summoning those of the elves.

It was to be a much smaller assembly than that which had met previously. For the dwarfs, only Morek and Haggar were present. As for the elves, Ithalred had preferred just Korhvale and Lethralmir, the latter captain present in spite of his injuries – the gash upon his forehead spoiling his aesthetically good looks.

'Abject failure,' growled the king to the warriors of both races. 'It is the only way I can think of to describe our ignominious defeat.' The words came through clenched teeth. There were no maps, no coins and no councils this time; just warriors, elves and dwarfs both.

'Had the elgi restrained themselves and not gone off like grobi chasing swine, the outcome may have been different,' said Morek, levelling his gaze at Lethralmir in particular. 'We had a plan, my king–'

'Yes, Morek,' snapped the king, before the hearth guard captain could finish, 'and it was found wanting in the face of the enemy. No single warrior can be made to shoulder the blame here,' he added, now regarding Prince Ithalred closely as he spoke. 'We were all culpable... All of us!' Bagrik breathed deep, the sound wheezing through his nostrils as he fought to stay calm. He then shifted in his seat at the discomfort in his leg.

'The bickering must end,' he told them, as his gaze drifted away to a different place, one where he'd rather not be. 'Nagrim's revenge demands it,' he rasped darkly.

'This horde is bent towards one aim, and one aim alone.' It was Ithalred who spoke, his deep and sonorous voice commanding attention. 'To destroy us,' he added simply. 'I saw it outside the borders of Tor Eorfith when we first fought these curs and I see it again now. There is a malign will guiding these beasts, and I do not speak of the heathen warlord, either.'

'The shaman...' said Bagrik. 'It is him of whom you speak.'

Ithalred met his gaze and perhaps for the first time since they'd met in the Great Hall of Karak Ungor, there was mutual understanding.

'Yes, but I do not think that the shaman is a "he",' said Ithalred, his face as stern as iron. 'I do not think *he* is mortal at all.'

'A *daemon?*' hissed Morek, scowling at the use of the word.

Ithalred looked at the hearth guard captain.

'Exactly that,' said the elf, 'Allied to Slaanesh, the lord of pleasures. My kin are familiar with its caress. The goddess Atharti bears much in common with it. We can all sense it. Those *creatures* that came from the mist are its hand maidens,' he added darkly, before returning to the king.

'I have been a fool, King Bagrik,' Ithalred admitted, 'encouraging the wilfulness of my commanders, even resenting your aid in the face of a common foe. It ends now,' Ithalred promised, a side glance at Lethralmir making it clear that this message was for him, too. 'The heathen northmen worship the Dark Gods of Chaos, but here one of their heralds walks abroad with them in human form. What's more he has chosen a champion, a vessel for their power. Make no mistake, we face anni-hilation. It was the same in the elder days when mighty Aenarion the Defender fought the daemon hosts of ruin and cast them back into the Realm of Chaos. You dwarfs, shut up in your mountain fastness, did not see it as we elves did.'

There was a ripple of annoyance in Bagrik and his captain's at Ithalred's last remark, but the elf prince ignored it and went on.

'It was only through *our* sacrifice that the world was kept safe. Is *still* kept safe,' he said, his voice impas-sioned. 'We can ill afford another defeat. I fear if we do, it will be our last.'

A snarl of displeasure had crept upon Bagrik's face after Ithalred had finished, and he spoke with his lip upcurled.

'Then we'll fight together this time. All of us!' His gaze surveyed the room. 'Daemon or no, we will crush these Norscans, we will crush them! So says Bagrik, King of Ungor! In Nagrim's name I make this pledge.'

'Then we will need a plan, my king,' said Haggar suddenly, the young thane clearly fired by Bagrik's rhetoric.

Ithalred smiled.

'Leave that to me,' he said.

'THEY ARE MOVING!'

The cry came from the dwarf rangers who had sat in silent vigil throughout the night and most of the early morning, watching the Norscan camp. The sounding of horns and rap of drums followed the announcement as all upon Broken Anvil Hill were made aware of it.

'Are you sure this is wise, my king?' Morek asked as he tightened the leather wrist strap of Bagrik's vambrace.

'Am I so old and infirm that I need the captain of my hearth guard to fight all of my battles for me?' the king replied.

Morek could find no response.

'Aye, it is wise,' said Bagrik, for him. 'Not so tight!' he added, wincing as Morek pulled hard on the king's gromril cuirass. 'Too much roast boar, eh lad?' he said with a half-hearted chuckle.

'Aye,' Morek agreed. Bagrik hadn't called him 'lad' since he was a beardling. The gesture was not lost on the hearth guard captain, who could not keep the sadness from his eyes, so he lowered them instead, pretending to check the king's weapons belt.

Bagrik had deliberately dismissed his armourers prior to battle, insisting that Morek be the one to help him don his ancestral plate and mail. It seemed fitting somehow, and Morek was only too glad to do his duty to the king.

'Then I will be by your side, my liege,' said the hearth guard captain, gruffly.

'You will not,' was Bagrik's curt reply. 'I need you out in the battlefield, driving our flank, not beardling-sitting an old longbeard like me.'

'But–'

'It is decided, Morek,' Bagrik told him, cutting the other dwarf off. The king clenched and unclenched his fists, rolled his shoulders as he got used to the weight and heft of his armour. Lastly, once his crown and helm were in place, Morek draped the boar pelt across Bagrik's shoulders, completing his panoply of war. The king clapped him on the arm when Morek was done, gripping it in his age-old fingers.

'You are my best warrior, Morek. You have served me well all these years, but I crave one last duty of you.'

'Please, my king, don't speak like this–' Morek began.

'One last duty,' Bagrik repeated, loud and insistent before his voice softened and the stone in his eyes that had been there since Nagrim's death lifted for a moment. 'Just one. Look after Brunvilda.'

Morek felt like his heart was clutched in an iron fist, so hard that he was unable to speak. Instead he nodded. The movement was barely discernable.

'Good,' said Bagrik. 'Now go and marshal my army and let us write this last bloody saga together.'

THE NORSCAN HORDE took to the field amidst jeering and yelled obscenities. The few prisoners they had captured, dead and alive, were paraded on their banners naked, their skins a patchwork of welts, cuts and bruises. The dwarfs had their beards shorn, the elves their hair shaven as all symbols of respect and nobility were cut away like chaff. The thump of the massive Norscan war drums beat like a raging heart as they strode across the plain in a mob.

Morek's suspicions as to their numbers had been proved correct, as the horde seemed even larger than it was before.

The warlord, on the back of his feral steed, rode between two enormous flanks of bearded and slope-browed warriors from a dozen or more tribes. Surrounded by his armoured huscarl retinue, the warlord paraded like a barbarian king amongst the brutish subjects of his court. Guttural warhorns heralded him as the sabre-tusk pawed hungrily across the plain. The surviving mammoths trumpeted in unison, stomping wildly with their massive hooves before they were goaded into obedience.

Despite its size, it was much the same host as they had faced before, though the riders who had outflanked them yesterday were moving with the main army now. Morek had sent parties of rangers out into the scattered rock debris on the extreme edges of the plain to lay traps and erect barricades. It seemed to have persuaded the flankers into joining their debased brethren, the Norscan warlord favouring a full frontal assault.

The allies had changed tactics too, though, and it was a different battle-line that greeted the Norscans this time. The dwarfs and elves had drawn their forces back, all the way to Broken Anvil Hill, a good two miles from where they had deployed previously. Here, the valley widened, and the mountains fell away as the lowland became hilly and scattered with gorse and pine.

During the night, the mercy parties had buried broken blades in the half mile of earth leading up to

Broken Anvil Hill and dug shallow pits festooned with
spikes to hinder the northmen's approach. Morek saw
one of the mammoths founder as its heavy footfall
broke through one of the pit tarps, concealed with a
light covering of earth, and fell, crushing several
screaming warriors beneath its shaggy bulk. In the end,
despite their efforts to raise it, they had killed the beast
and left its cooling carcass behind.

Morek smiled.

Already, the fragile order of the heathen army was
wearing down.

On the crest of Broken Anvil Hill, at the eastern-most
promontory, the archers, quarrellers and war machines
were arrayed. Just below, a ring of silver and bronze surrounded them as elf spearmen and dwarf clan warriors
and hearth guard stood shoulder-to-shoulder. There were
no cavalry this time, and none of the vainglorious eagerness to close with the foe. The face the mustering of dwarfs
and elves presented now was one of stoic resilience.

BAGRIK HELD THE apex of the half-ring of armour,
together with most of the hearth guard and the longbeards. Seated upon his throne, he was afforded an
excellent view of the battlefield. Haggar stood alongside
the king, next to the throne bearers, with the banner of
Ungor unfurled proudly, the fabric still stained black
with the previous day's warring.

Elf spearmen regiments were interspaced evenly with
those of the dwarfs, the proud warriors of Ulthuan facing the coming horde with unshakeable resolve. They
towered above their dwarf allies but together presented
a unified wall of shields and blades.

Casting his eye across the battle-line, Bagrik saw
Ithalred looking back at him far away on the left flank.

The dwarf king thought he saw the elf prince nod, so he returned the gesture. He was on foot, the hunter, Korhvale, at his lord's side amongst a thicket of upraised spears held by the elf warriors around them.

To the right flank there was Morek, the dwarf's armoured faceplate masking his expression. Bagrik knew it would be one of determination. Morek had never failed him. He led two hundred clan warriors, the hearth guard captain's presence amongst them designed to embolden them.

There atop their grassy hill, the crest of war machines and archers their tower, the locked shields below their walls and Bagrik himself the mighty gate, the allies stood in fortified unity.

'You will find the way is shut,' Bagrik muttered under his breath, as he willed the northmen to come. He would not have long to wait.

As IF POSSESSED, the Norscan horde charged across the last few hundred feet of open ground separating them from their foes with alarming speed. As the barbarians closed, a dwarf warhorn echoed across the field. It was quickly taken up by the clarion of further horns, and as one the dwarf regiments in the half-ring marched forward. Twenty feet ahead of the elves, the dwarfs jutted out like an armoured reef before a sheer metal-faced cliff.

Volleys from the war machines, quarrellers and archer remnants punished the edges of the loose Norscan formations, corralling them into long deep ranks. No shimmering fire burned down the arrows and bolts this time, the heathen forces were too close.

With shouted curses on their lips, the Norscans crashed against the dwarf bulwarks like pounding surf striking the rocks.

'Hold them!' cried Morek, ramming his shoulder behind his shield as the heathen men pushed. Somewhere above, resonating through his helmet, he heard a clamour of angry voices as the Norscans found themselves locked in a meatgrinder, and there were no better exponents of a battle of attrition than the sons of Grungni.

The Norscans hammered against them, but the dwarfs weathered the storm, paying for the held ground in blood and sweat. But hold them they did. Even with their rampaging mammoths and suicidal berserkers, the Norscans were pinned. Such an irresistible weight of pressing bodies could not be withstood for long, though, and soon a second cry split the air, this time from the shrilling horns of the elves.

With the enemy engaged to the front, the warriors of Ulthuan swept forward in a silver wave, filling the gaps left deliberately in the dwarf breakers, before crashing into the exposed flanks of the northmen.

Morek felt the weight lifted almost at once and was quick to lower his shield so he could cut down his foes with his rune axe. The hot, copper tang of blood filled his nostrils and he revelled in it. Severing heads, ignoring the battering against his armour as the northmen landed desperate blows, the captain of the hearth guard was like a whirlwind of death.

'Uzkul!' he roared furiously, 'Uzkul a umgal!'

THE BATTLE HAD slumped once more into a bitter grind, but now it was one of the allies' devising, fought on their terms. But despite the battering the Norscans were taking they showed no sign of breaking.

Bagrik winced as a green flash of sorcery erupted in the darkening sky, filling the air with a sulphurous stench. A counter spell seemed to ignite the breeze as Ithalred's mages on the crest of Broken Anvil Hill cast their own magicks. Scouring the battlefield, the king could see no sign of the shaman's whereabouts. Instead, his gaze rested upon another foe.

The Norscan warlord was carving his way through the dwarf and elf ranks with reckless ease, cleaved limbs flung from every swipe of his fell axe. While this chosen one of whatever daemon that favoured the horde lived, Bagrik knew the northmen would not falter. The warlord was only a few feet away and as their eyes locked across the sprawling carnage, Bagrik knew what he must now do.

Tightening the grip on his axe, he roared to his throne bearers.

'Forward! Bring my axe within reach of the heathen's neck!'

The hearth guard shield wall in front of the king broke up instantly, the dwarf warriors laying into the bondsmen and huscarls with brutal determination as they forged a bloody path for their king. Any that broke through were cut down by the throne bearers or crushed by the following longbeards.

'Stay with me, Haggar Anvilfist,' roared Bagrik to his banner bearer who stomped alongside him, cutting left and right through the swell of barbarians with his axe, the noble standard of Karak Ungor clutched firmly in his rune hand.

'Nagrim!' cried Haggar, 'Nagrim!' And the dwarfs around him shouted the dead prince's name.

Bagrik used it, allowed his memory to focus his anger in a burning sharp point at the end of his rune-encrusted axe.

'You and me, north-man!' the king snarled aloud, lowering the faceplate of his helmet and pointing his weapon at the onrushing warlord slaying a path towards him.

Seconds dragged into minutes but at last the two titans clashed, dwarf king versus heathen warlord, the sea of bodies parting around them as if at some unseen command.

One of Bagrik's throne bearers was torn down before it had really begun, the sabre-tusk biting off his startled head after smashing the dwarf down with its brawny body. Bagrik felt the throne wobble as one corner was suddenly left without support. A black blur raced across the eye-slits of his helmet and he parried the warlord's blow just in time.

Grungni's teeth, he is strong, thought Bagrik as the force of it rippled down his forearm, jarring his shoulder. A second blow *pranged* against his pauldron and he felt the blade bite his flesh. Blood started welling in Bagrik's armpit. Never had the king's armour of Karak Ungor been breached so easily. This blade the warlord wielded was like none Bagrik had ever seen. Black, but shiny like polished glass, its curvature seemed to follow his forearm, veins of darkness visible like adders writhing beneath his skin, the weapon nigh-on melded into his very flesh. It rose to a wicked curve, flawless and terrible as if death at that stygian blade would go on for eternity.

A violent shudder ran down the throne again as Bagrik fought the black spots at the edge of his vision. Another of his bearers was ripped apart by a claw-thrust of the Norscan's monster. Unable to bear the king's weight, the remaining warriors collapsed, and Bagrik was dumped unceremoniously to the ground. The Norscan warlord sought to pounce on the stricken dwarf king, have his beast rip out his leathery throat and end the fight, but Bagrik's throne bearers were on their feet swiftly and rushed forward to intercede. They were cut down in moments, their blood-gurgled screams short-lived and lost in the battle din.

Their sacrifice had not been in vain. Bagrik was back on his feet, though he favoured his good leg and used it to support his armoured weight.

'Not done yet, you ugly bastard,' he snarled, beckoning the warlord on with his outstretched finger. 'Come then, let us finish this…'

Roaring as its master urged it, the sabre-tusk lunged for Bagrik's throat, ragged meat strips hanging off its fangs from its kills. The dwarf king ducked and shifted his body at the last possible moment as he went down on his good knee. He carved his rune axe up the beast's stomach, opening it and spilling hot entrails as it leapt over him. Though buffeted to the ground, his head ringing inside his helmet, Bagrik had killed the sabre-tusk. The Norscan warlord was wallowing in its pooling viscera. Shrugging free of the beast's corpse, the northman emerged swathed in gore. If he had a face beneath that helmet of black iron, Bagrik fancied it might look displeased.

'Like I said,' the dwarf taunted, 'just you and me.'

The warlord roared in anger, the sound erupting from his skull-encasing warhelm tinny and strange.

Bagrik matched it with a challenge of his own, struggling to his feet just as the Norscan began to charge. The warlord's muscled gait spanned the distance between them quickly and he leapt into the air as he brought his black blade crashing against the dwarf king's upraised shield. Bagrik reeled from the sheer ferocity of the attack, staggered back as the Norscan followed through and used his shoulder like a battering ram.

Bagrik felt every ounce of the brute's bulk as he was spun like a weather vane struck by a fearsome gale. The dwarf almost fell, crying out in pain as he shifted too much weight onto his wounded leg. The white hot lance of agony brought him to his senses and he realised, readying himself to receive another charge, that his shield was broken. He shrugged the shattered pieces of wood and iron from his arm, and took his rune axe in a two-handed grip.

Bagrik felt his heart thundering in his head, resounding like a rock fall, and his breathing came in laboured gasps.

'For Nagrim…' he rasped, as he marshalled his failing strength.

The warlord came again, but this time Bagrik stepped aside, or rather almost fell, and hammered the spiked pommel of his rune axe into the meat of the Norscan's exposed leg. Without waiting, the dwarf wrenched the weapon free in a bloody spray and hammered a blow against the warlord's head that should have decapitated him. Instead, there was a cascade of sparks as dwarf-forged rune metal met Chaos black iron and the two combatants were flung apart in a backwash of power.

Smoke rose from Bagrik's body in tiny grey tendrils and his armour felt warm to the touch. But it was the dwarf king that was triumphant as he got to his feet and saw he'd chipped away a piece of the Norscan's helmet.

An eye, shot through with ugly pink and violet veins, the flesh around it white and smooth, stared malignly through the jagged hole in the warlord's helmet. At first Bagrik saw incomprehension there, even fear, but it was soon crushed by rage.

'Now we're even,' muttered Bagrik and spat a gobbet of blood against the inside of his faceplate, afraid that if he let down his weapon to lift it he might not be strong enough to wield his rune blade again. Even as the black spots tried to engulf his vision, he held his axe as steady as he could. He bit his lip hard, tasting blood, and the pain kept him going.

The Norscan made to rush at Bagrik, swinging the dark blade melded to his flesh around his head in a wicked arc, when the clarion of warhorns sounded. The duelling warriors faltered at the unexpected noise. The ground was shaking. Cries of panic came from the Norscan ranks, growing steadily louder and more urgent every second. A ripple of discord passed through the horde, palpable to all. The northmen had begun to flee. Fear rushed through the army like a cold wave. As they ran in their droves, like ants deserting a burning nest, the vengeful dwarfs and elves cut them down without mercy.

Before he could try and rally the army, the warlord's huscarl retinue surged forward, presenting shields and stern-faced aggression to the dwarf king, before hauling their chieftain away. At first the warlord resisted, roaring in defiant rage, but as he caught sight of something in the distance behind him he relented.

Bagrik followed the Norscan's eye and saw the shaman for the first time. Shawled in ragged robes, his thin fingers wrapped around a staff of gnarled bone, the lone shaman cut a wretched figure. As he moved, slipping from the dwarf king's sight, he seemed almost serpentine, and Bagrik swore the shaman's eyes flared like the green flash across the horizon line, before he slithered from view. It was but a fleeting glance, a sense of agelessness and malevolence lingering in the dwarf's mind once the shaman had gone. The skies then darkened for Bagrik, and the blackness he had held at bay finally claimed him.

CHAPTER FIFTEEN
No Mercy

THE FIELD BEYOND Broken Anvil Hill was like a charnel ground.

Norscan bodies littered the blood-slick earth, cleaved by axes or pierced by spears. Mammoth carcasses slumped alongside them, being feasted on by the carrion that had descended in the battle's aftermath.

Held in reserve at the western approach to Broken Anvil Hill, and concealed from the Norscans' view, the elf cavalry had ridden slowly through the sparse copses of pine. Once the enemy had committed to the attack, their flanks fully engaged by the elven spears, Lethralmir and his knights had sounded their advance. Exploding from the treeline the charge of the knights was irresistible. The warning cries of the Norscan outriders had been much too late, the feral horseman and their brutish steeds swept away in a red haze. The relentless vigour of Lethralmir driving them, the elf nobles had smashed into the rear of the northmen horde and shut the trap with a line of elven steel. Beset on all sides, the courage of the heathens had cracked like thawing ice pounded by a thousand hammers.

Lances spitted with quivering northmen bodies, their long swords slicked with blood, the elf knights had cleaved through the fleeing horde rending and killing at will. Panic had turned to fear and in moments the Norscans were fleeing with abandon, trampling their own warriors in their urgency to escape certain death.

The will of the enemy broken, the dwarfs and elves had surged forward, intent on dealing them a brutal parting blow, before the order to hold the line was sounded and the allies cheered victory and shouted curses at the disappearing Norscan horde.

Drenched in blood and the bodies of the fallen, the field was theirs.

BAGRIK OPENED HIS eyes and found that he was in the bed chamber of his war tent. Iron braziers burned quietly at the edges of the room. The dwarf king sat up and saw Morek at the foot of his bed, swathed in flickering shadow.

As Bagrik awoke, two priestesses of Valaya emerged from the penumbra at the recesses of the bed chamber. They carried salves and poultices, smiling benevolently as they approached the king.

'You're alive then,' said Morek, a flare of light illuminating his face as he ignited his pipe.

'You look as old as I feel,' Bagrik replied, scowling at one of the Valakryn as she dabbed the purple-black bruise on his shoulder where the Norscan warlord had struck him. The other uncorked the bottled salve and began tending the cuts and gashes on the dwarf king's body.

Morek grunted in half-hearted amusement.

'The elgi's plan worked,' he said, somewhat begrudgingly. 'The cavalry broke the northmen horde in the end.'

'Aye,' agreed Bagrik, 'after we had worn them down. Let them have their glory. We know the truth of it–' he began, but was interrupted with the Valakryn's ministrations.

'Enough fussing,' he snapped furiously, making the priestesses recoil. 'Can a king get no peace?' A confused look suddenly crept onto Bagrik's face and he looked beneath the hruk wool blanket covering his body. 'I am naked under here!' he cried, face reddening. 'Get these rinns out of here, Morek!'

The Valakryn retreated, backing out of the bed chamber quickly with their heads bowed.

'Worse than Brunvilda,' Bagrik muttered shamefacedly once they were gone.

Morek chuckled, smoke escaping from the upcurled corners of his mouth.

'*I* removed your armour and trappings, my king,' he said with a wry smile. 'Your dignity is safe.'

Bagrik groused under his breath and threw off the blanket. Grimacing, the naked dwarf king struggled from his bed.

'You need rest,' said Morek, his tone expressing the futility of his words.

His advice went unheeded as Bagrik hobbled over to his war attire where it lay draped on a plain stone statue. He took his helmet, encircled by his glittering crown, and set it upon his head.

'Gather my army,' said Bagrik, his back to his captain. It was a bizarre image, the dwarf king standing naked in the firelight, just wearing his warhelm. 'Tell the elves we are mustering.'

Morek stepped forward without need for request, and pressed the king's tankard into his hand. Bagrik quaffed the ale in one thirsty gulp, belching loudly as he wiped the foam from his beard.

'Now we chase these dogs down,' he growled.

VICTORY AT BROKEN Anvil Hill gave the dwarfs and elves the impetus they sorely needed. Forged on the altar of battle that day was an alliance of silver and bronze that would not easily be undone. Suspicion and mistrust were washed away by shed blood and sweat experienced mutually on the field, the emergent camaraderie between the two races galvanised through shared triumph.

Winter still refused to relinquish its iron grip on the land as the dwarfs and elves doggedly pursued the fleeing Norscan horde through the snow-capped mountains, through drifts and icy winds. The spring thaw had begun slowly, the white shrouded peaks filling the lowland rivers with their melt waters. At Lake Kagrad, known also as Blood Water, due to its rusted sheen and tang caused by the copper ore embedded in its basin, the allies caught the northmen rearguard. Unprepared, and with the fight beaten out of them, a rout quickly became a slaughter and Lake Kagrad became the Blood Water in more than just name alone.

As the dwarfs and elves pressed on with their campaign, moving ever northward, skirmishes between scouts became common. After several weeks of this guerrilla fighting along the cragged spine of the Worlds Edge, the allies brought the Norscan horde to battle again, upon an immense and lofty plateau surrounded by the soaring peaks of High Pass.

Thunder echoed around the mountains like the angry cries of gods, and lightning tore the sky apart in brilliant forked flashes. Clouds gathered and the rain swept down in a relentless barrage, rattling against armour plates and helmets in a frenetic din as the two armies fought.

Ten thousand northmen plummeted over the edge of High Pass that storm-wracked day, unable to resist the sheer fury of their determined enemy.

The dwarfs formed an impenetrable wall of shields and marched forward resolutely. At the flanks, elf knights and horsemasters killed any Norscans who tried to flee whilst archers and quarrellers thinned the host that was being slowly corralled before the advancing dwarfs. The back ranks fell first, screaming as they were pushed into mist-filled oblivion by their fellow northmen. Death was as inexorable as the passing of the seasons. Those that did escape survived only by virtue of an inexplicable mist that roiled over the edges of the plateau and filled the stony battlefield utterly. Though they were still many, the Norscans had been cut down brutally from an all-conquering horde to a band of raiders. Yet, the Norscan warlord and his shaman had eluded them again, and whilst they lived the dwarfs' and elves' task was not done.

Bagrik brooded in his war tent, a pipe cinched between his lips, still wearing his armour.

'This is not battle,' he muttered, undoing the straps of his gilded vambrace and letting it fall to the ground. 'It is massacre.'

The victory at High Pass was three weeks behind them and they were now travelling across country, having harried the Norscan horde across the lands of barbarian men and finally to within sight of the Sea of Claws.

'They are running out of earth to flee to,' said Morek, sat opposite his king in the close confines of the tent.

The dwelling was little more than a square-edged pavilion, much smaller and less ostentatious than Bagrik's tent at Broken Anvil Hill. With camp broken every few hours, there was not enough time to erect the larger dwellings. Most of the troops, in fact, shared makeshift bivouacs and were huddled together against the growing cold of the north and the icy rain that had persisted for six straight days.

'Aye, then I'll finish what we started at Broken Anvil Hill,' the dwarf king promised darkly. Since that day when he had fallen at the end of the allies' first triumph, Bagrik had sought his nemesis, the Norscan warlord, in every conflict. Thus far, he had been thwarted. His shaman, the supposed daemon that wore a man's flesh as the dwarf king would wear a cloak or pelt, was also proving elusive. It mattered not – he could wait. Patience was an easy thing for a dwarf. Bagrik knew the enemy he wanted was not so far ahead.

'Something troubles me,' Morek began, easing back on a stool as he regarded his king. 'Why leave the bodies behind, at the gorge I mean. Why leave Nagrim and those with him for the carrion?'

Bagrik's face darkened further.

'Who can say what drives these honourless dogs. I have more regard for beasts than these *north-men*.'

Before Morek could reply the flap to the small tent opened and a wet, bedraggled Haggar entered. He bowed once to his king and then thumped his chest in salute to Morek before he spoke.

'News from the rangers,' he said, breathlessly.

Bagrik imagined that the young banner bearer had run all the way across camp.

'The northmen are holed up in a vast cave that looks out upon the Sea of Claws,' he said. 'They are making their final stand there.'

Morek raised an eyebrow, quizzically.

'I honestly thought they would get in their ships and flee across the ocean,' he said.

'Be thankful they did not,' growled Bagrik. 'Both of you,' he barked, 'prepare your warriors. We march within the hour.'

ULFJARL SLUMPED UPON his throne, defeated. The noise from the Sea of Claws carried from the mouth of the cave as it boomed and thundered, funnelled through a wide cleft cut into the rock of the cliff. Salt-tainted air tasted bitter and cold in his mouth and every wave smashing against the deadly hidden reef near the shore sounded like mocking laughter.

The seat on which the Norscan now brooded was carved from the bones of his enemies. It was meant to be a trophy of his victory. Instead, it had become a painful reminder of his bitter defeat. Casting his gaze about the hollow cave, Ulfjarl saw his scattered huscarl retinue in the thrall of manifested daemonettes. Daemon and man in varying stages of licentious consort cavorted languidly around him, mewling, moaning, and crying out in pleasurable agony. His warriors were ensnared by the creatures' deadly charms as they flickered in and out of existence in the jade-coloured smoke hugging the ground beneath his feet. Ulfjarl refused their lascivious advances, only the force of his iron will keeping them at bay.

His army was beaten. Many had already fled. Those he had caught deserting he had killed – their flayed flesh was displayed on crude standards rammed into

the soft earth around the cave mouth as a warning to
the others camped outside, crouched silently around
dying fires. Only Ulfjarl's loyal Norscans remained; the
subjugated tribes were all gone. The mammoths were
nearly all dead. Destiny was slipping through his grasp
– the destiny that Veorik had promised him.

The shaman waited patiently in the shadows behind
him, almost part of the thickening darkness of the cave.
Though he had his back to him, Ulfjarl knew he was
there. He felt Veorik's emerald eyes boring into him.
The shaman's quiet displeasure was like insidious poison seeping into his body. Ulfjarl felt his glory fading,
together with the favour he had garnered through the
barter of his undying soul.

What had gone wrong? Had he not sworn his loyalty
to the Dark Gods? Had he not shown his might when
he had crushed the immortals and their craven watch
towers? Had he not demonstrated his will during the
slaughter of the elf army in the plains beyond their glittering city? He had offered up their souls as a gift to
Shornaal, and the Prince of Raptures had repaid him
with boons. Even now Ulfjarl touched the wound in his
helmet with tentative and fearful fingers. Through the
gaping crevice that the bearded king of the mountain
had gouged in him, Ulfjarl could see the world again
and the bright vista hurt his eyes. He had thought the
meteoric iron was indestructible. He had thought *he*
was indestructible. It was not so.

Only the bearded king of the mountain had ever hurt
Ulfjarl. At first he had felt anger, a wrathful desire to
rend and tear the diminutive warrior apart in the name
of the Dark Gods, but then anger had fled, eroded by
doubt and the threat of his own mortality. Ulfjarl was in
disarray, and Veorik was no longer any comfort or

guide. The Norscan warlord's strength, the strength of his rule, was slipping like the dread blade fused into his flesh. He felt it, the black glaive that had become one with his will, reject him. It was a constant struggle now, the black veins in his arm ever restless and eager for egress, to maintain his grip upon it.

The torches at either side of Ulfjarl's throne flickered wildly, their flames bent as if like fiery water rolling down a slope. Except... they were flowing the wrong way, against the wind. Ulfjarl looked up suddenly, his warrior senses prickling with alarm, and saw a sliver of shadow seemingly detach itself from the wall. At first it was like black smoke, an amorphous thing fashioned from the dark that crept slowly towards the Norscan chief like a wraith. Robes emerged from the dissipating smoke, curves and flowing lines that shaped a lithe body clad in iridescent violet. Only the suggestion of a face was visible beneath a voluminous cowl; the edge of a nose, the ridge of a cheekbone, picked out in the wan light.

Rothfeg, a huscarl still with some of his wits about him, noticed the apparition gliding towards his chieftain and hastily grabbing his warhammer charged the clandestine figure. Arms folded benignly across its chest, the enrobed one calmly took its hand out from where it was concealed in its opposite sleeve and Rothfeg was immolated by a flare of violet flame. The huscarl died swiftly, in agony and raptures, the fat of his flesh dripping onto the floor like wax where it first boiled and then cooled. Charred bone ash remained as the enrobed one passed the warrior and came before Ulfjarl himself.

Veorik had not moved. Leastways, Ulfjarl had not heard him move. The warlord raised a hand to stave off his other huscarls who had realised belatedly that their chieftain might be in danger.

'Ulfjarl, Chosen of Shornaal, you languish in defeat,' said the enrobed one, its voice androgynous, ageless and coming from everywhere and nowhere at the same time.

The sense of it was disconcerting and though Ulfjarl did not speak the language that issued from its mouth, he understood every word.

'Do you still desire victory and endless power?' it asked sibilantly.

Ulfjarl rose to his feet and nodded slowly, transfixed by the robed spectre in front of him.

'Slay the bearded king,' it told him. 'Slay him and claim your victory.' The enrobed one slipped its hand back into the folds of its sleeve and when it came out again held a long, serrated dagger. Carrying the cruel-looking weapon in two hands, the enrobed one proffered it to Ulfjarl as if in supplication.

Slowly, Ulfjarl reached for the weapon. He was about to touch the blade to gauge its sharpness, when he saw the leprous-yellow shimmer upon it and stopped short. Instead, reacting to his instincts, the Norscan took the hilt and handle in a firm grip. Removing the long knife from the sheath on his belt, he replaced it with the serrated dagger.

Seemingly satisfied, the enrobed one bowed once and backed away, melting slowly into dark ether as it became one with the shadow once more.

The ash that remained of Rothfeg stirred. Peering deeply, Ulfjarl saw the semblance of a creature within the huscarl's remains. Sobbing, chirruping in what sounded like debased laughter and writhing in agony, something manifested in that purple ash. Wretched and beautiful at the same time, the nascent thing grew at an exponential rate. Scar-tissue blubber, shot through with bruise-black veins, throbbed into a fat mass of flesh. Muscled haunches pressed outward from it, stretching glabrous skin and extending into saurian legs. Lastly, there came a head, emerging perversely from a crevice hollowed out in the blubber. Its eyes glinted wetly, either side of an equine skull and a thin, spine-like tongue whipped back and forth from its snout as it tasted the air. The flesh-thing reminded Ulfjarl of a giant flightless bird though there was the sense of something disturbingly human about it.

The enrobed one had left a second gift.

Ulfjarl got to his feet and clenched his fist. He felt strength there again. The black veins were no longer restive. Looking to Veorik, he found renewed purpose and knew what he must do.

Ulfjarl gazed down at his throne, raised the obsidian blade aloft and smashed the bone seat into fragments. In the flickering torchlight, he saw that his shaman was smiling.

CHAPTER SIXTEEN
A Final Reckoning

A BITTER WIND was blowing off the Sea of Claws.

King Bagrik was standing upon the war shield of Karak Ungor. Inscribed with ancient runes, the shield's gromril surface blazed with a polished sheen. Runic manacles clasped Bagrik's booted feet, steadying him so he could stand with his wounded leg. He wore a suit of gromril scale, and a mail coif beneath his crowned battle helm, the faceplate having been removed so he could better see the foe. Bagrik's rune axe was cleaned of blood and shone dully in the early dawn light. Its gilded glory did not echo the dwarf king's mood.

Over three months since he had left Karak Ungor. Countless weeks forced to endure bitter cold and spirit-sapping downpours. Seemingly endless nights camped in the wildernesses of the Worlds Edge Mountains, with sky and stars above his head instead of good, solid stone. Bagrik longed for the hearth of his Great Hall and closeness of his queen. All the battles against the northmen, the shed blood, the struggle to bring vengeance for Nagrim's death had brought him to this point.

This then would be the final reckoning, and Bagrik had chosen his shieldbearers with this very fact in mind. Morek and Haggar stood beneath him, shouldering the weight of their king as if he were naught with a feather-filled sack.

As he stared out to the sea, the rising wind disturbing the banner of Karak Ungor mounted on the back of the war shield, the dwarf king fancied he could see the shadow of monsters writhing in its stygian depths. Perhaps they had heard the call to battle; perhaps they too hungered for blood.

'This is where we'll end it,' he said dourly to Prince Ithalred.

'I will be glad of it,' the elf answered. 'The constant killing is not to my taste. Let us drive these beasts into the sea at last.'

The two generals waited in the no-man's land, a few hundred feet from the deployment of their allied army. It was a bleak day, the platinum sky filled with the threat of more rain.

Ithalred was mounted on a white Ellyrian stallion, the steed encased in ithilmar barding much like the armour of its master. A dark mood was upon the prince, the grave look on his face made more severe by the dragonesque battlehelm he wore, two great wings sweeping out at either temple. A long nose guard, fashioned into the dragon's snout, went all the way down to the prince's snarling lip.

Bagrik sensed that something else was on his mind, besides the impending battle, but chose not to voice it.

'Aye, we'll drown them all right enough,' the dwarf growled instead. 'This day the beaches will be stained in north-men blood. What are you seeking, Ithalred?' he asked, watching the elf as he surveyed the sky overhead.

'Ravens,' Ithalred replied.

'Ravens?'

'They bear ill-omen from the Crone, Morai-Heg,' the elf explained, though Bagrik was none the wiser.

'The skies are clear, elgi,' the dwarf king replied. 'Is that good?'

'Without my sister to interpret their signs, yes, it is good.'

The elf seeress had returned to Tor Eorfith after the allies had won their first victory at Broken Anvil Hill, citing illness and fatigue as the reason for her departure.

'Trust in this,' said Bagrik, patting his arm with an armoured hand, 'not in signs and portents. Are your forces ready, Ithalred?' asked the dwarf, his gaze returning to the horizon and the arc of coastline where the mouth of the Norscan cave was cut into the cliffs. Tendrils of smoke from doused fires drifted forlornly on the salt-tanged breeze over a broad expanse of frozen ground in front of it. Bagrik assumed the northmen were cowering inside.

'I yearn for battle, if only for an ending to all this, as do you, Bagrik,' the elf replied, facing the king. The many weeks campaigning had eclipsed their uneasy accord with solidarity, even something approaching friendship. But it had left the elf weary and with only bitter humour, as if a great burden weighed upon his mind and pulled at his soul.

The dwarf smiled grimly.

An ending to all of this…

'And yes, my warriors are ready,' the elf answered.

Bagrik's reply was gruff and curt.

'Then you had best join them now,' he said, 'for our enemy comes…'

From out of the mouth of the cave marched the remnants of the Norscan horde. Their warlord led them, riding in a bone chariot that was drawn by some fell creature of the ether that looked like a fleshless bird, only more grotesque and horrifically malformed. In the warlord's wake came a pair of shaggy mammoths, the last of their breed in the war host, followed by a ragged trail of bondsmen and huscarl warriors. Slithering amongst the heavily outnumbered northmen was their enigmatic shaman, though Bagrik kept losing him from sight even when he was staring directly at him.

'To victory, Bagrik,' said the elf prince, holding up his silver long sword.

'To annihilation,' growled Bagrik, and clanged his axe against the elf's blade in salute.

Ithalred gave a snapped command, turning his horse away and galloping to where his kinsmen waited for him. There he would join Lethralmir at the head of the dragon knights, Ellyrian reavers and silver helms alongside them in three deep lines of elven steel. Serried ranks of spearmen and archers, stretching half the length of the ice plain, stood silently in support of the nobles, clutching spears and bows with determination.

'For Nagrim…' Bagrik muttered, once the elf was gone.

Tramping across the frozen shore, its fringes still rimed with ice, the Norscan chief called a halt and the horde stopped.

'They're using the sea to protect their flank,' Morek observed from beneath the war shield, once they too had returned to their lines.

'Why don't they come at us?' asked Haggar alongside him, a hint of wariness in his voice.

'Because they are outnumbered and realise that their doom is upon them,' snarled Bagrik, answering for the hearth guard captain.

'It is madness,' said Morek, taking in the paltry army that opposed them, a mere fraction of its previous size.

By contrast, the dwarf regiments were immense and stretched back into many ranks and across numerous files. There was to be no subtlety, no grand tactics to this battle. The dwarfs would march until they reached the enemy, moving as an implacable wall of bronze and not stopping until the northmen were dead or had been driven into the water and drowned. 'No survivors' Morek had promised his king; it was an oath he fully intended keeping.

'Theirs is a lost hope,' he added. 'They would be better off casting themselves into the sea right now and save us the bother of slaying them.'

'Enough talk. We march,' Bagrik snapped. 'Khazuk!'

'Khazuk!' cried Morek and Haggar.

The war cry was taken up by the dwarf throng and echoed across the ice-bound shore like thunder.

The dwarfs and elves moved slowly at first as they advanced to within a few hundred feet of the Norscans and came to a halt. Still the enemy did not move. By now the chariot riding warlord was lost from view. His huscarl retinue, mounted on their brutish steeds, concealed him behind their shields. Banners were raised aloft throughout the allied army and the armoured front ranks of dwarf warriors and elf spearmen parted to allow a long line of archers and quarrellers through.

'At your order, my king,' said Morek, from beneath the war shield.

Bagrik's gaze was unwavering as he regarded the enemy. No battle cries, no curses or threats. It was as if the northmen knew they were finished and had merely come to play out the final act of this bloody saga.

'Make them run the gauntlet,' the king replied.

Morek took a breath and yelled, 'Loose!'

A flurry of red-fletched quarrels filled the air, pitching up and then down in a razor-sharp arc. The elf archers let fly too, in perfect harmony with the dwarfs.

Faced with the oncoming arrow storm, the Norscans raised shields as one in an act of uncharacteristic discipline. Bondsmen came forward to protect the horses from harm. Such was the sheer number of missiles permeating the air that casualties were inevitable, but the northmen weathered the attack well and once it was over lowered their pin-cushioned shields and roared in defiance.

Bagrik knew then that this was a different breed to that which he had already fought. These were the last of them, the warlord's warrior-brothers. He smiled to himself at a sudden thought – they would be much harder to break.

'Another volley,' said the king.

Morek responded with the order and the sky darkened again.

And again the northmen raised shields and did not falter in the face of whickering death from above. Instead, once the deadly rain was done, they charged, parting like a ragged wave as they ran and allowing the mammoths through their ranks. The earth shook as the beasts of the northern wastes tromped forward. Snapping hounds, let loose by their whelp masters, bounded in front of them. Swarms of hirsute and tattooed bondsmen marauders followed in their wake whirling axes and hammers, the masked berserkers amongst them. After that there came the armoured huscarls on foot, skull-faced death masks grinning madly as they ran in perfect formation. The mounted warriors were content to canter slowly behind the horde alongside their chieftain, and allow the foot-sloggers to bear the brunt of their enemy's initial wrath.

The allies responded with steel-fanged death, the elves loosing with such swiftness that the dwarfs could scarcely see, let alone try to match.

Peppered by a swathe of bolts and arrows, one of the mammoths rocked unsteadily. Its fore-feet collapsed in front of it and it fell hard onto the frozen ground, driving a furrow into the earth with its bloodied snout until at last the beast came to a dead stop and expired.

Within bow range themselves, the Norscans retaliated, small groups of bondsmen archers checking their runs and loosing off arrows into the dwarf and elf ranks. A scattering of warriors fell to their attacks, their death screams raking the air, but it was as nothing. Sling stones and javelins followed, and the unprotected allied missile troops took further casualties.

Bagrik was about to order the quarrellers back when an ululating cry ripped from the northmen ranks, and there was his nemesis – the Norscan warlord atop his chariot of bone, armoured riders trailing behind their chieftain towards the dwarf left flank.

'Take him down!' Bagrik cried, suddenly impotent in the thickly serried dwarf centre. Somehow, the Norscan warlord had manoeuvred behind his horde's advance and slipped from sight to strike at a weaker point in the dwarf king's wall of bronze.

The quarrellers aimed and shot but the few bolts that struck spun away from the hardened frame of the macabre war machine. The daemon beast driving it, charging like a flightless bird, carried the Norscan with unearthly swiftness.

Fast, thought Bagrik with sudden concern as he watched the chariot eat up the ground between him and the dwarf line like it was nothing; too fast!

'Quarrellers, fall back!' thundered the king, 'Armour… For-ward!'

Too late, the dwarf crossbows started their retreat. The chariot struck, scythed wheels churning a bloody path into the quarrellers and punching right through to the slow-moving hearth guard and clan warriors behind. The sudden assault shook the front ranks of the dwarf flank as they were spun and cleaved and crushed.

Laying about him, the warlord severed heads and limbs with enraged abandon. There was no time for the dwarfs to regroup as the mounted huscarls charged in after their warlord, exploiting the sudden gap in the shield wall, slaying the battered and exposed warriors in a blur of bloodshed and pitted metal blades.

From the far opposite flank, an elven battle cry tore into the building maelstrom. Ithalred and his knights were on the move. Bagrik saw them canter at first, then peel away and charge towards the approaching mass of northmen foot-sloggers, pennants snapping gloriously in the rising wind from their raised lances.

It was a call to arms, and slowly at first, but with gathering momentum, the allies not already engaged advanced forward. Though laboured, the dwarf warriors kept a steady pace, their armour clanking loudly as they picked up speed.

Closer and closer they came to the jeering northmen who barrelled at them from the opposite direction, war cries building to a crescendo.

The dwarfs roared in anger, while the elves gave voice to their own fury.

The din of clashing metal rose up like a thunderhead of sound as the armies met in a cauldron of blood and death.

BLADES FLASHED BY in a frenzy of motion. Screams filled the air that was redolent with sweat and breathless anger. Rage came like a wave, tempered by fear. The noise of war and the cries of furious desperation fuelled by a desire to kill, to live, gathered to a tumult. Death, endless death, reigned on the blood-soaked ice.

'Onward!' raged Bagrik, hacking down either side of his war shield as he and his hearth guard carved up a horde of bondsmen. Beneath the king, Morek and Haggar slew with all the fury of Grimnir reborn.

'None survive!' snarled the king as he buried his axe in the skull of a passing northman.

'Slay them all!' A second blow sent a severed bondsman head spinning off into the throbbing mass, a gory fountain erupting from his cleaved neck. Hate took Bagrik over as he spat diatribes against the Norscans and butchered the host.

From the corner of his eye, an arterial spray impeding his vision for a moment, Bagrik saw the chariot-riding warlord shredding the left flank. Such was the speed and ferocity of his daemon-driven war machine, the dwarfs arrayed against him could scarcely land a blow. They were dwindling slowly, yet the warlord's murderous vigour showed no sign of ebbing.

'Take me there,' said Bagrik, pointing his axe at the chariot as it scythed through the thinning throng of dwarfs. 'Morek, Haggar... for Grungni!' he thundered.

The dwarf thanes turned in their advance, the small cohort of hearth guard turning with them, and headed for the distant flank cutting a gore-soaked swathe through the horde. Bondsmen and huscarls were everywhere. Morek and Haggar parried, and hewed, and roared, driving through the Norscan mass like a battering ram. None that came before their blades, or the blade of their king, lived.

Morek sang, loud and strong, the sagas of the old heroes; of Skanir Helgenfell as he fought the Bloodtooth Tribe on the slopes of Ungor; of Duganar Umbrikson, slayer of the Green Wyrm; and of Thengaz Stonespike, saviour of the underway, who fought a horde of rampaging trolls single-handed. Haggar joined him, and the mournful dirge punctuated every blow, every axe fall.

Though impossible in the clamour, it was as if the Norscan warlord heard the war song, turning as he did in his bloody rampage. His swollen eye staring wildly through the gap in his black iron helmet found Bagrik and his thanes. Now he came for them.

The Norscan warlord drove headlong at the dwarf king, even cutting through his own warriors to reach him. His first charge rushed by like caged lightning, scythed wheels *pranging* violently against the axes of Bagrik and his thanes. Several of the hearth guard were crushed or eviscerated by the whirling blades. A severed dwarf head bounced off the bloody war shield.

Unwilling to be mown down by the irresistible chariot, the bondsmen and huscarls clamouring around Bagrik and his hearth guard withdrew. In their zeal to close with the Norscan warlord, the dwarfs had ventured deep into the enemy ranks and the small knot of warriors, shields facing in every direction, was like a bronze island surrounded by foes.

Reaching the end of the open ground that had suddenly appeared around him, the Norscan warlord turned his chariot and charged again. The attack came swiftly, and more dwarf warriors fell to the chariot blades without even striking back. Bagrik and his thanes were staggered by the brutal assault and the dwarf king nearly fell.

'While he rides that machine, we cannot touch the heathen,' said Morek, breathing hard from below the war shield. 'We need to upend him.'

Bagrik scowled as the foe rode out his momentum, gathering speed for another deadly pass. He quickly regarded the handful of hearth guard warriors that remained. From the edge of his vision, he saw the distant lancehead of elven knights falter, Prince Ithalred clutching his throat suddenly as if being strangled. The elf fell from his steed and was lost from view. He was in peril and the elf lay prone. This final reckoning was not unfolding as Bagrik had envisioned.

'Set me down,' he snarled at his thanes, returning to his own battle.

'My king, you can barely walk,' said Morek.

'Do it!' snapped Bagrik, ignoring the hearth guard captain's protests.

The thanes obeyed and put the war shield on the ground, the hearth guard that were left locking their shields together in a feeble wall of bronze and iron in front of them. Quickly, they unclasped the manacles around Bagrik's boots and the king hobbled off the shield to stand with his thanes. Looking over the shield wall, Bagrik saw that the Norscan warlord had whirled around and was coming again.

'Crouch down,' he said, stowing his axe and gripping the lip of the massive war shield with both hands. 'Here and here,' he added, nodding to either side for the thanes to follow his lead.

Stowing their blades, Haggar first yanking the banner of Ungor free and ramming it hard into the earth beside him, both dwarfs gripped the war shield like their king.

'When he tears through the hearth guard, lift the war shield up and get behind it,' Bagrik told them. 'Stay strong and don't give any ground, not even an inch!'

'We are unyielding...' said Morek.

'...strong as stone and steel,' Haggar concluded.

As Bagrik had predicted, the Norscan warlord smashed through the hearth guard wall, killing those unlucky enough to be in his path in a chorus of screams and showered blood. Beyond the slain warriors, he found a stern-faced dwarf king and his thanes waiting.

'Heave!' Bagrik yelled.

The three dwarfs lifted the war shield as one, thrusting it up at a high angle.

Carried by the momentum of his charge, the Norscan warlord didn't have time to slow and the chariot crashed against the gromril bulwark. Bagrik and his thanes roared together, ramming their shoulders against the underside of the shield, boots gouging into the frozen ground as they were pushed back. The crack of wrenching bone echoed dully through the metal, as the war machine lurched madly to its side, frame splintering when it struck the ground.

Gasping for breath, Bagrik staggered backwards and together with Morek and Haggar, let the war shield drop. It fell with a clatter of resounding gromril and was still. The three dwarfs turned on their heels.

The chariot was a broken mess of shattered bone. A spear of it impaled the daemon beast through its grotesque body. Ichorous fluid leaked from the wound.

Bagrik hobbled the few feet to the bone wreckage, unslinging his axe as he followed the long furrow gouged in the earth left by the chariot. He severed the mewling creature's head with a grunt.

Morek and Haggar were behind the king when the Norscan warlord emerged out of the carnage, skin cut in a dozen places but very much alive.

'Find the shaman,' Bagrik snarled over his shoulder at them, gaze fixed on his foe.

The clank of armour told the dwarf king that his thanes had no intention of leaving him.

'Find him now!' he snapped. 'Save Ithalred.'

MOREK'S FACE WAS set like stone. Haggar turned to him, unsure what he should do. In that brief moment, Morek saw that victory was close. A cohort of long-beards had broken through to them past the clot of bondsmen and huscarls. In the distance, he saw a band of triumphant slayers take down the last of the mammoths, its shaggy hide set ablaze by torches before they butchered it.

'Take the banner,' the hearth guard captain told Haggar. 'Lead them,' he said, pointing to the beleaguered warriors that had just broken through.

Haggar nodded, tramping back to the banner and wrenching it from the earth. Bellowing belligerently, he joined the embattled longbeards and waded into the fight.

'You,' said Morek, turning to the startled handful of hearth guard from the king's bodyguard that still lived, 'with me.'

Though he knew little of sorcerers and their distrustful ways, Morek was experienced enough to realise that their ilk often cowered in the rear ranks of an army where they could practise their magic unopposed. This, he felt in his gut, was where he'd find the shaman. Only a thin line of bondsmen stood between Morek and the rear echelons of the dwindling horde. Beyond that was only the sea. There was nowhere else left to hide. Gripping the haft of his rune axe tightly, he made for the foe he had in his sights, the name of Grimnir on his lips.

EMBOLDENED BY THE presence of the banner of Karak Ungor in their midst, the longbeards redoubled their efforts. As they fought the Norscans back, Haggar at their fore, a throng of clan warriors waded in on the flank, having slain a pack of vicious war hounds and their whelp masters. Together the dwarfs drove the northmen back, foot by bloody foot, to the crags at the bottom of the cliffs.

'Victory is near!' Haggar cried, determined to keep the banner aloft, the grip of his rune hand like iron. Blood spurting across his eyes, he saw one of the Norscan leaders raise a warhorn to his lips. A keening cry ripped out of the curled instrument, echoing discordantly across the craggy shore.

It was answered by a bestial call, throaty and reverberant. The sound of it hurt Haggar's ears and he winced in pain. From amongst the crags, from out of the shallow caves and dark hollows, monsters emerged.

Dank-looking skin, gnarled by warts, red scar-tissue weals and patches of discolouration swathed the tall and sinewy bodies of the creatures. Bent-backed with spiked protuberances erupting out of their spines, they loped forward in a gangling fashion. Long talons scraped against the ground at the end of rangy arms, covered in tufts of coarse hair. Flat ears, scarred and chewed, flared from ugly heads that snarled in anger.

'Trolls,' Haggar muttered with distaste, and knew that the fight was far from over.

BAGRIK SPAT ON the purple ash remains of the daemon steed.

'You need to find a stronger beast, north-man,' he told the Norscan.

Through the gouge in his black iron war helm, the warlord's eye narrowed in anger. He leapt over the wreckage of the chariot and threw a thunderous blow at the dwarf king.

Bagrik was taken off guard by the sudden attack and only just parried it. A punch swept in to his left temple and the dwarf blocked with his vambrace. Ignoring the pain seizing his forearm, he smashed his axe haft into the Norscan's stomach. It was like striking iron. The black blade flashed in a blur of movement as the Norscan rained frenzied blows against Bagrik's hard-pressed defence.

Waiting for an opening, after a second flurry of attacks, Bagrik smashed the top of his axe into the Norscan's armoured chin. The blow rocked him, and the heathen chieftain staggered only for the dwarf to shoulder barge him in the chest. Bagrik was about to end the move with an overhead strike when one of the warlord's huscarls from those gathered around them threw himself forward. Bagrik reversed his blow, stepping aside with his good leg, and cutting the huscarl in half as he charged past screaming. His legs ran on for a few seconds, before slumping over next to his steaming torso.

'Like I said at Broken Anvil Hill,' snarled Bagrik to the Norscan warlord, who had since recovered, 'just you and me.'

KNOTS OF STRUGGLING warriors littered the field now, order and discipline breaking down into individual combats. Morek dodged his way through the scattered melee of isolated groups of fighters. Hacking foes as he went, the hearth guard in tow, the dwarf captain reached the thin line of bondsmen. Cutting through them quickly, the small throng found themselves at the rear of the Norscan horde. Morek saw they were close to the right flank, where the elven cavalry had split. One force, mainly made up of the dragon knights, encircled the prone form of Ithalred. Morek caught glimpses of the stricken prince through the legs of the elven steeds. The second, led by Lethralmir, continued the charge, cutting through the northmen ranks with horns blaring.

Morek reasoned that if Ithalred was indeed ensnared by the shaman then the wretch must be close by. He headed for the dragon knights. It wasn't long before the dwarf got his reward.

Seemingly alone, scattered elf corpses littering the ground around him, Morek saw the shaman. Like summer haze, the Norscan shifted in the dwarf's eye-line. Morek blinked, twice, three times before he appeared to solidify. With his back to the Sea of Claws, the shaman gestured with needle-like fingers as he worked his sorcery.

He was only fifty feet away.

'Uzkul!' yelled the dwarf, axe upraised.

The shaman twisted to face the dwarf. His movements were clipped and rapid like a snake as he outstretched a hand with his palm facing out.

Morek and the hearth guard had run half the distance when the shaman closed his palm into a fist and the Sea of Claws exploded.

Erupting from the freezing depths was a fell creature of the deeps. A watery torrent announced the monster's sudden emergence, raining down in sheets from its long serpentine body somehow held erect in the thrashing waves of the sea. Its keening cry chilled the air around it and turned the blood in Morek's veins to ice water. Silver-blue scales shimmering wetly, the ice drake glared down at the pathetic dwarfs, its black orbs full of malign intelligence. Lowering its saurian snout, the monster opened its mouth, baring fangs. Its breath smelled like cold copper and rotting fish.

'Valaya's mercy,' breathed Morek, rigid with terror, as he realised he was already dead.

ANOTHER LONGBEARD LOST his head as a troll bit it off. Most of the clan warriors were already dead, so too were the Norscan bondsmen, as many eaten by the monsters as were slain by the dwarfs. Slowly, Haggar and the remaining longbeards were being forced back. One of the trolls reached for him, acidic drool dripping from its bottom lip that hissed as it struck the ground. Haggar hacked off its claw at the wrist. The creature squealed in agony, before the dwarf thane lunged forward and put his axe blade into its misshapen skull. The monster fell back, and was trampled by its ravenous kin.

To his right, Haggar saw a wretched plume of bile and fluids erupt from a troll's extended maw. Awash with the foul acid, a longbeard went down screaming. Another lost an arm as one of the monsters, its flesh already knitting together from the stomach wound the longbeard had delivered, ripped through his upraised shield and staved in his head.

'For Ungor!' Haggar cried, determined not to let his clan's honour slip again. But it was an impossible task. For every troll they slew, another with its wounds regenerated, came back at them.

'Hold the line in the name of the king!' he yelled, hoping that Morek was faring better.

MOREK WAS DEAD. Bones smashed against the ice-hard earth, blood oozing from his armour where the monster of the deep had mauled him.

Or so the dwarf had imagined his fate until he was thrown aside, the ice drake diving downwards like a spear. Chunks of rock and frozen debris erupted from the impact as the dwarf felt himself skidding on his armoured stomach across the ice-slick ground.

Slightly dazed, Morek came to his senses and found he was staring into the stern face of the elf bodyguard Korhvale. The dwarf captain nodded reluctant thanks, inwardly chagrined at being saved by an elf. The king may have found some peace with the fey creatures from across the sea; Morek had not.

Struggling to his feet, he saw that the hearth guard were up too, and charged the ice drake as it lurched upwards for another strike. Morek was running towards them, Korhvale in tow, when a blast of freezing air roared from the monster's gaping maw. Three of the charging hearth guard were frozen solid, weapons raised in attack. Surging forward like silver lightning, the last of the dwarfs was snapped up in the creature's jaws and devoured before he even had time to scream.

Morek ground to a halt, watching the beast warily as it rose up like a scaled column and chugged the hearth guard's body down its gullet.

'We must kill that thing,' he said to Korhvale, standing alongside him. From the corner of his eye, Morek saw that the shaman's attention was back on the elven prince.

'And that bastard is next,' he added, pointing him out.

The White Lion nodded, eyes flicking quickly from the shaman and back to the ice drake.

'One of us must try to distract it–' Morek began, but Korhvale was already running towards the beast. Upon seeing fresh prey the ice drake darted towards the elf, opening its hungry mouth for another morsel.

The creature was inhumanly fast.

Korhvale was faster. He sprang forward as the ice drake came for him, rolling beneath its jaws as they clamped thin air. Korhvale came out of the roll and onto his feet in a single fluid motion, unhitching his axe as he braced himself. The White Lion was mere feet from the creature, elf runes on his axe blade blazing white as he held it aloft.

'*Charoi!*' The dwarf heard him cry, as Korhvale brought his weapon down against the ice drake's neck in two hands. Scales sheared away like parchment as the blow went through skin, flesh and bone to emerge on the other side embedded in the rock.

The ice drake let out a surprised shriek before its severed head lolled over on its side, and the blood and viscera in its neck gushed out in a grisly flood.

'Or you could just lop its head off,' Morek muttered to himself, suddenly aware of a group of elves approaching.

'The beast is dead,' uttered Korhvale upon his return. 'Thelion of Saphery and his sword masters,' he added, gesturing to the new arrivals.

The elf called Thelion bowed curtly, his robes and trappings indicating that he was a mage. His warriors were a different breed however, clad in long coats of silver mail, wearing pointed helms and carrying great swords that were nearly half as tall again as Morek. Each one hefted the huge blade as if it were a feather.

'Sword masters indeed,' Morek said to himself. Muttering an oath to Grimnir for the fallen hearth guard, frozen and devoured by the slain ice drake, the dwarf turned his steel-hard gaze upon the shaman. He'd be damned if the elf was going to kill him, too.

A small band of huscarls, evidently seeing the shaman's approaching assassins, and having just despatched a vanguard of spearmen, charged Morek and the elves. The sword masters swept forward unbidden and carved the northmen up in a web of flashing steel. It lasted only seconds, dismembered limbs and impaled bodies already growing cold against the earth.

A cry ripped from Thelion's mouth and they surged towards the unprotected shaman, who now gave them his undivided attention. Korhvale fell in behind his kinsmen, a few feet back, whilst Morek brought up the rear unable to keep pace with the long strides of the elves.

Thin mouth curled into a snarl of displeasure, the shaman splayed his talon-like fingers towards the charging sword masters and a host of serpentine heads spat out on arcs of emerald fire. There was a gurgled cry as one of the sword masters was impaled, his impressive blade clattering to the ground beside his lifeless body. A second died with a flaming emerald band wrapped around his throat, armoured fingers clutching ineffectually at the sorcerous bindings. The last two sword masters were burned down like candles, their bodies engulfed in a green conflagration.

'It has power,' Thelion said to Korhvale and Morek, using Khazalid so the dwarf would understand him. 'Stay behind me.'

'A dwarf cowers behind no one, especially an elgi!' Morek raged, ignoring the mage as he strode forward.

An explosion of green fire knocked Morek from his feet, gromril armour smoking. Patting out the eldritch flames, the dwarf said, 'What are you waiting for, mageling, work your magic.'

At the shaman's bidding the flaming serpents snapped at the survivors, but they recoiled upon striking a shimmering azure shield.

Back on his feet, Morek saw that Thelion had stepped forward. Beads of sweat were dappling his forehead already as he forced the probing serpents back and flung a bolt of incandescent silver at his sorcerous opponent. The shaman caught and crushed it, the dying light of the spell exploding through the gaps in his fingers. He fashioned the writhing serpent forms into an emerald lash. Thelion cried out in agony as it wrapped around his outstretched wrist, bilious green smoke issuing from his seared flesh. Making a cutting motion with his free hand, an azure blade appeared and sliced through the binding lace, dissipating it.

'Go now,' the elf snarled, through gritted teeth. 'I can't hold it for long.'

Morek and Korhvale went around the mage, the dwarf flinging a throwing axe at the shaman's skull only to see it deflected by a glowing green palm. He saw Korhvale dodge an incandescent dagger, before sweeping his axe at the foe. Slithering away with preternatural speed, the shaman avoided the blow. Morek waded in moments later, a downward strike from his axe hitting dirt as the shaman's whickering body made a mockery of his skill.

Elf and dwarf threw attack after attack at the snake-like shaman, who twisted and weaved and undulated away from every one. Slowly though, he backed away, Thelion taking a painful step forward with every foot the heroes bought him. Thrusting his gem-encrusted staff into the air, the elf mage called down thunder bolts from the heavens to smite his foe, but to no avail. Using his body like a lightning rod, the shaman captured the ferocious energy and instead of being destroyed by it, released it back at Thelion. Struck by the cerulean barrage, the mage was brought to his knees. The last thing the elf saw was the shaman's eyes aflame with emerald fire... then there was only agony and darkness.

Morek saw Thelion immolated in a blaze of green fire. Finishing the mage seemed to take something out of the shaman, though, as Korhvale at last landed a blow, cutting a deep gash in his arm. The shaman staggered, dark green blood flowing from the wound, and Morek stepped forward. Sweeping his axe in a punishing arc, he cut the shaman in half, all the way across his waist. The two disparate parts flopped to the ground, spilling bloody intestine.

'Wasn't so hard,' said Morek once he'd got his breath back. The dwarf was about to congratulate himself when he realised that the shaman wasn't dead. The Norscan's hood had slipped off when the upper half of his body was severed. Beneath it was a serpent-like visage, utterly bald with scaled flesh, snake-slit eyes and fangs. The shaman laughed, forked tongue flicking back and forth from his lipless mouth, as his body shuddered. Morek and Korhvale backed away as the shaman convulsed and spasmed. Their eyes widened as something moved beneath his bloody robes. The thin, barbed tip of a tail emerged, growing steadily with each horrific moment. By the time they reacted, it was too late. The shaman lashed out with his new appendage, upending elf and dwarf.

Struggling to his feet, Morek saw the shaman had righted himself also and balanced on the thickening snake tail replacing his severed legs. As the dwarf watched, the shaman's robes fell away revealing a scaled body not unlike the Chaos gorgons of legend.

'*Mother Isha,*' whispered Korhvale as the snake-shaman loomed over them, its tongue lathing the air through its fangs.

Flicking out a talon, the creature sheared through the White Lion's gilded vambrace, severing the tendons in his wrist. Korhvale screamed, his axe slipping from his nerveless fingers. Blood began oozing through the shredded armour plate and he clutched it with his other hand to staunch its flow. Sweeping its serpentine body around in a swift arc, the snake-shaman took the elf's feet from under him again and put him on his back. Korhvale gasped as the air was punched from his lungs, and he writhed on the ground winded.

Roaring, Morek came at the snake-daemon with his rune axe. It dodged the first swipe, chittering in what sounded like profound amusement then raked a talon across the dwarf's face, putting four red gouges in his cheek and ripping off his battle helm. Morek shook his head, blinking back stars, and was about to attack again when the snake-shaman slithered towards him with blinding speed, sweeping his sinuous body around the dwarf and constricting in an eye blink. Morek grunted, dropping his rune axe as the snake-shaman crushed him in its serpentine coils.

The sudden wrench of metal filled his ears, and the dwarf felt his armour being slowly dented inwards. Despite himself, he cried out and smashed his balled fists against the scaled hide but the shaman would not release his deadly embrace. Instead, his glabrous head hove into view, a wicked smile curving his lipless mouth, sadistic malice in his slitted eyes.

Morek felt himself suddenly drawn to the shaman's penetrating glare, relenting in his struggles as sibilant whispers probed at his mind's defences, visions manifesting slowly in his consciousness...

An island wracked by terrible storms, its earth scorched by fire and drenched with blood...

An army of elves, hatred in their hearts led by a cursed and vengeful king...

A warrior of the line of Ithalred, fighting in the glittering host, a war cry on his lips...

A daemon, like a serpent fused with a man, run through by Ithalred's ancestor and cast screaming into the waiting void...

The image changed, bleeding away like streaks of paint across a slickened canvas, resolving itself into a new vista...

King Bagrik, lord of the under-mountain, stabbed by a poison blade...

A red-eyed goblin squatting on the throne of Karak Ungor wearing a pelt of beards, its kin capering around it...

Morek crowned king, Brunvilda in his arms cradling a beardling child, his heir...

Only Morek's innate dwarf resolve saved him from madness. Remembered pain came back and he growled in anger as the battlefield returned to him.

'Give in,' hissed the snake-shaman, 'give in to the Prince of Rapturessss...' it goaded sibilantly.

'Bugger off,' Morek snarled through gritted teeth and headbutted the snake-shaman hard in the mouth. Shrieking painfully the daemon recoiled, spitting out a broken tooth as it relinquished its death grip on the dwarf. Morek was dumped onto the ground and, despite the pins and needles forcing white hot pain into his body, took up his fallen axe and cleaved the snake-shaman's head in two. Without waiting, he ripped his blade from the cloven skull and hacked again and again, chopping the daemon into pieces.

When he was done, Morek bent over with his hands on his knees, a warm sensation spreading across his forehead, chest heaving as the snake-shaman dissolved into ichorous sludge in front of him. When he'd caught his breath, the dwarf walked over to Korhvale. Extending a hand, he helped the elf to his feet. He winced as he did it, realising that at least one of his ribs was broken.

The dwarf smiled despite the pain, the rune of Grungni that was inscribed just above his brow and usually concealed by his battle helm cooling.

'Now, he's dead,' said the dwarf, hoisting Korhvale to his feet.

Once he was up, the elf tore a strip from his robes and used it to bind his wound.

Morek stared around the battlefield.

'This way,' he said, already off and running.

Bagrik was alone. His king needed him.

BELLOWING THE NAME of Grimnir, the slayers fell upon the trolls with axes cleaving. Their death songs were like sweet music to Haggar's ears, and the thane made an oath to the ancestor god, himself. As they cleaved, the rampant slayers threw flaming torches, those left after the destruction of the mammoths.

Fire was anathema to trolls, their rugged flesh unable to regenerate if it was burned. The wretched creatures screeched and groaned in terror at the mere sight of it. Haggar marshalled what longbeards were left and set about surrounding the few remaining trolls, deliberately picking on the injured. Though formidable foes, once their will was broken, trolls were easy meat. The attack of the slayers with their fiery brands was enough to make the trolls panic and they fled, hooting and shrieking back into the caves. Not to be deprived of their worthy doom, the slayers gave chase.

'Hold here,' said Haggar, gasping for breath. He looked around and behind him, trying to gauge the stage the battle was at. To the distant right, the elf knights were carving through scores of fleeing northmen being crushed under hoof or spitted on lances. Lethralmir seemed to revel in the slaying. Nearby, the dwarf could see Ithalred being helped back onto his horse. Everywhere the final few Norscans were being cut down or driven to an icy doom, just as Morek had promised the king. In the middle of the carnage though, a last bastion of enemy resistance remained. Here were the majority of the warlord's best and most loyal warriors. Shields out and tightly packed, they were proving difficult to crack. Haggar knew that amongst the sea of foes Bagrik was fighting for his life. He knew also that they needed to hold this flank, ensure that nothing else emerged from the caves. Even so, the young thane was not about to leave his king to his fate.

'With me,' Haggar ordered, 'King Bagrik needs us.' With that he hared off, the longbeards muttering disparagingly as they followed, the banner of Karak Ungor swaying back and forth as Haggar ran to the throng of Norscans and to the king.

'HEH, HEH, IS that all you've got north-man?' Bagrik laughed, spitting a gobbet of blood onto the frozen ground. His chest felt heavy inside his armour, every breath an effort, and his old wound was now so stiff that he could barely move. Lamentably, Bagrik glanced at the dents and tears in his gromril scale from where he'd been a little too slow to parry the Norscan's blade.

Fifty years ago this cur would not have even touched me, thought Bagrik, using the brief lull to gather his strength. Only it wasn't fifty years ago, and the Norscan had cut him; he'd cut him deep.

In contrast the warlord was barely scratched. Every blow Bagrik landed was shrugged off or what should've been a killing strike manifested as a graze or nick. With every swipe, the king felt his strength fading, the power behind the blow lessening as if his muscles were atrophying aggressively all the while they fought.

One good hit, Bagrik thought, that's all I need.

In a blackened blur, the Norscan's blade fell upon Bagrik again, the brief amnesty in the battle having ended. The dwarf king struggled desperately to fend him off, knowing in his heart that he was losing. Blows rained in and Bagrik was battered to his knees. Gasping for breath as the Norscan sought to crush him, the dwarf king searched deep within himself for the last vestiges of his strength. There at the core of his being, he tapped into the one thing he had left that could save him. Anger.

Swiping madly, the dwarf caught the Norscan a glancing blow against his war helm, his enemy having opened up his defences when he'd believed that Bagrik was all but defeated. He spun on his heel a little, staggered by the dwarf's sudden lucky strike. Bagrik used it to his advantage. He managed to heave his good leg to a standing position, though the pain was crippling him, and with a roar of fury severed the Norscan's forearm in two. The obsidian blade clattered to the ground and shattered into glassy fragments, its power suddenly broken. Protruding from the lopped off stump of the Norscan's arm, his writhing black veins searched desperately for the weapon. Like a floundering fish gaping for air on the shore, the tentacled veins slowly ceased, flaking away into nothing.

Bagrik didn't stop. To stop now would mean death. He rammed the spiked pommel of his rune axe into the Norscan's thigh, tearing it open and felling the warlord to his knees. They were face to face. Bagrik snarled as their eyes met.

'Now you die,' he promised, aiming for the Norscan's neck. As he lifted the blade, he exposed his side. The warlord ripped another weapon from its sheath and stabbed the king. Bagrik felt nothing more than a pinprick, glancing quickly to see a serrated dagger in the Norscan's meaty fist. It was nothing. Even driven by the warlord's formidable strength, it had only grazed the dwarf king's flesh, slowed by his rune armour.

With a roar, Bagrik decapitated the Norscan. His armoured head *thunked* onto the icy ground and rolled, his body slumped over next to it pooling blood.

Then the poison hit. Coldness seized Bagrik's bones. Paralysis in his fingers saw the rune axe fall from his desperate grasp. The dwarf king reached down to the wound, though he could no longer feel it. The blood on his gauntlets, his blood, was tainted yellow. He gritted his teeth against sudden agony. Gripped by palsy, he fell. Barely able to keep his eyes open, Bagrik stared into the cold lifeless orbs of the Norscan's severed head. Huscarls still surrounded him. He could hear them closing.

ONE OF ULFJARL'S ambitious hurscarls, Heimdarr, had raised his axe and was about to claim the life of the bearded king, and with it lordship over the tribes, when he heard a heavy object spinning through the air towards him. Too late, he turned. Blurring silver was the last thing he ever saw.

'TO THE KING! To the king!' Morek cried, whipping his last thrown axe into the bestial brow of another Norscan. Korhvale was alongside him, severing heads and limbs one-handed with his hand axe, his wounded arm bound to his side, even as the dwarf barrelled into the huscarls hacking, punching and butting.

In seconds they had forged a way through to Bagrik. The hearth guard captain's heart held in his throat when he saw the ashen-faced king on his side, fearing his liege lord was dead. With relief, he noticed that Bagrik was still breathing, though it was with shallow, laboured gasps.

'Uzkul umgi,' he shouted, cutting down a northman as he dared to take a step toward the stricken dwarf king.

Together, elf and dwarf circled Bagrik keeping the foe back.

War horns rent the air as the back of the Norscan mob suddenly crumpled. From the north, Haggar emerged through a swathe of carnage with a band of dour long-beards. To the east came Ithalred at the head of his dragon knights, crushing Norscan skulls and cutting them down where they stood. In a few bloody moments, the battlefield was clear and the last of the northmen were being destroyed. Some were rounded up and slaughtered, others were harried into the sea. Desperately, these last remnants dove into the icy water. They only reached a few hundred feet from the shoreline before they were dragged asunder by the denizens of the deep, their screams eclipsed by the crashing waves. The Norscan beasts were burned, greasy smoke already staining the air black.

Satisfied the foe was vanquished, Morek went to his king.

'Victory my liege,' he said, thinking at first that Bagrik was only winded.

Far from it. The king was alabaster white. His fingers were shaking, eyes wide, as he hissed through gritted teeth, fighting to speak.

'Back to the camp,' rasped Morek, fear gripping his chest as he looked at Haggar. 'Back to the camp!' he cried.

ACT THREE
Elf Bane

CHAPTER SEVENTEEN
Broken Bread, Shattered Alliance

'How is he?' Morek asked. He kept his voice low; the king was only in the next room.

The allies had returned slowly and wearily to their encampment, twenty miles from the battle site upon a flat ridge overlooking the distant sea. A thin, lonely trail had led them down to the ice plain, now slicked with blood, and it was by this path that the victorious allies returned in dark mood. The camp was little more than scattered pavilions and sparsely dotted stone-ringed fires. Most of the troops had been committed to the final battle, only disparate knots of wounded and a paltry group of guards awaited the allies upon their return. Morek had sent rangers ahead of the war host to ensure that Bagrik's grand tent was put up, determined his king would have every comfort as he was tended to. The squat structure, smoke issuing through the chimney vent from an already stoked fire, dominated the flat ridge. Drifting in and out of consciousness, Bagrik had been taken there immediately and the Valakryn summoned in force.

'He'll live… for now,' replied Hetga, matriarch of the priestesses. She was a grizzled matronly woman, her robes and trappings cinched tightly around her impressive girth and bosom. Her long hair, bound into a tight bun, was once golden but had since faded to an elegant silver-grey. She carried several scars and much like her uncompromising appearance, didn't sweeten her words. 'The poison still runs through him. He's weak, but some of his strength may return given time. The cantankerous old bastard is awake though, refusing help and banishing my priestesses from his bed chambers, the prude. Truth be told,' said Hetga, lighting up a pipe and supping deep, 'there's nothing more we can do anyway. Whatever venom was upon that blade is beyond our arts to heal completely. Only Valaya, bless her name, can decide his fate now.'

Morek's face hardened. He'd hoped for better news.

'Tromm,' he intoned, bowing his head slightly.

'Tromm, Thane Stonehammer,' Hetga replied, bowing too, and took her leave.

The hearth guard captain took a deep breath before he passed through the flapped entrance to Bagrik's bed chamber.

'This is becoming an all-too familiar occurrence, my king,' he said with forced good humour.

Bagrik muttered a reply that Morek didn't quite catch. He gestured weakly for the dwarf to come to his bedside. Morek obeyed the pale-faced king, seemingly more old and frail that he'd ever known him. Bagrik looked even worse up close. Dark blue veins were visible beneath skin that was white and thin like parchment. Liver spots flared angrily as did the harsh purple bruises where his dented armour had nicked him. The king's eyes, though, were the worst. Rheumy and old, sunken into gaunt cheekbones, they lacked purpose and vigour. It was if the angry fire behind them had died in the hearth.

Bagrik reached out and grasped Morek's tunic, dragging him close. It seemed the old king had strength in his body yet.

'Get me... out of this... damned bed,' he snarled. Every word was an effort, but Morek was still taken aback by the king's vehemence.

'You have to rest,' he told him, shaking his head.

Bagrik tightened his grip. Morek felt his collar pinch his neck and his breathing get a little more difficult.

'If I... am to die,' said Bagrik, gritting his teeth against the pain, 'then... I'll do so with the rock... of the mountain above me, not on this Grungni-forsaken plain... Now, help me up!'

Morek swallowed with effort, managing a nod as he hooked his arms beneath the king's and lifted him out of the bed.

'Enough...' Bagrik said breathlessly, content to sit on the edge of the bed for a moment to gather his strength. 'I need a moment...'

'My king, are you sure–'

'A moment!' snapped the king, cutting Morek off as he glared at him.

When he was ready, Bagrik nodded and Morek heaved him off the bed and helped him into his boots and robes. As he did so, the hearth guard captain saw the ugly yellow wound that had been caused by the poison dagger. It was only small, little more than a graze, but the flesh around it festered and stank.

It reminded Morek of what he'd been shown when in the shaman's thrall. He thought about confiding in his king but in the end decided against it. Bagrik had enough to worry about. Knowledge of the future foretold would avail him nothing.

'Throne bearers!' cried Morek, once the king was back on his feet and the crown of Karak Ungor upon his head.

Four hearth guard marched into the room, the king's seat carried aloft between them. When they reached their captain and the king, they set the throne down and kneeled, heads bowed. Morek assisted Bagrik as the king mounted his throne, then draped heavy furs, together with the boar pelt over his back and shoulders.

'This'll keep out the cold,' he whispered, pressing a tankard of ale into the king's wasted fist. Bagrik had to clasp it with both hands, but as he drank he straightened, eventually holding the tankard in one hand, as if some of his strength was returning.

'A good drop,' remarked the king, some of the colour coming back to his cheeks as he wiped the foam from his mouth. 'I'll need more if we're to travel,' he added, forcing a determined smile.

Morek filled the tankard. The king raised it to his lips.

RUGNIR DRANK THE last of the broth, upending the warm cauldron into his mouth, allowing rivulets of the thick soup to run down his face only to be sopped up by his beard.

Whilst in the cave with Craggen, time had lost all sense of meaning. Drifting in and out of consciousness, it could have been days, weeks or months. Rugnir simply did not know. He knew only that he had to return, and with all haste, to Karak Ungor.

When he was finished, the dwarf set the cauldron down and belched.

'You're a fine cook, Craggen,' he noted.

The old hermit was watching him from the shadows of the cave, smoking his pipe as ever.

'Perhaps I can recommend you to King Bagrik, upon my return, and once all of this sorry business is behind us,' Rugnir added, getting up from where he'd been sitting. At last his strength had almost returned, his wounds had nearly healed and he could even walk without aid. Probably believed dead, Rugnir was finally ready to leave. He only hoped it wouldn't be too late.

'There's a pack for you,' said the gruff voice of Craggen.

Rugnir turned towards where the old hermit was pointing and found a leather knapsack resting against the cave wall.

'Provisions,' he explained, 'ale, stonebread and the like. You'll find rope too, as well as a little pipeweed for the journey.'

Rugnir turned back towards the old dwarf and bowed deeply.

'*Gnollengrom*,' he intoned. 'I am forever in your debt, Craggen.'

'Bah!' scowled the dwarf. 'I'll be glad to be rid of you. Least now I can get back to the grobkul,' he said, shuffling off his rocky perch and tromping over to where the other dwarf was standing.

'Here,' said the hermit, 'it's no heirloom, but it'll kill urk and grobi right enough.' The old dwarf pressed the haft of a hunting axe into Rugnir's hands.

The younger dwarf's face conveyed his deep honour at the gift.

'Nah, don't worry on it,' snapped Craggen, tramping away again. 'Plenty more where that came from,' he said, his voice slowly fading as he was engulfed by the darkness of the cave until he'd disappeared from view.

'I won't forget you,' Rugnir promised, stowing the axe and then hoisting the knapsack onto his back before he left the cave, blinking into the harsh morning light.

RUGNIR FOUND HIS bearings quickly. Only just over an hour on the trail that led off from the cave and he saw a cluster of crags he recognised. Incredibly, it seemed, he was not that far from his hold. A few days solid march across the mountains and he would be able to see the gates of Karak Ungor again. Rugnir's jubilation at his imminent homecoming was tempered, however, by the thought of what he might find there and what he must do as soon as he was back.

Walking with a heavy heart, Rugnir crested a rocky rise and saw corpses strewn upon a battlefield below him. Most were picked clean, bones bleached by the sun. Huge pyres littered the darkened plain, their fires long since gone out. Scattered weapons lay strewn about, along with fallen banners.

Rugnir knew this place. He had been here before, long ago. It was called Broken Anvil Hill.

A HUGE CHEER erupted from the gathered warriors as King Bagrik and Prince Ithalred entered the Great Hall of Karak Ungor. Together, their crowns glittered like halos in the flickering torchlight of the hall. Both lords wore robes and ceremonial armour plate with runes of dwarfish or elvish design as appropriate. Ithalred came on foot, whilst Bagrik was carried upon his throne.

Where Ithalred wore a cape of star-blue silk, Bagrik shouldered the boar mantle of his namesake.

The king's health had improved slightly each day since leaving the encampment near the edge of the Sea of Claws. Dwarfs were fast healers. There was little that didn't kill them that left them debilitated for long. Even still, Bagrik was a shadow of the dwarf he once was, a constant grimace cast upon his face like a mask as his every moment was pained by the poison inside him. The onlookers surrounding him, except the few that knew the truth, would assume it was his natural wrathful demeanour that forged the king's expression.

The hall was teeming with dwarfs and elves, mingling with one another as a mood of solidarity pervaded. By joining blades with the dwarfs, through the blood they'd shed on the field, the elves had atoned for their previous dishonour. And while it would never be forgotten, at least the relationship between the two races could move forward. They exchanged words, patted one another on the back and shoulder, even laughed together. Some, mainly the dwarfs, were sombre and reflective, seeking isolated corners to raise their tankards or goblets in remembrance of the deeds done and fallen friends. Others, predominantly elves, were ebullient and self-aggrandising, enjoying the moment for what it was – a celebration of victory.

Captains followed in the wake of their conquering lords. First Morek, clad in his finest gromril armour and best tunic, then Haggar similarly attired, the banner of Karak Ungor held up proudly. Other thanes and clan leaders followed behind him in a dazzling array of battle helms, ancient mantles and ornate regalia. For the elves there was Korhvale, the hunter wearing a magnificent lion pelt across his bare shoulders and a silver ithilmar cuirass over vermillion robes. Lethralmir followed him, the other elf nobles stepping into line after him. The raven-haired elf wore a perturbed expression in addition to his silver-trimmed azure robes and gilded headband, at being only second in the processional column behind his prince.

Of the original elven delegation that had come to the hold several months before, the ones who had not fallen in battle, only Arthelas was not present, deciding to stay in solitude at Tor Eorfith until her brother had returned for good. This fact had only further soured Lethralmir's already caustic demeanour.

Morek noted the look in the raven-haired elf's face, following his venomous gaze as it came to rest on the ambassador, Malbeth. The hearth guard captain reserved his own ire for the dwarf alongside him.

Kandor, you ufdi, he thought. *Where were you when the call to war was sounded? Preening your beard, no doubt!*

He scowled as the ambassadors were the first to receive the triumphant heroes, offering their weak congratulations and honeyed platitudes. Kandor brought a tankard of ale for the dwarf king, and Malbeth a goblet of wine for his prince.

'From the vineyards of Eataine, Prince Ithalred,' said the elf, his tone respectful and not obsequious.

The prince nodded his thanks.

'From Brewmaster Heganbour's finest stocks,' chipped in Kandor, proffering the tankard to his king, who took it with difficulty. 'You gift me with ale from my own stores and expect me to be grateful?' Bagrik growled.

Morek smiled to himself, and then followed the gaze of the king as it pierced the throng and came to

Brunvilda waiting patiently upon her throne. She was a sight for sore eyes, right enough. Though outwardly composed, Morek saw the relief at the return of her husband fracture her guarded expression, the suggestion of tears glistening in the corners of her eyes.

The hubbub fell to a dull murmur in the Great Hall, as the doors were shut and Bagrik addressed his hold.

'Long have we fought,' he said, 'far from our home, far from our hearths.' The king lingered on Brunvilda. 'The north-men are dead!' Bagrik stated flatly. 'And Nagrim...' Bagrik's voice was nearly cracking, 'and Nagrim,' he repeated after he'd regained his composure, 'is avenged.'

Solemn muttering from the dwarfs greeted the pronouncement, amidst much head nodding and beard biting.

Prince Ithalred spoke up, breaking the melancholy mood with his musical voice.

'Alliance,' he said, 'is an easy word to use. It is much harder to *mean*. This day, we asur have forged that alliance. It is a bond of hot iron, cooled and hardened by blood,' he continued, the analogy not lost on the attentive dwarfs. 'But it is more than that.' Ithalred turned to face the dwarf king, and offered his hand. 'It is friendship.'

Bagrik nodded, and clasped the elf prince's hand in his own and then embraced him.

Malbeth was still translating Ithalred's words into Khazalid when the roar from the crowd drowned him out. The gesture between king and prince said far more than words ever could. The dwarfs and elves in the Great Hall followed the example of their lords and a warm air of camaraderie slowly filled the massive chamber.

'Drink for all!' bellowed the king. 'We drink to battles won, and to the passing of kith and kin. Remember them, one and all.' Bagrik nodded once to Ithalred and the lords made their way together to the King's Table where Brunvilda waited for them.

'I am glad you are safe,' she whispered into Bagrik's ear once the throne bearers had set him down.

'Aye lass, as am I,' the king replied, grimacing as he went to pat Brunvilda's hand.

She didn't know about the battle on the ice plain.

'You're hurt,' said the dwarf queen, her face awash with concern as she leaned over.

'It's nothing.'

'No, you're wounded–'

'Please Brunvilda,' Bagrik snapped, then lowered his voice. 'It is over now,' he said, looking out to the celebrating throng. 'Let them have their moment.'

Brunvilda bit her tongue, leaning back and facing the crowd with a stony expression.

MOREK WATCHED BRUNVILDA'S face darken and knew that she had discovered the truth about the king's injury. As she surveyed the crowd, her eyes met with the hearth guard captain's and she smiled weakly. Morek chastened himself. Averting his gaze, he found himself locking eyes with Grikk Ironspike. The captain of the ironbreakers, his face smeared with a thin patina of soot, folded his arms in reproach. This was not the triumphant return that Morek had hoped for.

THE FEAST WAS over an hour old before Brunvilda slipped away from the Great Hall. She padded quickly on soft sandals, weaving through the darkened corridors of the hold in silence. Hearth guard warriors gave her murmured greeting as she passed them, but none dared impede the Queen of Karak Ungor. Soon, she had reached the lower halls and the entrance to the vaults. Pausing at the iron-bound door, she reached for a hanging lantern. Her heart was pounding. The Grey Road lay beyond, and the ironbreakers who Bagrik had stationed there to guard it. But neither them, nor the fear of that lonely place would stop her from seeing her son.

Braving the shadowy catacombs of the vaults as she trod the Grey Road unaccompanied, Brunvilda browbeat every ironbreaker patrol that sought to challenge her. Even the guard at the gate, the one who bore the key to Lothvar's dungeon, fell victim to her withering iron-hard stare.

With the door yawning open, its guardian unable to meet her gaze, Brunvilda covered her mouth against the stink from within and went inside. The place was much as she had left it, dank and smeared with filth. She'd seen pigs in the sties of the overground farms at Zhufvorn and Undvarn in less squalor. Ignoring the rank surroundings, Brunvilda stepped quickly to the opening in the floor that led down to Lothvar's cell. When she looked inside, she found the pitiable dwarf with one misshapen ear pressed hard against the cave wall.

'I hear noises from above,' he said, in halting speech. 'Are we under attack? Does my father need me? I am ready.'

Despite his obvious afflictions, Lothvar possessed far superior hearing and olfaction than other dwarfs. Evidently he had heard the merrymaking far above, even through the many thick layers of stone between the Great Hall and his wretched pit. As if to prove his other 'natural' aptitude, Lothvar sniffed suddenly at the rancid air of his cave.

'I can smell elgi. Are we at war, mother? Lend me an axe and I'll drive them from the hold. Nagrim and I will do it. No enemy of Ungor can stand against us brothers!' he declared proudly standing tall, at least as tall as he was able to given his misshapen spine.

'Nagrim is dead,' Brunvilda told him softly, leaning down over the hole and bringing the lantern close, so that Lothvar could see her. It was dark in the cave, night having fallen over the mountains, but Brunvilda could still make out her son. Unlike Lothvar, her nocturnal vision was excellent. 'To a northmen ambush,' she said. 'I told you this long ago.'

'Dead?' Lothvar gasped, halted in his belligerent posturing. The dwarf's face twisted as he struggled to comprehend at first. 'Yes, I remember…' he said at last, falling into a sudden melancholy, '…Gazul, guide him to the Gate.'

'Lothvar,' said Brunvilda, patiently, 'I came to tell you that your father has returned, that he is safe.'

'Did he slay the elgi?' the dwarf asked, sorrow turning to aggression in an eye blink.

'No. The elves are our allies, our friends.' It was like coaxing a frightened mule though it was a timid naïve dwarf Brunvilda goaded, and towards understanding and the truth rather than the edge of a lode tunnel.

'I wish I could have fought beside him,' Lothvar bemoaned wistfully, his earlier melancholy returning.

It was worse than usual. Lothvar was barely lucid for a moment, before he drifted back into the imagined history of his inner world. His speech devolved into muttered ravings, and he shrank back into the darker shadows.

Brunvilda could endure no more of it.

'Give him this,' she told the guard, who lingered at the portal behind her.

She left a bundle of food wrapped lovingly in cloth, and returned to the Grey Road in silence.

BRUNVILDA'S MIND WAS tormented. Seeing Lothvar so debilitated, sinking ever deeper into a mire of madness, was an agony she felt scarcely fit to bear anymore. And what had it driven her to? Defiance of her king, skulking in the shadows like a thief? Perhaps Bagrik had been right... perhaps it would have been better if Lothvar had been exiled and left to the beasts of the mountain. No, he was her son, she could not countenance that, even if it meant going against tradition and ritual, even if it meant lying to Bagrik. Her husband or her son, it was no choice for anyone to make. Brunvilda was so preoccupied agonising over her thoughts that she failed to see Morek standing in the passageway in front of her.

'If the king finds you here, he'll know you have been to see Lothvar,' he said sternly, standing outside the antechamber that led back to the Great Hall.

Brunvilda was startled by Morek's voice, but calmed down as soon as she realised it was him.

'Have you been taking him morsels from the feast, again?' he asked.

Brunvilda nodded, 'And to tell him that his father has returned, and remind him that his brother is dead...'

A fissure was cracking through the queen's resolve that she could not prevent. She sobbed and broke down.

Morek couldn't watch Brunvilda suffer. He came forward and held her in his arms.

'I fear for him, Morek,' she confessed. 'I fear for Bagrik.'

The hearth guard captain paused, unwilling at first to voice his concerns should speaking them suddenly make them real.

'I cannot lie, Brunvilda,' he replied. 'The king's wound is grave. Whatever poison was on that blade–'

'Poison!' She recoiled, though Morek still held her, albeit at arm's length. 'I knew nothing of this–'

The creak of an opening door echoed dully behind them.

'Do you covet my queen, Morek Stonehammer?' asked a dour and sonorous voice.

Morek and Brunvilda stepped away from one another as if scalded, and turned to face the speaker.

Bagrik emerged from the shadows, the door to the antechamber closing quietly behind him.

'You should not be without your throne bearers,' Brunvilda told him, walking towards him. The queen was stopped in her paces by Bagrik's wrathful glare.

'I've strength enough to stand, rinn!' he snapped. 'Though, you obviously think me weak in mind as well as body if you believed that this... *deceit*,' he snarled waving his hand over them both, 'would go unheeded.'

'You misunderstand, my liege,' Morek told the king firmly, putting himself deliberately in Bagrik's eye-line. 'I love my queen,' he said, 'as I love my king. I would gladly give my life for either. It would be the greatest honour you could bestow upon my shoulders,' he said vehemently. 'I have served you for over one hundred years. I cannot believe you could think this.'

Bagrik's face was hard as stone at first but then his resolve cracked, and his weary shoulders sagged.

'My line is dead, Morek,' he said, close enough to rest his hand upon the hearth guard captain's pauldron for support. 'And I am so very tired...'

Catching sight of his queen again, Bagrik's demeanour changed.

'Your continued defiance of my will is not excused!' he raged, before she approached any further. 'Where else could you have been but visiting that *thing*. I was wrong to spare its life. It should have been cast out long ago.'

'If only you would speak to him,' Brunvilda pleaded. Morek stepped out of the way. It was unwise to get between a dwarf king and his queen.

'And say what?' asked Bagrik. 'What sense would it make to a *zaki*?'

'Don't call him that,' she warned.

'You'd prefer nubungki? For that is what *he* is.'

Brunvilda was furious. Morek feared the heat from her face and her fiery glare would melt the iron in Bagrik's ceremonial armour.

'He is *our* son,' she said calmly, through clenched teeth.

There was no time for a bellicose rejoinder. The door to the passageway was thrown open and Kandor barrelled through with several other dwarfs behind him. Amongst them were the king's throne bearers. Mercifully, Kandor's sudden arrival had dispersed the pressure cooker of building tension.

'King Bagrik,' he said breathlessly. 'You must come quickly.'

'What is it?' growled the king, annoyed by the interruption.

'Rugnir,' Kandor replied. 'He's alive.'

ABJECT SILENCE FILLED the Great Hall as all within awaited the return of Rugnir Goldmaster. Against all odds it seemed, he had survived the northmen ambush

and found his way back to Karak Ungor after almost
four months in the wild mountains.

Runners had been sent ahead to the outer gateway hall
– Rugnir was to be brought before Bagrik at once. The king
would know of the final moments of his son Nagrim.
All would hear of it. Apparently, the dwarf had said little upon
his arrival back at the hold. Only that he must see the king
with all haste on a matter of the direst importance.

Bagrik steepled his fingers, bent low over the arms of
his throne so that his broad back was arched and his
chin nearly touched his knees. Gargoyle-like, he stared
at the double doors to his hall without moving. After
what felt like an age, remarkable given the patience and
tenacity of dwarfs, the sound of booted feet could be
heard echoing down the long corridor beyond. A few
minutes later and the massive gates to the Great Hall
were thrust open, a group of six hearth guard trooped in
beside the lone ambush survivor.

Rugnir kept his gaze level and straight ahead. He met
the eyes of his king and did not falter as he strode down
the narrow aisle and past the tables thronging with
dwarfs, some confounded, their mouths agape or
scratching their heads; others thoughtful as they supped
on pipes, longbeards muttering disapprovingly. The
elves alongside them looked disconcerted.

Morek noticed two in particular, Ithalred and
Lethralmir, sharing a dark glance between themselves
furtively.

There was no announcement, no herald to usher him,
just Rugnir, alone, with the hearth guard left behind
him.

The dwarf, still laden with Craggen's pack, his hunting axe in a loop on his belt, bowed before his king at
the edge of the stone dais beneath his throne.

'Approach,' Bagrik growled, taking the utmost care not to look at Brunvilda sitting beside him.

Rugnir rose quickly and moved forward to kneel at the foot of his liege lord, placing the knuckles of both fists on the ground as he did so.

'*Tromm*, King Bagrik,' he uttered, head bowed, his voice harsh and rasping like grit.

The dwarf king squinted at him with one eye, before he leaned forward and prodded Rugnir hard on the shoulder. It made the dwarf look up. Satisfied that Rugnir was indeed corporeal, Bagrik leaned back again, and began stroking his beard.

'You are no apparition then, Rugnir Goldmaster,' declared the king. 'Welcome back,' he added, somewhat belatedly.

Morek was watching the entire display intently, between glances at the elf nobles, who seemed so stiff as to be easily mistaken for petrified wutroth. Rugnir, though, seemed different. No raucous pronouncements, no drunken swagger. Even the alcoholic cherrying of his cheeks was gone, replaced by a rawness, a hollowing out of something inside. Something had happened to him, and it was more than just merely surviving the ambush.

'I bring news,' said Rugnir, when it was clear he was expected to speak. 'Of Nagrim's death and the ambush in the gorge,' he added, much louder than before.

'Tell me, Rugnir,' urged Bagrik in little more than a harsh whisper as tears gathered at the corners of his rheumy eyes. 'Tell me what happened to my son.'

'My king,' Rugnir began, standing to his feet as his voice cracked with emotion, 'it was not northmen that attacked us in the gorge, though that is what you were meant to think no doubt.' He turned to face the elves and levelled an accusing finger at Lethralmir. 'It was them.'

Shocked silence descended like an anvil.

'Ridiculous,' Kandor piped up. 'He is raving,' he said, getting to his feet as other dwarfs also started to voice their dissent. 'Most likely drunk, as well.'

'He's sober, right enough,' said Morek, his words carrying over the growing hubbub. He shook his head, saying, 'And I've never seen him like this before.'

'The elgi are our allies,' Kandor protested, clearly unable to believe what he was hearing. 'They fought with us against the northmen hordes.'

Morek sniffed derisively at the remark.

'You feast with vipers,' Rugnir roared, taking a step towards the King's Table before a pair of hearth guard interceded. 'Dawi slayers and murderers sit at your table... Thagi!' he cried, glowering at the elves with fists clenched. 'Thagi!'

'No,' said Kandor with half an eye on Malbeth, who seemed stunned into silence. 'Impossible. Nagrim was stuck with northmen arrows,' he petitioned the king, 'We all saw it.'

'Arrows, nothing more,' said Rugnir. 'Shot by the elgi,' he scowled. 'I saw it with my very eyes,' he added, pointing at them with two fingers.

'The dwarf lies,' snapped Lethralmir, getting up from the table.

'Sit down, Lethralmir,' Ithalred ordered in an undertone.

'Whilst we are accused of murder and treachery?' replied the raven-haired elf. 'I will not, my lord.'

'Do as your prince commands,' Malbeth told him, the ambassador rising too so that he was level with Lethralmir.

A clamour of disgruntled voices – both dwarf and elf – was gathering momentum throughout the hall. The mood, so genial at first, had soured swiftly and was becoming more riotous by the minute.

'Watch your temper, Malbeth,' Lethralmir warned, sneering, before he turned his attention back to Ithalred. 'We are insulted,' he said, continuing the earlier theme, 'and I demand to know what is to be done.'

'Nothing,' said Morek simply. 'Nothing will be done, until we get to the truth of this.'

The hearth guard captain was already standing. He had moved to within a few feet of Rugnir – the dwarf looked ready to snap at any moment.

'For isn't the truth that the northmen came here for vengeance and not conquest at all,' said Morek, remembering the visions bestowed upon him by the Norscan shaman. 'That we dawi were never a part of whatever fell purpose drove them. You,' – Morek pointed at Ithalred – 'you were the one the daemon sought. There was a debt against your blood, ages old.'

'I can't believe this,' said Kandor. 'How is it possible you know this, Morek?'

The hearth guard captain turned on the dwarf merchant. His eyes were like blazing coals of vehemence.

'I know it, because I saw it when the daemon tried to addle my mind!' he hissed through his teeth.

Kandor could only gape.

Bagrik turned his gaze on Ithalred. The king was stony faced, bereft of all emotion. Morek had never seen him look more dangerous.

'Did you murder my son?' he said with a level voice, looking the elf prince in the eye. 'Do not lie to me, elgi,' he warned, shaking his head then nodding as he narrowed his eyes, 'for I will know.'

Ithalred mustered as much presence as he could, matching the dwarf king's steely glare as one lord to another.

'It was not supposed to be this way,' he admitted with profound sorrow.

The Great Hall exploded in uproar. Like a rampant summer flame over dry fields of wheat and corn, the furore swept across the entire chamber. It infected everyone like a virulent contagion, with anger, belligerence and hate. Everything that had been built over the many months, all the painstaking endeavour to bring the two races together, the warrior bond forged on the fields of blood against the Norscans came tumbling down like a fortress with its foundations cruelly ripped away.

Quickly, the elves found their fellow kinsmen and banded together in protective circles, surrounded by mobs of wrathful dwarfs. The longbeards demanded action and swift vengeance.

Korhvale, seeing the imminent danger, cried out in elvish and he together with a handful of the prince's bodyguard gathered to Ithalred. But because the two lords were still sat next to each other, the elves fought for position with the hearth guard. Both sets of warriors were only inches away from one another, bristling with anger, one wrong step, one slight away, from going over the edge to bloodshed.

'In Lileath's name, Ithalred I beg you, say this is not true,' pleaded Malbeth from within the circle, anguish etched upon his face.

The prince's eyes were hollow.

'I cannot.'

Frantically, desperate to salvage something, anything from this abject disaster, Malbeth turned to Kandor.

'This was not known to us,' said the elf, looking down at the dwarf beside him. 'We came here out of a desire for lasting peace.'

'You knew of it,' spat Lethralmir, the vitriol was palpable. 'You were as complicit in this as any of us.'

Malbeth's face went as white as chalk, as the life seemed to drain away to be replaced by something colder and harder. To look at him, you would think he had died suddenly. In many ways, he had. The elf's eyes grew wide. All the pent up rage, the dark desires of his past he'd kept at bay for so many years were finally unleashed in a flood of red-hazed catharsis.

'Lying scum!' Malbeth flew at Lethralmir, flinging one of Ithalred's guards aside who had been unfortunate enough to get in his way, and smashed a heavy blow against the blade-master's exposed cheek.

Lethralmir was thrown to the floor under the savage impact. Sprawled on his back the raven-haired elf, supported by his elbows, craned his neck to regard his attacker. A thin drool of blood hung from the corner of his mouth. Lethralmir touched it with his naked fingers, before licking off the hot metallic fluid with his tongue.

'See the killer,' he said, eyes on Malbeth the whole time. 'He even slew his own wife, *murdered* her in cold blood. He is the worst of us all.'

'*Elethya…*' Malbeth scarcely uttered the word. He was breathing raggedly, as he searched in his robes for something. When he couldn't find it, he locked his gaze with Lethralmir. The raven-haired elf smiled, oh so slightly.

The entire hall was enrapt for the moment as Malbeth and Lethralmir played out the tragedy. The elf ambassador was about to reach for a blade to finish his raven-haired aggressor, when he felt a presence on the arm of his robe. Without thinking, Malbeth lashed out. Blinking back the crimson rage that blanketed his vision, he was horrified when he realised he had struck Kandor. The dwarf shrank away from him, rubbing his jaw. Malbeth watched as something died, there and then, in Kandor's eyes.

With the performance over, Morek decided to take matters into his own hands.

'Dreng elgi,' he snarled, unslinging his axe, 'Dreng thagi!' Scraping metal resounded in the hall as the hearth guard drew blades; Rugnir, too, and any other dwarf that carried a weapon. Those who were unarmed balled their fists and chewed their beards in fury. Some of the elves unsheathed daggers, Korhvale amongst them. Lethralmir slipped a hidden blade from his vambrace. Ithalred didn't move as his kin made to defend themselves.

'Cease!' The gravel voice of King Bagrik stopped the fight before it could begin. 'Stow your blades,' he growled at length, glowering around the room at every dwarf in his eye-line. 'Do it now or be entered into the dammaz kron for defying your king,' he promised. A side glance at Grumkaz Grimbrow, the leathery chief grudgemaster, confirmed to Bagrik that the old granite-faced dwarf had his quill readied.

No other dwarf in the Great Hall of Karak Ungor had greater claim to blood for the elves' heinous deeds than Bagrik. His bellow for cessation of hostility was not about to be challenged and, for now, the dwarfs lowered their axes.

'You saved my life, Ithalred,' the king told the elf prince, speaking to him as if they were the only ones in the mighty room, 'and for that I grant you one concession,' he added, raising a gnarled finger for emphasis. The king abided for silence, waiting until even the recalcitrant longbeards had stopped their pugnacious grumbling.

'Get out,' he said simply. 'Take your kin and go. But mark this: do it quickly. I am a hair's breadth from killing you all in this very chamber,' Bagrik promised. The king's eye was twitching as he said it, drawing on all of his will not to just cut the elves down where they stood and let that be an end to it. 'But I will not stain its legacy with blood, especially that of thagging traitors. There has been enough shed in my hold to last me five lifetimes,' he added with the faintest trace of lamented remembrance.

'Go, now. Seven days hence, I will meet you on the field of battle on the lowland outside your city. Then…' he muttered, nodding darkly to the prince, 'then you can atone in full for this treachery.'

Wood scraping on stone announced Ithalred as he rose from his seat in silence. His gaze lingered on Bagrik for a moment longer, before he turned, waiting for the surrounding dwarfs to back away – who did so eventually, but only at Bagrik's snarled urging – and walked down the aisle, up to the gate and through it to the halls beyond.

A hearth guard escort accompanied the elves. Morek was ordered to go with them should any get the idea to take matters into their own hands. Once at the outer gateway hall, the elves were stripped of any armour or weapons, aside from Ithalred's ancestral blade, which Bagrik had allowed him to keep out of respect for him saving his life, and cast out. The elven trappings were then piled up on a mule cart and taken to the lower deeps where they would be melted down in the forges and remade into bolt tips and arrow heads.

The accord between the dwarfs and elves was at an end, their victory over the Norscan hordes a pyrrhic one. In seven days' time, Karak Ungor and Tor Eorfith would meet again, and there would be blood.

'CURSE THE WILES of Loec and his perfidy,' muttered Ithalred as the elves tramped listlessly from the dwarf hold. 'How did this happen? There was to be no survivors, no chance of the truth of what we did coming out.'

All told, almost three thousand elves were banished from Karak Ungor and its slopes. Many of the warriors, mainly rangers, spearmen militia and archers, were encamped in the crags around the hold. The reaction to the treatment of their lords when they'd emerged from the postern gate bereft of their belongings was one of dismay and anger. The elves' belligerence had cooled somewhat though when the ranks of quarrellers had appeared in the watch station overlooking the great gate and the towers and sky-bridges either side of it. Once the ballista and stone throwers had been wheeled into position, the elves packed up their fluted pavilions and elegant tents and marched away.

It was a few miles down the road before Ithalred gave voice to his frustration. By now he, and the other exiles from the Great Hall, had been given travelling cloaks, weapons and armour.

'It was inevitable,' said Lethralmir.

'How so?' Ithalred stopped walking and rounded on the raven-haired elf. 'Did you let one escape?'

'I meant, my prince,' he said, subtly clearing his throat, 'that war with the mountain-dwellers was inevitable.'

Ithalred backed down, seemingly satisfied. About to continue on his way, he noticed Malbeth trudging down the road towards them. He appeared catatonic, staring straight ahead at some unseen horizon, one foot in front of the other like an automaton. After the elves had been expelled from the dwarf hold, the ambassador had immediately started scrabbling around in his baggage. Ithalred had paid him little mind, he had his own crisis to contend with. Whatever Malbeth had been looking for, the prince assumed he had not found it.

When he approached the two nobles, Ithalred saw a flicker of recognition in the ambassador's eyes and the blank slate expression fell away, consumed by rage. A roar of anguish ripped from Malbeth's lips as he tore a sword from the sheath of one of Ithalred's guards and lunged at Lethralmir. The raven-haired elf saw the attack late, but was swift enough to weave his body from the killing stroke. Instead, the blade grazed his ribs and he cried out in pain.

Like lightning, Korhvale, the prince's shadow, seized Malbeth's wrist before he could strike again.

'Drop it,' he growled. The White Lion had seen the attack a fraction before it took place. Only he knew that he had delayed for a second to see if Lethralmir got what he deserved, before he'd intervened. When Malbeth didn't relinquish the blade immediately, Korhvale twisted the ambassador's wrist and the weapon fell from his agonised grasp with a yell. The White Lion was about to let him go when he saw Malbeth's expression twisted with fury, his eyes full of hate and loathing. He tried to break free and Korhvale, fearing that he would, called for help. Two more guards came to his aid, holding onto one arm whilst Korhvale grabbed the other.

'Khaine has him,' snarled Lethralmir, staunching the blood from his wounded side as he watched Malbeth struggle. 'What's the matter,' he said quietly, drawing close to the pinioned elf, 'have you lost your medicine?' he asked, smiling.

Malbeth thrashed against his captors, screaming curses at Lethralmir as his rage swallowed him utterly.

'Hold him down,' Ithalred said calmly. 'You,' he added, nodding towards a gaping onlooker, 'bring rope to bind his legs and arms.' The prince looked back at Malbeth with pitying eyes. '*By Isha's grace…*' he whispered, realising that he regarded that which dwelt in all the asur, their raw warrior spirit and violent potential. Here was the Bloody Handed God made manifest. It had destroyed Malbeth, engulfed him with rage and a desire to kill.

Ithalred averted his gaze and found Lethralmir looking back at him, still clutching his bloodied side.

'And get a surgeon for this one,' added the prince, lip curling in distaste. 'You'll get your war with the dwarfs, Lethralmir,' he promised fatalistically. 'I'm going to need every sword.'

Ithalred stalked away. The skies overhead were darkening. Ravens circled.

CHAPTER EIGHTEEN
Fallen Lion

ITHALRED STARED OUT across the plain from the tallest tower of Tor Eorfith. He was naked barring the thick velvet cloak that trailed all the way to the marbled floor. It chilled his bare feet, but the elf hardly noticed. Ithalred felt numb, and not from the cold stone. Below he heard the sounds of battle preparation, of spears and longbows being racked, the dry-loosing of bolt throwers and the clank of hammers as forgesmiths fashioned suits of armour. Saddles were made ready, horse barding polished, lances and arrows stacked. The entire population of Tor Eorfith, man and woman, bustled in quiet urgency. For come the morrow, they would be at war with the dwarfs.

Eyrie Rock was the other, perhaps more prosaic, name for Tor Eorfith. It was a fitting appellation. The beauteous bastion was set upon a vast rugged spur of basalt and granite. Seven silver spires pierced cloud and soared into the stratosphere as if reaching for the very stars. The

wondrous towers punctuated a stout outer wall of
smoothed alabaster and grey-veined marble. Minarets
branched out from the main towers that also supported
many balconies. Those edifices that stood behind the
outer wall were joined by narrow arching bridges,
dripping with ornamentation and bejewelled
downward-thrusting spikes. Gem-encrusted obelisks lay
sunken in the verdant earth beyond the elven city. They
were waymarkers and potent magical foci through which
Tor Eorfith's mages could practise their arcane arts.

When he left Ulthuan, Ithalred had brought some of
the finest mason-artisans of Lothern and Eataine with
him. The glorious citadel where he now stood, this city
of silver and jewels, was the glittering fruit of their
labours, a masterpiece of the aesthetic, protected by
enchanted wards and bound with spells of resistance.
As the elf prince stared into the wind at the distant fires
of the dwarfs, as they made their encampment a few
miles from his gilded gates, he wondered if those magicks would be enough to stop them.

'Ravens flock to the towers, my prince,' said the grim
voice of Korhvale from behind him. The two warriors
were alone on the balcony. Ithalred chose to no longer
keep company with Lethralmir, preferring solitude.

'They foretell our destruction,' intoned the elf prince,
his golden hair disturbed by the growing breeze. 'Do
you think we are doomed, Korhvale?' he asked, facing
the White Lion.

'We reap what we have sown,' he answered tacitly.

'We faced annihilation at the hands of the northmen,
what else was I supposed to do?' asked the prince.

'We acted with dishonour.'

'It is not so black and white, Korhvale,' Ithalred
pressed, becoming more animated. 'You saw the

aftermath of their attack on the watch towers. And what of Hasseled's hawk ships? Fifteen vessels led by our finest naval captain, gone, destroyed. Our army was not strong enough to defeat them.'

'Had I known of your plan to kill the dwarf prince, and trick his kin into a war that was not theirs to fight, I would have stopped it,' Korhvale told him.

'It is much too late for that,' Ithalred scoffed, laughing despite himself.

After a brief silence, Korhvale said, 'We should leave. Take what ships we have left and return to Ulthuan. Your sister ails more by the day, she is constantly fatigued. She has not been seen out of her chamber for weeks. Isha knows it is her home that she craves.'

'*This* is her home, Korhvale,' Ithalred snapped, pointing to the marble at his feet. 'As it is yours and mine, and all of the other damned souls within these cold walls.'

He showed his back to the White Lion.

'Begone,' the prince said brusquely. 'I tire of you, Korhvale.'

The White Lion's lightened step made little sound as he walked away.

For over an hour after Korhvale had left, Ithalred looked down on the dwarfs below. They milled around like ants, tramping back and forth in their armour, raising their tents and unshackling cavalcades of ballista and mangonels from a string of draught mules. Ithalred's keen eyes discerned it all. The armoured dwarfs were like a blanket of bronze and iron blighting the verdant green of the land for miles. Hawk-eyed as he was, though, the elf failed to notice a figure moving through the rocks, several miles away from where the dwarfs were camped, but getting steadily closer.

* * *

KORHVALE HEARD THE soft tread of his own boots echo down the lonely corridor from the spire where Prince Ithalred had made his eyrie. It was a doleful refrain to the beating of his heavy heart. The White Lion was in disarray. His conscience warred with his sense of duty. No warrior wearing the pelt could ever be accused of disloyalty. For was it not the woodsmen of Chrace who went to the aid of Caledor the First, saving him from death at the knives of druchii assassins? But slaying in cold blood… the very act stuck in Korhvale's craw and no matter how he rationalised it, the White Lion could not dislodge the feeling that such a deed made them no better than druchii themselves.

To face the dwarfs meant certain death. A pang of fear seized Korhvale at the sudden thought. Not for him; the prospect of mortality held no terror for a White Lion of Chrace. No, it was Arthelas whom Korhvale feared for. He could not leave her to be slain along with the rest. A desperate plan began to form in his mind. If he could get her onto a boat, there were Lothern sailors eager enough to leave the Old World to ferry her. He could smuggle her away in secret, ensure that she was safe. It was dark enough now for that.

As he plotted, the simple act of it leaving an uncomfortable sheen over his skin, Korhvale remembered the scroll he had hidden beneath his cuirass. Stopping in the darkness he reached for it tentatively. The parchment pages seemed so innocuous rolled up in his hand. Yet they held his desires, his yearnings; the profession of his true feelings for Arthelas.

Her quarters were not far. It might be the last chance he would ever get. Full of purpose, Korhvale returned the scroll delicately to its hiding place and went off swiftly down the shadowed hall. He had only passed a single sentry on his way to Arthelas's chambers in the next tower. Most of the warriors were below, watching from the battlements or making their final preparations for the fight to come. Korhvale had said nothing to him, he'd not even made eye contact so obsessed was he with his mission. First he would tell her of his feelings and then he would get her away from this place.

Korhvale was so anxious by the time he arrived at Arthelas's door that he felt sick. He was about to knock, when he thought better of it. It was deathly silent in the corridor, though the White Lion heard some muffled noises from within the room – perhaps she was singing – any commotion, however insignificant, might rouse unwanted attention. So instead, he eased his weight against the door. To the elf's relief, it was unlocked and opened quietly.

Stepping inside Korhvale closed the door behind him, making only a dull thud as the wood came flush against the alabaster arch. It was gloomy inside and a pungent aroma permeated the air in a thick violet fug. Thin veils were suspended from the ceiling made from gossamer and silk that obscured Korhvale's view into the room.

'*Arthelas*,' he whispered, searching for her in the pastel-hued darkness.

Korhvale thought he saw the hazy glow of fettered lanterns or perhaps candles with their wicks shortened to dull the flame. Passing through the first wall of veils, he noticed carafes of wine, platters of half-eaten fruit. A lyre lay discarded on a wooden bench carved into the effigy of a swan. Through a second layer of overlapping veils, and the muffled sound he heard outside the door became louder and more discernible. It was not singing. Rather, it was more breathless, repetitive but without harmony.

Beyond a narrow arch, through a circular anteroom festooned with plump cushions, was Arthelas's bed-chamber.

A final azure veil impeded him. There was the shape of two figures moving softly beyond it. Pulling back the drape, Korhvale whispered again.

'Arthelas…'

The words died on his lips. He'd found his true love, the woman he had watched from a distance for all the years he'd been in Ithalred's service. She was in the bed… with Lethralmir. The two of them writhed like adders beneath the orchid, silken sheets.

'Korhvale,' said Arthelas, noticing the White Lion first. The perverted serenity on the seeress's face brought a fresh rush of nausea. Then Lethralmir, with his back to him, looked over his shoulder at the Chracian and smiled in malicious pleasure. With her fingernail Arthelas had carved a symbol in Lethralmir's back in blood.

Korhvale recoiled in horror.

It was the mark of Atharti, the underworld goddess of pleasure.

The White Lion felt the scroll of parchment fall from his nerveless fingers, those words and feelings made cheap and worthless in the face of his horrified revelation. He couldn't breath and clutched at his chest in sudden panic. It was as if a dagger had been thrust into him. Korhvale wished he could take that dagger and use it to cut out his eyes.

'No…' The sound issued from his mouth was a gasp, but it was raw and primal. Tears fled from Korhvale's eyes, the corners of his mouth curling in disgust.

'Noooo!' he roared with such anguish that it rent his heart and left it forever ruined. Mortified, the White Lion fled. Lethralmir's mocking laughter echoed after him, like wraiths tugging at the Chracian's resolve. Korhvale was a veteran warrior. He had fought countless battles, alone in the mountains of his homeland and the forests of Cothique, on the shores of Nagarythe against the druchii and now for his lord versus the northmen hordes, but Korhvale had never before been wounded like this.

ARTHELAS'S SMILE SOURED into a scowl as she lay beneath the sweating body of Lethralmir and watched Korhvale claw through the veils.

'Don't let him escape,' she hissed urgently. 'Ithalred must never know…'

The smirk on Lethralmir's face vanished. The raven-haired elf grabbed his sword from where he'd left it alongside his discarded armour next to the bed, and leapt naked from the sheets after the White Lion.

Lethralmir knew his way around the chambers. He was also well-accustomed to the soporific fumes that laded the air. Weaving through the veil like a serpent, his narrowed eyes like slits upon the White Lion as he blundered in blind grief, Lethralmir caught his prey.

THE SILVER FLASH of a sword blade reflecting off the lanterns caught Korhvale's attention. Instinct took over, burning through his tortured misery like a beacon. A hot line of pain seared his side and the White Lion realised he had been cut. Grabbing a fistful of veils, he tore them down and threw them into Lethralmir's face. The raven-haired elf sliced through them with ease, his diamond-sharp blade paring the fabric like he was slicing through air. It slowed him long enough though for the White Lion to unsling his axe.

Chest heaving with the effort of his grief, Korhvale regarded his enemy a few feet across the pastel chamber. Despair boiled away, turning into something more substantial; something the White Lion could use – hate.

'I'll tear you limb from li–'

A FLASH OF light blossomed swiftly, lighting up the chamber, and then died. An actinic aroma, merged with the stench of burnt flesh, overwhelmed the soporific musk.

Lethralmir, blade poised at the ready, looked down at Korhvale's chest and saw why the White Lion had ceased his threats so abruptly. A gaping crater of cauterised flesh and blood existed where his torso should have been. Metal from his ithilmar cuirass fused with bone and boiled viscera. Smoke eking from the terrible wound, Korhvale slumped first to his knees and then fell face forward onto the ground. Arthelas was revealed behind him, draped in a violet gown, crackling tendrils of black energy fading slowly across her outstretched fingertips.

The surprised expression on Lethralmir's face turned amorous.

'Murder is such an aphrodisiac,' he purred.

'Get him up,' Arthelas snapped, in no mood for copulation. 'We must dispose of his body before he's missed.' She swept quickly to her bedside, let the gown slip from her shoulders and put on her robes and trappings.

Despondent and frustrated, Lethralmir set down his blade and threw the White Lion over his shoulder.

'He is heavy,' he complained through clenched teeth.

'Quiet!' Arthelas hissed, adding, 'In here,' as she opened the lid to a large ottoman.

Lethralmir dumped Korhvale's corpse inside unceremoniously and shut the lid.

Arthelas had moved back over to the scene of the fight. She scowled at the blood-stained floor.

'Clean it,' she snapped, looking around her chambers for further evidence of Korhvale's presence there.

'What about this?' Lethralmir asked as he crouched over the bloody smear left by the White Lion. He held a scroll of parchment between his fingers and showed it to Arthelas.

'Burn it,' she told him coldly.

'GONE, MY LORD,' said Commander Valorian.

'"Gone", what do you mean "gone"?' asked Ithalred, strapping on his final leg greave.

The elves were mustering. The arched gates of Tor Eorfith were open and its drawbridge lowered to enable snaking columns of dragon knights, silver helms and reavers to sally. Squadrons of chariots from the partly sundered realm of Tiranoc followed; phalanxes of spearmen and archers in their wake. Bolt throwers, aptly named 'reapers' were wheeled out along the bridge and bedded in quickly upon the high ground. After the war machines marched the sword masters, their massive blades held in salute as they encircled Tor Eorfith's mages who trod solemnly within the web of steel carrying their orbs, staffs and other magical arcana. Though there were just a handful of the warrior-scholars, their deadly great swords could shear through even the thickest dwarf armour.

Tor Eorfith's spellweavers were led by the silver-haired archmage, Rhathilan. He was Arthelas's teacher and mentor though unknown to Rhathilan she had since surpassed him, yoking her power from darker sources. Having seemingly overcome her fatigue, the seeress had insisted she be allowed to fight in the battle. Ithalred had wanted to keep her safe behind the gates of the city, but even they would not persevere forever. In the end he had relented, and so she too joined her fellow mages behind the sword masters' steel circle.

As the elves filed out of the city gates they arrayed themselves upon the plain in disciplined ranks and formed their regiments, banners snapping in the wind. Several miles to the south were the army of the dwarfs, waiting patiently for the elves to finish mustering.

'Precisely that, my prince,' Valorian replied. The warden of Tor Eorfith would be taking command of the interior troops during the first sortie. 'Korhvale is no longer in Tor Eorfith,' he concluded.

'Fled?' Ithalred's voice was tinged with disbelief as he donned his golden hawk-helm. 'He expressed his reservations about this conflict with the dwarfs... that was the last time I ever saw him. But to run?' the elf prince shook his head. 'It is not his way. Something is amiss,' he muttered.

'Would you like me to investigate the matter?' Valorian asked.

'No,' Ithalred decided, looping his foot in the stirrup of his mighty great eagle. The magnificent beast was called Awari, and he was one of three rookery brothers. To forge a bond with such a creature was not easy and no one other than Ithalred ever rode these eagles. Awari was his favourite – intelligence and nobility shone behind his avian eyes. 'There is no time. Marshal the defences,' he said, swinging into the saddle, 'when the dwarfs beat us outside the city you'll need to be ready to interrupt any pursuit so that as many of us as possible can get back behind the walls.'

It sounded fatalistic, but Ithalred was not so vainglorious as to be unrealistic. The dwarfs drew upon all the armies of their entire hold. The elves, though their colony was large, had no such force at their disposal and no time to request reinforcements. Such negative strategy was prerequisite when so badly outnumbered.

With nothing further to say to Valorian, Ithalred arched his head back and uttered an ululating command that shrilled like a bird cry. His great eagle spread its mighty wings, its armoured head and beak glittering in the morning light. With a piercing shriek the ancient creature rose magnificently into the sky to join its unmounted rookery brothers, Skarhir and Urouke, amidst the darkening cloud.

IT WAS FIVE days since the elves had been expelled from Karak Ungor in ignominy. Brunvilda thought it a rare miracle that none had lost their lives in the Great Hall, that scarcely no blood had been shed.

In a few hours Bagrik's armies would leave Karak Ungor for the long, slow march to the elven city. The road to the north would take around two days to travel, two short days before the grand dwarf army would assemble on the lowlands before Tor Eorfith. Using his influence and power as king, Bagrik had assembled such a force as to leave the hold almost empty, barring a skeleton company of thinly spread miners, clan warriors and ironbreakers. There were some, amongst the most venerable ancestors and longbeards, that would also remain but few in the Delving Hold had seen or heard of them in many years.

The scarcity of troops patrolling the corridors was to Brunvilda's advantage as she hurried towards her destination. The queen was shrouded in a thick cloak of hruk wool, voluminous enough to hide what she needed it to. Cowl drawn over her head she moved anonymously, down into the farthest deeps. Brunvilda suppressed a pang of regret and sorrow. It would probably be the last time she ever did this.

Dimly, she recalled her last conversation with Bagrik, what had passed between them now fully occupying her thoughts. After the elven treachery had been revealed, Bagrik had slipped into a bitter melancholy. Brunvilda, once she had him alone in their royal quarters, had tried desperately to bring him out of it, but to no avail. Instead, she had only worsened the king's buried choler.

'Please, I beg of you, don't go into battle,' she had urged him. 'Let Morek reckon this misdeed of the elgi. You are not fit enough–'

'I am fit enough!' Bagrik had raged. 'You'll never meet the dawi king that is not fit enough to reckon his own deeds. I'd have to be dead before I allowed another to settle this grudge,' he vowed. 'My son... Nagrim was slain by these pointy-eared, pale-arsed bastards. His kinsdwarf left for dead, too. And that,' he had told her, his eyes widening with vehemence as he wagged his finger, 'was their biggest mistake. They reckoned on a dwarf being as soft and effeminate as their own silk-swaddled race. What folly!' Bagrik laughed, but it had been a bitter, mirthless expression. The coldness of it had struck to Brunvilda's core.

'I feel for Nagrim, too,' the queen had assured him. 'I loved him dearly, and I would see these elgi pay with their lives for what they did, but I would not see you give up yours so wastefully.'

'It is not profligate to avenge one's kin, Brunvilda,' Bagrik had barked. 'My only son is dead. My *only* son,' he repeated, with a warning in his tone as he had turned away from her to face his armour. 'Upon my return, the other will be exiled,' Bagrik had said without emotion, 'left to die in the mountains, as it should have been years ago.'

Despite her impassioned protests, Bagrik had not listened. Reason had fled in his mind. Whether caused by the poison running in his veins that would surely kill him, or the fact that his heart and soul were hollow lifeless husks, Brunvilda did not know. All she was certain of was that she could not allow Lothvar to be so callously discarded. If he was to die then at least it would be upon the field of battle, fighting for the honour of his father and his clan.

The door to the Grey Road had come upon Brunvilda swiftly. She took no lantern this time; she would need the darkness and the shadows to conceal her. Silently, with only her nocturnal vision to guide her, Brunvilda moved down the long subterranean passageway that led to Lothvar's cell. Approaching the corona of light cast by the hanging lantern at the door, she noted with some dismay that the guard was still present.

Swathed in her dark woollen cloak, the ironbreaker did not see her until she was almost upon him.

'Hold–' he began, starting to show Brunvilda his armoured palm in a gesture for her to stop.

Brunvilda swung the hammer she carried out from beneath the cloak and smashed it, two-handed, against the ironbreaker's helmet. When he didn't go down from the first blow, she struck him again. This time, he went to his knees and his arms dropped to his side. Whilst he was still dazed, Brunvilda pulled off his helmet and then smacked him again over his bare, bald pate. That did it. The ironbreaker fell onto his back unconscious.

Satisfied he was still breathing, and would only be nursing an unearthly headache when he eventually awoke, Brunvilda, leaving the hammer behind, stepped over the prone dwarf and into Lothvar's cell using the key stolen from the guard.

Using the wooden bucket and some patient cajoling, Brunvilda got Lothvar out of his pit. She brought a bundle of tightly wrapped clothes: a coarse jerkin, some woollen leggings and boots. Flicking anxious glances back in the direction of the supine guard, she dressed her son. Though it was a struggle, she managed it quickly and with a few quiet words of encouragement took Lothvar out of the dungeon for the first time in over eighty years. Brunvilda forgot to douse the lantern outside as they fled and Lothvar cowered against the light. She had been tempted to extinguish it, but her son would need to get used to it if he were to achieve the destiny she had in mind for him.

'Where are you taking us, mother?' asked Lothvar, holding Brunvilda's hand as she led them through the Grey Road as fast as she dared.

'To see your brother,' she promised. 'Move swiftly, Lothvar. No one must know you have gone… not yet, at least.'

'Does our father need us?' he asked. 'Together, we will drive the grobi from our gates… No, wait…' said Lothvar, his sudden bravura overcome by solemnity, 'Nagrim is dead…'

'Quietly now, Lothvar,' Brunvilda told him, gripping his malformed hand just a little tighter, 'we are leaving the Grey Road.'

Lothvar did as his mother asked and together they used all the seldom trodden paths, the forgotten corridors and dust-clogged passageways of Karak Ungor, moving in secret until they had reached their destination.

When a noble of a dwarf hold was slain, tradition demanded that a long period of mourning be observed before the dead were allowed to pass into the Halls of the Ancestors. Like with everything, dwarfs took their time over this ritual. Nagrim's internment had been interrupted by the sudden need for war, the abrupt desire to mete out vengeance in his name. So it was then that he had remained in the Temple of Valaya, beneath the goddess's watchful gaze.

Between the magic embedded in the runes of that sacred place and the unguents and oils lathering his body, the dwarf prince was kept preserved and had not decayed even slightly when Brunvilda and Lothvar finally reached him.

'Nagrim,' breathed Lothvar, setting eyes on his younger brother for the very first time. He staggered forward, limping free of his mother's grasp to stand before the cold body of his sibling laid in quiet repose.

'He looks like he's sleeping,' said Lothvar, reaching out with trembling fingers.

'Don't touch him, my son,' warned Brunvilda. 'He is awaiting his ancestors' call. Gazul will guide him when the time comes.'

Lothvar wept, though it was a brief mourning. As he wiped away the last errant tear from his ravaged face, he turned to Brunvilda.

'Why have you brought me here?'

Brunvilda smiled warmly. Out of the corner of her eye she could see the ancestral armour of Karak Ungor, that which by right and tradition would go to the heir of Delving Hold, he who was eldest of the king's offspring upon reaching his eightieth winter.

Lothvar was over eighty winters old.

'I've brought you here for your destiny,' Brunvilda told him. 'Now listen to me Lothvar, listen carefully to what you must do.'

CHAPTER NINETEEN
For Vengeance

AT LAST THE elves were ready. Regal dragon knights glared imperiously astride shuddering steeds, vermillion armour gleaming as if aflame. Silver helm knights, with lances upraised and banners dipped, shimmered in their ithilmar mail. The spear tips of the elf infantry shone in forests of silver spikes. Archers stood motionless, a long unbroken line of sapphire and white. This was an army of the elder race, the immortal sons and daughters of Aenarion from across the Great Ocean. Truly, it was a wondrous sight.

'The glittering host,' Morek growled from atop the ridge, voice thick with contempt. He was standing alongside King Bagrik in his full hearth guard regalia, battle mask drawn over his face. The dwarf stroked the runic talisman around his neck with absent-minded affection. Below him were the batteries of war machines arranged in half-rings. The quarrellers were beneath them strung out in ragged lines to compensate for the uneven terrain. Below that was the sheer wall of iron and bronze that Morek would use as a hammer to crush the elven host and send them fleeing back behind their walls.

'T'would be a pity to bloody them,' remarked the hearth guard captain after he'd received his final orders from the king.

Bagrik grunted beneath his own battle mask.

'But bloody them we will,' he promised darkly, 'and more besides.'

The horn call rang out like clear thunder on a summer's day. It split the air and signalled the first advance. Dwarf trumpets bayed in response, and the staccato beat of drums was struck up in earnest. The sons of Grungni were moving.

The battlefield was dominated by a broad expanse of flat lowland consisting of coarse grass, isolated copses of pine and scattered rocks. Hillocks formed a shaggy undulating spine across the far left flank, developing into much heavier-contoured ground that culminated in the ridge of sparsely grassed rock where Bagrik watched and waited. To the right was the rocky debris of the mountains, eroded by weather and age to encroach a fair distance onto the killing field.

Alongside King Bagrik there stood his runelord, Agrin Oakenheart. The venerable dwarf had said nothing during the long trudge from Karak Ungor. He and his apprentices had kept their own counsel, maintaining a watchful eye on the Anvils of Doom as they were hauled by mules to the battlesite. Skengi and Hurbad were below, amongst the main dwarf throng. The two master runesmiths would be needed to counter whatever sorcery the elves might throw at them.

'There's a change in the earth,' growled Agrin, his voice like metal scraping rock. 'I fear this will be the end of it.'

'The end of what, old one?' Bagrik asked.

'The end of all we know,' replied the runelord, 'and the beginning of change.'

Blinking, Agrin gazed up into the sky, where a pale yellow sun struggled to shine through the gathering clouds, and scowled.

'S'been a long few years since I've seen the sky, felt the wind on my face,' he remarked. 'Now I know why.' Expression souring, he returned to his silence.

STONE FELL IN a relentless hail from the dwarf mangonels arrayed on the hill. It blotted the limpid sun before crashing down like rock-hard thunder against the elven reapers. The bolt throwers were smashed into elegant kindling, their crewman maimed or pulped in the sudden avalanche of granite. Isolated elven mages endeavoured to protect the war engines with shimmering magical shields but their attention was divided between attack and defence. Occasionally thwarted by the efforts of the dwarf runesmiths, the elves could only do so much.

Punitive strikes against the elven machineries had been one of Bagrik's priorities. It had proven a wise stratagem, for even depleted as they were they spat a deadly fusillade that tore up dwarf armour like parchment. Even the stoutest shields were rent apart. Reapers – they were well named, for theirs was a bitter harvest.

'DO YOU REMEMBER what that is for?' Morek shouted above the clang of chafing armour and rattled shields, as the hearth guard marched up the left flank.

'Aye, I've not forgotten my axe-craft, Thane Stone-hammer,' Kandor growled back at him. The dwarf merchant wore an open-faced helmet with a long nose-guard that showed off his reddening cheeks as they puffed and blowed.

'A little thick around the waist, too, I see,' observed the hearth guard captain. 'More fat than muscle, I'd warrant.'

Kandor looked down at the suit of lamellar armour bulging at his girth and frowned.

'I don't see why we must go to the elgi. Why don't we let them come to us?' he grumbled.

Kandor had joined the army at his own request. His dealings with the elves had left his honour in tatters. Already, his name had been entered into the book of grudges for his singular lack of wisdom in entreating the foreigners. Kandor himself felt partly to blame for what had transpired. Short of taking the slayer oath, he would exact his toll of revenge against those who had tricked him with honeyed words and gilded promises in blood. It would not erase the stain of his ignominy, but it would at least settle some of his account when he met with Gazul at the Gate.

'Ah,' replied Morek conspiratorially, tapping the nose-guard of his battle mask with a gauntleted finger, 'that's because our king has a surprise in mind for the pointy-eared bastards,' he explained. 'Don't worry, ufdi, I'll make sure you live long enough to reap a tally that'll see you into the Halls.' Morek laughed loudly, the sound oddly metallic through his helmet.

This will be a grand battle. Nagrim would have wanted to fight in it, thought Morek sadly, as the man-gonels continued their barrage.

* * *

HAGGAR ANVILFIST HELD the dwarf centre. The banner of Karak Ungor was clenched firmly in the thane's iron grip, and swayed as he moved. The clan warriors arrayed around him followed it like a beacon. This was a day of destiny; Haggar felt it as sure as the rune axe in his hand and the armour on his back. Facing the northmen had been a time of trial, which he had passed. Already, he felt the mark that Thagri had made against his clan's honour lifting. Here upon the fields outside Eyrie Rock that legacy would be forever expunged and a new saga of honour forged in its place.

A violent fulguration erupted before the thane, arresting his thoughts. Haggar watched arcs of lightning dissipating into sparks on the ground as they earthed into Skengi's outstretched runestaff. The thane nodded his thanks to the runesmith whose beard was spiked from the sudden bolt charge. Further down the dwarf battle-line, Haggar saw a distant regiment of clan warriors succumb to the fury of an elven firestorm. The entire front rank died in the conflagration, the dwarfs' magical defences breached at last. Dourly, the clan warriors behind stepped over the scorched remains of the dead and raised their blackened banner in defiance.

'Keep with me!' Haggar shouted to his own warriors, looking to see that they were holding firm. Musicians beat their drums, dictating the pace of the march and clan leaders reaffirmed the thane's orders further down the file. Arrows loosed by the elven archers whickered into their ranks, the occasional gurgled cry indicating that some found their mark, but the dwarfs were unperturbed. Haggar kept them moving until they reached the standing point, the one that Bagrik had shown to all of his captains when they had convened in his tent for the war council.

The thane called a halt, signalling with the banner. Horns blared, carrying the order, and the drummers beat a frantic staccato until they too ceased. Three hundred dwarfs, twenty ranks deep, spanned across the ironclad centre of King Bagrik Boarbrow's army in their regiments of fifty. And this was just Haggar's throng. Two more, equally massive, infantry cohorts bolstered the armoured lynchpin either side, with three further throngs behind them as reserves.

'Here we stand, rocks of the mountain,' Haggar cried to his warriors, 'unshakeable, resilient. Let none through. Smash them on your shields!'

Reverberating horn blasts greeted the declaration, and the dwarf warriors cheered.

'They come now,' Skengi said calmly, hefting his forging hammer.

The earth was trembling. From out of the glittering host there arose a terrible thunder. Heavy-armoured dragon knights surged from the elven centre, their silver helmed kinsmen galloping in their wake. Either side of the lancehead there rumbled vast squadrons of war chariots, scythed wheels shimmering dangerously in the light as they raced. Several of the machines were crushed by boulders flung from the dwarf mangonels. The missiles rolled through them or ploughed into the earth to create immovable reefs upon which several chariots were dashed. But there were simply too many to hope the stone throwers could stop them all.

As the elven cavalry closed, hurtling along the open ground, the elven infantry regiments closed the gap in the line behind them and followed on swiftly. Mere feet from the dwarfs, the elven knights lowered their lances for the final charge.

'Raise shields,' roared Haggar, the tumult of galloping steeds filling his ears as the wall of iron and bronze went up. 'Give 'em nothing!'

BAGRIK SAT PENSIVELY upon his war shield watching the battle slowly unfold. The aged king, grown more ancient in these last few months than all of his one hundred and eighty-six winters, felt a sharp twinge in his side from where the Norscan had stabbed him. Gritting his teeth he forced the pain caused by the poison in his dying body to the back of his mind. He only needed to stay alive long enough to exact his revenge. Nothing else mattered anymore.

The initial advance had gone well. The dwarf centre and both its flanks had reached the standing point, making their shield walls in front of the enemy. Volleys from the stone throwers had all but destroyed the elven reapers, though their archers were still taking a heavy toll. Bagrik was all but ready to order the master engineer to concentrate on them when a war cry echoed to the king's far right. Out of a small cluster of trees emerged a mounted group of reavers, the horsemasters of Ellyrion, loosing arrows and javelins. Two dwarf crewmen slumped dead over their machine already, the remaining journeyman and sighter taking cover behind the stone thrower's carriage.

Another shout rang out, though this time it was followed by dwarf curses, as a concealed band of rangers burst from their hiding places amongst a dense thicket of scrub. Bagrik had learned his lesson against the northmen. He'd deployed these reserves purposely to protect his machineries and dissuade ambitious saboteurs. The dwarf king would not be outflanked by skirmishers so easily again.

Thrown axes thudded into the foremost reavers as the rangers attacked, the elven steeds panicked by the sudden ambush. The elves rallied quickly though, making a feigned flight to draw out their attackers before regrouping and driving at them again. Though slow, the dwarf rangers unslung crossbows and soon had the horsemasters pinned. A second harass of steeds with heavier-armoured, spear-wielding reavers undid their well-employed strategy.

Unable to handle both groups of reavers, the rangers were forced into retreat whilst the elves ran rampant amongst the dwarf war machines. Bagrik scowled at the carnage just a hundred feet from his vantage point, as his devastating stone thrower barrage was brought to an abrupt halt. Though the dwarf crews put up stern resistance, showing no signs of being overrun, they were locked at an impasse with the elves.

Bellowing for quarrellers, the dwarf king was determined to break it.

MOREK WATCHED THE mass of elven cavalry break away from their main battle-line, only for the gap to be filled a moment later by onrushing units of spearmen and bolstered by a smaller regiment of sword masters. The hearth guard captain's foes were closing too, though at a much slower rate than the knights. Another large block of elven spears was coming Morek's way, with more sword masters too. He counted one of the mages amongst their ranks, a silver-haired elf that seemed to radiate power. The dwarf looked askance down the line, to where Hurbad waited silently with a regiment of longbeards. Stroking the talisman around his neck, Morek hoped the runesmith would be able to staunch the elf's sorcery long enough for him to remove the mage's silver-maned head from his shoulders.

Swinging his rune axe in readiness, Morek's attention went back to the dwarf centre and Haggar's clan warriors. The elf knights had passed through the gauntlet lain down by the war machines and quarrellers, who were now curiously silent. They struck the shield wall in an avalanche of steel and armoured horseflesh. Morek felt the ripple of the elves' charge all the way down his own flank.

'Hold them, lad,' he muttered to himself. 'Stand your ground, Haggar.'

HAGGAR'S SHIELD WALL crumpled. Driven by the impetus of their onrushing steeds and the will of the elf noble leading them, the charge of the dragon knights was irresistible. Burnished red armour flew by in a furious blur and the clatter of steel and the discord of screams filled the thane's ears. The gradually widening hole torn in the dwarf centre was further exploited by the immediate wave of silver helms that followed. The dwarf warriors were afforded no time to recover and more were trampled, or spit on sharpened lances as the elven knights ripped through them.

Haggar was nearly pitched off his feet in the initial assault. Staggering, he managed to steady himself and level his shield before the chariots hit. The war machines ground through the dwarfs, only the hardiest or the fortunate spared death or maiming beneath their steel-shod wheels and razor-sharp scythes. The elves aboard the chariots loosed arrows or lunged with spears as they raced past, adding further to the death toll.

Devastated in the wake of the cavalry charge, the dwarf centre rocked, like a pugilist put on his heels by a body blow, and began to falter.

'Hold,' cried Haggar, 'hold!' The command was voiced in desperation as the thane thrust the banner of Karak Ungor into the air.

'Skengi Granitehand, are you still alive?' called Haggar through the chaos when he thought the immediate moment of crisis had passed.

'Aye,' bawled the runesmith. 'Just.' A savage gash across the dwarf's forehead was leaking blood down the side of his face, and Skengi held his hammer-wielding arm close to his chest.

Haggar nodded, before shouting, 'Close ranks!'

Looking behind him, he saw the elves had punched right through with few losses. The noble at the elves' head must have been a skilled rider. He had managed to maintain the knights' impetus and angled their approach so that they tore out of the dwarfs' flank, into a regiment from the second throng, and then clean through into the open ground.

Haggar watched through a sea of bobbing helmets, axe blades and banners as the elf cavalry cantered swiftly along the dwarf rear, bolts and quarrels whipping by harmlessly as they kept out of bowshot. Using their momentum, the noble led the knights around to the dwarf right flank, darting audaciously in-between the two separate throngs. Distant clan warriors reacted to the sudden threat, urgently sounding trumpets to signal the change in formation. The dwarfs showed their shields to the elves prowling alongside them, but were ignored. The dragon knights were coming around for a second charge at Haggar's still regrouping throng. It seemed the noble at the fore wanted to claim the banner of Karak Ungor for himself.

'You'll have to prise it from my cold dead hand,' Haggar muttered as the dwarf warriors drew in around him.

The dragon knights were building up speed. They were coming, only this time the elven infantry would be right behind them.

Haggar closed his grip even tighter on the banner and made an oath to Grungni that he would not let it fall.

'Here they come again! Dwarfs of Karak Ungor, dig in and stay with me,' he roared.

The adrenalin rush as the dragon knights bore down on the dwarfs was almost overwhelming. The hoofbeats from their armoured steeds hammered the ground like deafening thunder.

Skengi the runesmith stepped forward from the shield wall when the elves were just a few feet away. Haggar shouted out to him but his cry was lost in the bellowed avowal of rune rites as Skengi rammed his staff into the ground. The sigils inscribed down its shaft blazed into life and a moment later the earth shook as if with the footsteps of giants.

The dragon knights ran straight into the tremor as it rippled from Skengi's staff, their surefooting lost as the ground trembled beneath them. Elves were unhorsed in the quake, crushed as they struck the unyielding plain, or trampled by the steeds of oncoming knights. Others were driven into comrades alongside them, careening dangerously out of control, only to clatter against dwarf shields acting as breakers.

Suddenly the cavalry charge had faltered. Some, like the elven noble at the head, kept their balance and drove on with lances levelled, but the attack had paled in its power and ferocity. Even the chariots were undone, few getting through, most crashing to a halt or upended and destroyed against the stalwart dwarf warriors. Within the morass of iron and bronze, the elven knights found themselves mired.

No glorious charges to win the day. No lightning attacks to rend the foe asunder. This was the grind. Now it got ugly.

HIGH ABOVE THE battlefield, Ithalred gazed down at the struggle below. He soared through the grey heavens on Awari's back, the wind whipping against his face and whistling loudly through the curves of his ornate hawk-helm.

Bursts of magic erupted in the dust-filled chaos beneath him, just ephemeral sparks of lightning or spits of flame such was Ithalred's altitude. The enemy seemed equal to the elves' sorcerous barrage as bolts rebounded against iridescent shields and fiery conflagrations withered into smoke with the dwarfs' counter-magic.

Pinnacle of the glittering host, the elven cavalry led by the dragon knights had become trapped amongst the dwarf infantry. Ithalred watched with displeasure as a silver helm was dragged from his saddle and slain. He considered intervening to try and break the deadlock when elven battle horns announced the arrival of a massive block of spearmen and sword masters following up after the horse. Arcing back on himself, the elf prince turned his attention elsewhere.

A dense patch of cloud loomed in front of him. Ithalred leaned down in the saddle and whispered into Awari's ear. The great eagle pushed with his wings as they surged through it. Wisps of grey-black cumulonimbus tugged at the elf prince's armour, and peeled in misty tendrils from Awari's wings, as they broke free. The great eagle's rookery brothers gave chase and emerged seconds later. The dark vapour still clinging tenaciously to their magnificent bodies dissipated into ether as Ithalred plunged Awari into a sharp dive.

Skarhir and Urouke followed him, maintaining close aerial formation. The great eagles' beaks were dipped like down-thrusting arrows, their wings pinned back, before Ithalred let out a sharp screech and they arrested their descent, wings fanned and claws outstretched in front of them. Buoyed by warm currents of air, the eagles were content to glide as their master surveyed the carnage.

Directly below him, Ithalred saw a stricken band of reavers battling against a group of rangers and the sweating crewmen of the infernal dwarf catapults. Reaching over his left shoulder the elf prince pulled out his longbow, an exquisite weapon forged in the temples of Vaul at Caledor. He swiftly nocked an arrow and loosed. Ithalred smiled darkly as one of the dwarfs, an engineer clad in gilded armour and wielding an immense warhammer, fell dead with a shaft protruding from his neck. The elf prince's enjoyment at the deed was fleeting as he took another arrow and let fly. This time he aimed at the rangers. As the missile flew it broke into many pointed shafts and hammered against the dwarfs in a barrage, who fell in their droves.

Ithalred didn't wait to see what would happen next, his gaze was locked on the still struggling reavers, now being pin-cushioned by dwarf quarrellers. Against the relentless volley fire, the elf cavalry fled. Already the surviving dwarf crews were back toiling at their war machines, preparing to resume their assault. Ithalred narrowed his eyes and trilled aggressively through clenched teeth.

Here is where my sword will fall hardest, he thought as the great eagles dove earthward. The dwarf stone throwers were doomed.

MOREK WINCED AS a surging column of fire flared and then died before his eyes. No sooner had Hurbad dispelled the magicks, the silver-haired elf mage had conjured a luminous golden spear. Concentration etched on his face, the elf lunged with it at the runesmith. Hurbad cried out in agony as the enchanted weapon pierced his gromril armour and dug deep into his thigh.

He fell as the weapon was removed. Morek stepped in its path before silver-mane could finish Hurbad for good. Eldritch sparks danced and spat from the two blades as the hearth guard captain parried another thrust with his rune axe.

'Get him back!' he yelled, and saw two dwarfs come forward and pull the injured runesmith from the fighting rank and out of his eye-line.

'Hold 'em!' cried Morek, as he aimed to cleave the elf mage's neck but was thwarted by the gilded shaft of his magically summoned spear.

Morek's order was easier said than done. The hearth guard were hard-pressed, the warrior-scholars of the elven sword masters weaving about them, cutting and hewing in whirlwinds of deadly steel. Several dwarfs were already dead, no match for the elegant killers.

Kandor was holding his own, though the dwarf merchant was fortunate to be facing off against spearmen rather than the elven sword masters. Morek had deployed him farther down the line when he'd seen the enemy's approach. Kandor was an ufdi, yes, but he deserved a fighting chance at survival and redemption all the same.

'You'll live longer this way,' Morek had joked, calling out to him just before the elves had hit.

Kandor hadn't answered. His eyes had been fixed on the charging elves, knuckles white as he'd gripped his axe. The time for talking had ended.

Landing a punch in silver-mane's midriff, Morek was rewarded with a grunt of pain from his duelling partner. As he drove home the blow, he saw a dwarf cast a throwing axe at one of the sword masters, only to see it rebounded by a spinning arc of silver. The hearth guard fell dead, his own weapon lodged in his neck. Morek found he was still able to force a grave smile. Silver-mane had lost his golden spear. It evaporated into iridescent yellow dust in his spidery fingers.

'You'll lose a lot more than that,' Morek promised then felt his bravura ebb as the mage retreated, allowing two sword masters to take his place.

The dwarf's reaction was terse.

'Bugger…'

DEATH… DEATH WAS everywhere. It was the reek on the breeze. It was the screaming in his ears. It was the hot red haze in his eyes. Death was redolent. It permeated everything, soaked every pore. Death revelled with the savage ecstasy that filled Haggar's thumping heart as he killed.

The elf knights were pinned and had lost the advantage of the charge, but they were still fearsome foes. Well-armoured, high up on their steeds, they would be no pushovers. Even still, Haggar dragged one from his saddle by the boot and applied the death blow with his axe. One of the beasts rammed its muscled flank into him, but it obviously hadn't reckoned on dwarf tenacity and Haggar pushed back with his armoured shoulder, making the steed rear up and unhorsing its rider. Skengi, fighting just ahead of the thane, was quick to dispatch the fallen elf with a blow from his hammer.

It was hard fighting. Probably the hardest that Haggar had ever fought. The elves were skilled, disciplined and phenomenally fast. Dragon knights jabbed down with swords and lances in a crimson blur, piercing dwarf armour with their accurate blade thrusts. Steeds kicked and trampled. It could go either way.

Though the dwarfs fought for all they were worth, the arrival of the spearmen and limb-reaping sword masters had dented their resolve, pushing them to the edge. Haggar could feel the warriors hanging on the brink of retreat. Only the banner of Karak Ungor, the shame of fleeing from it and allowing it to be taken by the enemy, held them... at least for now.

'I'll be damned if I see you put us to flight,' Haggar snarled under his breath at the nearest elf in his eye-line.

With some satisfaction, he watched as the dragon knight was brought down. Another figure loomed out of the battle haze behind him, cutting at either flank with his shimmering, gore-slicked blade. Carving a path through a band of clan warriors, he found the dwarf he was looking for. The noble, he who had led the charge of the dragon knights with such ferocity and skill, levelled his long sword at Haggar. A ruby of blood peeled along the edge and fell ominously onto the ground in front of him.

The dwarf thane roared a challenge, thumping his chestplate and then brandishing the banner of Karak Ungor meaningfully.

'Try and take it you pointy-eared swine,' he cursed, 'I dare you.'

Haggar recognised the warrior. A black mane issued from beneath his stylised dragon helm. He even maintained the cocky swagger in the way he approached the dwarf on his steed. This was the raven-haired blademaster, the elf called Lethralmir.

A shrieking war cry tore from the noble's lips, sounding tinny through his helmet. Lethralmir stirred his barded horse and charged. Though it was only a short distance through the melee, Lethralmir's first blow struck with all the force of an avalanche. At least that's how it felt to Haggar, as he was battered, barely able to turn the blade aside from his neck.

The smallest of gaps had developed in the bloody struggle for the centre. It was through this that the elf noble brought his steed around for a second pass. Though he couldn't see the elf's face hidden by the snarling visage of his dragon helm, Haggar was sure he would be smiling.

Bastard, step down off that bloody horse and we'll see what's what, he thought, working the tension out of his axe-arm where Lethralmir had managed to strike him on the pauldron.

Three short strides and Lethralmir was upon him again, angling his blade in a vicious downward thrust intended to find the gap between the dwarf's gorget and battle helm. But Haggar was equal to it. He fended off the elf's attack, turning the sword with the flat blade of his rune axe. The impact jarred Lethralmir's arm, forcing the elf to take a tighter rein on his steed. As he pulled up, Haggar was able to stay on his feet and whirled his axe around, raking it down the beast's barded flank as it sped past. Armour chinks cascaded like red rain and the dwarf was rewarded with a whinny of pain from the elven horse. Haggar looked down at the freshly reddened edge to his axe blade and smiled.

Lethralmir's steed staggered and nearly fell. The ragged wound in its side was making its barding and armoured rider an intolerable burden. Even so, the elf hauled on its reins to bring it around. Despite loud protests, the steed obeyed. Blood was running freely down its flank now, the enforced exertions tearing its wound ever wider. Suddenly its forelegs bunched beneath it, fetlocks collapsing under the weight it could no longer bear, and Lethralmir was dumped onto the ground in front of it.

The elf blade-master rose swiftly, in spite of his heavy armour, dispatching a pair of clan warriors that came at him out of the melee, axes swinging. Two expert blows, the first whilst he was still on one knee striking the groin and the second rising to his full height, preceded by a deft pirouette that made the dwarf's axe strike seem slow and clumsy, followed by a brutal arcing slash that took the warrior's helmeted head from his shoulders.

Haggar blanched when he saw it – the elf's long sword had sheared straight through the decapitated dwarf's chainmail coif.

'You'll find me a sterner test,' he promised, growling beneath his breath as the elf stalked towards him.

RIDING ON AWARI's back, Prince Ithalred bolted from the sky like a spear of lightning. With a wicked swipe, he cut the head from the shoulders of a dwarf loader, the stone he was lumbering over to the catapult thudding at his feet before his body toppled back. An engineer brought a mechanised crossbow up, only for Ithalred to swat the weapon aside, sending the quarrel off harmlessly to impact into the war machine's wooden carriage, before impaling the dwarf through the throat with a second blade. Awari raked a third crewman with his talons, ripping apart the dwarf's leather apron like damp parchment. Skarhir and Urouke dove down a moment later, rending with beak and claw. In the few short seconds since the descent of the great eagles, the entrenched stone thrower battery had become something more akin to an open air abattoir.

As he butchered the hapless dwarfs, Ithalred gazed further up the hill and saw King Bagrik glaring at him. The dwarf was stood with a small retinue of warriors and the ancient runesmith of his hold. It would be a simple matter for Ithalred to take flight with his eagles and kill the dwarf lord where he sat upon his war shield. For Bagrik to leave himself so exposed smacked of arrogance, or perhaps it was merely grief that had blotted out his caution and sense. It mattered not. Here was Ithalred's chance to slay the enemy general and win this fight in one clean stroke.

Acutely aware of the dwarf quarrellers beneath him, about to draw a bead at any moment, the elf prince was poised to order the attack when Bagrik raised the faceplate of his battle helm and smiled. Ithalred followed his gaze, to a cluster of large wicker baskets above the stone throwers, further up the hill.

The elf prince had seen them briefly as he'd dove to attack the war machines, but assumed they were filled with ammunition, rock carved from the mountainside in readiness to fling from the launching arms of the catapults, and gave them no further thought. When the lids of the baskets were thrown off and the front and sides fell away to reveal a second battery of war machines, heavy dwarf ballista with bolts primed, Ithalred's words caught in his throat.

The elf shrieked the order to ascend but the dwarf machineries had already loosed. Skarhir got two feet off the ground before his left wing was shredded and he crashed down again. Vindictive quarrellers pinioned him with crossbow bolts until the great eagle ceased floundering. Urouke fared no better and was struck through the neck, the triumphant whoop of the dwarf engineers drowning out the noble beast's death scream.

Awari took to the air with panicked urgency. A missile from one of the ballista grazed his side eliciting a squawk of pain but the great eagle kept on rising. Ithalred felt a crossbow bolt *thunk* into his armour, and knew that some of the volley must have struck his mount too. Already Awari was flagging, doing his best to duck and weave as he sought altitude and the relative safety of the clouds. Weakened though, and losing blood, the great eagle was unable to dodge a bolt that raked across his wing and sent him dipping towards the ground.

Ithalred roared, impelling his beloved mount onwards. They only need reach the safety of the walls of Tor Eorfith…

Awari drew deep on his reserves of strength, managing to put some distance between them and their attackers. But even gliding was painful, every feather ruffled by the wind sending daggers of agony through the proud beast. Ithalred could feel Awari's heart beating faster and faster as he pressed close to the great eagle's body and whispered encouragement. They pitched lower as a strong gust of wind almost sent them crashing earthward, but Awari held on. The white walls were close and the battle seemed dull and distant behind them. Ithalred urged his great eagle for one last effort as he struggled for loft, the high battlements their only remaining obstacle. Spiralling madly, elf prince and great eagle clawed their way over and plunged headlong into the courtyard below. As he fell, Ithalred thought he heard the distant clarion of horns…

To THE EAST, dwarf battle horns echoed through the mountains as another force erupted from the hidden caves and crags on the elven left flank. Grikk, captain of the iron-breakers was at their head with a vast and heavily-armoured host. Travelling through the subterranean ungdrin, the dwarfs had been able to move unnoticed and arrive at the standing point where the elves were currently embroiled in fierce fighting against the main dwarf army. They struck up pipe and drum, and raised banners in salute of the king, who watched grimly from his distant vantage point.

Grikk's flanking force made the ground between them and their foes quickly and fell like a gromril wave upon the already embattled elves, massive cohorts of iron-breakers and stern-faced clan miners hewing and rending with axe and pick.

Outflanked, outnumbered and with their general already fled, the elves sounded the retreat.

HAGGAR HEARD THE bellowing horns of Grikk's battle company and breathed an inward sigh of relief. He and the elf blade-master merely stared at each other, still within striking distance, as the elves began disengaging. To their credit, the enemy retreated in good order, raising shields and adopting a defensive stance as they fell back. For their part, the dwarfs were content to let them go and consolidate their own position. It would be dishonourable to stab a foe in the back, even an elf.

As they slowly withdrew, Haggar's attention was suddenly drawn by one of the many small battles still petering out in the wake of the mass elven retreat.

Arthelas was fighting alongside a band of sword masters. He watched her rise up on a pillar of coruscating fire, eyes ablaze with white lightning. She was… magnificent, and for a split second Haggar took his eye off the foe. It was like he and she were the only ones upon the field.

Haggar shook away the glamour quickly.

'I'll see you aga–' he began. The blade in his chest prevented Haggar from finishing his threat.

Mere feet away, Lethralmir's eyes flashed behind his dragon helm with murderous satisfaction.

Sudden shock paralysed the dwarf as a warm sensation spread across his lower body. He felt the wound with his hand and brought up blood on his armoured fingers. It was pooling in his boot.

Lethralmir twisted the blade then yanked it free, before drifting away like a wraith.

Haggar spat blood onto the underside of his faceplate and gagged for air. His vision was fading. The blade had gone right through, piercing his armour as if it were nothing. He wanted to scream out, find strength in wrath but his mouth felt like it was stuffed with ash.

Instead, with the last of his life's blood oozing from his body, Haggar rammed the banner of Karak Ungor deep into the earth so that it would not fall. As the world broke away and darkness smothered him, he thought he could hear singing, like from the old days in the ancient hearth holds of his ancestors…

SKENGI FOUND HAGGAR slumped against the battle standard. It stood proudly like a spire of rock, the dragon banner snapping defiantly in the wind. The thane had not allowed it to fall. The honour of the Skengdrang clan was intact. It had cost Haggar his life.

CHAPTER TWENTY
Tighten the Noose

HAGGAR'S DEATH HIT Morek hardest. The young thane had been one of his charges. He had taught him axe-craft and taken him under his wing. Now he was dead, and there was nothing Morek could do to change that fact. At least he had kept his clan's honour. Another of the Skengdrangs had been chosen to carry the banner of Karak Ungor in Haggar's stead. It was small cause for joy.

So, the captain of the hearth guard was more sullen and morose than ever as he stood at the king's table in his war tent. The elves would pay in blood for all the dwarf lives they'd taken. Morek had seen the dragon-helmed noble at the head of the elven knights. He knew it was the raven-haired blade-master that had fought and killed Haggar. When the elves had retreated the hearth guard captain has lost sight of Lethralmir in the crowd, but he knew in his heart they'd meet again. The slaying of Haggar was ignoble, and the raven-haired elf had a reckoning coming his way for that and more. Such a thing could not stand and Morek promised the young thane vengeance. Even if he could no longer claim it himself, Morek would do it in his name.

Morek's growing canker was further unleavened by the fact that Bagrik seemed now to favour Skarbrag Ironback for war counsel. Skarbrag was old and wise for sure, but the great beard had long since succumbed to senility and hadn't fought on the battlefield for over a hundred years, let alone taken command of one. The king's sudden magnanimity upon finding Brunvilda in Morek's arms had obviously been feigned. Either that or Bagrik had found time to brood upon it during the battle and chose now to exact his grudge against the hearth guard captain.

'The elves are fragile,' stated Skarbrag, 'their towers and walls will crumble swiftly beneath a determined assault.'

Bagrik nodded sagely, pipe cinched between his lips and gestured towards his war table.

'Here,' he announced to the assembled throng of thanes, captains and masters in his presence. 'This is where the fighting will be hardest.' Bagrik wheezed as he spoke, and had grown more ashen in these last few hours than in all the days he had been at Karak Ungor since being wounded by the poison blade. Many amongst the war council exchanged grave glances with one another at the king's condition, but dared not voice their concern. Bagrik was not to be denied. His will would ensure he would see the course.

The king had pointed to the elven gatehouse. The entire structure of Tor Eorfith was rendered in finely carved blocks of stone and set out upon a map of the battleground drawn by Bagrik's cartographers.

Since the fight outside the elven city the dwarfs had pushed up, bringing their camp with them, and laid siege to Eyrie Rock. Even as the dwarf lords debated their tactics, work crews could be heard through the walls of the tent constructing rams and ladders, gathering rope for grapnels and digging trenches. Rangers had already been sent to the nearby forests to hew more wood. Stone was being carved from the mountain and rocky escarpments of the land then collected in baskets for the stone throwers.

Smoke drifted through the tent flaps redolent with the aroma of iron, bronze and gromril as it was tempered in white-hot forges and bent to the dwarfs' will. All metal workings fell under the iron-hard gaze of Agrin Oakenheart and his apprentices – Morek had been glad to learn that Hurbad had survived his wounding by the silver-maned elf mage, though the runesmith now walked with a pronounced limp.

Racks of quarrels and thick-shafted bolts appeared by the hour and were stacked in makeshift armoury tents before being distributed amongst the dwarf crossbow-men and ballista crews. Piquets had gone up almost immediately, surrounding the elf city, all roads in and out watched by heavily-armoured patrols of hearth guard and longbeards. None could enter; none would be allowed to leave.

'I would not wish to be stationed there,' muttered Kandor beneath his breath, though Morek caught the gist of his words and couldn't help but agree. Taking the gate was a brutal task; certainly elven resistance would be at its fiercest before the gatehouse. Leading such an assault would be something of a death sentence. A pity the slayers could not do it, but no self-respecting dwarf with a death oath would ever cower beneath the mantlet of a battering ram. That was not their fight.

'High walls,' said Kozdokk, guildmaster of the miners. He stroked his chin as he spoke, as if pondering a solution, 'we'll need siege towers,' he added.

Morek was about to answer when Grikk Ironspike chipped in ahead of him. 'We could undermine the walls. I doubt the foundations are deep.'

Bagrik nodded his approval as did Kozdokk, the guildmaster's eyes narrowing with respect for the iron-breaker captain.

Morek cursed under his breath. He had been about to suggest the very same thing in the hope of trying to get back into Bagrik's good graces, but here Grikk had beaten him to the punch. It was galling.

'The elven towers present a problem, also,' growled Skarbrag. 'I saw thrice-cursed sorcery in the windows. They are a haven for elgi wizards.'

'Our stone throwers will put paid to them,' declared Bagrik, followed by a bout of coughing. Once recovered, wiping away the blood from his mouth on his sleeve, the king fixed them all with his steely gaze and announced the deployments for the siege. He came to Morek last of all.

'You'll be here,' he told his captain of the hearth guard in a snarl, 'at the gate.'

THE NIGHT WAS many hours old by the time Rugnir was moving through the camp. He had fought at Grikk's side in the flanking force, assisting the captain of the ironbreakers in negotiating the ungdrin caverns in order to ambush the elves swiftly, and was glad of the chance to fight. But still he wanted more. Nagrim was like a brother to him, one he loved dearly. Only he amongst all the dwarfs of Karak Ungor had been there at his death. It was a bitter memory, made harder to bear by the fact of his enforced sobriety, and one he planned to assuage with elven blood.

Rugnir was not the only dwarf awake and abroad that night. Few could sleep, it seemed, as the final preparations were being made for the siege of Tor Eorfith. The ex-miner walked solemnly past the numerous tents and workshops. To the east he saw the distant elven city. Lantern light glowed dully in the windows and along the parapets and battlements where patrolling spearmen paced back and forth in syncopated rhythm. Both elf and dwarf launched ranging shots into the darkness with their war machines but these were not intended to hit home, merely prepare the field for the following day and ensure the maximum amount of slaughter would be reaped on both sides.

Rugnir felt a strange empathy for the obvious anxiety felt by the elves. He felt it too and decided that he hated being sober, but hated the elves even more. Perhaps when all this was over, when he had sated the latter; he could indulge the former. Memories of Kraggin Goldmaster, Rugnir's father, sprang unbidden into the dwarf's mind as he walked. Rugnir gripped his father's rune pick in his hand. It was an heirloom, borne by Buldrin, his grandfather, and his grandfather before that. Remarkable that Rugnir had not hocked it already, that the entropic dwarf hadn't drunk or gambled it away. It was called Skrun-duraz, or *Stone Hewer*, and it had seen much better days. The pick blade itself was badly tarnished, encrusted by age and a thick patina of rust and grime. The gilded shaft no longer glimmered in the torchlight; rather it was dull and smeared by years of disuse. Rugnir wrenched his eyes away from the forlorn-looking weapon and pressed on with a heavy heart.

When he reached the metalsmith's forge, at the middle of the dwarf camp, Rugnir stopped. Stepping before the hot coals of the furnace, having been given the metalsmith's blessing, he beat away the rust and the age-tarnished sheath around Skrun-duraz. Sweating over the blazing forge, Rugnir hammered and chipped and honed for several hours. When he was done, he cooled the rune pick in a large metal water basin and let the steam from it wash over his face. It was like being reborn – just like Skrun-duraz had been reforged, so too was Rugnir.

Only when he retrieved the venerable weapon did he notice Agrin watching him from the shadows. The runelord was sitting on an upturned rock, studying Rugnir silently under his gimlet gaze. The ex-miner nodded at the aging dwarf, who may have reciprocated. It was impossible to tell. The older a dwarf became, the less pronounced his gestures were. And Agrin Oakenheart was amongst the eldest of all dwarfs.

Moving on, Rugnir had one more errand before he could retire for the night. As he left the forge, though, he felt as if someone was watching him. It wasn't Agrin. It was something else. Rugnir decided to ignore it, chalking up his paranoia to the fact that he hadn't had a drink in months. Right on cue, his dwarf stomach groaned in sympathy.

RUGNIR HEARD KING Bagrik before he saw him. The sound of a hacking, phlegmy cough rattled from his war tent as the dwarf approached. Rugnir was about to enter when another dwarf stepped out of the king's abode and into his path. Hetga was the matriarch of the priestesses of Valaya, and her old but handsome face was grave as she regarded Rugnir. Clearly she had been ministering to the king and, judging by her expression, to little avail.

'Don't keep him long,' she warned brusquely. 'He needs his rest. Though I dare say the cantankerous old bugger will be awake all night anyway.' The matriarch shuffled past him and was gone into the dark.

'Come then,' growled the voice of the king as Rugnir stood outside, wary of entering Bagrik's presence all of a sudden. Swallowing deeply, Rugnir went inside. 'Morek, if you've come to protest over the-' the king began. 'Oh, it's you,' he said, scowling when he saw Rugnir.

Bagrik was sat on his throne, a thick blanket draped over his knees and another across his shoulders. He looked smaller and somehow diminished since Rugnir had seen him last, and now he was divested of his armour. The king had been poring over the 'dead lists' when the other dwarf had entered. His face was fixed in a scowl and his foul mood was obvious. The dead lists were the records of all the slain, all those who would be returning to Karak Ungor beneath a tarp to be then entombed forever with their ancestors in the vaults. A great many leaves of parchment littered the area around Bagrik's throne and upon his lap. The death toll during the battle against the elves had been high and costly it seemed. Rugnir also noticed that Grumkaz Grimbrow was sitting in one corner of the room, stooped over the book of grudges transcribing all the recent edicts of the king.

'Ignore him,' snapped the king, when he'd followed Rugnir's errant gaze. 'He has much to occupy him and cannot hear us. What do you want at this hour, Goldmaster?'

'I have heard that we plan to undermine the walls of the elf city,' he said. 'And that you'll need expert tunnellers for the excavation.'

'What are you proposing, Rugnir?' asked the king shrewdly.

'That I lead the dig,' he answered boldly. 'There are none better than I, no dwarf as fast,' he reasoned.

In his heyday, Rugnir and the Goldmaster clan were peerless miners and excavators. Lodemasters all, they excelled in the business of digging. It was how their clan had prospered so quickly in the first place. Bagrik knew all this, just as he had known Kraggin and Buldrin, Rugnir's sires. This was a changed dwarf before him – no longer raucous and ebullient, nor frivolous or leeching.

'You loved my son – you loved Nagrim?' asked the king softly, seemingly older in that moment.

'Like he was my own kin,' Rugnir vowed, chin upraised proudly. 'He was hard as grimazul, your boy, but with courage and heart.'

Bagrik appraised the dwarf for a spell, judging him, making his decision.

'You'll lead the dig,' he told Rugnir. 'Bring that wall down for me. Bring it down for Nagrim,' he added, and the bitterness in his voice returned.

WHEN RUGNIR HAD gone, Bagrik sagged in his throne.

'Just a little longer...' he breathed, looking at the statue of Grungni set up in his war tent. The Ancestor God was depicted holding aloft a huge chunk of rock veined with silver. 'I'll need your strength,' said Bagrik as he met Grungni eye-to-eye.

The link was broken when Bagrik got the feeling he was being watched. A quick glance at Grumkaz showed him the grudgemaster was still engrossed. Other than that, he was alone.

Must be getting old… he thought, and went back to the grim business of the dead lists.

BAGRIK DIDN'T SEE the shadow figure retreating from the confines of his war tent. None noticed it slipping quietly through the camp and back into the foothills.

FIVE DAYS THE dwarfs had pounded the city of Tor Eorfith. Five days they had flung rock, rammed the gates and assaulted the walls. Still the elves would not yield. Even when their towers had been toppled by stone and lightning, they didn't give in. Even when their warriors died in droves and the dwarfs pressed relentlessly, they would not capitulate. The foundations of Eyrie Rock had been proven strong. They matched the will of its inhabitants. The elves, despite the dwarfs' earlier confidence, would not be easy to break.

'Loose!'

Morek heard the gruff voice of Master Engineer Lodkin as he shouted for another volley. Over a dozen hunks of mountain rock idled through the air from the stone thrower battery on the ridge above, seemingly in slow motion, before crashing against Tor Eorfith's walls in showers of marble and granite.

The hearth guard captain followed their trajectory with some satisfaction as the elves patrolling the parapets were crushed or fled before the barrage. Sat upon a small rise with his cohort of fifty hearth guard, Morek was glad of the view and the respite from ramming the gates. It seemed nothing, not even the gromril-headed battering ram forged by Agrin Oakenheart, could break down the door to the elven city. After their latest attempts had yielded little, Morek had been ordered back from the siege lines to protect the dwarf war engines whilst they loosed in concerted volleys.

Occasionally the chunks of spinning stone would be blasted apart by the elf mages on the battlements casting fireballs or lightning arcs, and the air would be filled with shards of falling rock. A few hundred feet in front of the stone throwers, Morek and his warriors raised shields as another granite shower rained down on their heads.

When it was over, Morek returned his attention to the elven city walls and saw a banner upraised. From behind a line of spearmen there emerged a host of elf archers. Immediately they began pouring arrows in a steel-fanged torrent towards the stone throwers. Even at extreme long range, the sweaty dwarf crews were forced into cover by the elven volleys. As they retreated and the stone thrower barrage abated, another banner went up. It was followed by the peal of horns.

'Valaya's golden cups!' Morek spat the pipe he was smoking out of his mouth then hurried to his feet and took up his axe.

The gates to Tor Eorfith were opening.

Morek was already shouting orders, rallying his hearth guard into defensive positions. Drummers rattled out the formation in sharp staccato beats as the dwarfs moved in front of the entrenched war machines and into the path of the elven knights hammering out of the city. The dwarf trenches and abatis were nigh on empty. Most of the troops were away from the battleline preparing for the next big push whilst the war machines tried to soften the hardy nut the warriors needed to crack. Only Morek and his hearth guard stood between the elven sortie and the annihilation of the stone throwers.

'Shields together,' he cried as soon as the hearth guard were ready and in position. Unwillingly, Morek's mind returned to the earlier battle on the plain. He had seen what the elven dragon knights could do. He stroked the talisman around his neck without thinking then took a firmer grip on his rune axe and shield.

RUGNIR HEARD THUNDER through the many layers of earth between him and the surface. Though the din of the drilling engine was loud, the sound from above carried well and the miner felt it as much as heard it. It had taken five days to get to this point. Sweating at the rock face, digging deep into the bowels of the world, Rugnir had brought the dwarf excavators to within a hundred feet or so of the foundations to Tor Eorfith. He expected to hit rock in the next hour. From there they would undermine the walls and send them crumbling to the ground for King Bagrik's reserve forces to exploit.

'Hard work eh, ufdi?' Rugnir remarked to Kandor with some of his old cheek.

The dwarf merchant had offered to join the mining expedition almost as soon as it was mooted. He had long since stripped out of his finery and adopted more practical attire of course garments and a rugged miner's helmet.

'You look almost like a proper dwarf,' he joked with good humour.

'We Silverbeards know gold,' Kandor said by way of explanation, 'and we know tunnelling also. It is long past due that I got my hands dirty again,' he added humbly.

Kozdokk, head of the Miners' Guild, smacked Rugnir on the back before he could reply. Rugnir was stripped down to tabard and breeches, a black pot helmet on his head with numerous candles affixed to it by their waxy emissions. He was sweating profusely and wiped a swathe of dirt across his forehead as he turned to the guildmaster.

'Not far,' Rugnir cried above the crushing of rock and the churning of earth.

Kozdokk nodded, chewing on a hunk of stonebread as he watched the work of his miners keenly. The guildmaster had brought the drilling engine all the way from Karak Ungor. A solid metal chassis supported an iron plated cage that ran on large, broad wheels. At the end was a gromril drill, tipped with diamond. A series of mechanical cranks and roped pulleys drove the engine itself, pure dwarf sweat and hard labour needed to turn it in order to build momentum. Teams of sappers worked either side of it, hauling back chunks of discarded rock to the waiting strings of mules that were led from the tunnel fully-laden and to the waiting baskets of engineers that supplied the stone throwers and shored up the dwarf entrenchments. Other miners worked with pick and shovel in tandem with the machine. Under Rugnir's expert guidance, progress was swift.

The large cohort of ironbreakers behind them, with Grikk Ironspike at their lead, would not have long to wait.

MOREK FELT THE ground trembling beneath him as the elven knights charged. The hearth guard had locked shields, anchoring themselves around the captain, their lynchpin. As Morek peered through the gap between shields, he saw the warrior leading the dragon knights.

'Lethralmir,' he spat beneath his breath. 'I hope you're watching this, Haggar...'

The elves rammed against the dwarf defence like a hammer hitting an anvil. Despite the power of their driven lances and the fury of their sudden attack, the dwarfs would not yield before them.

'You…' Morek cried, stepping out of the shield wall to level his axe in Lethralmir's direction as dragon knights and hearth guard cut each other down around him.

The raven-haired elf turned in the dwarf thane's direction and his eyes narrowed in the shadowed confines of his helmet.

'Face me!' the captain of the hearth guard roared.

Lethralmir dispatched a dwarf warrior impudently with his longsword in what might have been a gesture of acceptance. He called out a curt command to his knights and they backed away.

'Hold!' bellowed Morek in turn and the hearth guard disengaged, glowering hatefully at the enemy as they withdrew.

The warriors of both races knew a challenge when they saw it. Martial honour dictated that it be observed and that none other than challenger and challenged would fight. No one could intervene until one of the duellists was dead.

Morek was banking on the elf's arrogance to deliver him into the vicinity of his rune axe. When Lethralmir reared up on his steed and came at him, it seemed the dwarf's gambit had paid off.

The elf's first blow was swift and it glanced off Morek's shield with a loud *prang*. A second thrust was aimed at his neck, but the dwarf blocked that too, this time with his axe blade. Aloft on his steed's saddle, Lethralmir tried to press his height advantage. A low swipe arced over the dwarf's head. As he ducked only then did Morek make his move, ramming his shield into the horse's armoured chest. The beast neighed in pain and surprise, buckling onto its fetlocks. Lethralmir had no choice but to go with it. As he hung forward in his saddle, Morek severed the elf's neck as he scrabbled desperately for the reins.

Lethralmir's head fell from his shoulders to bounce over by Morek's feet. The expression on the dead elf's face as it rolled from his helmet was one of profound disbelief.

'I can fight dirty too,' muttered Morek, spitting on the decapitated head before smacking Lethralmir's half-panicked steed on the rump, sending it barging through the other knights and back towards the gates. At the sight of their leader so ignominiously dispatched, his headless body lolling in the saddle as his steed galloped away, the resolve of the dragon knights failed them. They fled, the sounds of jeering dwarfs dogging them all the way back to the city.

The attack on the war machines had failed. One of their nobles was dead and soon the tunnellers would reach the walls.

Slowly, the dwarfs tightened the noose.

CHAPTER TWENTY-ONE
Siege of Blood

DUST MOTES DRIFTED from the ceiling, covering Ithalred's pauldrons in a grey patina. The elf prince's armour was dented, his body bruised since his flight over the walls on Awari's back. Alas, the great eagle had not survived the fall and died in Ithalred's arms shortly after. Awari had been ancient, older than Ithalred, who himself had enjoyed a long life. The elf prince stumbled as a tremor ran beneath his feet. The barrage was unrelenting. The arcing foundation stones shook with the dwarfs' anger. Even through rock, Ithalred could hear the pleas of the dying and the clamour of battle from above. It was a constant reminder of his plight. So desperate was it that it had brought him here, to the lowest depths of Tor Eorfith, the nadir of Eyrie Rock itself.

The elf prince was not alone in the half-dark. Commander Valorian, warden of Tor Eorfith in Ithalred's absence, had joined him.

'He is lost to Khaine,' the elf commander muttered darkly. Resplendent in his silver ithilmar armour, chased with gold and with the lower half of the breast-plate rendered in the image of a surging phoenix, he looked distinctly incongruous. Swathed in shadows, Valorian was standing next to his prince outside a prison chamber.

Shining a silver lantern into the depths of the gaol, Valorian revealed a ragged-looking elf in the lamplight. His eyes were bloodshot behind a hungry, desperate mask. His once beauteous silvern mane was now lank and wretched. Strips of cloth lay all about him on the floor where he squatted; they were the shreds of his robes, ripped from his body in a maddened rage. Long gashes throbbed angrily from where the elf had raked his skin with his nails.

Ithalred stepped towards the bars of the cage and regarded the feral creature before him without emotion.

'Still no sign of Korhvale?' he asked quietly with his back to Valorian.

'None my prince, though I have searched the city as best I can. For whatever it is worth, I do not believe a White Lion would ever abandon his post. A Chracian would rather die first.'

'That is what I'm afraid of,' Ithalred whispered to the dark.

Valorian didn't hear him and continued with his report.

'The last of the towers have now fallen, my lord, and I do not think the gates will endure much longer.'

Another tremor added credence to the commander's remarks.

'Arthelas?' asked the prince, without even acknowledging the slow disintegration of his city.

'She is hidden away from the fighting as you ordered. Though, I have not seen her since before the siege began...' replied Valorian, pausing a beat, before saying, 'perhaps the seeress was distraught at the news of Lord Lethralmir's death.'

Ithalred grunted dismissively.

'The hour draws near when we must make our final stand against the dwarfs,' said Valorian.

'Then we'll need every sword, won't we, commander?'

Ithalred's gaze was fixed upon the caged elf.

'Are you ready to fight, Malbeth?' he asked.

The elf ambassador nodded slowly and showed Ithalred his manacled wrists.

'Release him,' Ithalred said to his commander, 'and when the dwarfs break through here... give him his swords.'

THE GATE WAS down. And silver-mane was long dead. Morek had felt a measure of satisfaction upon seeing the mage plunge to his demise.

Recompense for Hurbad's limp, he thought grimly.

Weathering the fusillade from the elven reapers, Morek charged into the levelled spears of the elves that had now moved in front of it. His mouth described a battle cry as he and his warriors barrelled forward. A dwarf charge was a rare thing, likened to a boulder rolling down a steep hill – slow at first but with enough momentum, it could shatter any barrier. Only the elf spearmen stood between them and the city. This close, the captain of the hearth guard was not about to be denied.

Morek smashed one spear aside with his shield, hacked another in two with his rune axe before launching himself at the enemy proper. Dwarfs were impaled on the forest of spikes, twitching in their armour as the elves stabbed and lunged, but it wasn't enough. Inspired by their captain, the hearth guard trampled the well-ordered elf defence with brutality and sheer fury.

Morek could smell blood in his nostrils as he killed, when the spearmen's resolve finally broke and they ran. The dwarfs' momentum carried them further into the city. They wrecked the twin reaper bolt throwers, hacking them to kindling with their axes and dispatching any crew that lingered behind without mercy.

'Sound the horn,' cried Morek to his musician, 'the elgi gate has fallen!'

BAGRIK WAS ALREADY moving down the ridge when the signal that the gatehouse was taken pealed through the air.

A foothold in Eyrie Rock, thought Bagrik darkly, *now all we have to do is keep it.*

As he rocked from side to side with the march of his shield bearers, biting back every twinge of pain and clinging to his fading strength, Bagrik watched the battlefield roll by.

A storm was already brewing in the darkling sky when the hearth guard rear rankers stormed through the broken gate. Rain drizzled in sheets, tinkling against armour and soaking cloth. Sporadic lightning flashes illuminated the elf archers hunkered down either side of the gatehouse on ruined spurs of parapet, loosing arrows in desperation. It was but a feeble shower to the determined dwarfs, no more deterrent than the rain.

Further warriors surged from trenches and behind abatis, swarming towards the open gate in their hundreds to support the hearth guard.

Across the walls, lines of stout siege towers were locked in position and disgorged warriors into the hard-pressed elf spearmen atop the battlements. Alongside them were racks of ladders with further hordes of armoured dwarfs climbing resolutely to back their kin.

Overhead, the barrage from the stone throwers and ballista had abated. So too had the volleys from the quarrellers below them. Together they loosed sporadically, picking off isolated pockets of resistance, as across the entire battlefield the dwarfs made the final push.

At the south wall, Bagrik's reserves waited patiently. Five cohorts of one hundred clan warriors, plus all the hold's longbeards led by Skarbrag Ironback, bided for Rugnir's sappers to collapse the wall and open up Tor Eorfith completely.

Much to the king's annoyance, and despite the fact that the walls were overrun in places and their gate was now largely ornate tinder, the elves remained steadfast and refused to capitulate. Such tenacity would be laudable had the king not sworn an oath to bring the city down and slay its potentate. The dwarfs needed that south wall down, and soon.

BELOW THE EARTH, the dwarf sappers were nearing their goal. Rugnir had ordered the drilling engine removed from the tunnel. He and the miners would finish the job with picks and shovels.

'A few more feet,' he said to Kandor, digging alongside him. The merchant thane only nodded, intent on the rock face. Kandor had proven his worth during the excavation, not moaning once and unrelenting in his labour. Rugnir sensed he was not the only one trying to make up for past mistakes.

'Bring up the *zharrum*,' added the miner, and waited for a small group of engineers to make their way forward. They had fat satchels slung across their backs. Within were clay fire casks, roughly spherical pots filled with oil and other flammable materials that the dwarfs would use to burn the foundations of the city. Zharrum, or fire drums, generated incredible amounts of heat and cracked stone in minutes, burned down wood in seconds. They were the last element of the dwarf sabotage and would ensure the collapse of the south wall.

'We're almost through,' Rugnir announced. Flecks of ambient light were visible in the fragile earth wall that stood between them and their goal.

'Ironbreakers, prepare for battle!' cried Grikk Ironspike, the captain having only just returned from making his report to King Bagrik and already marshalling his troops. The dwarfs were expecting resistance.

They were not to be disappointed.

As the earth wall crumbled a flurry of arrows spat through the ragged hole leading into the bowels of the elf city. Several miners, unprepared for the sudden attack, were felled instantly.

Pushing past the sappers – Rugnir, Kandor and a few of the others dragging back the dead and wounded – Grikk and his ironbreakers made a shield wall. More elf arrows rained from the gap, breaking harmlessly against Grikk's gromril bulwark. The dwarf veterans stomped forward as one and bellowed, 'Khazuk!'

The elf archers loosed again, now just visible behind the curtain of earth dust and falling rock.

Arrows rebounding off their shields, the ironbreakers took another step.

'Khazuk!'

A third brought them level with the breach.

'Khazuk!'

Retreating swiftly, the elf archers made way for their second line of defence.

Rugnir saw a flash of silver at first then heard a tinny scream as one of the ironbreakers was spun around, nigh on bifurcated in his armour.

Weaving their web of steel, a group of elven sword masters forced the ironbreakers back, their deadly blades carving red ruin in the dwarfs' serried ranks.

Iron-shod boots dragging furrows into the earth at their feet, the ironbreakers had little choice but to give ground against the elven onslaught. Grikk duelled with one of the elven bladelords – the cloak and plumed helmet he wore marked him out as the leader – but was getting the worst of it, battered into a desperate defence.

The elves had more. From out of the sword masters' ranks there emerged a maelstrom of bloody death. Naked from the waist up, a feral creature, an elf with twin blades, cut and hewed and killed. In the few short moments in which he had stormed into the tunnel, the possessed elf had slain a dozen ironbreakers. Blood rained across his body, criss-crossed by arterial spray, as he revelled in the slaughter.

'Miners to arms!' shouted Rugnir when he realised the sword masters, courtesy of their rampant slayer, would break through.

THE DWARFS WERE on the brink of victory.

Above, in the courtyard of Tor Eorfith's gatehouse, Morek and his hearth guard drove onward. He heard the tramp of booted feet behind him, the clamour of dwarf voices, and knew the rest of the army were following.

'Hold the gatehouse,' he cried to his warriors, 'keep the way open for King Bagrik!'

The hearth guard ground to a halt and stood firm with shields ready.

Across the flat stone of the courtyard, elves were storming from arches and alcoves to repel the dwarf invaders. Amongst them was a band of deadly sword masters. Prince Ithalred was leading them.

Stroking the talisman around his neck, Morek offered a pledge to Grungni that he would not been found wanting.

ITHALRED FOUGHT IN a blur. Every blow was precise; each and every strike was measured. It was as if the elf prince had choreographed the entire fight and already knew the outcome. In the few short moments it had taken Ithalred to parry Morek's first clumsy attack, and riposte with a shimmering arc, slicing the dwarf's forearm and opening him up completely as he dropped his shield, Morek knew he was outmatched.

The hearth guard couldn't even get close.

Ithalred killed them, coldly and efficiently, where they stood. The elf prince betrayed no arrogance in his skill, there was no flourish or swagger, no raw and murderous aggression like with the late Lethralmir; he was something else entirely – a very near perfect warrior.

'Grimnir's teeth!' Morek cursed, barely managing to fend off a searching lunge by the elf prince. Had it fallen, the blow would have impaled the hearth guard captain and it would all be over.

'Rally to me, rally to me!' the dwarf cried, acutely aware that his warriors were bearing the brunt of a serious battering. Morek backed off for a moment, unwilling to step into Ithalred's death arc just yet, and used the time to catch his breath. Clan warriors were forcing their way across the moat and in through the gate. Though in their wake, the elves had filled the gap left by the victorious hearth guard with spearmen. Even now, Morek knew his dwindling cohort were surrounded, that the elves had allowed them to get inside the courtyard so they could butcher them. As he cast about, he thought he saw a flash of armour, a lone warrior upon a sparsely guarded section of wall. It was only a glimpse out the corner of his eye, and with no time to look further Morek dismissed it as nothing.

Deeming he'd had long enough to gather his wits, Ithalred came at Morek again. The hearth guard captain was breathing heavily; he nursed a raft of small cuts and his armour felt hot and heavy. The elf had barely broken a sweat.

Morek blocked left then right, more by instinct and sheer desperation than through any strategy. Ithalred shaped for an overhead strike and the dwarf thought he had the drop on him at last.

No one's that good, he thought, already dodging to the side and preparing to counter with an axe blow to the prince's exposed back. Ithalred's attack never came, at least not the one the dwarf was expecting. Instead, he brought his sword around to lash at Morek's side, a second short blade seemingly emerging from nowhere to stab into the dwarf's opposite flank.

Morek felt the hot metal pierce armour, skin and flesh. Searing agony gave way to a sudden numbness and the hearth guard captain fell, his rune axe clattering to the ground after him.

With their leader down, the stubborn resolve of the hearth guard fractured and the unthinkable happened.

They fled. The sight of the veteran dwarf warriors abandoning the fight and running for their lives sent waves of panic rippling through the dwarf army. The elf spearmen at the gate parted, allowing the fleeing dwarfs through who stumbled into the pressing clan warriors and swept them up into the chaotic stampede.

Dwarfs fell screaming from the bridge into the molten silver moat as the broken warriors pushed their way out. Weighed down by their armour, they sank like bronze stones. In a matter of moments, one decisive act had turned the tide of the battle against the dwarfs and to the elves' favour. Hearth guard and clan warriors fled together and in their droves.

BAGRIK ROARED FROM atop his war shield. The wrathful dwarf king was only scant feet away from the abject retreat.

'Turn, Grimnir damn you! Turn back and face the foe!' Bagrik scoured the faces of the panicked warriors, making a mental note of every single one. They would be remembered forever in infamy in the pages of the book of grudges. Grumkaz Grimbrow was nearby, clasping the mighty tome. As Bagrik called out each name, the grudgemaster wrote it down. But it did no good, the dwarfs kept on running.

From his vantage point, Bagrik could see his lines were suddenly in danger of fragmenting. He wanted this over quickly. A defeat, like the one the dwarfs were close to, would only galvanise the elves. Bagrik had no desire to re-fight the siege again. In his heart, he knew he would not last out a protracted battle. Even raging at his fleeing warriors sapped at his strength – the poison had nearly done for him. He was about to order in his reserves, in spite of the fact that the south wall still stood, when a horn rang out into the blood-hazed night. Its pitch climbed above the thunder, clear as the first hammer strike against the anvil. Bagrik followed its source all the way to the top of the elven battlements.

'Not possible...' he breathed, as tears filled the old king's eyes.

MOREK THOUGHT HE was dead. All around him the clamour of voices drifted in and out. Peering through a dense fog, his gaze went to elven battlements directly above him. When he saw who stood there, shimmering in his ancestral armour, the hearth guard captain knew he was but a breath away from Gazul's Gate.

'Nagrim...' he rasped through bloodied teeth, and passed out.

'NAGRIM!' THE CRY went up from one of the fleeing hearth guard as he pointed to the battlements. In the frantic press to win the battle in the courtyard, the walls had all but been abandoned. The prince of Ungor stood there alone, the corpses of elf sentries slumped around him.

Other dwarfs took up the chorus swiftly and it built to a powerful crescendo as all those close enough to see gazed upon the slain hero of Karak Ungor in fear and awe. The legacy of the hold, personified in iron and gromril, had come back from the dead to fight alongside his kin in their hour of need. In one hand, Nagrim held his battle horn; in the other, a warhammer. Raising the weapon aloft, it was a rallying cry the dwarfs sorely needed and they cheered as one.

The effect was miraculous.

Drums sounded, pipes rang out and the warriors of Karak Ungor held up their banners once more and returned to the fight. The hearth guard found their courage at last, and turned, thundering back to the gate even as their hero descended the battlement steps to meet the foe.

BAGRIK WAS STUNNED into silence. He did not even notice the slowing of his shield bearers as the apparition of his dead son disappeared from sight.

'Not possible,' he muttered again, when he'd found his voice. It wore Nagrim's armour. Bagrik's warriors had cried his name. But…

The king's face darkened abruptly as he remembered how 'Nagrim' had cradled the battle horn. He hadn't noticed it at first. He had been too shocked by what he thought he had seen. The hand that gripped around that horn was crooked, Bagrik recognised it even beneath the dwarf's armoured gauntlet.

'*Lothvar…*' he snarled, face creasing into a scowl.

Brunvilda had defied him again.

Bagrik was close enough to the gate now to see over the heads of his clamouring warriors and the elven force within. Through a gap between banners, he recognised Ithalred. The elf prince was battling furiously, slaying dwarfs with every stroke. Lothvar had descended into that melee. It could be him falling beneath that sword next.

'Lothvar,' Bagrik said again, though this time his tone was urgent. 'Get me through the gate,' the dwarf king raged at his shield bearers suddenly. 'Do it now!'

IN THE TUNNELS, the miners and ironbreakers were taking a severe beating. Dwarf corpses littered the ground, for precious little reply. Alone, the sword masters were few and eminently defeatable, but with the half-naked elf blade-master they had the edge.

Rugnir ducked the swipe of an elf greatsword, before ramming the head of his pick into the startled sword master's chest. He wrenched it out, the wound spitting gore, and stepped over the still-cooling body into another fight.

'Stay with me, ufdi,' he said to Kandor, who fought at the other dwarf's back and was just trying to stay alive. Old Kozdokk was already dead, skewered by a flurry of elven silver. Rugnir tried to keep the guildmaster's bloody carcass out of his eye-line.

Kandor nodded, too tired to speak as he heaved enough breath into his lungs to fight.

Somewhere in the madness, Grikk and his ironbreakers were struggling. Rugnir had lost track of the ebb and flow of the battle almost immediately.

Tunnel fighting was chaotic at best. Sound resonated in the blackened confines of the subterranean; it echoed off the walls and fell away abruptly to nothing. In the gloom, shadows became real and foes became as shadows. The stench of blood and death was intensified. The effect was disconcerting. Hard enough to fight grobi in the dark places under the earth; battling a foe like the elves and their murderous talisman was proving almost impossible.

And then there he was... a crimson phantom, his blood-slicked body shimmering like red oil. Eyes white with crazed fury bored into Rugnir like daggers and the dwarf felt his courage draining.

'Name of Valaya,' he whispered at the spectre of death stalking towards him.

Salvation came from an unlikely source. Kandor appeared at Rugnir's side and one word from his lips saved them both.

'Malbeth?'

The feral elf stalled and recognition dawned upon his face.

'Kandor…'

Anger bled away, supplanted by anguish. Malbeth lowered his blades and let his arms drop to his sides.

'*End it*,' he mouthed to his erstwhile friend and shut his eyes.

A half dozen dwarf axes fell upon the elf, cutting him down at last. Kandor's had been the first. The merchant thane was sobbing by the time it was done. Rugnir gathered the other dwarf to him, putting a meaty arm around his shoulder, and let the miners and ironbreakers past him – now freed with the death of Malbeth – to finish the sword masters. Advantage had swung back into the dwarfs' favour. The elves were few, and though skilled, could not last long.

It was over in a matter of minutes. The tunnel was theirs. Engineers with the zharrum were rallied swiftly. Now, the south wall would crumble.

BAGRIK HAD GAINED the gate when the south wall of Tor Eorfith came down. Trumpets sounded loudly in the chaos as the dwarf reserves piled through the breach. The dwarf king did not need to see it to know that the elves' doom was now sealed. Strangely, it gave him no pleasure. Though he had tried, Bagrik could find no sign of Lothvar amongst the fighting or the fallen. He hoped that Grungni favoured him in all the ways that he had not. There was but one more thing left for Bagrik to do. Across the courtyard, he saw Prince Ithalred. The elf was tiring now. No warrior, however skilled, could reap a tally like he had and not feel fatigue. Bagrik's own malady evened the scales. The king was glad it would at least be a fair fight.

Cutting through a regiment of spearmen, the remaining hearth guard having gathered around their king as soon as he had arrived, Bagrik at last found himself face-to-face with his true nemesis.

There was no need to bellow a challenge this time, no pithy words or caustic insults. The elf prince knew this was coming and faced the dwarf king with dignity, offering a salute with his blade which Bagrik did not reciprocate.

The old king unclasped the faceplate from his helmet and let it fall to the ground. He wanted the elf to be able to see his face when he killed him.

Pleasantries over, Ithalred fell upon Bagrik. Blows came and went in a flurry, elven deftness and speed versus dwarf strength and aggression. Ithalred lunged, thrust, cut and sliced as his sword flashed like silver lightning. Bagrik weathered the barrage with typical dwarf obstinance, using his haft and blade to parry, getting in swings between the elf's blindingly fast attacks. The shield bearers did not intervene; they merely kept their king aloft while he fought.

Ithalred tried to open up Bagrik's defences by crafting an intricate array of attacks, but the dwarf king was equal to it. He replied with a forceful assault of his own. Such was the dwarf's fury that Ithalred felt every bone-rattling strike like a hammer blow.

Bagrik knew the elf's endurance was waning. No creature alive could match a dwarf for tenacity. As Bagrik pounded him, raining blow after heavy blow against Ithalred's improvised defence, the elf began to flag and sought a swift end to the duel. Waiting for a gap in the dwarf king's relentless assault, Ithalred lunged aiming for Bagrik's exposed neck. It was the moment of recklessness that the dwarf king had been waiting for. Feigning loss of balance, Bagrik allowed the elf to stretch and lead with the point of his sword. At the last moment, though, he twisted and brought the flat of his axe down on Ithalred's unprotected grip. The sudden blow forced the elf's sword aside. It grazed Bagrik's gorget before Ithalred dropped it from his nerveless fingers. Fashioning a return strike, Bagrik first caught the elf's wrist, as he went in from the dwarf king's blind side with his short sword, and snapped it. Ithalred suppressed a scream of agony when his wrist broke. He gasped blood when Bagrik finished the move, bringing his rune axe down onto the elf's exposed shoulder, cleaving through his armour and embedding bone.

Ithalred was breathing hard, the rune axe still lodged in his clavicle and his broken wrist limp in the dwarf king's iron grip.

Spitting blood, he rasped, 'Allow me a warrior's death.'

Bagrik's eyes were cold and lifeless.

'You killed my son,' he replied. Bagrik ripped out his rune axe with both hands and roared as he beheaded Prince Ithalred.

'Behold,' yelled Bagrik, once he had caught his breath, pointing down to the decapitated elf at his feet, 'your lord is dead!'

Nearby a few of the elves and dwarfs stopped fighting to look.

'Behold, Prince Ithalred is slain,' declared the king, as more and more warriors turned to face him. 'Cease now... Cease!' he cried. 'It is over. You elgi are defeated.' Across the length and breadth of Tor Eorfith, throughout the battlefield mire beyond, in the lowest depths of the city's foundations as the sound of Bagrik's declaration carried, elves and dwarfs together lowered their weapons and stopped fighting.

RUGNIR HAD EMERGED into the courtyard with Kandor, Grikk and the other survivors of the tunnel battle in tow. It had stopped raining and night was fading, giving way to a rising sun in the east. His warrior band was not far from the king, and he saw the pained expression on Bagrik's face as he spoke, knew that the poison ravaging the king's body was all but done with him as he mustered a final effort before the dawn.

'Leave this place,' shouted the king, his voice echoing around the courtyard. 'Go back to your island in shame. Your treachery has blighted any friendship, any accord with us dawi. You are no longer welcome in the Karaz Ankor.'

THE DAMNING WORDS of the dwarf king fell harder than any blow. Valorian, the sole surviving elf noble issued a clipped command in his native tongue and his warriors sheathed their swords and shouldered their weapons. There were precious few left in any case to make any kind of last stand. Though, truthfully, the elves had lost heart. Valorian had not been aware of their betrayal at first; he was not party to Ithalred's desperate plan to garner the dwarfs' martial might.

He knew it now, he had known since before the siege and it had sat ill with him even then, just, he suspected, as it had with Korhvale. It was his greatest regret that the Chracian had not been found. Elven horns sounded mournfully and the survivors of Tor Eorfith gathered into a bedraggled column with Commander Valorian at the front. The noble marched his warriors out, together with all who remained of the elven colony. They would head for their ships still at dock along the river to the east and from there back across the Great Ocean to Ulthuan.

'SET ME DOWN,' Bagrik growled, grateful for an end to the rocking of his war shield. He took off his helmet, watching the dwarfs in front of the gate parting to let the elves through. Reaching over without looking, he took a fistful of earth in his hand and clenched it tightly. Letting his rune axe slip from his fingers, Bagrik closed his eyes and exhaled a lingering breath. It was to be his last.

EPILOGUE
All Hail the Queen

KARAK UNGOR WAS silent as a tomb. The workshops were quiet. No clatter of hammers or ringing upon anvils could be heard. No voices called out, no murmuring of longbeards, no scrape and clash of picks on stone. No clank of armour as warriors patrolled. Even the gold counters were stilled. The hold had simply stopped so that all within could bear remembrance to their king, Bagrik Boarbrow. Such a thing was unprecedented. Never in all the days of the Delving Hold had utter quietude descended, but descend it had and like a bitter black veil.

In the days since the siege at Tor Eorfith, Bagrik had been returned to his hold. Grikk found him sat upon his shield, slate-grey eyes glaring sternly forever more, a fistful of earth in his leathery grasp.

The king is dead. The solemn pronouncement had rung around the battlefield like a mournful bell.

The king is dead.

As Bagrik's body was taken up by his shield bearers, a tearful Morek had led a slow procession from the city all the way to the camp and from there to Karak Ungor. In his wake, the miners and engineers had descended, smashing rock and hewing stone, finishing what the siege engines started and leaving Tor Eorfith a ruin.

Upon the dwarfs' return, Bagrik was entombed with Nagrim. There was a palpable wave of relief at the sight of the slain prince. There had been those who swore they had seen him battle the elves, even fought by his side, but none could remember what happened to him after the siege. He had simply been lost from sight.

Some, the overly superstitious or gullible, suggested Nagrim's body might not be in the temple of Valaya when the dwarfs came back, that he had somehow taken leave of his own death. It was not so. Rangers had scoured the battlefield afterwards, and the crags beyond, but no sign could be found of Nagrim or his apparent spectre. There was just his suit of armour left inexplicably in a shadowy alcove, laid out with reverence and respect. It too was taken back to the hold and entombed in the vaults.

Only Brunvilda knew the truth of it, and she would not say.

In time, missives would be sent by the High King Gotrek Starbreaker of Karaz-a-Karak pledging his support and expressing his grief. A new liege lord of Karak Ungor would be chosen by the elders, but for now it was Brunvilda who ruled. Addressing her throng in the wake of her husband's death was her first royal act as matriarch.

'We dawi stand alone,' the queen began.

She too was alone, stood before the throne of Ungor in the Great Hall.

Brunvilda was glorious. Clad in her ancestral armour, the shimmering crown set upon her brow flashed like a star of fire. Bedecked in jewels, clasped with vambrace and greave, she was every bit the warrior queen. A short cloak hung heavily from her shoulders; heavy like the dour mood that pervaded throughout the hold. In her hand, stone head held downward to the floor, was Brunvilda's rune hammer.

The vast chamber that stretched in front of her was teeming with dwarfs. They stood shoulder-to-shoulder like a mighty iron sea. All the clans were present; all the longbeards, the veterans, the craftguilds, masters, artisans and merchants. No dwarf that day, save for the gate guards – and even they had their heads bowed and their bodies still – wasn't present for the queen's address.

Such was the magnitude of the gathering that the huge double doors to the Great Hall were thrown open wide and the dwarfs trailed back down the long corridor beyond for as far as the eye could see.

Flickering torches cast a weak and sombre light on the scene in the Great Hall. Even the statues of kings appeared bowed and subdued.

'Like the mountains we stand alone,' Brunvilda said, 'and like the mountains we will endure. We are rocks, you and I. Neither man nor elgi, nor grobi, nor any other creature of the world that looks upon our domain with jealous eyes will ever break us... ever!' Her voice echoed loudly through the massive chamber, resonating in all those present.

'They will find us resolute and belligerent. They will find a wall of iron and bronze, rooted in the bedrock of the very earth. Such things do not yield to force.' Brunvilda paused. Looking around the room, her gaze was as hard as her words, as hard as iron.

'Dark days are ahead, make no mistake about that,' she warned. 'We must look to ourselves for salvation. When the enemies of the Karaz Ankor come, and mark me they will… we will not bow to them, nor will we be put asunder. We are dawi! By all the Ancestor Gods, we will smash our foes to dust should they come to our walls. We are steadfast. Together, we will never be defeated. Never! So says, Brunvilda, Queen of Karak Ungor!'

She thrust her rune hammer into the air and the throng roared in affirmation.

The sound was deafening. It shook the walls and made the earth tremble. The dwarfs were defiant; their anger and their bitterness gave them strength and solidarity. But dark days *were* coming, and they were closer than anyone could have known…

TOR EORFITH WAS like a skeleton of shattered rock and broken spires. The former glory of the elven city had been smashed utterly from the face of the world. The miners and sappers led by Rugnir had set about their task with extreme prejudice.

Within the shadows of the bowels of a ruined tower, Lothvar awoke and found he was trussed to a slab of fallen stone. He remembered only snatches of how he came to be here. Like his mother had told him in the Temple of Valaya, he had found the battlesite by following the trail of his kinsdwarfs and fought with his father against the elves. His heart had sung, unshackled for the first time, exultation filling the dwarf prince as his kin had cheered. It did not matter that they shouted his brother's name; all that mattered was that he was there and had rallied the army. Lothvar had never been happier in all his miserable, mistreated life.

A presence in the hollowed-out tower got his attention and wrenched his thoughts back to his predicament. Once the battle was over, Lothvar had slipped away. He had wanted desperately to stay, but his mother had forbid it. Lothvar didn't really understand her reasons as she had explained them, but he did not wish to bring shame to his father by exposing the lie of his existence, so he had disappeared.

It had not been difficult; all eyes had been upon his father when he had retreated back over the wall. Once on the other side, he had hiked away from the battle-field. Both armies were spent, and none had the strength or inclination to follow him. Once out of sight, Lothvar had removed his ancestral armour, and placed it carefully out of the way where he knew it would eventually be found. Moving quickly, a hand before his eyes to ward off the painful light of the rising sun, Lothvar had tracked his way through the crags using scent and sound to guide him. There within a shallow gulley, beneath the shadow of a rocky promontory, he found the knapsack he had secreted before the siege began. There was a hooded cloak, which he had donned at once drawing the cowl to fend off the bright sun, food and weapons. He slung the crossbow over his back and cinched the hand axe to his belt. Then he began to make his way into the mountains.

Recollection became hazy after that. Lothvar had kept off the path, using seldom trodden ways and keeping to the shadows. It was within a copse of scattered pine, in the lee of an overhanging rock that he heard the crunch of stone. Something had moved in the gloom around him. He had reached for his hand axe, sensing danger, but all too quickly the shadows became warriors and the warriors subdued him. He had woken here, alone in the cold and merciless ruins of Tor Eorfith.

* * *

ONCE PAST THE dwarf piquets, Arthelas had found her followers quickly. In the confusion of the coming siege, she had slipped away from the citadel and beyond the city's walls. Using sorcery, she had adopted the form of Craggen the dwarf hermit, the guise with which she had duped Rugnir so easily. Unleashing him at precisely the right moment to bring about discord and war amongst the elves and dwarfs had been easy too.

The cave where she had held, and ministered, to him was found and secured by her followers already at large in the Old World. Magically transporting herself from Tor Eorfith to the cave for Craggen's appearances had been taxing, but not impossible, and vital to her lie.

Foolish Ithalred – he had no concept of her true ability. Now, it no longer mattered.

Swathed in purple robes, Arthelas stood at the apex of a triangle of three. Her two acolytes were standing silently at the opposite points. Between them, at the nexus of the triangle, was the dwarf sacrifice.

'With this blade, I invoke Hekarti,' she said in the sibilant tongue of dark magic. 'By the Cytharai, by Ereth Khial and all the fell gods of the Underworld, I beseech her power. Let blood seal the pact.'

Arthelas cried out, throwing her head back. Her face was twisted into a howl of pure malice. In her outstretched hand she clasped a jagged dagger. It was not so dissimilar from the one used to stab Bagrik and poison the dwarf king.

LOTHVAR'S EYES SNAPPED wide open when the blade went in, when it pierced his pale naked skin and entered flesh. A warm cascade flowed across his body at first, before it cooled and chilling numbness took hold.

As he slipped away, his life blood pooling below the slab, Lothvar hoped he would see his father and brother in the Halls…

HER FACE WAS dashed with blood. Arthelas left it that way, staring wild eyed at the slain dwarf beneath her. She felt empowered, her mind awash with visions of war. Malekith would be pleased. She and her small coven had sown dissension between Karak Ungor and the elves of Ulthuan. Though in truth, Ithalred had been an easy dupe. His arrogance and desperation had led him down the path; Arthelas had only to show him the way. Lethralmir was an easy pawn in that regard. Love-sick and amorous, the blade-master had bent all too effortlessly to her will. Atharti, underworld goddess of pleasure, was well sated by their lustful desires.

It was all just the beginning of a much larger plan. Arthelas was wise enough to realise the small significance of her part in it. For she knew that all across the Old World her dark kin were making ready to ensure any lasting peace between elves and dwarfs would be fleeting. Malekith had willed it.

GLOSSARY

Beardling – Young dwarfs, no more than fifty winters old, are known as beardlings, since beard length is an indicator of experience and wisdom.

Dammaz kron – Literally 'book of grudges', though the word has two meanings and can refer to the Great Book of Grudges, that which resides in the dwarfen capital of Karaz-a-Karak and records all the wrongs and misdeeds ever perpetrated against the dwarf race. It can also refer to a particular hold's book of grudges as each and every dwarf realm has one to record that hold's specific grievances.

Dawi – Literally meaning 'dwarfs'.

Dawongi – Literally translates as 'dwarf-friend'. Given rarely to creatures of other races, the receiver of this title is trusted as if they were a dwarf. It is a great honour to be regarded as such, and not something that should even be given or taken lightly.

DEEPS – The levels into which dwarf holds are divided.

DRENG TROMM – Translates literally as 'slay beard'. It refers to a very serious lamentation during which a dwarf expresses his profound sorrow and desire to tear at his beard in shared remorse. The sentiment can also be conveyed more solemnly to indicate when something is a great shame or to acknowledge a profound loss or misdeed.

ELGI – Elves, but also means weak.

GNOLLENGROM – This greeting is a mark of respect afforded to a dwarf who has a longer and more spectacular beard. Commonly, it is a term used when in the company of longbeards or ancestors, but there are instances of it being used to address a dwarf of high station such as a king or runelord (who is likely to be a longbeard in any event).

GRIMAZUL – Translates literally as 'unyielding iron' and is generally accepted as the dwarf word for steel.

GROBI – Meaning 'goblin'. The word grob, of which grobi is derived, also means green and can refer to greenskins in general.

GROMRIL – Also known as 'hammernought' or 'starmetal', gromril is the hardest substance in the known world and can only be fashioned by the craft of the dwarfs. The metal is incredibly rare and exceptionally valuable.

GROBKUL – Derived from the word 'grobi', meaning 'goblin', grobkul means 'goblin hunt' or literally 'the art of stalking goblins in caves'.

THE HALLS OF THE ANCESTORS – These are the legendary feast halls where the ancestor gods, Grungni and Valaya sit for eternity. All dwarfs believe that, upon their death, they will pass on to the Halls of the Ancestors where they will feast with their ancestors forever more. Only if a dwarf's tomb is desecrated or some past deed undone will they be unable to enter the great halls, which is why the dwarfs view the sanctity of the dead with such seriousness.

HRUK – A hardy breed of mountain goat, reared on overground farms, from which the dwarfs harvest milk, wool and meat.

KARAZ ANKOR – The ancient realm of the dwarfs, encompassing all the holds of the Worlds Edge Mountains and beyond.

KHAZUKAN KAZAKIT-HA! – War cry of the dwarfs, literally meaning 'Look out, the dwarfs are on the warpath!'

KHAZUK – The shortened version of the war cry 'Khazukan Kazakit-ha!'

KLINKARHUN – Describes the core dwarf alphabet, but also refers to their numerical system. Literally means 'chisel runes'.

KRON – A book or tome, a record of history or deeds.

NUBUNGKI – A largely forbidden word, seldom used in dwarf circles, nubungki are beardling children that are 'afflicted' with some physical or mental impediment such as albinism or alopecia. Instances are rare and almost never recorded for the fear of the great shame a nubungki would bring to clan and hold. Regarded by dwarfs as outcasts, they are banished in the wilderness according to strict ritual.

RECKONERS – Those dwarfs charged with ensuing proper payment is levelled and paid for the grievances of other dwarfs. Each reckoner keeps a tally of deeds done and recompense made in his log or on stone tablets.

RINN – A dwarf woman or king's consort.

STONE BREAD – Granite like victual that forms part of the staple diet of the dwarfs. Such is its hardness and robust texture that only dwarfs have the constitution to consume it. Not unlike eating rock but will never soil.

THAGI – Literally means 'murderous traitor' and is derived from the verb 'thag' which means to slay by an act of treachery.

TROMM – Meaning 'beard', but it is also a respectful greeting.

UFDI – This is a term used to describe any dwarf who labours over preening their beard. A vain dwarf, one who is overly concerned with appearance and likely cannot be trusted to fight.

UMGAL – Meaning 'man' as in the race, and derived from the word for men, 'umgi'.

UNGDRIN – Also known as the underway, the ungdrin or ungdrin road is the massive network of subterranean tunnels wrought by the dwarfs in ages past to make travelling from one hold to another much easier and more expedient. As the ravages of orcs, goblins and skaven had taken their toll on the dwarf empire, much of the ungdrin is in a state of disrepair or been made into the lair of monsters.

URK – Orc or enemy. This word also translates as 'coward' as all enemies of the dwarfs are considered as such.

UZKUL – Commonly meaning 'death', but can also be used to mean 'bones'. Often used as a warning to chambers where there are known dangers.

VALA-AZRILUNGOL – Ancient Khazalid name for Karak Eight Peaks, meaning 'Queen of the Silver Depths'. It was once the greatest and most vaunted of all the holds of the dwarf empire, greater even than Karaz-a-Karak, but fell after over a century of bitter warfare against skaven and greenskins.

VALAKRYN – Warrior-priestesses of Valaya, the Valkryn are a rare dwarf warrior sisterhood who minister to the wounded and the fallen on the battlefield, providing mercy to dying dwarfs but swift vengeance to the enemy.

WANAZ – The opposite of an ufdi, a wanaz is a dwarf that has an unkempt beard and is known to be disreputable. An insult.

WATTOCK – An insult meaning a down at heel or unsuccessful dwarf.

WAZLIK – An insult meaning an honourless dwarf that borrowed gold from another and did not pay it back.

WAZZOK – Foolish or gullible dwarfs, those who have been duped in matters of business, exchanging valuables for something of little or no worth, or who are easily parted from their gold in a doomed venture, are called wazzocks. Much like other dwarfish derogatory terms, this is regarded as an insult.

WUTROTH – Also known as 'ironbark' and 'stone trunk', this wood of dwarfen origin is incredibly rare and exceptionally strong but also very pliable.

ZAKI – The zaki is the dwarf that has lost his mind and wanders the mountains. Many dwarf hermits are often described thusly, as are those guilders who deviate from the strictures of their guild (quite a common occurrence amongst journeyman engineers).

ZHARRUM – Literally meaning 'fire drum'. Zharrum are metal spheres containing lamp oil or other combustibles and used like rudimentary bombs to spread fires quickly. In mining, they can be used on wooden supports to collapse tunnels.

ABOUT THE AUTHOR

Nick Kyme hails from Grimsby, a small town on the east coast of England. Nick moved to Nottingham in 2003 to work on White Dwarf magazine as a Layout Designer. Since then, he has made the switch to the Black Library's hallowed halls as an editor and has been involved in a multitude of diverse projects. His writing credits include several published short stories, background books and novels.

You can catch up with Nick and read about all of his other published works at his website:
www.nickkyme.com

WARHAMMER

GOTREK & FELIX

THE FIRST OMNIBUS

Buy these
omnibuses or read
free extracts at
www.blacklibrary.com

TROLLSLAYER · SKAVENSLAYER · DAEMONSLAYER

WILLIAM KING

WARHAMMER

GOTREK & FELIX

THE SECOND OMNIBUS

DRAGONSLAYER • BEASTSLAYER • VAMPIRESLAYER

WILLIAM KING

ISBN 978-1-84416-417-2

GRUDGELORE

A HISTORY OF GRUDGES AND THE GREAT REALM OF THE DWARFS

NICK KYME AND GAV THORPE

ISBN: 978-1-84416-503-2

Presented as an artefact from the Warhammer World, *Grudgelore* contains a wealth of associated background about the dwarfs and in-character tales of heroism and desperate battles. It's a must-have for all Warhammer fans.